About the Author

BOB FLAHERTY is a freelance writer, cartoonist, and comedian. Born and raised in Boston, Bob lives in western Massachusetts, with his wife, Annemarie, who seems to understand him. They have three sons.

Puff

a novel

BOB FLAHERTY

Perennial
An Imprint of HarperCollins*Publishers*

HarperCollins books may be purchased for educational, business, or sales promotional use. For information please write: Special Markets Department, HarperCollins Publishers Inc., 10 East 53rd Street, New York, NY 10022.

FIRST EDITION

Designed by Nancy B. Field

The Library of Congress Cataloging-in-Publication Data

Flaherty, Bob.
    Puff / by Bob Flaherty.—1st ed.
        p. cm.
    ISBN 0-06-075152-5
    1. Young men—Fiction. 2. Brothers—Fiction. I. Title.

PS3606.L343R43 2005
813'.6—dc22   2004053415

    06 07 08 09   ❖/RRD   10 9 8 7 6 5 4 3

for Annemarie

I'd like to thank

Kate Travers,

Joy Tutela,

John Stifler's writing workshop,

and the _Hampshire Life_
Short Fiction Contest

Contents

puff

1

Mole

I am aware of the moles. I am aware of the moles because I am covered with moles. Why, I have no idea. Not one member of my family has even so much as a blackhead, and here's me, a walking sheet of Braille. I am also keenly aware of the poster. The poster of the mole. The poster of the mole I see on the Red Line coming home from Catechism Wednesday nights. The poster that magnifies the mole about 350,000 times, depicting the mole in various stages of metamorphosis, with big serious black letters beneath each stage warning: SEE MOLE. SEE MOLE CHANGE. SEE A DOCTOR. I am now so aware of the moles I can practically see them changing before my eyes. Changing color, changing texture, changing size. Threatening to bubble over in hideous disease. I can feel them incubating on the small of my back like a colony of ticks. I look at them in the morning before school, with mirrors and magnifying glasses, making detailed mental notes of the slightest variations: the deepening crease on the one under my left nipple, the ever-multiplying cluster of them under my armpit, the one three inches from my navel I've never seen before in my *life*. It's like trying to identify constellations on a chart of the midnight sky. I feel compelled to give them names. I am thirteen years old. In the prime of my life. Moleridden.

Certain I am soon to die, I spend a lot of time praying. On my knees. Beside my Roy Rogers–Dale Evans bedspread in the Wild Bill Hickock–wallpapered room I share with my brother. I pray Our Fathers. I pray Hail Marys. I pray and pray, eyes closed, trying to block out my brother's derisive laughter from the bunk above. "Why dontcha use yer rosary beads, Bishop Sheen?"

"Because they remind me of moles," I say, and that just about kills him. Of course, everything kills Gully. Laugh, laugh, laugh. That's what everybody calls him too. *Gully*. From about the minute he was born. It's short for Gullivan, which is our last name. Nobody calls *me* Gully, even though I was born first, by about two whole years. I'm just John, always John, unmistakably John. Who lives not in Boston, mind you, but about 350 feet from the sign that says: ENTERING BOSTON, in a place called Morton, which, by Bostonian decree, is pronounced "Maught'n" by exactly everyone.

Our family prophecy is pretty much spelled out on Dad's panel truck. It has GULLIVAN & SON DISTRIB. painted on both front doors and it has our phone number too. The *son* in Gullivan & Son is Dad. What he "distribs" are newspapers, everything from the *Boston Globe* to the *Christian Science Monitor* to those dinky little AFL-CIO rags that always have front-page pictures of fat guys receiving plaques. Trucks start bombarding him with bundles about four in the morning at his little hole-in-the-wall news agency off Dot Ave. He spends the rest of the morning breaking the towering mess into smaller bundles, which he then carts off to storefronts and subway entrances and to the minions of paperboys who work for him. By then the *afternoon* mess is in.

The *son* part was painted on while Dad was in the navy, but he assumed the *Gullivan* role the day he got discharged, which, as luck would have it, was the day Granddad decided he couldn't work anymore on account of his back. (Or on account of his zeal for the sauce, depending on which of my relatives you talk to.) Dad's vision is that one or both of us will one day become the "Son" and he mentions it all the time. That is, when he's not seething. The business he's in goes along smoothly enough until it snows, or rains, or the *Herald*s are late, or he loses his wire cutters, or the truck blows a head gasket or fifteen of his snotty minions call in sick. Otherwise, he's calm as an egg, smoking Chesterfields til the walls turn brown.

Gully thinks the whole affair's a laugh-a-minute riot. And when Gully's not laughing at Dad, he's busy laughing at me. Me and the moles. Then, inevitably, somewhere between ten o'clock at night and two in the morning, the only time when Dad is asleep in his bed, old Schoerner's dogs from the kennel next door start going at it like the Ray Conniff Singers. Dad shrieks behind his closed bedroom door. Ma picks up the phone and starts yelling. And Gully just about dies.

But I pay him no mind. That's all he does half the time anyway. Laughs like the gull he is. I blot it out like a black first baseman at Caddigan Park. Laugh all he wants.

But then we go to church. I have not had huge success blotting out the laughter in church. Nor, for that matter, in any public, solemn place where people sit expressionless and listen to pins drop. My brother's gut-clutching giggling becomes as contagious to me as mumps. Which is why the two of us are kept far apart when dragged there, sitting at opposite ends of the family pew—three immaculately dressed sisters, two parents and old Aunt Fran between us. But in this dreary and sorrowful place, where white-haired monsignors drone like South Station dispatchers, where old men snore and little kids squirm and organists play selections from *Frankenstein*, all it takes to get Gully in gear is for the fat old guy in back to start blowing his sausage-sized nose like Tarzan summoning the elephants. By the time Dad pinch-hits for one of the ushers and proceeds to slam old lady Flambeau right in the puss with the collection basket, my brother is completely buckled over, and, sadly, so am I, drowning in hysteria with things coming out of my nose.

Ma thrashes us on the way home, it goes without saying, sometimes all the way home. Sometimes on the way to church as a preemptive strike; with anything she can get her hands on—her pocketbook, her shoe, a Sunday paper—while Dad drives with his arm out the window and smokes.

Despite all that, we were positive angels, I swear, all during our first family tragedy, Granny's death, not two weeks ago. Not that dramatic a tragedy, I'll give you, not nearly as heart-clawing as the ones God would throw before us in the not-too-distant future, but *Granny's,* this had been our first. You should have seen how we faced up to it. Not a tear shed, not by Ma, not by Dad, not by any of us. We buried her and had people over the house. Finished and done. But the way she died, that's what killed me. She just hobbled upstairs after not touching dinner, sat herself down on the commode in her room and dropped dead. I had never given Granny much thought—she'd been ancient and untalkative for as long as I can remember—but I felt so sorry for her there on her toilet as a houseful of firemen and ambulance guys pawed over her before lugging her body away. A dead body. Right here in our house on Knoll Road. Chilling, shocking, *yes,* but the next part, the part where they prepare the dead body for viewing—this is the part to be avoided at all cost, particularly if the dead body is yours. Prying eyes all over you. People who wouldn't have given you the time of day—NOW they look at you. They practically *study* you, you and your withered self. And you can go without warning, that's the thing. Watching *Dragnet* one minute, dead the next on the commode Dad ordered from Sears.

My dreams have been different too, not the usual trauma of being chased through jungles by soldiers, natives, spiders or wolves. Now I wake up drenched in sweat with visions of *Ma* laid out in that coffin, plain as day, her arms crossed like Granny's, everybody staring, her privacy washed away like bleach. I go to her wake too, boy. I go in

there swinging a baseball bat at the crummy mourners. I've been seeing these things for almost a week now, night and day. Sometimes it's
a different family member, but mostly it's Ma, suddenly dead, leaving
us all to fend. But then I'm reminded of my cavalcade of moles and
know I'll be the first to go.

And so today I am praying. I am *really* praying. I am
kneeling by my bed and I am praying. Praying for a sign. Something.
Anything. My sniggering brother would be struck down dumb.
Anything that'll convince me that what I am praying to is God and
not just a bedspread covered with cowboys. And then my mother
bursts into the room.

"Johnny!" she screams. "That was Monsignor Burke! They want
you to serve Mass on Sunday! THIS Sunday!"

My brother looks up from his comic in disbelief, "You mean like
as an *altar* boy?"

"Yes!" she cries. "The eight-thirty tomorrow morning! Ohh, I've
got to call Aunt Fran and tell her we'll pick her up for the early one and
I'll shine up your good black shoes and I'll pick up some Beau Junior
to put in your hair and I'll call Pop-Pop and Uncle Tut and ohhhh, I'm
just so proud of you!" And she kisses me all lipsticky on the cheek and
races downstairs. My brother hangs upside down from his bunk, opens
wide his arms and says, "Forgimme Faddah, for I have sinned! It's been
thirteen months since my last confession!"

"Shut up," I retort.

"But I took the Lord's name in *vain*!" he rails. "I took it today,
twice yesterday, and fifty Christ-forsaken times last week!"

"Say three Hail Marys, two Acts of Contrition and hang yourself."

He goes back to his *Hulk*. And laughs.

I vaguely recall signing up for altar boys. I remember taking the
classes on Saturday with Father Gillipede and three or four other
kids, but I never got called because I was rotten at it. I never both-

ered learning the little Latin responses you were supposed to say back at the priest (I just went "ooby-dooby ubba-dubba"). And I was never sure exactly when you were supposed to ring the little bell, or how many rings you were supposed to give it, or when you were supposed to get up and move the priest's big hooby Bible from one end of the altar to the other, while he just stood there reading words off it, his arms upraised like some quack about to take out somebody's gall bladder. And I never understood why the priest just didn't move his *own* bible, instead of leaving it up to little scrawny kids like me—a rib cage with a cowlick—who struggled with the thing as if it was a refrigerator.

For me to get assigned to serve Mass, a Sunday Mass at that, can only mean that an outbreak of diphtheria or something has bowled through the rest of the altar boys like a plague of hail and locusts. And to be called in now, in my darkest hour, while I'm on my knees praying to God knows what, wondering which of my two million festering moles will be the one to do me in, can be nothing less than a *sign*. "Abandon your worries, my son," it appears to be telling me, "For soon you shall dwell at the right hand of God!" And I close my eyes and picture myself kneeling in church, surrounded by the stained-glass mosaics of all fourteen stations of the cross, with Jesus being ratted out in this one and spat at in that one and whipped and scorned and crowned with thorns and stuck with spears and nailed to the cross like a specimen in a bug collection—when suddenly I get it. I *get* it. All that thee-thou Catechism stuff that's been crammed into me since my Christening is as clear now as the wounds on Christ's hands. The life-after-death part. The Jesus-died-for-your-sins part. I get it. I get all of it. And, okay, I wouldn't mind finding a *fifteenth* station, where Jesus jumps down off the cross, pounds his chest, bares his teeth, rips the cross out of the ground as if it were no more than a stalk of corn and beats the brains out of every last jerk in

Rome with it—but I GET it. I am swelling with newfound faith and Christianity. I am ready to face my death. And the life beyond.

The newfound faith is still with me the next morning, Sunday morning, and I am up with the honk of the horn. The honk is coming from the Gullivan & Son panel truck, which is idling outside with my father in it. He generally picks up my mother and the rest of us *after* he's done with the papers. Then we travel to worship in style. He's up against it today, though, because this is the early Mass. The truck is still half-full of the Sunday edition. We all get to ride back there reclining on bundles (a vast improvement over the bare metal floor) reading *Li'l Abner* and *Cicero's Cat*. My older sister Dee Dee is sitting on the pile right in front of me. Her name is short for Jean, which she has never been called. Oddly enough, in the back of the truck on the way to church is about the only time the Gullivan siblings actually talk. Oh, Gully and I exchange conversation a little bit with them at home, I guess, but that's more in the way of taunting, set to song and verse.

"Ma's really proud of you," whispers Dee Dee, leafing through a *Parade* under one of the dome lights.

"Yeah," says sister Cassie, "you'd think you were being ordained."

Madgie just sucks her thumb and rolls her eyes at the very idea. Gully sleeps, his body shagged across three stacks of *Globe*s and a twisted nest of packing rope.

I look at Ma in the passenger seat up front, her eyes on the road like a ranger, all the while fretting over the smudges of newsprint that're likely to end up all over her daughters' dresses. But when we stop to get Aunt Fran, Ma crawls in the back with the rest of us, stroking Madgie's hair as she smiles at me, an Easter Sunday smile, all the way to St. Ukelele's.

The papers have to be delivered to three different churches by half-past eight but I, luckily, won't be taking part in the drop. I have to be at the rectory by eight to get dressed. Dad pulls up to the curb, swings open the rear doors and lets me out. And the females in the family wave good-bye. An unusually dramatic wave. A going-away-to-Princeton wave. A Johnny-we-hardly-knew-ye wave. My posture seems straighter as I turn to climb the steps, inhaling maturity with every breath of air. I decide to open a checking account on Monday.

The maturity stays with me, along with the posture and the new-found faith, carrying over to the moment that I and Floydie Simmons (another rookie) escort Monsignor Burke in an organ-accompanied procession out of the sacristy, looking for all the world like miniature monsignors ourselves, freshly scrubbed in our frilly white surplices and our long, black, buttoned-down-to-the-shins cassocks, with only part of our pant legs and wrinkled socks revealed. Amazingly, a lot of the maneuvers I thought I'd never learned in practice come back to me right off the bat in the *actual* Mass. I'm not entirely sure if I'm following Floydie or he's following me—all I can tell you is that we seem to be bowing in breathtaking precision and kneeling in just the right way. Of course, young Father Gillipede's over in the wings directing the two of us with gestures and head feints, but after a while, even he seems confident, which is good. Father Gillipede is stocky and quiet and seems invisible next to Monsignor, who breathes fire. His sermons are different too, real personal and everything. I saw him do one about this kid he used to hang with who got his lips burned off. I remembered it for two whole days. He was also pretty good at training altar boys and I can tell right now he's smiling. Floydie and I silently pray our way over to our assigned seats off to the side, and sit quietly all during Monsignor's sermon, just like we'd been drilled, as rigid as Buckingham guards.

I glance out at the packed house before me. Aside from my beaming red parents and my grandfather, sisters, aunt, uncle, and softly giggling brother in the third row, I recognize none of these gloms. (We never go to the eight-thirty Mass.) I've seen a couple of them around town, I guess, but never here, all gussied up in their caked-on makeup and their ill-fitting suits. Monsignor's monotone rasp, though, early *or* late, still sounds like botulism. When he leans over the pulpit with every inch of his lengthy frame, with furrowed white brows that look capable of ringing your neck all by themselves, and hisses, "My dear friendzzzzz in Chrissssszzzzt. . ." it sounds like profanity. All of which makes my eyes wander further, darting from pew to pew to pew, before screeching to a halt at the sight of a woman, an enormous mahogany-haired woman, all by herself in the very first row. Stuffed into a bathroom-wallpaper-print dress (pink and green amoebas against a navy blue background) with a huge necklace of skeeball-sized pearls pinching her gargantuan neck, and a pocketbook as big as a mail sack at her side. But her face, her sweet angelic face, is as pretty and kind as a kindergarten nun. She glimmers with bracelets and brooches and earrings, and, at first, I mistake the thing sticking out of her neck as more of the same. But wait a minute, I say, how can a piece of jewelry stick out of a neck? I steal another glance, and another, and another. My body and my head remain motionless, staring straight ahead, fixed on nothing but Monsignor. Only my eyes move, returning again and again to the thing, which was REAL, which was attached to a STEM, and which quivered each time she exhaled. My God, it hits me, the damn thing's a MOLE! A swollen, pinkish, peach-fuzzed monstrosity the size, shape, and color of a Boston Baked BEAN! On a STEM! In MOTION! My peripheral vision tells me that my brother is in convulsions, but I don't look at him. I just look at the lady. I just look at the mole. I can hear the Monsignor drone on. I can feel Floydie Simmons fidget. But I can't take my eyes off the mole. Then a thin ray of sunlight filters down from a crack in the stained glass to a spot on the tip of my freshly shined shoe. I am certain I'm receiving a sign. And the sign says, "My son, you are going to live! You shall go forth and enjoy a long and prosperous life!" For it suddenly makes crystal-clear sense to me that if this poor unfortunate woman can sit here, right in front of every clodhopper in town, and survive to a reasonable age with a thing on her neck like a dart from a pygmy's blowgun, then none of *my* puny little moles are gonna amount to anything. I can hear my brother squeaking and tittering and desperately holding his sides, but it has no effect on me at all. I feel like a weight has been lifted. I feel pious. I feel saved. I feel I may enter the priesthood. Stone-faced I sit there, as if my portrait's being done, feeling the Savior all around me—as Monsignor honks and honks, Floydie picks his ears, and my brother laughs and laughs.

I move effortlessly through all the other parts of the Mass, lugging the Monsignor's hooby old book like it's nothing and giving old Floydie the heads-up when it's time to ring the bell. I recite Latin-like gibberish that almost *sounds* like Latin, and when it's time to pray, I pray bowed over, like a Turk in some mosque, my genuflections sweeping, majestic acts of adoration. And when it's time to serve Communion and I accompany Monsignor to the railing to assist him in the serving of it, I see my family lining up; I see the wet-eyed pride in my mother's and Aunt Fran's faces; I see the Vatican in my future.

My function in this last part of the Mass involves a tray—this small, flat, gold-plated dish the size of a Ping-Pong paddle that you're supposed to slide under the chin of each communicant as they kneel at the railing and open their mouths to receive. You steady the tray there to catch any crumbs or drool that may come spewing out, and right down the line you go. Nothing to it. Floydie's down one end with Father Gillipede and I'm over here with Monsignor. Easy as pie. But the *tongues*. I am not prepared for the tongues. I have not, in fact, up to this point, ever had a solitary thought about tongues. Or, if I'd thought about them at all, it was always the "Th-Th-That's All, Folks!" model that stuck in my head, the happy-as-hell fire engine–red kind with the dazzling white highlight. But these pale, pockmarked abominations before me now, wriggling hungrily out of the mouths of one seventy-five-year-old parishioner after another, are making my hair stand on end. "Put those despicable slabs of uncooked octopus meat back in your yaps!" I want to shout. "You remind me of birds in a nest waiting for *worms!*" I begin to shake. Sweat. Hyperventilate. And each tongue we come upon is more disturbing than the last! Tongues. *Tongues.* A chorus line of papillary slime! And I am in this particular frame of mind when we arrive, the Monsignor and I, at The Lady With The Mole.

Her eyes being closed, I am able to study the atrocity in minute detail. My God, I inhale, it's actually furry! But, like the stroke of a harp, an unexpected serenity comes over me. A quieting. And although my brother is waiting his turn at the railing right behind her, tears of hysteria glistening on his cheeks, I am oblivious. The tray, which had been shaking in my trembling hands, was now still. I had been calmed by the thing on this sweet large lady's neck.

But then, as she opens wide her jaw to receive the precious host from Monsignor's steady fingers, something extraordinary happens. The mole, suddenly, sharply, and without warning, *disappears*! Slaps itself against the side of her neck as if on a hinge. Conceals itself behind her ear like it never existed. And as she closes her mouth to chew, I stare in wide-eyed disbelief as it comes swinging back out like the sign at a railroad crossing, quivering like a willow in wind.

"Jesus Christ!" I gasp, loud enough to be heard. "The mole has a life of its OWN!"

Looking back on it, I knew it was wrong to just stand there, jaw dropped in stupor, arms hanging at my sides. I knew it was wrong for the Monsignor to have to nudge me in the shoulder, trying to snap me back to business. I knew it was wrong to release my grip on the tray's handle, sending it clanging to the rug in front of my parents and all creation. But I knew it was very, very wrong to even think about gazing in the direction of my brother, who was helplessly pissing his pants and whimpering, four or five feet away. But gaze I did. His eyes met mine. And all was lost.

2

Ten Years Later

The "van" is a splotchy, bathtub-colored Econoline with one bumper, two cracked mirrors, a flame-charred roach clip dangling from the engine hub like a cowboy necktie and a speedometer stuck on twelve. The cargo space in back offers no windows, no lighting, and basically two options for seating: the spare tire—which sits on its side collecting refuse like a giant clam—or the couch, this black vinyl embarrassment we lifted out of the K of C Hall and normally set aside for the random skank one of us may chance to seduce off the seawall at Wollaston Beach. At the moment, though, my brother's crapped out on it by himself, with his feet in the air, ignoring the *motion* of the couch, which, depending on acceleration or braking, scrapes back and forth along the van's ribbed metal floor like furniture on a sinking ship. I know. I rode back there last week, during Gully's most recent attempt at a driver's license. Which brings up the central dilemma that Gully has lived with: he is drawn to machinery, all machinery, but is virtually incapable of operating it. Something to do with depth perception. All motorized craft seems to him much larger than it actually is and anytime he has a steering wheel in his fists he feels all the world's power unleashed. A girl he sometimes goes with, Gina Sookey, who also happens to be Ma's twice-a-week caretaker, lent him her car for his *first* try at a license. The car, a '67 Galaxy that started up like a cattle drive and spewed black smoke out of both exhausts, shook so violently that the Registry cop giving the test spilled coffee on his pants, got mad, and canceled the whole thing.

"And that was fine with me," said Gully. "Driving that fucking bomb woulda been like landing a fighter on the SS *Kearsage*."

For my brother's second attempt, we took the van. I sat on the vinyl couch and ate Fritos as he started her up and adjusted the mirror, the cop checking off boxes on a clipboard. "Okay, Steverino, pull out of the parking lot and hang a right onto Pearl."

Gully yanked the steering column nervously into *drive* and eased slowly toward the street. He came to a gradual stop. Looked to his left, looked to his right. Looked again to his left. Unless you counted the two cars about a half mile in the distance, he had the road to himself. Apparently he was counting the two cars in the distance, though, because he just stayed put and studied them, casually looking again to his right, then back to his left. Good, I said to myself, he's being cautious. Maybe a little *too* cautious, if you ask me, but you can't be cautious enough when you've got cops in the passenger seat. The cars got closer; the first one a four-door Toyota with a vinyl roof, the other a dark-green station wagon with a CB antenna. You wouldn't have been able to tell that from way back where we first saw them. Now, you could tell that the guy driving the four-door had a hat with a feather in it and the dog with its head out the window was a Lab. And now my brother gunned it and screeched out to the street.

"*Jesus!*" he yelled, as the two cars seemed to come out of nowhere, taking him completely by surprise.

"*Jesus Christ!*" screamed the Registry cop, as Gully struggled frantically for the vehicle's control, bouncing off the median strip with both left tires as the Toyota tried valiantly to swerve around him on the right. The van swung back to the other side, brushing the wagon on the left fin before coming to rest on the lawn in front of a blue house, largely because the cop grabbed the wheel with one hand and turned off the ignition key with the other. He then stared at Gully for a very long time, waiting for his breathing to return to normal. "Do *you* drive?" he turned to me.

"Yes," I said, picking myself up off the floor.

"And you possess a valid license from the Commonwealth of Massachusetts?"

I showed it to him.

"Good. Drive me back to the Registry and drop me the hell off."

My brother resigned himself then to a lifetime of riding shotgun and that is where you will find him, night after night, his feet on the dash.

But on this night, Gully is on the couch. Chiefly, because his regular seat is occupied by no less than Ma. The van has never been a conveyance our mother has looked forward to traveling in, not even in its "distrib-uting" heyday, when the lettering on the sides was still dark blue and you could still make out our phone number—but here she sits, up front with me, biting her nails, riding her imaginary brake, adjusting her 99 percent human hair wig, one hand resting on the handle of the green-and-beige suitcase between us. An occasional snowflake zooms out of the darkness, splatting off the windshield as if some wiseass chucked it. The loudmouths on the radio are all over it, blathering about the *storm of the century* and *record-breaking snowfall*.

"It don't look like much *now*," cautions Ma, in what's left of her voice, "but it's gonna be a beaut!" Gully scoffs out loud, having about as much faith in meteorologists as he does in the sanctimonious quacks who'll carve great big hunks out of half of your organs, suck every cent of your life savings like a wet-dry vac and then tell you with a straight face that they'll shrink the rest of your cantaloupe-sized tumors by zapping you three times a week with something worse. I drop him and Ma at Emergency—the only entrance open this time of night—and go looking for a space. In the time it takes me to accomplish this, in the time it takes me to advise Harry the rent-a-cop to go shit in his fist, I park here all the time—Gully has already gotten into it with the admitting nurse, calling attention to the black-and-purple radiation burns the length of Ma's neck with: "It's a vasectomy she's after, lady, what the hell do you *think* brings her in?" They pretty much have her wheeled onto the elevator by the time I walk in; so we blow her a little kiss, snag a couple Sky Bars out of the vending machine and get the antiseptic Christ out of there.

"I got no problem calling the girls at Aunt Fran's if you call Dee Dee," yawns my brother from his usual shotgun position up front.

"I'll call the girls," I say, "but I'll let them call the D. I ain't about to get into no discussion about this shit with the D." The flakes are coming harder now, with greater frequency, and sideways at that. I am almost forced to use the wipers.

"Storm of the century," sniffs my brother. "Balderdouche."

It snows like the End of the World. A blinding, strafing, blitzkrieging snow, of a kind not seen before. Three nights and three days does it rage, nonstop and nearly horizontal, as if it were attacking from across the sea. You can barely stay out in it long enough to move the rabbits to the cellar, so hard and unforgiving it is. And it seems to want *in*—clawing at the shingles, rattling the doors, sandblasting the storm windows, forcing you to go full volume on the TV. It drifts halfway up utility poles like time-lapse photography, foot by foot by foot, shutting down business, halting all trains, stranding hundreds of motorists out on 128, and paralyzing the City of Boston and its surrounding communities like the King

Kong Queen of all blue laws. Not until the early hours of Thursday does it subside. Gully and I ride out most of it in bed, or watching the Stooges, or smoking what's left of the weed. My brother also spends a lot of time on the phone, whispering and giggling with Gina Sookey.

Noon. In the middle of Knoll Road. In it up to your waist, wearing your father's old reindeer sweater, your mother's fur-lined gloves. Squinting across an infinite ocean of white. Shivering. Breathing. Listening. To nothing. There are no cars, no mailboxes, no traffic islands, no *sound*. The triple-deckers are double-deckers and everything's muffled and buried and gone. You yell and you are the only one yelling. The only one breathing. The only one there. The faint chime of a city plow in the distance. The wail of one of Schoerner's penned-up hounds. But no one is with you. No one to contradict you. And you dare to close your eyes and fill up your lungs with winter, your destiny before you like a map of the world. And the wind seems to whisper promises, and you, with arms outstretched and chin to the heavens, swear oaths back to the wind— little things, like fulfilling prophecies and charting new courses and going forth from this time and this place to do great and wondrous things. But first, of course, it will be necessary to get high.

"We're in luck," said my brother, as I shook off the snow on the kitchen floor. "I just got off the horn with Worms Faulkner, who, it may interest you to know, has available one exceedingly fine ounce of Dominican Sin, and if we can get ourselves there by four, it's ours."

"Worms Faulkner?" I said. "Are you crazy? They're not allowing any vehicles on the road. How the fuck are we gonna get to Worms Faulkner's house all the way the fuck out in Braintree?"

"Don't have a miscarriage," said my Gully, who, when it came to the pursuit of getting high, could plan an itinerary worthy of the Billy

Graham Crusade. "I also just got through talking to Doody Levine, who, as you may know, is employed by the Red Cross. You know, they got him teaching that Heimlich shit on Saturdays."

"What the hell does that have to do with Worms Faulkner and his exceedingly fine ounce of Dominican?" I tried to keep up.

"Doody's on his way over with Red Cross armbands and logos and stuff," explained Gully. "We'll be able to ride around like we're the fucking mayors!"

"To the shovels!" I decreed.

Using landmarks and a crude version of dead reckoning, we were able to come up with a reasonable approximation of the spot we'd skidded the van into several nights prior, and, after a few furious minutes of dog-like digging, our calculations proved to be correct.

"Eureka!" wheezed my brother. "I think I just unearthed the antenna!"

"Excellent!" I panted. "Then this must be the right rear tire over here!"

In less than an hour, I was behind the wheel, stomping my boots on the floor, making the sign of the cross, turning the key—and spitting out a cocksucking string of motherfucking modifiers when the piece of cancer failed to start.

Schoerner, the veterinarian, whose imprisoned fleabags barked day and night and should be blamed more than *us* for putting our old man in his grave, forced open his front door and neighborly peered out at us as if he thought we were about to go over and shovel him out next. "Fuck his ancient ass," said Gully, and I stopped to recall that fateful March night, when Dad, who was a middle-aged knot of frustration as it was, charged out to the driveway in his pajamas at 1:17 a.m., screaming, "SHUT UP! SHUT UP! SHUT UP! SHUT UP!" through clenched skullish teeth, which only inspired the unseen dogs to reach greater heights in their shrilly cacophony, their excited toenails dancing back and forth along the bottom of the plywood fence like the fingers of Ferrante and Teicher. He desperately tried to hurl a barrel of trash at them, but it was half-full of rain, the weight got the better of him on the backswing, and *he,* not it, went crashing into the kennel wall headfirst. There was a strange but peaceful look on his face when we got to him, tongues flicking out from under the fence to lap at the blood, trash everywhere, a rusty metal handle in one fist.

"Either he was gonna get those dogs or they were gonna get him," sobbed Ma, as we waited in the chill for the ambulance. Fuck Schoerner.

I came pretty close to my *own* meltdown trying to start the mostly frozen van, pounding on the dash with both fists, attempting to wrest the sun visor from its overhead mount with every ounce of my inherited anger, and, just when it seemed about as hopeless as finding oil in the sand with a stick, the dented dirigible came shuddering to life, pent-up exhaust vomited from the wildly shaking tailpipe, and a five-foot section of snow got blackened. Gully signaled touchdown and the both of us roared.

It was right about this time that Doody Levine, holding a yellow plastic shopping bag high in his hand, came breaststroking up our driveway. He held tightly to the bag, not willing to relinquish its contents until we both swore an oath that we would never divulge how this material happened to come into our possession no matter what methods of interrogation were used, and that we were gladly prepared to die like martyrs before even breathing the *name* Doody Levine.

"Sure, Dood," said Gully, "Whatever you say. We solemnly swear and everything. Now what's in the fucking bag?"

"These babies are magnetic," he said, whipping out a pair of large white placemats with a big red cross on each one. "You slap 'em right on the doors like this, see? And these are your armbands, one for each arm. And, need I remind you, you two assholes owe me, like, *big time*. When you get the shit from Worms, stop by my place. I got a pipe big enough to fucking sleep in."

"Pencil us there," I assured him.

"And one more thing!" yelled Doody, as he fought his way back down the driveway. "Wear something *white!* It looks a lot more authentic if you wear something *white!*"

This presented a slight problem. My brother and I were not exactly of the white-collar variety, and neither was our father before us. The only white clothes we owned, in fact, other than our little First Communion suits that hung in Ma's closet, were our blood-stained old smocks from our days at Frannie's Fine Foods, which stood not a block from Dudley Station, right smack in the heart of Roxbury. Very few Caucasians in the world, particularly Caucasians from our Irish/Jewish/Intolerant neck of it, were known to venture very far into *any* part of Roxbury, much less to Frannie's Fine Foods. But Gully and I, all but unemployable in our home town since the sudden and unexpected liquidation of Gullivan & Son Distrib., ventured there several times a week, grabbing an exhaust-scorched bus out of Mattapan Square, squeezing our white but soulful behinds onto the elevated train at Egleston, then stepping out onto the sun-dappled platform at Dudley—another language, another Stax-Volt soundtrack, another world.

We were stock boys. Our days and sometimes nights were spent ripping open cases of beans or cauliflower or pig's feet, stamping smudgy prices on the cans, stacking the cans on stained and sticky shelves and slowly, deliberately, in the same go-fuck-yourself style of the black kids we worked with, dragging ass back to the stockroom for more. Occasionally we (that is, Gully and I) would be ordered to roll this revolting mountain of entrails and gizzards down to a huge, foul, fly-ridden receptacle in the basement. That's where the smocks came in. Our boss was a large, purple-faced, mean-spirited, cigar-chomping, Dumpster-shaped glom named Leonard Bernstein (which Gully and I thought was rich beyond belief, since we couldn't imagine the hairy-backed buffoon having the musical wherewithal to whistle "Three Blind Mice" without assistance).

Bernie, as we all called him, was more than accustomed to putting up with a great amount of lip from the many brash young black kids who worked under him, but drew a very distinct line at taking any lip whatsoever from any brash young kids who were the same basic color as him. But my brother and I were feeling exceptionally brash this particular afternoon, having been screwed out of eighteen minutes of overtime we'd put in two weeks back, and we both gave it to Bernie pretty good. *Adjectives* were used. Ones like *hemorrhoid-faced,* as I recall. We were fired. Together. As a team. Bernie brought us our time cards and methodically ripped them up in our faces, letting the little pieces fall to our feet as if he were symbolically destroying our lives. "*Now take off my smocks!*" he bellowed, the cigar stub rolling out of his carp-like mouth like a turd, "*and get the hell out of my store!*"

All this, it must be said, did not take place in the privacy of Bernie's office. Nor did it occur in the cavernous stockroom out back. Nor in the employees' lunchroom, or out on the shipping dock or in the shithouse under the stairs. It happened right smack-dab in the middle of Frannie's Fine Foods at two o'clock in the afternoon, with all the young black stock boys and the young black checkout girls and the heavy black women with their overstuffed shopping carts and the three bald Jewish butchers behind the meat counter and the seven sad lobsters bubbling away in the holding tank, all looking on silently to see what form, if any, our response would take. A response was in order, there could be no doubt, but we'd pretty much used up all our adjectives in the *first* go-round. So we took the only action we could take: spun on our heels in gorgeous synchronization, snatched two Slim Jims and a bag of Doritos from a nearby dolly and marched right out of Frannie's Fine Foods with our

Frannie's Fine Foods smocks still on our backs, with Bernie right on our tail, screaming, "*I'll see you in jail, you disheveled bastards! You'll never get away with this! I'll see you fry, you thieving sonovabitches! Do you hear me?! You're gonna fry! Fry! FRY!!*"

And out into a teeming Dudley Street we strode, masters of our own destiny, striking a blow for oppressed workers everywhere, proudly wearing our smocks. Our dirty, smelly, frayed, blood-spattered, chicken liver–stained Frannie's Fine Foods smocks.

Which looked remarkably snazzy, we now observed, with Red Cross armbands fastened to the sleeves.

They'd plowed the main roads a dozen times a day during the storm, and, though it had largely been a losing battle, I was almost sure they could be navigated. The side streets, on the other hand, which had barely been touched, were another matter. We lived on a side street. Being fairly skilled at this sort of thing, though, I wagered if we could just get up enough momentum coming down our rather steep driveway to carry us across the Boston cream pie of Knoll Road, and swerved into the intersection at just the right time, we'd hit Mallard Avenue in good shape and follow the main roads all the way to Braintree. Gas might prove to be an issue, especially since Spid and his 67.6-cents-a-gallon highway-robbery Sunoco was still shut down, but we'd take our chances.

We hung Doody's red crosses on each door. Adjusted our armbands. Gazed out onto the horizon. My brother turned up the radio real loud. I spit in my hands, tightly gripped the steering wheel, rev-rev-revved the engine 'til it threatened to explode, and put the van in gear.

Shrieking like madmen, the Swedish bobsled team hurtled down the slope into the wall of white, great gobs of snow slapping at their sides like sharks at the *Kon Tiki*. Grinding, groaning, whining, the van lurched, fought for yardage, and almost turned over, then heaved itself into Mallard on two wheels and we were underway. The only vehicle on the road. Hunters on the Serengeti Plain. Grim, lonely men were beginning to dig out from under and stopped to look at us as we drifted slowly by.

"See?" said my brother. "We are cool. We are cool. We are completely fucking cool."

I agreed. I'd been a little concerned about the three bald tires we hadn't taken off the van since Dad died, but they seemed to be handling reasonably well. The pace was excruciatingly slow but we made up time by going right through any and all traffic lights. I even went so far as to drive left-footed for a bit and rested my right foot on the engine hub, so overwhelmingly cool did I feel.

We had only traveled maybe a half mile, past nearly buried two-families and a barely recognizable post office, when, up in the distance, there appeared to be a *man,* a short, middle-aged man, without a coat, frantically waving his arms out in the middle of the street.

"What's with the birdbrain up ahead?" laughed Gully, and I laughed with him. The awful realization hit us at the same time.

"Oh *shit!*" I said, dropping my forehead to the steering wheel. "This dickhead thinks we're real Red Cross guys! He wants us to *help!*"

"We *can't* stop!" shouted Gully, panic rising in his voice. "He probably wants us to set his fucking *leg! Can you* set his fucking leg?! I can't set his fucking leg!"

"Look," I said, sitting up straight. "We blow him off; he calls the cops and has us arrested for impersonating someone who gives a shit. Let's just see what he wants." I slowly pulled the van up close to the shirtsleeved man as Gully rolled down his window.

"Whatsa problem, man?" asked my brother.

"It's my mother!" gasped the man. "She can't breathe! She's all out of oxygen! She has to get to the hospital right away!" He paused to catch his breath. "The ambulance says they'll get here when they *get* here! What the hell does that *mean*?! Can you fellas take her in?"

"Sorry, pal," said my brother, "we'd really like to help, but we're sort of on our way to a CPR convention and we can't be late."

The man stared at my brother. Then he stuck his head way into the van and stared at me. Then back at my brother. Then at the much-abused black vinyl couch we kept in the back of the van for romantic purposes and then back at me. He was giving us The Look. The same look we used to get from Ma when she'd bag us smoking bones behind Schoerner's. Great. We hadn't so much as encountered a *seed* in seven hours and here we were getting The Look. We would have to think fast.

"Well, look," I said, "my associate and I would be glad to take a peek at your mother."

"Good," said the man. "Follow me." He pushed away from the van, did a little skip-jump through the path he'd cut earlier with his snow-blower and waited impatiently at the foot of his steps like Lassie leading the search party. I was now getting The Look from my brother.

I tried to check the time on the snow-covered clock up the street before climbing down and joining Gully and the little man on the porch. He swung open the heavy glass door to the right. The name over the doorbell began with a *W*, ended with a *Z* and had pretty much the rest of the alphabet in between. We entered into a dark, drab, yellowy hallway and climbed creaky, treaded stairs to the second floor. The door to the apartment was open. Sheets of hard thick plastic, the kind used by offices to protect carpets from the ravages of swivel chairs, formed an intricate pathway throughout the house from one room to another. We trailed the man down this yellow brick road to the far bedroom and there found the mother, propped up in bed, under a paint-by-number picture of two Mexicans taking a siesta, holding a large blue handkerchief to her mouth.

"Sophie, these men are here to help you," the man said, rushing right past her to a closet in the back of the room. (I imagined calling Ma by her first name—wouldn't *that* get a laugh?)

"Vat are dey, doctors?" rasped the large old woman.

"No," said the man, emerging from the closet with a black fur coat and a large blue pocketbook, "they are going to *take* you to the doctors."

"Did dey take off dere shoos ven dey kem in or are dey just drippeenk de snow all ofer de rug?"

"Sounds like she's got plenty of wind to me," said my brother.

"Here, lady," I said, offering my hand, "let me help you up."

The woman looked over to her son with an expression of absolute horror and began wheezing into her handkerchief.

"Oh, she won't be able to walk," said the man. "We'll have to carry her out." He draped the coat about her shoulders and started fumbling under the bed for her slippers.

"*Carry* her?" exclaimed Gully. "Look, buddy, whattya think we are, circus elephants?!"

"Uh, my associate and I need a moment to confer," I said, drawing my brother into the living room. "Shit almighty, we've come this far. She don't appear to be all *that* heavy."

"*Heavy*?! She looks like Hoss Cartwright with a Jewish accent! I'm not getting involved in this!"

"What if she croaks?" I reasoned. "Can you live with that?"

He gave me a hard look. Then he peeked in at the poor, confused, gasping old woman on the bed. "You always have to bring death into it, don't you? Okay, let's go. She's gonna croak anyway when we drop her down the gaddamned stairs."

We spit in our hands and went to work. With the man and I on either side of her and Gully holding onto her ruined feet, we got the wheezing, frightened old thing down the stairs, out to the street, into the van and onto the mildewed old couch in the time it takes to pee. My brother lost one of his armbands on the turn coming out of the hallway, but had no interest in retrieving it.

"Drive," he said.

What normally would have been a five-minute ride to the Crawley took nearly three times that in the heavy snow. "So how long have you folks been living in our fair city?" I asked the passengers on the couch, trying to make conversation, something I always did when I used to pick up fares for Morton Cab.

"You drife too goddamn slow," said the woman.

The hospital loomed in the distance, its icy brick facade looking colder and more impenetrable than usual.

3

Full

The first of my family's many outings to Crawley Hospital came the day after Dad had taken us on our yearly *blueberry*-picking outing in the Blue Hills. Of all our annual one-day excursions into nature, the blueberry one was tough to beat. The cool pine air drugged us like catnipped dogs. Ma and the girls and the girl next door, Dally Schoerner, who had a mustache, giggled and laughed and acted out songs from *South Pacific*, all the while counting out loud to see who'd pick the most. My brother and I ran around chucking acorns at chipmunks and urinating on trees. Dad smoked. Way up high on a rock. With his hat pulled down over his eyes.

Later that night Ma made three good-sized pies and I ate one. I'd been breathing in their succulence half the night as they slowly cooled in the pantry, and I could stand no more. I crept downstairs in the pitch dark and felt around for a knife or a fork or a garden spade for that matter, and tore, with a vengeance, into pie number one. I didn't mean to down the whole thing. I just did. The first bite was the Second Coming and it went uphill from there. Everything about it: the *filling;* the *crust;* the soggy sweet underbelly that floated on your palate like the watercolor backgrounds in *Pinocchio*. I devoured every inch of it without so much as a burp. Then I calmly wiped my purple face on the dish towel, wiped my hands on my shorts, thought for a second about breaking into pie number two, but caught myself, turned away from the remaining delicacies and crawled back into bed, a hugely satisfied mammal.

My stomach started asking questions the minute my head hit the pillow. "*Why?*" It demanded to know. "Why, Johnny, *Why?* Why did you do it? Why? Why?! *Why?*!" Sections of intestine I never knew I had tentacled up from the bodily depths, punching and clawing at my abdomen for any possible way to escape. *air . . . air . . .* must . . . have . . . *air . . .* must . . . have . . . *air . . .* must have— *air!!* Hot molten lava sloshed audibly from my bowels to my esophagus like seawater into a cave. Faster . . . Faster . . . It whirlpooled into my solar plexus. Rippled under my newly sprouted pubic hair. Churning . . . churning . . . faster . . . faster . . . "*Christ . . . Jesus . . . GOD!*" I clutched at the springs under Gully's bed and gurgled for my mother as the world and all its continents exploded from every possible exit in my body, and the cowboy-papered room ran red. Gully got up on his knees screaming for help like a guy trapped on a rock in a fast-rising flood. Lights went on. Parents in pajamas came toe-stubbing, elbow-banging and swearing down the hall. A sister cried out: "*whatizzit?!*" Another: "*Are we in a fire?*" Pets poked their noses in and recoiled from the horror with tails between legs. And still the purple-red agony spilled helplessly out of me, from both ends, with no end in sight.

"*Jesus and Mary!*" gasped Ma, who tried to hold me down like a boated tuna as she barked for Dad to call an ambulance. Dad's bewildered bloodshot eyes had now witnessed all there was to see. He did as he was told and rushed from the room.

"My *God*, Johnny, what's happened to you?" cried my mother, squeezing the crucifix that hung from her neck, trying to make sense of the war-torn scene.

"Pie," I managed to wheeze between convulsions. Please, Death, come soon, I was praying to myself—the warmth of my mother's arms cradling me all the way to heaven.

Her blue eyes looked questioningly into mine as she yanked up my head by a fistful of my vomit-drenched hair and said, "Pie? Did I just hear you say *pie*?"

"Yeah," I continued to spew. "*Piiiiiiieeeeeeeeeeeeeee . . .*"

She was up with a shot. "*Dee Dee! Go down to the kitchen, gather up all the pies and throw them into the garbage!*"

"In the *garbage*?" came my sister's voice. "But we picked nearly three and a half gallons of . . ."

"*Now!*" screamed Ma, "before your father, the dog, or anyone else gets into them!" The guilt on her stricken face was obvious. She had unwittingly poisoned her own son. And the son, nearing unconsciousness, was in no shape to explain that it was the amount eaten and not the pie itself. She prayed as loud and as fast as she could—pieces of this prayer, snatches of that, casting out devils in the name of the Lord who dwelleth in high places and reigneth over heaven and earth—as the Blue Hills flowed relentlessly onto my rug, my table, my bed, my windowsill, all over our much revered issue of *Fantastic Four* #44 ("The Battle of the Baxter Building") and into my sneakers, shoes, jackets, socks, and anything else that happened to be in its path.

"Will we have to move?" Madgie asked, holding her nightgown to her mouth and nose.

"The ambulance is on the way!" said Dad, who hesitated at my doorway like a deer at a clearing.

"We can't wait!" cried Ma. "He's turning *blue*!" And she suddenly became Haystacks Calhoun and gathered me off the bile-sullied bed like a sandbag. "Grab the girls, get the keys to the truck and let's go!" I could feel my eyes rolling back in my head as they wrapped me in swaddling sheets and, together, hauled me down the stairs. In a manger of day-old *Herald*s they lay me, like the Trumbull painting of *The Death of General Warren,* my organs continuing to expunge on a rotating basis. Ma held my wildly trembling hand and begged the forgiveness only God could give.

"There goes the ambulance," Dad observed, toot-toot-tooting to let them know we had their assignment in tow. The rest of my family was huddled against the side doors, as far away from the assignment as possible. Dee Dee made a sign of the cross and the girls and even Gully followed suit, the four of them staring dumbstruck, like they were watching hippopotami breed.

Dad swung the panel truck right in and backed it up to the emergency room like he was Eddie the ambulance man. Two large women in white thrust open the back doors and reached for me, not wasting any time telling Dad that he'd have to get his jalopy out of there pronto because a stabbing was coming in. "Busy, busy, busy night," they felt obliged to tsk-tsk-tsk as they wheeled me in, apparently trying to convey a message to all involved that the loss of all bodily functions had a long ways to go to compete with a stabbing. Working in sinister tandem, they tore off my underwear, sponged me down like a shaved dog, tied me up in a red, white, and blue–striped johnny and stuck a thermometer in my mouth. It was their way of gaining the upper hand, I saw right away. Humiliate you with ridiculous clothing and stuff something in your yap to shut you up, well aware that you haven't the strength to resist. It seemed I was also deemed ready to receive visitors, as they flung open my curtain and presented me to the world, a large silver receptacle at my side, "In case he's got any more in him."

Gully laughed so hard when he saw me he hit his head on the railing that kept me from falling out. Nice. Of all the possible courses of action they *might* have taken—pump what was left of my stomach, give me the last rites of the church, amputate something—they go with the johnny. Then, with the mob that is my family hanging onto my gurney like pallbearers, they roll me right out into the hallway, for all the bald-headed gawkers in town to file past me like I'm lying in state.

The main reason I was parked there and not on the operating table where I belonged was because the vomiting had somewhat subsided and, despite my barely detectable breathing and four-days-dead complexion, they were figuring I would live. That and they had bigger fish to fry. Through the sorry slits of my eyes, and the crack in the hallway door, I could see all the way back into emergency. Even in my semi-comatose state, I clearly saw a guy's socked feet sticking out from a squadron of doctors, I saw a Morton High football jacket lying nearby, and I saw a fat lady at the foot of the guy's bed pointing and yelling and crying and pleading. And as one of the nurses reached frantically for something on a lower shelf, I saw blood, red as hamburger, soaking through clothing and sheets.

Words like *pulse* and *switchblade* and *vital organs* came blow-darting out to the waiting room and I heard Madgie and Cassie climb on board underneath, hoping to cash in on the same view as me. Then three guys in Morton football jackets slapped through the swinging doors and the word "Niggers!" made it on to the list, then "Look what them fucking niggers *did*!" and the three turned hard to go. The woman tried to block their path but they faked her out with two quick moves and were back through the exits as fast as they'd come in. Without saying a word, Dad followed them out. We could see him talking to them out in the parking lot, offering them ciga-rettes, which they all took, and lit, on one match. I then recognized the biggest one as Drake "Prick" LaPinza, who'd been one of Dad's most valued paperboys a few years back, a big tireless pack mule, capable of running two and three routes at a time. He wasn't called Prick then but he was definitely called Prick now, a mean and mas-sive pink-faced carnivore with a size-34 neck so scarred with acne it looked like hanging meat. He came by his famous nickname, it was said, by depositing about a quart of his own sperm into the gym sock of Gunther Malstreum, then putting it back into Gunther's gym locker for the unsuspecting lad to wear that very afternoon in a spiffy game of crab soccer.

Prick didn't seem to be buying a whole lot of what Dad was selling out there in the Crawley lot, but you could tell he was getting through to the other two because they were nodding a lot and looking down at their shoes. When Father Gillipede showed up, they trailed him back inside; and a disgusted Prick LaPinza threw down his cigarette and surged off into the blackness, leaving Dad smoking by himself in the cold. We shifted our positions on, and under, the bed. The lady (Mrs. Gerfalts, it turned out, which would make the guy swimming in blood Grady Gerfalts, tight end and linebacker) wailed Hail Marys as Father took the two guys by the shoulders and gently pushed them in the direction of the door. *Our* door. They came out real sullen-like and gave everybody a real good sneer, before spotting the color TV in the far corner and slouching down on the couch underneath it. Rex Harrison and Audrey Hepburn were singing, "The Rain in Spain Stays Mainly on the Plain," which caused one of the guys to mutter, "I'd plainly like to see you naked, you raven-haired tomato." And the other guy laughed out loud and so did Gully, who got knuckle-swatted by Ma, who'd just come back from filling out a Bible's worth of paperwork at the desk.

A nurse came over to tell us that arrangements had been made for me to stay overnight, so they could "monitor my condition." This horrifying news brought shrieks of fear from the girls below me, causing Ma to loudly wonder who allowed them to go down there in the first place. Dad asked the nurse if she thought the Gerfalts boy was going to pull through. She drew him aside. "Good Christmas, dearie," I heard her whisper, "not in front of the children."

They stuck me in room 327 with a very old guy named Fred who was in the process of coughing up a lung. It wasn't like he bothered me, though. I closed my eyes, exhaled like a harpooned whale, and fell asleep forever. My usual nightmares and premonitions were with me, of course, but they didn't keep me up.

The Fred guy was still coughing when I woke up. The sun was streaming through the venetian blinds. And Ma was there to take me home. She'd had to borrow old man Schoerner's station wagon to make the run because Dad and the panel truck were at work. Dally Schoerner was in the front seat with Dee Dee, Cassie, and Madgie, and I crawled in the back with the dog cages and Gully.

Dally turned around and gave me a big Hallmark card that she and her father had signed. Dally looked different, somehow. I couldn't put my finger on it. She was wearing a pale green cotton shirt with a white turtleneck underneath and the sleeves of the turtleneck showed on her dark forearms and her black hair hung down shiny and straight, except where it curved up at her shoulders and she looked different, real different, is all I can tell you.

My brother leaned over. "She bleached out the mustache," then added, "Maybe you should try it on the moles."

And as Dally Schoerner turned her gaze back to the road before us, I looked at the back of her jet-black head and read her card five, six, and seven times.

It's safe to say my family treated me like a king from there. I stayed up in Granny's old room convalescing for two whole days while they aired mine out. Gully got stuck with the couch. They brought me thin soupy things to eat and *Mad* magazines to read. Periodically, I looked out the window. Periodically, I looked over at the house next door. I had never seen it from this high up. All that was familiar about it seemed new. The swinging yellow sign with the panting brown dog; the matching blue dog bowls in the chain-link runs out back; the cluttered porch with the busted swing; and the third floor bedroom directly, *exactly*, across from mine. Then I noticed the clothesline. The clothesline that ran on an old rusted pulley from a hook just outside my window to a hook just outside hers. I remembered Dally telling us when we were little that both her granny and ours used to meet at the clothesline every day, cackling gossip across the great divide in their right-off-the-boat accents, one pulling laundry in, the other pinning it on. Ma once said that the day Sears Roebuck delivered the brand-new washer and dryer to Schoerner's back door was the last time the two ever spoke. "Thinks she's too damn good for us anymore," Granny was known to have said. She then had Dad put in a new line on the other side of the house, from the porch railing to the tree, so as not to give old lady Schoerner the satisfaction of seeing Granny's soaking wet pantaloons flapping over the driveway.

I continued to watch for the school bus like a pet terrier. I saw Dad pull in for lunch about sixteen past two. I saw Ma go across the street in her blue-and-green scarf to wait. It showed up right on time. My sisters and brother and Dally Schoerner, and the kid from Roland Street, who wore earmuffs all year round, got off it. Dally waved to the others and went in, hugging her schoolbooks tightly to her chest, as if she really, really liked them. Nineteen minutes later she appeared at the window and took off the red ribbon tie that was part of the uniform at St. Ukelele's, and then the patent leather shoes and the knee socks, first the left one, carefully rolling it down her calf like the unfurling of a potted palm, then the right. I got out of bed, fell to my knees, and, with what little strength I had, pried open Granny's long-neglected window and stuck out my head. I knew she saw me because I could see her waving out of the corner of my eye. But I never looked her way. I was far too occupied gazing out at the telephone pole and at the old vacant lot on the corner of Roland and at the fire hydrant on the island in the middle of Mallard. If I'd had one of Dad's Chesterfields, I'd be taking one of those squinty one-eyed Hollywood drags and flicking the ashes into the warm Morton air. I craned my neck out and looked far below, where Dad was under the panel truck draining out the oil while old man Schoerner, in his unbuttoned white vet's suit, rested his foot on Dad's bumper, lit his pipe and pestered him.

Slowly and painstakingly, my eyes allowed themselves to roll up the side of Schoerner's house, working their way from shingle to shingle until they suddenly locked on to Dally's brown eyes and I mouthed the surprised words, "Oh, hi!"

She mouthed back: "How are you feeling?"

I made like I couldn't hear. When she forced open her window with both arms I thought she was gonna start hollering. But she too took a peek at the proceedings down below, saw her old man and the lower half of mine and made a shushing gesture. She then ducked back to her desk and composed a quick note. Taking a bobby pin from her hair, her tongue licking her upper lip in determination, she reached way out, fastened the note to the clothesline and brought the prehistoric pulley to squeak-squeak-squeaking life. I had to strain out pretty far to retrieve it. Rendered in purple felt pen, with handwriting as big and gorgeous as the founding fathers, it asked, in all sincerity: **"How do you feel?"**

I ran across the room and tore apart Granny's old dresser looking for something to write with. I came up with lipstick, darker than lamb's blood, with the fragrance of all the old women in church. On the other side of the very paper she'd sent me, in my weak recuperating scroll, I scrawled, **"I'll live."** Then I pinned it to the line with an old sun- bleached clothespin I conveniently found on the windowsill and sent it squeak-squeak-squeaking back. I did not allow my lungs to breathe as I watched her haul it in. She smiled as she read it, sniffed it even, and, much to my relief, continued our correspondence. Squeak—squeak—squeak—

I snatched it off the line like a private at mail call.

"**When will you be coming back to school?**" it wondered. The **i's** were all dotted with teeny little hearts. I was aware of my moles, which were tingling, like a hatchery of gnats.

I wrote back: "**Maybe Friday . . . Probably not 'til Monday . . . I'm pretty much day-to-day.**" I tried dotting my **i's** with little hearts too. They came out looking like wrinkled little asses. Squeak.

Dally's reply came caterpilling right back: "**Everyone's been asking for U.**"

I had a hard time buying that one. I looked straight into her eyes for verification and they said: Yes! I said U! U, U, U! I rummaged through Granny's drawers until I found an unworn yellow blouse that had one of those cardboard rib cages inside it to keep it stiff. I tore off a hunk and scribbled: "**And how is the great and powerful Mother Superior?**"

This time she took about five minutes and dashed off a manifesto: "**As TEN COMMANDMENTS as ever! There was trouble at the school today, though. Mother had to call the police because Prick LaPinza showed up at recess looking for the cousin of the kid who killed Grady.**"

The word "*Prick*" jumped out of the page, throbbed like a Combat Zone marquee and stopped my heart in its tracks. No girl I had ever known had actually said Prick's name aloud. Everyone *knew* his name, of course, but the only people who called Prick Prick were the boys. The girls, just like the P.A. announcer at the football games, called him Drake. It was like catching a glimpse of Worms Faulkner's dog-eared copy of *Candy* that he kept in his locker and let you look at for twenty-five cents a pop. I ripped off a bigger piece of cardboard and casually inquired: "**What happened to PRICK? Did PRICK get arrested? Did PRICK get taken away?**"

The reply came squeaking back: "**I don't think so, but all three of our black kids are lying low.**" I swear the little hearts over the i's were beginning to look like the genitalia in Miss Grauster's health class at the YMCA. The exchange continued. The pieces increased in size. The pace got faster. The questions got more and more brazen. The subject matter got more and more adult.

"**Did you get the new Stones record yet?**" Squeak-squeak-squeak . . .

"**No, but has anyone ever told you that you look just like Keith Richard?**" Squeak-squeak-squeak . . .

"**Not lately.**" Squeak-squeak . . .

"**Yes! It's the *eyes*, I think, and the way your mouth curves at the corners in a perpetual frown is just WILD!**"

"**You should hear me sing.**"

"**What would you sing me?**"

"**Let's spend the NIGHT together,**" I said. She laughed out loud and hugged the message to her bosom like a geometry book.

Then she read it again, unconsciously unbuttoning the top two buttons of her blouse as she wrote: "**I just got a new bathing suit down at Maloof's. A *pink* one.**" Squeak-squeak . . .

"**That must look** (get this) **like the Cape Cod sky against your dark skin.**" Squeeeeeeeeeeeek . . .

"**Do you want to see it?**"

"**In the worst possible way!**"

She disappeared for about a four-minute eternity and returned to the window wearing it. The birds-and-bees talk I'd never actually had with Dad I was now having with myself. I began thinking thoughts about hickeys. French kisses. Gunther Malstreum's gym sock. She sent a new message. It simply asked: "**Well?**"

I came back with: "**Well, WELL!**"

She ran her left hand up the suit and back down it as her right hand wrote: "**It's Lycra, you know. It's so soft on my body I could die.**"

"**I'm already dead just *looking* at it.**"

"**You make me feel *sexy*.**"

"You make me want SEX"

Rolling her eyes, she wrote: **"I can plainly see why they say you've got the *Devil* in you, John Gullivan!"**

And I replied, on the biggest piece of cardboard in my dead grandmother's room—the old green ink blotter from her canvas-covered mahogany desk: **"And I'd plainly like to see you *naked*, you raven-haired TOMATO."**

Squeak-squeak . . .

And then something gave. Maybe the sheer weight of the blotter, I don't know. Maybe I tugged on the line with just a little too much torque. One way or the other, this particular piece of mail was not about to get through. The screws that held the pulley in on Dally's side shot suddenly free from their moorings, and the entire ensemble—rope, pulley, cardboard, and clothespin—came raining down on the ribbed roof of the Gullivan & Son panel truck like a buckshot goose from the sky.

It was over in seconds. I rested my chin on the windowsill, looked over at the shade-drawn window across and contemplated the many changes and conditions that were now due to come my way.

Dally would wear the bathing suit again in a few weeks, up at Houghton's Pond, but I never saw it, grounded as I was. She was wearing it when she saved Gully from drowning, believe it or not, something I would have given all my hair to see. She was the only one who saw Gully struggling in deep water gulping for his life, and she dove in like Tarzan's Jane, yanked his head into the crook of her arm and towed him to shore. It was the biggest thing that had happened at Houghton's Pond all day, maybe all summer, and I was home watching *Candlepins for Ca$h*. Ma took over from there and got Gully to cough up water and the crowd started cheering and Dad was hugging Dally and cops came and asked questions and my sister Cassie said she got a real good look at one of their guns.

The thing is, though, Gully wasn't happy at all about having his life saved and has a whole different take on things. He claims he was just out there playacting, like a shark had him, and wasn't in trouble at all until the showboating Dally jumped in and half-nelsoned him. "I was the victim of an unwarranted rescue!" he cried, and will always maintain.

To that, Dally huffed, "Well, then, you must have gills, Gilly, because your lungs were taking in water when I got to you." Dee Dee told me the consensus of the crowd was that Gully was faking it to save face and that Dally was a true hero. The crowd also got a kick out of the new nickname "Gilly" but it died out after a few days and never took. (I don't think girls are as obsessive as boys are about *making* nicknames stick.) At any rate, Gully and Dally were not on speaking terms after that, and then she was gone, first to camp, then to some private school a plane ride away.

But this was before all that. This was the day the incriminating correspondence slammed down on the roof of Dad's truck. This was the night my brother fell asleep laughing, woke up in the middle of the night laughing and was still laughing when the blue jays started up in the morning. The first words out of his mouth were, "I'd love to see you naked, you raven-haired *tomato*."

As for me, what would I love to see? The next note on the pulley. That's what I'd have given anything to see.

4

Oath

The problem with driving the most pitiable vehicle in town is that no sane person will believe it when you try to dress it up as something else. This thought hit us as we snaked our way up the snowy ramp to Emergency, the gigantic red crosses standing starkly against the van's pissed-on doornail finish like the pope's hat on a whore. The old lady on the couch gasped for air as we skidded and spun, her fretful middle-aged son hanging onto Gully's armrest with his fingertips in order to prevent the couch from sliding the length of the van and crashing out through the back doors with the two of them still on it.

"Are ve at de doctors?" rasped the old bird, as half the personnel of Crawley Hospital, dragging oxygen tanks, wheelchairs, and other unidentifiable apparatus, descended upon us like gulls at a trawler.

"Yes, Sophie," sighed the son of Sophie, "we are at the doctor's. And they should have everything ready for you."

They even knew her name. Like they knew she was coming. It was: "And how are we today, Mrs. Wzionkowitz?" And: "Be careful stepping down, Mrs. Wzionkowitz." And: "Gracious! That was some storm, wasn't it, Mrs. Wzionkowitz?" She just grabbed for the oxygen mask and dismissed the rest of their chitchat with a wave of her hand. They barely glanced at me *or* my brother as they wrapped her up and whisked her away. The authenticity of the Red Cross armbands, which stood out like the Stars of India against the sleeves of our gore-stained smocks and the rest of our unkempt selves, was never questioned. "It's a good thing you got her here when you did, Mr. Wzionkowitz," one of them said as they maneuvered her mastodonian girth through the revolving door. "Another minute longer might've been critical." Then the Son of Sophie looked back at us and sort of nodded, with his chin out, as if we'd all fought together at the Alamo.

I was feeling pretty worthy as I shifted into R. Accomplished, even. I was about to suggest that we lock up the van and hike up to Intensive Care to see Ma, but then realized that the conditions in the mostly deserted and semi-plowed parking lot would be absolutely ideal for putting the van through some 360's, the same sort of recklessness that recently cost me my job at Morton Cab.

"No, you are *not* doing donuts," said my brother.

"Just a couple," I insisted. "We're heroes, for Chrissakes, we need to celebrate."

"Celebrate? We dragged some poor old wretch out of her deathbed so they can butcher her here like a hog. The only celebrating we'll be doing will occur when we manage to dogsled this shitcan across three town lines and dive headfirst into Worms Faulkner's bag of Dominican."

I was forced to agree, and began driving in a sensible way. I adjusted the mirror, shifted into first, turned up the radio, and SLAMMED ON THE BRAKES! She was right in front of us. A nurse. One of the nurses from the emergency room. The one who was a good deal younger than the others and who had Irish Setter–colored hair and a smile white as soap. She ran to my window, holding up a tiny white parcel tied with string.

"Oh, I'm so glad I caught you!" she said, and began talking to us like we were five-year-old jeebers learning a fire drill. "This is *in-su-lin*. It needs to go to an elderly woman named Mrs. *Ku-pun-ska*. She lives on *Do-ber-man* Street. Can you take it? She really needs it. It's like really really really important!" She started bouncing on her toes to fight the cold.

My brother leaned across, "Look, lady, we'd really like to lend a hand, but we're on our way—"

"We'd be more than happy to take it," I said, snatching the package from her hands and passing it to Gully. "You'll probably be reading our names in the obituaries, of course, but we'll get it there one way or the other. Now what was that address again?"

"Three-thirty-four Doberman. Oh, God bless you both! I knew you'd help! You're a couple of lifesavers is what you are!"

"That's why we work for the Red Cross," I said, and winked. *Winked.* Then I rolled up the window all cocky and loose and set a course for the unknown.

"Have you lost your fucking *mind*?" squeaked my brother in his seldom-used Vienna Boys Choir contralto. "Braintree?! Do you, by any chance, remember *Braintree*?!"

"Don't have yourself a hernia," I said, giving the wheel some play. "I'm beginning to get a feel for this snow. We can run over to Doberman, drop off the poison to the hag and still have plenty of time to get to Worms's. And for Chrissakes, that was a nurse back there! A *nurse!* A standing member of the medical fucking profession, and there you go starting in with that crazy story about a CPR convention!"

"All I know," said my brother, looking straight ahead, "is that we have exactly one hour and forty-five minutes to make it to Braintree. If, for some reason, we do not make it to Braintree in one hour and forty-five minutes, we will not be sitting down with our good friend Worms Faulkner, we will not be coming within sniffing distance of his remaining ounce of Dominican, and we most certainly and with-out doubt will not be getting high. And if you think I have any inten-tion of coming back to this hellhole to visit Ma in anything less than a completely fucked-up condition, you can think *again*!" And with that he turned up the radio full blast, put his feet up on the dash and uttered not a word all the way to Mrs. *Ku-pun-ska*'s house on 334 *Do-ber-man* Street.

Which was okay by me because the passage to Doberman was treacherous. You had to cross all these side streets, none of which had been plowed more than twice. And you had to hit them with a full head of steam and hang on like a guy on a bull, steering wildly out of skids and away from parked cars, pump-pump-pumping on the brake pedal like Ginger Baker on "Toad." It was exhilarating fun of the highest order, and pretty good training to boot. If my only marketable skill was driving, becoming the best that I can be made sense.

The reason why Doberman was so easy to find in a neighbor-hood buried in white was because Doody Levine, who risked his one-day-a-week job to *furnish* us with the Red Cross stuff, also lived on the street, number 265. We located his house (the ever-running color wheel in the bay window a sure landmark) and basically counted our way to 334. The color wheel had been introduced to the Levine household the year Doody's father got murdered. It came with a three-foot-high aluminum Christmas tree, silver in color; the idea being that you'd prop the tree up in the front window, turn off the lights, plug in the wheel and bathe the whole thing in constantly rotating shades of red, blue, and gold. The Levines had been forbid-den to celebrate "goyim" holidays when Mr. Levine was alive, but when he died they made up for lost time. The first thing Mrs. Levine did was volunteer to make Styrofoam snowmen for St. Euclid's Christmas bazaar. The second thing she did was to go to the bazaar and take a two-dollar chance on the wheel and tree. And the third thing she did was to plug it into an outlet and run it—morning, noon, and night. The showing season got stretched more and more every year until she was eventually putting it out the day after Halloween and riding it all the way to Saint Patrick's Day. Doody began to be embarrassed by the spectacle around age twelve.

"Red, blue, gold," he complained. "Red, blue, gold. It never changes. It never *stops*. It's like living inside the Citgo sign."

He had a greater appreciation for it, though, in later years. Many a night the three of us—Doody, Gully, and me—would sit in the van and just watch it. "I never realized how beautiful the blue was," Doody once observed. "When it comes, it's like the ocean washing away all the bullshit, I swear to God. I find myself fucking *yearning* for it when it leaves. I mean, I like the gold and everything; and the red is fucking pissa. But when that blue shit comes around I get as willified as a bastard." I was quick to concur. And so was Gully.

We found the Kupunska house, argued for about five minutes over which one of us would have to go, and then ended up going together swearing and slogging through the snow like the Slobbovians in *Li'l Abner*. The van we left running, right out in the middle of the street. We had to push aside about a half-ton of snow just to get *up* the steps, let alone the mountainous drift that blocked the front door. When at last we uncovered the doorbell, we found it to be frozen useless, and had to knock. Gully did the honors. Loud as all Christ. With his shod foot.

It took a while for the old lady to make her way through the house and begin unlocking the endless series of dead bolts and chain locks, so my brother and I had time to chat.

"We'll be as old as her by the time she opens the fucking thing," he shivered. "Let's just shove it in the mailbox and screw."

"Patience, my son," I said.

The overwhelming stench of boiling cabbage and roasting mammals hit us like a piano from above as squat little Mrs. Kupunska pried open the door and looked us up and down.

"Oh you *boys!* You goodt goodt *boys*" she cried, gently cradling the box of insulin in her swollen mitts like a newborn kitten. Then she pulled us into the house. "Come! Come! Come! Come with me to the kitchen so I can put this in the icebox!" (And for some reason we *bought* this—like it'd be disobeying *Ma* or something if we didn't.) "Oh you goodt goodt *boys!*" She moved surprisingly fast, in rapid little steps, like a diaper-brat one week into walking.

"I have the diabetes, you know," she said, as we trailed her through the house, "and I wouldt not be making it to tomorrow if I did not have this. Oh you boys, you goodt goodt *boys!* I want to give you something for your trouble."

She opened wide her refrigerator. On every shelf were pies, sponge cakes, cream puffs, chocolate éclairs, and I don't know what else. My mouth was watering and my stomach was ready to growl. I was about to make my selection, in fact, when she swung the fridge door good and shut, grabbed a large wooden ladle-type thing and made a beeline for the foul, gurgling pot on the stove.

"What you goodt goodt boys need on such a day is something nice and hot. I have been all day making the *golompkies!*" And with that she went deep into the great cauldron and came up with a heavy, dripping, steaming, hideous, brackish-gray monstrosity and dumped it on a plate on the table. Then, turning around, went back into the column of smog and fished out another. "Now you boys sit down," she said, sliding out chairs and opening cupboards in one frantic motion, "and I will get for you some bread and some forks and some napkins."

The look I was getting from Gully was chilling.

"Uh, thanks, lady," I said, "but we can't stay. We've got like emergencies to rescue and legs to set and stuff."

"Then you shall be taking the golompkies *with* you!" she

declared, and shifted into a gear we wouldn't have used running from cops. Sweeping the abominations into a pail from under the sink, she threw a lid on it, handed off the whole shebang to me like she expected me to run for yardage, loaded up my brother with the napkins and silverware and pushed us through the living room and down the hall. "You can eat them as you are driving down the *road!*" she sang, holding the front door. "God bless you, you goodt, goodt *Boyss!*" Our last image before diving back into the drifts and finding a suitable spot to dump the golompkies, was the old family portrait of Mrs. Kupunska and her enormously eared husband and sons that hung from the wall in the hallway.

We talked as we trudged.

"Did you get a load of the ears on the mister?" I said.

"Jesus!" said my brother. "Like how much ear does a fucking guy need?"

"And the *sons!*" I said. "Their lobes must flap when they go outside!"

"How do the poor bastards stay on the ground?"

And then he grabbed my arm. And I saw the flashing blues. And the cop car, idling, with the door open and the radio squawking, right in front of the van. And the cop, the very very very *big* cop, leaning up against the side of the van, cigarette clenched in his teeth, arms folded across his unreasonably big chest. And then I had a heart attack and died.

"This is the day we go to jail," I said. "This is the day we go."

"And look who it is," said Gully as we neared. "Prick LaPinza! For Chrissakes, he's liable to kick the dogshit out of us first and drag our *guts* to jail!"

"Let me do the talking," I said. "He has a brain the size of a gall-stone. I might be able to outwit him."

"Sure, give it a go," said my brother. "Maybe you can hypnotize the sonuvabitch into going to Braintree and grabbing the stuff *for* us."

Normally, in this situation, we'd run. *Take* the van. *Take* it, we'd say, and whatever evidence you find inside it, and tow it the hell away. We won't be going with you. Chase us deep into the woods, if you must, and all around the quarries—we can run forever. But *here*, trapped between our vehicle and the canyon walls of snow on all sides, there would be no running. There was nowhere to run.

"Well, well, well," said Prick LaPinza. "If it ain't the Fabulous Furry Fuck Brothers. Now tell me, how do two useless jiboneys like you get in with the Red Cross?"

"It's our civic duty, Officer LaPinza," began Gully. "It's something we take very seriously and—"

"Actually, Prick," I quickly cut in, "it's part of our community service. We got sixty hours, you know, for that shopping-cart thing."

"Yeah," said my brother, getting on the same page. "We'll probably knock off a good twenty today alone."

"Well now isn't that nice," said the officer. "Living and breathing pillars of the fucking community right here in the goddamn flesh." We nodded with conviction and shivered, as he took a nice long drag from his cigarette and gazed on down the road. "You know," he exhaled, "I believe I may have some work I can send your way, something right up your alley, as a matter of fact." (Drag. Gaze down road. Exhale.) "It seems that his Holy Eminence, the good Monsignor Burke, is in dire need of someone to take him on his rounds, and, by Jesus, you two immediately come to mind. Now why don't you birds point your shitbox in a southerly direction and go pick his ancient ass up?"

Monsignor Burke? Spectre of our haunted Catholic youth? The dread. The horror. Jail was starting to look good.

"Look Prick, I'm gonna level with you," I began, knowing full well I'd have to come up with something very clever and convincing. "We've got this CPR convention to get to and—"

He held up his hand, made the shushing noise with his finger, and moved his immense steak-colored face so close to mine it cut off all the cold air around us and made me blink like a nest of parakeets. In an ominously hellish whisper, he spoke: "I've already called ahead. His Magnificence is expecting you. Now get in your scumbarrel and turn it around before I take you by your scrawny fag necks and shove you up each other's ass."

"Jeez, I don't know, Prick," my brother petitioned. "This snow and shit is practically impossible to drive in."

"Give it a rest, ballsuck," said the cop, never taking his eyes off mine. "I seen your big brother drive in snow before. Ask him if he recalls a certain incident two winters ago behind Caddigan Park." He glanced at his watch. "I figure you fucksticks to arrive at the rectory in fifteen minutes. Have the good Father say a rosary for me." He swaggered back to his car and said something into the microphone. We looked forlornly back at Mrs. Kupunska's house, number 334, and realized, by the way she quickly shut the door and peeked at us from behind a little corner of the curtain, that she'd been watching the whole thing. I passed the pail of golompkies to my brother.

"What am I supposed to do with this?"

"Put it in the back for the weight," I said, and we slowly climbed in.

The Monsignor, the Monsignor, the *Monsignor.* Coming upon us as we drew fat naked nuns in chalk on the walls of the rectory garage, or, worse yet, finding us in the middle innings of Pinky Ball Strikeout— balls and strikes determined by how close you came to hitting the bust of Saint Francis of Assisi in the schnozz. Out of the hedges he'd charge, eyes ablaze, swinging a hickory cane like he was driving the snakes out of Ireland. "*Vermin!*" he'd be screaming. "*Filthy vermin! A disgrace you are to your families!*" And his wrathful voice would be ringing in your ears for blocks as you and the other rats ran.

• • •

Gully had even more to think about. His involvement with the Monsignor, though indirect, was a bit more recent. The Selective Service had this insidious lottery system based on birthdates and Gully's birth date made Ma wish he had never been *born*. He got a 23. He would go early, he would go fast, and the idea of him and his unpredictable personality dropped into a jungle in the middle of Southeast Asia was as frightening to Ma as the end of the world. "He'll be the first one they *shoot!*" she wailed, and went to the Monsignor for guidance.

Out of respect for Ma and the memory of Dad, who'd passed the basket at the ten-thirty Mass for years, the Monsignor pulled some strings. He rang up an old shipmate, a Lieutenant Commander Conyers or somebody, and got Gully in the naval reserve. He'd have to go away to some base in Maine for six months of basic training, after which he'd only be required to report for duty at some seaside resort for about one weekend a month.

"Sounds cushy enough to me," said Gully.

The whole family attended the first couple of meetings with Lieutenant Commander Conyers at the Farragut Building. Gully had to recite the Pledge of Allegiance and memorize about twenty other promises and oaths and swore to defend America's shores from those who would cause her harm, and agreed not to question our government's policies and answered everything with a *yessir!*

"And you know," said Lieutenant Commander Conyers, with a wide Kentucky grin, "all that long greasy hair's gonna end up on the barber shop floor like a big ol' bale of hay." And we all laughed and laughed and laughed. Then the lieutenant commander pointed to a circled date on the calendar, *August 26,* the day of Gully's induction into the naval reserve. Which practically gave us the whole summer for mayhem.

But then, not three weeks later, a postcard came to say that the date had been moved up. *July 13. 0800 Hours. Be On Time.* The postcard did not go over well with my brother.

"I was mentally prepared to go away August twenty-sixth. I was mentally prepared to be *bald* on August twenty-sixth. I am prepared for neither on the thirteenth of July. I have loose ends up the wazoo, I have tickets to the Stones at Boston Garden, and I assure you I will be in my seat when the lights go down."

Another message came telling Gully he had to report to the Farragut Building on July 5 for preinduction orientation. Gully pondered. Since a *pre*induction was not exactly an induction, Gully decided that it wouldn't hurt to go through the motions; it'd buy some time until he figured what his real course of action would be. I drove him in at seven o'clock in the morning, parked the van on the corner of Summer Street, and slept on the vinyl couch until his return. Which was about five minutes later.

"Son of a *bitch*!" he seethed, slamming the door. "Drive me the fuck outta here!"

I obliged, quickly, as he told me how well it went. How he went in, got a special ID at the desk, and reported to room C7A, where the rest of the recruits were quietly sitting around a large wooden table, reading important pamphlets, waiting for Conyers. In the middle of the table was a tray full of glasses and a good-sized silver pitcher filled to the gills with ice water. Naturally, a terrible thirst came over Gully and he reached for the pitcher to quench it.

"*That's for after the meeting, you imbecile!*" the lieutenant commander's voice roared from the back of the room. "*Who the hell do you think you are?!*"

Startled by Conyer's sudden personality change, Gully almost dropped the whole thing as he let go of the handle and said, "Sorry."

"*Sorry? That's what you have to say? You show up at an induction ceremony in ripped dungarees and hair down to your goddam POOPSHOOT and all you can say is SORRY?!*" No one was looking at pamphlets anymore, it goes without saying.

Gully, in careful, measured, completely non-wiseass tones,

replied that, number one, he understood this to be a *pre*induction ceremony, not a real one, and number two, didn't the navy take care of all that head-shaving baloney *themselves?*

But Lieutenant Commander Conyers (the "crew-cutted cock-sucker") persisted: *"We're talking about coming into a military establishment looking like a lily dipped in SHIT! We're talking about insulting every single man in this ROOM! Now get your candy-coated ass to a barber and be back here by 1100 or go to bloody HELL!"*

By rights, that should have been it. But on the way home, after he had denounced Lieutenant Commander Conyers, Richard Nixon, most of the Founding Fathers, and all military personnel, he began to search his soul. He went on and on about Ma, and how this would probably kill Ma, and how he wouldn't be able to live under the same roof as Ma, and how Ma would never be able to look the Monsignor in the eye again. We ended up at Simpy's Barbershop in Mattapan Square. The same Simpy who cut our hair when we were little. He gave Gully the exact same haircut he gave him then—the clip-clip-buzz-buzz First Communion special—while I read *Reader's Digest* and suppressed hysteria. He got back in the van mad, *scalped* and mad, and stayed mad all the way back to the Farragut. It didn't help his disposition much when Lieutenant Commander Hard-on still had the attitude.

"I thought I told you to get a haircut!" was the first thing he yelled at Gully as he came through the door.

"What the hell are you *talking* about?" said Gully. "I left about a yard on Simpy Pollard's *floor!*"

"I told you to get a REAL haircut, shit-for-brains, not a dainty lit-tle PIXIE-BALLS job like this!"

Gully threw up his hands and appealed to his fellow recruits for backup, but they buried their heads in their pamphlets and did not look up. That pretty much did it for Gully. He called the Lieutenant Commander a real long descriptive name ending in *"Cub Scout,"*

sent the precious pitcher of ice water crashing to the floor with a
hard forehand slap, and ran. Two burly MP's gave chase, spurred on
by Conyers: "*arrest that man!*" but gave up long before Gully
reached the van.

"What about Ma?" I asked him.

"We'll cross Ma when we get there," he said, between breaths.

"What about the Monsignor?"

"Fuck the Monsignor," he said, and put in a tape.

But now, barely three years later, in a world awash in white, we
found ourselves in the same van, talking about the same Monsignor,
wondering how in the hell we were gonna get to Braintree. The
scenery went by like the stations of the cross.

"Look," said Gully. "This completely sucks. Let's just blow him
off and get the fuck outta here."

"I would," I said, "were it not for the fact that kindly Officer
LaPinza's been right on our bumper since Doberman." (I lost him once
in a chase through Caddigan Park and he's never forgotten it; as far as
I'm concerned, it wasn't *my* fault his cruiser got stuck in the snow, and
I certainly was not to blame for his crashing into Major Caddigan's
statue before he *got* stuck.)

We didn't even have to honk the horn for the Monsignor. The
cadaverous old relic emerged from the rectory's big oaken door the
second we pulled up. Clutching the collar of his black overcoat with
one large bony hand and grasping the snowy railing with the other, he
gingerly lowered himself down the neatly shoveled steps and made his
determined way to the van. A wide black fedora hid the great shock of
white hair—but the *eyes,* the cold, penetrating, silver-blue bloodshot
eyes, you could spot a mile away.

"Jesus Christ," I trembled. "It's the goddamn Prince of
Darkness. Who kicked me out of altar boys when I was thirteen and

bagged me and Doody putting Dee Dee's bathing suit on the statue of Virgin Mary not a year and a half later!"

"Oh for Chrissakes, he ain't gonna recognize either one of us the way we look now," said my brother, as he kicked open his door for Monsignor Burke and dove onto the couch in back. "Besides, just look at the son of a bitch. He's fucking ninety if he's a day. He don't remember which hand to wipe with."

"Good afternoon, John. Good afternoon, Stephen," said the Monsignor as he pulled himself aboard. "We'll be starting at Mrs. Carroll's place over on Bell." Then, ceremoniously placing his hat on the dash along with his bible, he unbuttoned his coat and pulled out a small gold chalice, which we knew to contain the body and blood of Our Lord Jesus Christ, and rested it on the engine hub, where it reflected shards of light from six directions at once and threatened to part the snow before us like the sacred staff of Moses.

5

Newsprint

The day the Gullivan & Son panel truck became simply known as "the van" came shortly after the demise of Gullivan & Son Distrib., which came hard on the heels of Dad's night in the driveway with the dogs.

We were alone, just Gully and me, driving back from the Registry with my brand-new, freshly minted Commonwealth of Massachusetts driver's license, when Gully suggested we stop for the guy thumbing. The guy with the Davy Crockett jacket and the three-foot tall birdcage. Except that the birdcage, upon closer examination, contained a monkey, a wild-eyed screeching bastard about the size of a GI Joe, flinging itself from one corner of the cage to the other, in four-fisted madness. Colonel Crockett slid it in through the cargo doors, tossed a green knapsack in after it and got in himself. It was then that we noticed the *rabbit,* the plain, brown, bored rabbit, sitting all the way down at the bottom of the cage, nibbling on a pellet made of hay.

"Nice rabbit," I said to the guy.

"Nice ape," said Gully.

"Extremely nice van," said the guy, who leaned back, rested his head on the edge of the spare tire and took in the surroundings, especially the ceiling and walls, which still bore the addresses of dozens of drops, with key drop times underlined and exclamation-pointed, all in Dad's frenetic scrawl. "Yessir, this is one goddamned nice van. You use it for pleasure or business?"

"Pleasure, business, what's the difference?" said Gully, feeling pretty cavalier, apparently, in the presence of a guy in a Davy Crockett coat.

"Good point," said the guy, "but you should fix up the fucker in any case. Glue in some ruggery, for starters—my ass feels like it gained another crack." But what he said next stopped time. Froze the stars and all planets. Changed the course of history. What he said next was: "So, you fine young businessmen care to smoke some tea, or what?" And the monkey gripped his bars tightly, showed us his gums, and bobbed up and down like a fiend. We drove the guy to Montpelier.

My brother and I had been groomed for our careers as newspapermen at a tender age. On Sunday mornings, when we were old enough (basically, right after our Confirmations), Dad brought us to work. He'd wake us up at three o'clock in the morning and go out to warm up the panel truck. The only time Dad used profanity, we observed, I mean *real* profanity, was in these early-waking moments when the truck got uncooperative. In snowy weather, when it would be necessary to fit chains on all four tires, the truck became downright noncompliant and Dad let out a steady fire-breathing glossary of four- five- and six-letter words, which alluded to the reproductive systems of every species in Darwin. The fact that Ma strongly objected to our taking *part* in this predawn arrangement made it as exciting as getting up for Christmas morning to peek at the tree. And, besides, being tapped as heirs to the Gullivan & Son empire was not to be taken lightly.

Dad's first stop would always be for honey-dipped donuts, which went down like tuffets of pure tree sap, and his second stop was for Ward Belvoir, who'd been his main helper for years. Ward was big, fat, about ten years older than us, and retarded. He lived with his mother, father, and grandmother in a gray two-family on a residential street in Lower Mills.

Ward slept on the second floor and he slept deep. Only a very loud alarm clock could wake him, but the very idea was out of the question because it had been tried more than once and always ended with Ward leaping out of bed in abject horror, screaming, "WHAT THE FUCK?! WHAT THE FUCK?! WHAT THE FUCK?!" as he ran through the house in his pajamas, jumping up and down on coffee tables and pulling mirrors and cuckoo clocks right off the walls. Tooting the horn out front at this ungodly hour only served in waking the rest of the street, so my father and Ward Belvoir devised a plan: Ward would hang a length of rope out his bedroom window before retiring and tie the end of it to his big toe. All Dad had to do was pull up, walk across the yard, give the rope two or three good yanks, and a shivering, half-asleep, mostly dressed Ward Belvoir would soon appear at Dad's window, reporting for duty, not always entirely sure what duty he was reporting for.

"Climb in," said Dad.

"Okay," said Ward Belvoir, and he would.

Ward got to sit up front but he never had too much to say, on account of his being half-asleep and all. Dad always saved him the last donut, which he stuffed in his considerable mouth and then fell *completely* asleep, his head bobbing on his chest, the un-devoured honey-dipped confection bulging from his teeth like a sugary mask— taunting, practically daring us to go over and pick at it like common starlings.

Our contribution to Gullivan & Son Distrib., for which we were paid five dollars and fifty cents, was to put together the Sunday edition. The *Boston Globe* truck showed up about the same time as us, followed by the trucks from all the other papers, and the race was on. The bundles were tall and the bundles were heavy—*full shovels of wet snow* heavy. There were whole sections—like "Living" and "Leisure" and "Travel"—that were fatter than an entire *paper* during the week. And the inserts, which included the comics, magazines, ads for RadioShack and flyers for fertilizer, arrived separately. The only thing occupying space in Dad's little hole-in-the-wall agency other than canyons of newspapers and a potbellied stove, were the long workbenches that lined all three walls. That's where we piled the inserts, one after another, freeing them with wire cutters as the assembly line kicked in. The idea was that you'd start by taking the top *Parade* off the pile, pinching it between your thumb and forefinger, as you dipped over to the next pile, taking on a "Bridal Fashion," then on to a "Lechmere Sales" and then a flyer and a flyer and a flyer and a flyer, as your left hand held open the maw of the main paper like a giant clam. FLOOP, your collection went in, *that* went to another pile, where Ward stuffed them into the comics section, and that pile went to Dad, who roped them into new bundles with a skill that bordered rodeo star. Then it was your right hand back on the *Parade*s and flippy-flippy-flippy-flippy-FLOOP right back to Ward. This would go on, basically, forever. Flippy-FLOOP, flippy-FLOOP, flippy-FLOOP. You could go into a trance. The problem was the comics. Dad did not allow us to read the comics until the work was all done. The fact that they were irresistible was lost on him because he paid them no mind at all. He learned at a very young age to hate them because they were a pain in the ass to work with. We *loved* the comics. Even the lousy ones like *Brenda Starr*. And the only thing we loved more than the comics was Ward Belvoir's reaction to the comics—he laughed so hard at *Mutt and Jeff*, layers of cream formed on his gums. We'd be forever sneaking glances at *Judge Parker* or *Terry and the Pirates* or *the Katzenjammer Kids*, which may cause us to lose our place here and there with the inserts, depriving an unsuspecting customer of his/her rotogravured cover

story of "Julie Nixon: My White House," while loading another with
four full-color flyers of Luber Pharmacy's 3-day sale on Hickman rods.
When Dad's bladder got so full of Chock Full o' Nuts he had to run
down to the basement to pee, we read the comics in *earnest*. Then,
when he and Ward left to deliver a load, it was all over. Gully and I
hopped up on a bench and devoured every word balloon, acting out
our favorites aloud, with convincing sound effects, discussing the plot-
ting devices of "Fearless Fosdick" and *Pogo* like Ma's monthly meeting
of the book club. We needn't panic. When necessary, my brother and I
could cram inserts with the speed of flying fish. We knew when Dad
was due back. We'd easily have another load ready. So we mostly just
read and laughed and drank forbidden coffee, with gobs of nondairy
creamer and fistfuls of sugar. Which directly brought up the dilemma
of the bathroom in the basement. There were no lights in the basement, just a toilet and a roll of toilet paper, and you had to feel your
way around in the dark, well aware that other things—rats, spiders,
beetles, and probably scorpions—were feeling their way around in the
dark with you, waiting for you to make a mistake, to *fall* perhaps, at
which point they'd move in and skeletonize you by the time the toilet
quit flushing. The most courage either one of us could muster was to
stand at the top of the stairs and urinate into the blackness. Dad would
blame the smell on random bums like Red Rand who were known to
crawl through the basement window in inclement weather and bed
down there for the night. *Bums.* The very thought of *them* down there
made us do half our peeing into the potbellied stove upstairs, which
produced sound effects of the highest order. A bowel movement was
another project entirely, too complicated to go into here.

 We knew, of course, that, were we to succeed Dad as proprietors
of Gullivan & Son, as the plan was laid out, we'd have to come to
terms with the unspeakable horrors belowdecks. But for now, the situation was pretty much manageable.

 One April night, when I was about fifteen, things took an unexpected turn. A baldheaded guy named Norm showed up and Dad immediately started explaining the business to him, showing him how to tie packing rope without getting splinters in your hands, and where to keep your wire cutters so you never lose them, and how important it was to hit the churches on time and how screwed you would be if you were late delivering to Waxman's Grocers or Trenier's Italian or Benny Lepcio's Newsstand by the Neponset River Bridge. Then he introduced Norm to the rest of us, explaining that Norm was going to take over things all next week while Dad went in for tests, and then they left with a fully loaded panel truck, leaving a crestfallen, disenfranchised Ward Belvoir behind with my brother and me.

"What kind of tests is Dad taking?" wondered Gully, who grabbed an armful of reading material and jumped up on a bench.

"I don't know," I said. "Maybe they're gonna grade him on how good he ties rope."

I started pouring coffee, as a still motionless Ward, his arms at his side, looked out into the bleakness of Dot Ave. and hung his head.

Gully and I were generally fond of Ward and, therefore, didn't mind, when Dad wasn't around, asking him sensitive questions, such as: "Do retarded people *know* they're retarded?" or "Do all retarded people pick their nose as much as you?" or "Do retarded people like novelty songs?" or "Do retarded people like girls?" or "Do retarded people like *retarded* girls?" or "If retarded people have kids, do the kids come *out* retarded, and, if so, do the kids get grounded if they do something retarded?"

Ward'd usually just shrug his shoulders and keep his mind on his work. He'd started out as one of Dad's paperboys, but ran into trouble when gorillas like the Gerfalts brothers harassed him and played keep-away with his collection bag and threw his papers up on somebody's roof. Ward's mother begged Dad to find him some sort of job where he'd be safe from such cruelty and Dad came up with the

Sunday morning idea, which gave Ward such a prestigious résumé that other part-time positions, like scraping pigeon droppings off the air conditioners at the Ruslan D. Loneberry Elementary School, came flooding his way.

Ward was a fellow of few words, but very much enjoyed using the phrase: "Hum job."

Mary Tyler Moore or Elizabeth Montgomery might be on the cover of *This Week on TV* and one of us would hold it up and yell, "*Ward!*" and Ward would look up and say, "Hum job," and Gully and I would spend about the next ten minutes laughing up lungs and then Ward would emphatically repeat the phrase, and all three of us would be screaming. Sometimes, though, he'd be talkative as a seal, in his funny little four-year-old voice, sharing with us intimate moments of his life.

"My mom yelled at me all day yesterday."

"What did you do?"

"I whizzed all over the toilet seat. Again."

"What did she say?"

"She said I was a farm animal."

"What kind of farm animal?"

"I dunno. Just a farm animal. A big, fat, dumb, smelly FARM ANIMAL!"

"What did *you* say?"

"Hum job."

While Dad was gone showing Norm the ropes and we used the time to catch up on our reading, coffee drinking, and urinating, a series of unfortunate events were put into motion. The first concerned artwork. My brother was in one of his creative-genius moods and grabbed one of Dad's laundry markers and began expressing himself. The only thing Gully was good at drawing, however, were penises. Big pineapple-sized things shrouded in large, hairy, vein-popping scrotums, usually dripping or squirting or both, with *faces*. Gully drew one of these penises, sitting up straight, in a car with Mutt and Jeff. Squarely in between Mutt and Jeff. With the exact same horrified expression on its face that Mutt and Jeff had on theirs as their little buggy seemed headed off the edge of a cliff with them in it. Gully then quietly slipped off the bench, placed the masterpiece on the top of the pile that Ward would soon be working on, and announced, "Okay, scabs, the boss is due back soon, let's get back to work."

Ward's reaction was more than we'd hoped for. He took the first comic off the pile, stuffed the *Globe* inside it, put it where it belonged, and froze. The thing is, he'd already *seen* Mutt and Jeff, so the next few moments were confusing for him. He played it back in his mind, one hand on his chin, the other acting out the sequence, from panel to panel to panel, ending up with Mutt and Jeff sitting in the pond, with only the cars' windshield and steering wheel show-ing. Try as he may, Ward could not remember a *third* passenger in Mutt and Jeff's little car. He finally returned to the pile he'd just left and stared and stared and stared. When his eyes arrived at the panel with the penis, Gully broke the silence with, "Hum job," and Ward Belvoir entered into another dimension. Laughing could not describe it, nor screaming, crying, speaking in tongues, or epilepsy. Holding his stomach as though bayoneted, he crashed to the floor, rolled around in the wire and rope and toppled high columns of unfinished Heralds with all 237 of his pounds. Every part of him that could flail, *did* flail, in upside-down-june-bug delirium, and he seemed incapable of stopping.

At this point, a crucial decision was made. It would be dangerous for this to continue; Ward in his present state was likely to destroy Dad's whole agency, and portions of the street outside. Our safest bet was to try and calm him down, and our best way of doing that would be to calm *ourselves* down, blow our noses, pick ourselves up off the floor, wipe the hysteria from our eyes and start cleaning up.

Instead, we reached for the markers. I drew a penis in an MP helmet, chasing Beetle Bailey and Killer through the base, and Gully had one atop Prince Valiant's horse, its testicles straddling the beast like an English saddle. When we presented our humble offerings to the quivering mass known as Ward Belvoir, the agonized wails and howls of the sanitarium visited the narrow confines of Gullivan & Son Distrib., and there was no turning back. Ward hit piles of paper six feet high like a fullback into the line, pages and sections flying in all directions possible, portions of one paper commingling with parts of another, inserts and travel sections and editorials and coupons swirling about the room like a hurricane in Autumn.

Aunt Fran used to say that if you got too close to a retarded person, you might end up a retarded person yourself, that it was contagious. Ridiculous, my mother used to say, and I believed her. Until the night my brother and I stepped into Ward Belvoir's world, and sampled freedom. A world with no consequences, where you can't control yourself, you simply can't control yourself, you are not expected to control yourself, and you have no *intention* of controlling yourself. A world where one can toss a 146-page Sunday newspaper high enough in the air that some of its sections end up hanging from the overhead fan and then fling another one even higher. A world where penises appear in Spiro T. Agnew's cuff links, and whole schools of the things show up on the cover of *TV Cavalcade* swimming with Jacques Cousteau. Retardation? It's an all-out frenzy of retardation. Your long morning of flippy-flippy-flippy-FLOOP is now the pillow fight of the century.

And the way that we embraced Ward's retardation with our own seemed special to him, you could tell. It was like that movie where the guy wins the wolves' favor by adopting their diet and eating rats. There would be no going back.

But when Gully climbed up on one of the few piles still standing and attempted to leap to the other one, and Ward, in his enormous blue Hush Puppies, appeared to be following suit, the sane part of me came rushing out of my mouth like a bat.

"Stop!" I screamed. *"Enough is enough! Look at this! Look at what we've done! This . . . must END!"*

But then my brother, with the most solemn expression, held up the ad for Gilchrist's Basement, which featured three blond women wearing bras, and said, "Hum job." Ward, straddling *Traveler*s, responded by pulling his shirt up over his head, revealing breasts three times bigger than the ones in the ad. And I knew, from the way I collapsed to the floor in drool, that retardation was a gift. It is the New Year's eve that never ends. The lamp shade dance forever.

But then Ward Belvoir stopped. He had a loose bundle of Saturday's leftover *Monitor*s over his head, about to toss them down the cellar stairs, and he stopped. He put the pile down. Looked at it, sat on it, put his face in his hands, and sobbed. Long and hard and mournful and loud. It was awful.

"Ward!" I said. "What's wrong? What is it?" (Allowing him to tear Dad's business apart like Jesus in the temple was one thing, but *this,* this pitiful, high-pitched bawl was something else. This was *unbearable.*)

"Don't worry, Ward," said Gully, "we can pick the papers up! See? I'm picking them up! See? *Johnny's* picking them up! We're gonna need about a week and a half, but *look,* we're *doing* it! We're picking them up! See? *See?* Hum job! Hum job! *Hum* job!"

And still he sobbed and sobbed, a hunching, rocking, naked-from-the-waist-up display of tears and gums and snot. What if he never *stopped?* He *had* to stop!

"C'mon, Ward, ol' buddy," I said, helping him wipe his nose with a roll of paper towels, "it'll be all right."

"Oh no it won't," Ward blew, between sobs. "It's his heart."

"His heart?" I thought he said. "Whose heart?"

"Jimbo Gullivan's," he said. "That's who."

"Dad? What's wrong with Dad's heart?"

"It's bad!" he gasped, and unrolled more towels.

"How bad?"

"He's going into the hospital!" he gestured with finality. "That's how bad!"

"Dad is going to the hospital? Who told you that?"

"My mom. And it's *true!*"

"Let me get this straight," I said. "*Your* mom told *you* that *our* dad is going to the hospital?" And suddenly, *everything*, from Ma's yelling at him all last week as he was dressing for work in the middle of the night, to his fainting at High Mass last month and spilling the contents of the collection basket all over the bewildered old couple in the last pew, to this baldheaded guy named Norm, made sense.

And I knew exactly what he'd look like at the moment of death. I knew because I had a premonition of it seconds later—the stricken expression on his face as he and bald Norm came through the front door, took two steps, and hardened. The stark, unbelieving look in his wind-whipped bloodshot eyes as they swept over the holocaust of newsprint and fixed on the three figures by the cellar stairs, Ward's boobs jiggling in the middle like walrus calves.

"Get out."

It was a whisper, really, but a whisper that could be heard to Jamaica Plain. A whisper suggesting that if we failed to obey its wishes by, say, the count of three, the situation would advance directly to triple homicide with no time-outs. It strongly suggested that we should accomplish this very quickly, all three of us, we three retarded brothers, that not a word should be spoken, that we should go directly home, or maybe to someone else's home, or maybe to church, because church was something we still did back then.

Red Rand, the bum from the cellar, a stooped, whiskered, urine-soaked booze-monkey in torn brown clothing, was on the corner blowing his nose. Dad knew Red from their *boxing* days, he claimed, which is why he got to sleep in the cellar in the first place. Ma told us to stay far away from him and to never accept any of his grimy little gifts, these spruced-up toys and stuff he salvaged from the dump. He wasn't offering anything this morning, though. He was just glaring right at us as we passed, muttering something about being kept up "half the goddamn *night!*" We just kept on walking.

"I don't wanna go to Saint Euclid's," said Ward, as we walked, a flicker of morning sun dancing off the statue of the sailor by the park. "Everybody knows me there. I don't wanna go no place where anybody knows me."

So we went to Holy Shepherd. We stood in the back in our lousy work clothes. And we left at Communion, Gully and me, dipping our ink-stained fingers in the holy water, while Ward, sobbing for redemption, folded his hands in a humble, prayerful way and got in line to receive the Body and Blood.

6

Rounds

The silence in the van was tick-tock-ticking like the timer on an iron lung. You could hear the *pages* turn, I swear to God, as the Monsignor, riding shotgun, sifted through his Bible, marking his Deuteronomy 7's and Luke 23's with one of the ribbons that spilled from the old book's binder like a fiery tail. He looked up only once or twice, pointing out lefts and rights with one long marrowed finger but he never so much as grunted in our direction. An eerie, clammy, submarine-like quiet had entered the van. Everything that was wrong with it—the bad ball joints, the rust-eaten muffler, the Frankensteined front end—could be unmistakably heard, crying out in metallic agony as we bushwhacked through the snow. To further compound things, I could feel my brother's eyes burning pictures and words on the back of my neck: "It's your fault," they accused. "It's your fault that—of *all* the goddamn people in the world— Monsignor Burke is sitting in the passenger seat picking out prayers while I am back here on the couch gnashing my teeth about the long-lost ounce of Dominican we shall never know. It is your fault that we stopped for a shirtsleeved wingnut in the middle of the street in the first place, and that we then agreed to deliver medicine to some poor misbegotten douche who'll be six feet in the ground by next week anyway. And it is your fault that we are listening to slipped rotors and a doomed transmission and a cracked water pump and a pleading exhaust." Usually, the stereo drowned out such noises. It was made up of no less than five speakers, mounted in door panels, under seats and God knows where else, and had been installed by Floydie Simmons, who worked for beer. And it *screamed*. Decibels like the end of Pompeii. Even back in the days when *Dad* drove the van, and all it had was an AM radio and a cigarette lighter, the thing blared. Juicy Bradley in the daytime, the Red Sox of Boston in the afternoon, and jazz, jazz, jazz all night. The only time problems were detected at all was when the van roared into Spid's Sunoco for gas and Spid himself said, "Jesus Christ, what the hell am I smelling *now?*"

We skidded to a long grinding stop out in front of this Mrs. Carroll lady's house and the only thing preventing us from plowing into the trunk of a brown Corvair was the pile of snow around it. Which we hit like Pie McKenzie. The Monsignor closed his Bible, kissed it, put his hat back on his head, opened his door, and stepped down. "This may take some time," he said. "You'll come in too."

"Uh, that's okay," I said, waving him off, "we'll just wait out here."

But the Monsignor, oblivious, was already halfway up the walk, motioning over his shoulder for us to follow like he was captain of the goddamned cavalry. It seemed we had no choice.

In stony silence the three of us waited on Mrs. Carroll's screened-in porch. We could hear her and her walker approaching: tap-tap-*moan*, tap-tap-*moan*, tap-tap-*moan*. We listened as she fumbled with the endless assortment of locking devices, one by one. Finally, she creaked open the door. And there she was. The corpse they forgot to bury. Squinting up at us with uncomprehending eyes that were as yellow as the remaining teeth in her involuntarily nodding head. But she brightened like a tulip when she saw that it was the Monsignor, made a sign of the cross and opened her heart wide as Ireland. That is, until she noticed Monsignor's bodyguards, and rigor mortis set back in.

"Why, my dear sweet Virginia," twinkled the Monsignor, in this weirdly gentle voice, holding out his ring for her to kiss. "You're looking more radiant than ever. You remember Jim Gullivan's boys. They're giving me a lift today." He put great emphasis on the *Gullivan* part and it seemed to reassure the old girl. If we had been the Steffanzi brothers or, worse yet, the *Blooms,* we'd have been left to shiver on the landing like squirrels. "Come in, come in," she said, and we joined the inch by inch, tap-tap-*moan* procession to the kitchen for hot chocolate and mincemeat pie.

"If you have any small tasks around the house that need doing," said Monsignor Burke as he sipped his cocoa, "these fine young lads would be pleased to tend to them."

"Oh, well, now, let me see . . ." said Mrs. Carroll, scratching an old chin that had thick random hairs sprouting from it like busted guitar strings. "I'll bet I can think of a few things."

She thought of a few things.

She thought of the toilet that needed plunging and the bathtub that had rings. She thought about the laundry that hadn't been folded and the garbage that hadn't been tossed. She told us where to find the Epsom salts and the deep blue pan, and, while Monsignor heard her vastly detailed confession on the living room couch, we helped her misshapen, varicosed feet into the hot water, where they soaked like Alaskan crabs. To say we dried these same feet afterwards with a striped towel would be too grotesque to recall.

Things didn't improve any at the next stop, old lady DeLisle's, two houses down. She had us vacuuming half-bald rugs and watering hanging plants and cleaning the cage of her pet canary Phil, whose foul, ammoniated existence made us want to set the bastard free. Layers and layers of canary dung were piled up in perverse formations as if they'd been built by tiny, drunken masons. It was everywhere: on Phil's water bowl, on Phil's perch, on Phil's mirror, and on Phil himself. And the headline on the damp, brownish newspaper at the bottom of the cage said something about Douglas MacArthur and the 38th parallel. There was a sad confusion in Phil's eyes as we scraped it all out. Like we were removing his life and all its belongings.

And shoveling? Have I mentioned the shoveling? The worst occurred at the Moakleys, a husband and wife team in their nineties, the only house on Monsignor's route that didn't have a widow living inside. The Moakleys did have one foot in the grave, though, judging by their constant shaking, and a bastard of a driveway, with a big hump in the middle and a turnaround. Mr. Moakley found the shovels in the breezeway, issued one to each of us, and held the door as we bent our shoulders to the icy wind. Gully's shovel, one of those old pointed spades made for digging holes, broke off at the handle two strokes into the job.

"Well that's it for me," said my brother, and started back inside to get warm.

"Not so fast," I said, continuing to throw snow, "We can take turns. One of us shovels for a few minutes, then the other takes over. There. There's my turn. You're up." I handed him the shovel.

It went well. A couple minutes of human bulldozing followed by moments of reflection, filling your lungs with Antarctica air. Not so tough. The only complaint reared up when I became sidetracked on the Moakleys' front lawn, which had this funny little slope that went from the hedges down to where the sidewalk should be. So smooth it was, perfectly rounded, completely unblemished. Ripe for artwork. So I stepped on and just stomped, first in one direction for awhile, then another, throwing distinctive little touches in as I went.

"What the hell are you doing?" said my brother, who'd spent *his* last coffee break urinating in the snow.

"Drawing," I said, expending no less energy than he was with the shovel.

"What does that mean—drawing?" he panted, resting his chin on the handle.

"I'm drawing a Christmas tree on this lawn," I panted back.

"That a fact? At what point do you think you might be taking your turn over here, Rembrandt?"

"When I'm done with my Christmas tree," I said, and that seemed to quell discussion, my brother knowing better than to bother me when I'm in the throes of genius. And the reason it was easy to do this particular drawing was because I had recently done a picture of a Christmas tree, my Christmas present to Ma. Since I had also recently been fired, I didn't have enough money to buy Ma a decent present so I found some drawing paper and a half-dozen colored pencils, spent about two hours on it, and slipped it under Ma's bald head while she slept. Yes, this *is* something that a nine-year-old might do, but my artwork won Ma over and made her cry, especially details like the snow on the branches and the shine on the ornaments. See? I *was* a good son, capable of giving my sick mother a moment of joy on her last Christmas on earth. In fact, the tree I was carving out right now on this sloping white lawn was also meant for Ma, though it'd be painfully corny to say so. Maybe my talent *was* meant to be shared. There was a time when it was.

"Nice tree," conceded Gully, when we got back in the van. Monsignor glanced at it but said nothing.

Stop number four was at Mrs. Audrey Walsh's over on Weld. She had a few ideas as well, and they all ended up with me and Gully down in the cellar, sponges in hand, peeling off layers of grime by the decade. Mrs. Walsh's middle-aged daughter Iris was, by all accounts, moving back in and with her came a teenaged son named Lyle. Lyle was getting the cellar, and *we* were getting the cellar ready for Lyle. To make it somewhat bed-worthy, thirty-one years of the late mister's collection of *Popular Mechanics* had to come upstairs and be stacked in the breezeway for St. Ukelele's annual Knights of Columbus paper drive.

When a young man is placed in such hopeless, grueling, chain gang–like situations, his mind naturally dreams of freedom. When that man has a bag of Dominican Sin waiting for him in the nearby town of Braintree, freedom is all he can think of.

"One of us needs to go over the wall," said my brother.

"Come again?" I said, already resigning myself to a lifetime of KP.

"One of us needs to crawl out that fucking window and get help."

I wasn't sure what he meant by "help" but I imagined it had something to do with Doody Levine.

"One of us slips upstairs to the old lady's bedroom and puts in a call to Doody." (My brother never disappoints me.) "We tell Doody in no uncertain terms to get his TV-watching ass down here in record-breaking time and scarf the van."

I was missing something. "Doody is going to steal the van?"

"Correct," said my brother.

"Doody Levine couldn't hot-wire a joy buzzer. How the fuck is he gonna steal the goddamned van?"

"Because my brother John is going to climb through that window and get him the fucking keys."

"Why me?" I wanted to know.

"Because I'm going upstairs to call Doody," he said, grabbing a big stack of *Popular Mechanics,* and the plan was afoot.

My involvement in this phase of the plan called for me to camp out at the top of the stairs with my own stack of mildewy mags, watching the Monsignor and Mrs. Walsh through the crack of the door. If it looked like one of them was getting suspicious and got up from the kitchen table to investigate, I was supposed to burst loudly through the door, drop everything all over the hallway floor and cough like Red Rand. Thus alerting Gully to get off the phone.

The Monsignor's back was to me but you could almost swear by the way his tern-colored hair bristled at the corners that he knew exactly what was taking place behind him. Mrs. Walsh had been busy showing him each and every picture from her daughter Iris's wedding, and she'd been pretty much narrating the whole thing: "Oh, and look how thin she looks here. And look how happy they are. God, Father, weren't they a handsome couple? Mary and Joseph, you should see her now. Rear end like a love seat. Here's one of Ken with the wedding cake. He had lovely eyes, Ken. I don't much blame him for leaving, Father, I really don't. That Lyle of hers is a handful. I don't think Ken knew what he was getting into with that conniving little no-good . . . just like his father, he is too. As shifty as Judas."

The sight of Gully in the hallway with her dear departed husband's books, though, had stirred up other memories in Mrs. Walsh. "Oh, God, Father, I miss Donald like blood."

"I know, dear," said Monsignor. "He was was a saint sent down to earth." He sounded consoling and all, but he was kissing his rosary beads, rearranging his Bible, wiping his reading glasses, and basically just looking impatient to start the sacramental portion of the program and get the hell out of there.

"Oh, Father, I'm afraid. I'm afraid to get up in the morning. I can't face the day-after-day anymore, Father, I just can't make it. God forgive me, I don't want Iris here. Donald could handle Iris, he always could. It's no good. I can't make it, Father . . . I don't know how."

"Nonsense, woman," Monsignor said, trying to bless away her problems by chopping the air with his palm while he read. "You've done it all your life, you'll do it again. God has nothing but faith in you."

"Faith? You don't understand, Father, he *was* my faith. He was my *strength*. He was all I had. When we lost Philip in Korea, *he* was the one got us through it. Not Jesus, God help me, it was Don!" She started to sob and stuff.

Monsignor just patted her hand and there-there'ed her, as if that's all she needed. Then, after draping his stole round his neck in a ceremonial way, whispered that he'd hear her confession now. It was getting close. He was bringing it home. We didn't have much time.

Hands clasped in prayer, the old woman recited the words she'd known since she was seven: "Forgive me Father, for I have sinned . . . It's been seven days since my last . . . since my . . . last . . . since my . . ." Then she blurted out: "Can't you *See?* It's no good! *Jesus* doesn't hold me in the dark, Father, *Jesus* doesn't do one . . . damn . . . Oh Father, I can't go on another minute praying to the air outside my window! It doesn't work anymore, Father! I don't believe . . . I don't believe in *Jesus!*"

I figured it was about time for the old bird to get her penance. He'd heard about all he was gonna hear and now he was ready to lower the boom, pronounce sentence and save her blasphemous soul. It'd have to be something big, like fifteen Hail Marys and a dozen Our Fathers, a rosary every night for a month and an hour or two of self-flagellation. She'll be so busy wailing to God for forgiveness she won't have time for doubting. He put aside his Bible and specs and took the woman's bloated hands in his. He looked into her eyes for a real long minute.

"Audrey, I've got something to tell you," he said. "Something that happened on a cold, rainy night so many years ago it seems like another lifetime. Donald came to see me. It was the night young Philip died. He knocked on the door of the rectory until Mrs. Corcoran let him in, and he dripped on the rug in his work clothes, soaked to the very skin."

"My Donald!" Mrs. Walsh stifled a gasp, as the memory of a punishing black rain washed over her, and the air in the skies over Korea seemed as familiar as the trees in Caddigan Park.

"He said, 'Father, I can't make it,'" Monsignor went on. "He said he had nowhere to turn, that his faith wasn't strong enough to bear the loss of this child, that God had deserted him, that he didn't see how he could go on with his life. And he got angry, as angry as anyone who's ever been in my presence, and then he became profoundly sad, and then got mad all over again. Mad at God, mad at me, mad at the whole blessed world."

"Wh—what did you say to him, Father?" asked the old woman, who couldn't have been more enrapt if he'd put her in a trance.

"I told him to go home and be with his wife. Because his wife had enough courage and faith for the both of them." Mrs. Walsh buried her face in her hands and leaned into the Monsignor, who took her in his arms and patted her back. "Whatever strength the good man had, Audrey Walsh, he got from you."

And then my brother flung open the door, and with a fiendish, tight-lipped, ventriloquist-like grin, said, "Doody's here in five. Let's go."

"What about the Monsignor and the old lady?" I asked, as we vaulted down the steps.

"He's got her sobbing into his lap, for Chrissakes. Her confession alone's gonna take a half hour. We're *miles* away from Communion."

"So, now let me get this straight," I said. "Doody Levine, who has enormous difficulty with manual hedge clippers, is gonna swipe a three-quarter-ton vehicle, pilot it through the snow to Braintree and come back with Worms Faulkner's ounce?"

"Don't be ridiculous," said Gully. "Doody can't drive the goddamn van."

"So you mock me purely for your own enjoyment, is that it?"

"Look," said my brother, "even Doody should be able to steer the fucking thing down to Caddigan Park, am I right?"

I conceded that, under certain conditions, this could be done.

"Fine. We go out the front door, you, me, the Monsignor. One of us gasps: 'Oh, my heavens! Our van has been stolen!'"

"Or we could say, 'Well I'll be darned,'" I said, my contribution to the conspiracy.

"Stolen! From right under our noses! In *broad* daylight!"

"Son of a gun!" I ad-libbed. "Son-of-a-*gun!*"

"Fine. Then we start kicking things and blaming each other and screaming for the cops; the old lady starts dialing 911, and we're free as fucking birds."

The "free" part eluded me.

"With the van now out of circulation," explained Gully, "the Monsignor has no further use for us. He waits for the cops and drinks cocoa, we book like a bastard, meet Doody, back on the fucking beam."

"Don't you think Burke will see through our little caper like the black-hearted sin it is and make us stay here ourselves and wait for the cops?"

"There is that possibility, of course, but we hafta try, man, we gotta *try!*"

To reach the window, you had to get up on the workbench and climb up on a stool. Then you rolled up the window and stared face-to-face with the packed-in snow. The idea called for me to burrow through it in feverish rhythm like Charles Bronson in *The Great Escape.* Clawing a tunnel to freedom. I was disoriented within seconds. I couldn't tell up from down or east from west. And then I couldn't breathe. Flailing like a madman, I slid back through the window and onto the bench in a gasping avalanche of hair and dungarees, knocking paint cans and power tools to the floor.

"What the freak is the deal?" said my brother, brushing off the snow that was now all over him.

"It's impossible," I sputtered. "It can't be done."

"What can't be *done?* You keep mole-ing snow 'til your head pops through."

"You can't see, you can't breathe, and it can't fucking work!"

"Of *course* you can't breathe! You gotta hold your breath til you get there."

"I refuse to be the first dipshit to ever drown on Weld Road," I said. "Your plan's an abortion."

The door opened at the top of the stairs. "Everything all right down there?" the Monsignor wanted to know.

"Yeah," answered Gully. "Used a little too much elbow grease on this here workbench is all, Father, we're okay now."

The door closed.

"We are many fucking moons from okay," Gully fumed. "Now what the Christ do we do?"

"What about the breezeway?" I lightbulbed, thinking about the little screened-in room off the kitchen where we were stacking the mags.

"What about it?"

"If it's anything like the breezeway at the canary lady's down the street, it's got a door. A door to the outside. A gateway to salvation."

"Let's go," said my brother, grabbing another slew of magazines. Plan B was in motion.

It took a one-two-three grunt to force open the little door, and, just like that, I was tasting freedom and inhaling Arctic air. *Free.* The driveway'd been plowed, I noticed, but you still had to slug your way across three state lines to get to it. It occurred to me that I'd spent more time slogging through snow on this one day than in twenty years of tobogganing down Hicks Hill. I was wet, cold, and miserable, I was wearing the smock from Frannie's Fine Foods, but I was free. Once out to the driveway I started doing *the walk.* The walk I always do to keep time with the Screamin' Jay Hawkins playlist that rotates in my head. The height of the plowed snow was enough to keep the occupants of the house from seeing me, so I just sort of whistled and threw back my hair and did the walk and acted like I was being filmed, in black and white, by the guy who made *On the Waterfront*.

Gully must have made his message to Doody pretty clear because there he was, walking in a stiff-armed shiver, with no coat, hat, gloves, boots or sweater. He *owns* all these items, of course, but preventing pneumonia never gets in the way of his loyalty to someone who can get him weed.

"I see you silly bitches didn't get very far," he said, blowing on his hands. "But don't tell me—I'm too fucking cold to listen to one of your stories. Just gimme the keys."

"Here," I said. "And you gotta pump it like seven times and then floor it or you'll be here all goddamn day."

"Fine," he said.

And then, like a ghost, this guy appeared out of nowhere, a trail of white behind him. No car, no nothing, just this guy. This tough-looking Latino guy, in a short brown jacket and ridiculous white scarf, all mad and heaving and vengeful. "You mothers seen a dark-haired bitch and a stupid little dog?" he said. And I was real glad we hadn't. We just gave him the half-assed shrug so he stomped on down the street spitting out a frustrated string of F's and MF's, peering down each alley of snow as if the objects of his search would suddenly appear. Doody jumped behind the wheel and I started back up the driveway. But not hearing anything resembling ignition, I stopped in mid-stride. "Shit!" I said. "I forgot to tell him that you have to wiggle the key in the hole until it catches." I went back to set him straight.

Apparently, his wiggling method was okay because the engine started the second I opened the door. But the stricken expression on his face said four-alarm fire. "Get in! Get in! Get in!" he shrieked. "It's that eyeballin' old priest on the porch with your brother!" I practically dove, pulling the door hard behind me and ducking down low.

"*Drive!*" I screamed. "*Put the pedal to the floor and go!*" I peeked out the side window as we fishtailed away. All three of them were in the doorway—Gully, the Monsignor, Mrs. Audrey Walsh—and they all looked equally confused.

"Did they see us?" said Doody, his voice choked in fear, his feet not certain which pedals did what.

"I'm not sure," I said, "but things're gonna start dawning on them soon."

And then I heard the whimper. As if it was my baby sister when we all used to ride back there. Except that it was unmistakably a dog. One of those little pipsqueak things with a pushed-in face like a cruller. Wearing a damn coat? The leash it was attached to led to the spare tire way in back. There sat the girl. The girl with the boots, the jeans, the long gray coat, the scarf, the beret, and the ribbons of black hair falling over her collar.

"John?" she said. "Is that you?"

I hadn't seen her since acne. They'd sent her to boarding school after our last get-together and then it was on to Rutgers. Word is she hadn't even made it home for the last three Christmases. But I wouldn't know.

"Yeah," I said, "it's me."

"I *knew* it was the truck!" said Dally Schoerner. "I just wasn't sure if you still owned it. How on earth have you been?" Her speech had changed. Much more cultured-sounding, a little deeper, and a whole lot theater-major. She got up and steadied herself over to the couch, so she could get a real good look at me.

"So who's the dog in the jacket?" I asked, getting a real good look at her.

"Oh, that would be Ca-Ca," she said. "And don't think I'm not embarrassed to be seen with the fully dressed little shit."

"Who's your friend outside with the long white scarf?"

"That would be Pelo," she said, pulling Ca-Ca up on her lap. "And Pelo, my dear, is no friend of mine."

Then Doody said something about the traffic light ahead and should he apply the brakes when he gets there or pump intermittingly all the way in?

"Just punch the fucking thing," I advised, looking into Dally's eyes. Funny, I don't remember Dally's eyes from before—were they ever this striking? They take you in, sort of, deep and wet, like they're trying to tell you something. All I saw as a kid was her mustache, then, later, a pink Lycra bathing suit. But her eyes—they hold honesty, somehow, and when they lock onto you, you are the only thing left standing and the rest of the world is mere scenery. Everything is smooth, they seem to be saying, nothing can happen, all is okay.

Which came in real handy right about now. With purgatory fading fast in the distance, the gates of hell ahead, and Doody Levine at the wheel.

7

Puff

Gas and the running out of gas has always been an issue for Gullivans. The sight of Dad angrily walking streets with a gasoline can in his hand was a familiar one to area residents. They hardly ever pulled over to give him a lift either, the bastards, no doubt sensing the mood he'd be in.

This tradition got passed, without fanfare, to his heirs. Who repeatedly ignored the warnings: the needle tap-tap-tapping into the *E* zone; the red *FUEL* light flashing like ship-to-shore. But, dammit, you'd get caught up in things. The home half of the seventh, for instance, or, in our case, the last five tracks of *Quadrophenia*. Or better still, cheesing it from cops and clergy in a seemingly stolen vehicle with Red Cross insignia on the sides.

"Are you aware that your needle's on *bone dry*?" sighed Doody, the earlier panic in his voice giving way to a wizened expectancy that every possible thing was going to go wrong.

And then the animal crossed our path.

"What the Jeezis Fuck was *that*?" Doody swerved to miss the broad-shouldered beast, damn near overturning us in the process. I caught a glimpse of it. Big as a beaver, but more upright, and striped.

It seemed to *sneer* at us as it slipped under the right wheel. And then I knew. It was Puff. Our cat. Who was named, like so many other tiger-striped cats of the era, for the good-natured tabby in *Dick and Jane*. *See Puff. See the blue yarn. See Puff play with the blue yarn.*

Our Puff did not play with yarn. Our Puff did not *play*. Our Puff was a snarling, ill-tempered hornet's nest of evil. Our Puff was Puff the Impaler, Inflicter of Deep, Scabrous Wounds.

Puff was part of a litter born in the florist shop at the foot of the Neponset River bridge. Her mother was Molly, a yellow meowing lump that went through the motions of chasing the mice in old man Weaver's greenhouse. Puff's father, most suspected, was Spike. *The* Spike. The mauling, brawling one-eyed tough who roamed Neponset's banks at night and dragged full-grown river rats back to his lair. Puff came to us in a box with a ribbon—just a kitten, maybe six weeks old, frisky as a jar of crickets.

"Look how she goes after my hand," laughed Dad, as Puff bit into it with all the muscles in her neck. "Oooh, those little teethes are sharp! Ha-ha-ha-*owww!*"

We came to know these teeth well, my terrified siblings and I. It wasn't even halfway grown when it began lying in wait—lurking under the dining room table, carefully selecting its victim (usually the one with the most leg exposed) then springing out and latching onto its prey, hugging your shin like a tree surgeon, clawing and biting with demented glee. It got *craftier* as it grew, spreading out its attacks, lulling you into complacency, and then striking as you emerged from the bathroom in a towel. Ma would have to hit it with something to make it let go, and it skulked back to the shadows, low and satisfied. What was left was shredded skin, blood on the floor, and wailing, bawling victims with irreversibly damaged nervous systems. One memorable ambush took place about ten Halloweens ago, when Doody, done up like Barney Rubble, gorged himself at our living room table on candy corn and Cheez Doodles, unaware that his tapping bare foot under the table was calling to poor Puff like a nest of hairless shrews. Doody ran screaming into the kitchen with Puff all over him, his purple face contorted into an expression we recognized at once.

We would have voted, Ma included, to get rid of Puff. We had a vet next door, for God's sake, who would've put her down for free. But Dad liked her and she seemed to like him, curling herself shamelessly round his leg when he came home from work, rolling on her back to be scratched by his rough, ink-stained fingers, purring like a damn pet.

Out of Dad's gaze our cat was a growling, malevolent scoundrel, who, we believed, had one ambition: to murder us in succession and drag our scarred, punctured corpses behind the couch before Ma could save us.

I once saw her kill a squirrel—a hapless rodent who ventured up to our screened-in porch. Puff pounced from the lawn—the animal had nowhere to go—and death came swift. African-safari swift. Puff didn't toy with the thing or torture it, prolonging its agony like any other cat in the world would. She hit it like an outboard motor, tearing it limb from limb, gnashing out its innards with tyrannosaurus-like purpose. Part of its gaping-mouthed head banked off the windowsill, little arms and legs were flung against the bookcase, and fur flew. She then carried a good portion of the squirrel's carcass down the steps, across the street and into the woods by the bus stop. Life was cheap on Knoll Road; tense, uncertain, and perilous.

But now, in the twilight of her life, it appeared our precious pet was trapped under our wheel. I had Doody pull over so I could get out and make sure.

"Do you think she's dead?" asked Dally from the couch.

"I don't know," I said, flinging open one of the side doors, "but even *that* steely-eyed bitch couldn't survive an ass-kicking like this."

And then Puff leapt into the open van without a scratch on her and, for a moment, strutted.

"Hi, Puffy!" said Dally. "Why, don't you look pretty! I don't believe I've seen her majesty in years."

Puff ignored the small talk and took a few seconds to look about the place; for all I knew, she hadn't been inside since the Gullivan & Son era. Her bored, seen-it-all eyes fell on this and that—the dangling roach clip, the liters of Pepsi, Doody's feet. She even let me scratch behind her ears, a modest privilege she'd granted to me and only me after Dad died. I cooed, "That's a nice Puffy . . . pretty Puffy . . . that's a pretty little Puffy-Wuffy."

But the thing in Dally's lap suddenly moved, and the beady eyes of Ca-Ca were upon the eyes of Puff, and her ears pinned back like bat wings. Is it a rat? she seemed to be asking, her great head cocked to one side. Its head's too big for a rat, its snout's too damn flat, but it *couldn't* be a dog, it . . . just . . . *couldn't*. Then the dog stood on all fours on the edge of the couch and let out a yip-yip-yip! And Puff zeroed right in on the little blue coat and entered the realm of unreason. She lunged at Ca-Ca like a tiger through a flaming hoop, tearing the despised jumper from the dog's skinheaded body and digging into its fleshy meat with unleashed relish as frightened squeals filled the air. Not 'til I shook a new jug of Pepsi and hosed down the maniacal beast did she let go, scooting out the door and back into the snow like a hunted weasel.

"Jesus!" cried Dally. "Look what the fiend did!" The dog had deep gashes on his belly, neck, and back and there was no certainty about his penis. "We gotta get him someplace *fast!*"

"We'll take him to your old man's," I agreed. "It's only a couple streets over."

"My father? In a pig's ass we will."

"He's a vet, isn't he? Where else are we gonna find a goddamn vet in the middle of—"

"Number one, he's a *retired* vet. Number two, the ignorant quack *should* have retired ten years ago when he put the wrong two Irish setters to sleep, and number three, my father and I are not, nor will we ever be, on speaking terms."

"Look," I said, "we're in a bit of a tight spot here. Don't think for a minute that we got time to take the little cur to Angell Memorial."

"We'll take him to the Crawley," she decided.

"Crawley *Hospital*?" laughed Doody. "Last I checked, Princess, they don't take the four-legged."

"Well, this one's gonna need about twenty-five stitches and a shot," Dally persisted. "It doesn't matter who does the honors—the nurse, the orderly, or the freaking proctologist—just get me there and I'll take care of the rest."

The dog was whimpering, for God's sake, *and* shivering, its royal blue garment in tatters at Dally's feet. And his eyes were slowly closing, as if life were ebbing away.

"Oh Christ, Doody," I gave in, "gimme the fucking wheel."

"In that case," said Doody, pulling over, "I shall take my leave. I will come to visit you in jail, though, I promise. I simply have no need to be fingerprinted alongside you." He thrust open the door, bid farewell to "M'Lady" and was gone with his shirtsleeved self into the cold. I drove away.

With Doody out of the picture, Dally suddenly opened up her life story—or at least the last three weeks of it—in one detached breath, her eyes fixed on the rearview mirror above me, Ca-Ca fading fast in her lap.

"Ca-Ca, in case you're wondering, is not mine," she began. "Ca-Ca belongs to Ethel Vierstra, a friend from school, who I brought home Monday to escape the clutches of her ex-boyfriend Pelo, who makes threats, talks like he's in the cast of *Grease*, and has taken to barging right into her biology class and yanking her out by the hair."

"You're telling me you've been home since Monday?" I interrupted.

She rolled her eyes in the mirror. "It doesn't help to restore Ethel's faith in men when my father appears in the hallway by her door wearing the top to his vet suit and nothing else from the waist down."

"You've really been home since Monday?"

"Pelo finds us, of course, mine being the only house on Knoll Road with the occupants' last name on a yellow sign out front. We slip out the back door, into the carport, and try to escape in Ethel's car, but there he is, right in front of us, and now he's getting in the backseat, through the only unlocked door. Ethel screams, 'Pelo, this can't go *on*! It's *over*!' and Pelo says, 'Yeah? Well then I'm gonna take what's mine. We'll start with that little fucken pisspot dog!' Ethel pulls the dog tight and says, 'You *can't* have Ca-Ca!' And he reaches over and starts pounding the dog with his open fist, yelling, 'I-brought-that-shitbag-into-the-house-and-I'll-take-his-ugly-fucken-ass-*out*!' And Ethel says 'Here! Take him! Just don't kill him, Pelo, please don't kill him!' She sort of tosses the dog at him and he backhands it through the air and it winds up with me, and, I don't know, some basic Annie Oakley instinct takes over, and I'm suddenly running down the street with Ca-Ca in my arms and Raging Fucking Bull behind me."

I couldn't believe she'd been home since Monday.

My brother was waiting at the next corner with his hands crammed into the pockets of his smock as if it was a planned stop. He got in.

"How is this possible?" I had to ask.

"I saw my opening and I took it," he said, stomping snow on the floorboards.

"You had an opening?"

"Yeah, basically. Monsignor was looking down the road awhile like he expected the van to turn around and come back or something, and then he turns to me and says, 'Where is your brother?'"

"We hadn't rehearsed the 'where is your brother?' question," I said.

"That's right," he said. "We really hadn't. Especially since my brother was supposed to be in the house *with* me. So I go, 'Uh, he's still downstairs.' And Monsignor says, 'Well, go and get him, then.' And, on the way, I slip out the same door you did, and here I fucking am."

"So, we're pretty much an all-points-bulletin by this time?"

"I would expect," said my brother, and put one foot on the dash. Then he cocked his head to ask Doody how much he enjoyed his brief stint piloting the van and was surprised to hear a woman's voice coming back.

"That's Dally Schoerner back there, isn't it," said Gully.

"It is," I confirmed.

"And there is no doubt a very good reason for this development?" I shrugged.

"And there is, of course, an *extremely* good reason for us to be pulling, once again, into the emergency entrance of Crawley Fucking Memorial Hospital?"

"Well," is about all I remember saying.

It took about a minute and a half for the never-take-no-for-an-answer Dally to get from: "You're going to have to treat him—everything else is shut down!" to: "Where do I sign?" One nurse passed him to another nurse and they and Dally all went through the swinging doors together, whispering far more encouragement to the semiconscious little fleabag than I had ever seen them give to anyone else.

"So what happened to Dally's dog?" asked Gully, making his way to the vending machines. "And what was that shredded piece of shit on its back?"

"Puff happened to Ca-Ca," I said, "and that, such as it is, was a coat."

"I see," said Gully. "And how is it that Puff is running around in the snow?"

"Beats me," I said. "She must've slipped by us when we went out to shovel."

"I don't recall seeing her *in* the house."

"Haven't you been feeding her?"

"Me? I thought Ma fed the fucking thing."

"Ma? For Chrissakes, Gully, Ma's been in *here* since Monday! Are you saying Puff's gone hungry?"

"Look, I was all set to give her some of my tuna fish the other day and the cunt hissed at me. Whattya want me to do?"

Someone looking an awful lot like our older sister Dee Dee was pulling a scalding cup of coffee out of the Hot! Hot! Hot! machine in the corner. The reason it couldn't be Dee Dee was because Dee Dee lived in Gloucester and couldn't possibly be here right now.

"Oh good!" said Dee Dee. "You got my message!"

"What message?" one of us said.

"From your friend Doody. He said not only did he know where you were, he was on his way to see you. This never took place?"

"No, we saw him," said Gully, "but he didn't give us any message."

"Then you showed up to see Ma on your *own?* That's almost sweet!" (She practically spilled her coffee.) "She's taken a turn for the worse—you must have sensed it!"

"Yeah," I said. It took a real clairvoyant to hone in on that one. Ma's turns have been getting steadily worse by the month. Her frail arms and legs would suddenly balloon with swelling, and visiting nurses or Gina Sookey (when she wasn't having sex in the van with Gully) would come and wrap her up in yards of Ace bandage and call her "Dearie." She'd bravely and feebly climb into a taxi to be taken to her chemo session and come back in a state of fever and nausea worse than malaria. The baldness was a nice touch too, in the string-'em-along-til-they've-wheezed-their-last process. It's not enough they bleed you like a raisin—they need you to look like Nosferatu the Vampire to boot.

Ma's courage through the ordeal, we think, came from movie stars. She'd been affected by John Wayne's heroic battle with cancer and by Susan Hayward's and Gary Cooper's and Humphrey Bogart's. She'd made up her mind to battle hers heroically too. She'd seen the other way. Her friend Edna from Sodality, a stout little wirehaired woman with a French accent, had a husband with the disease. He died at home because they had no health insurance, and it took him about two years to do it, screaming at Edna the whole time about how she caused his cancer in the first place by making him take the assistant painter's job at E and Y Auto Body. Apparently she made him smoke too, because he inhaled about five packs of Lucky Strikes a day.

Ma felt sorry for the penniless Edna afterwards and decided to hire her as a housekeeper a couple times a week while Ma took a part-time job cashiering at Flynn's. This point was lost on Dad. Why anyone would take a job and then turn around and give half the proceeds to the widow of some shiftless sourpuss was beyond him. This was how our parents quarreled too. He'd rail on about the many things that were beyond him and she'd iron blouses and hum Richard Rodgers. The Edna arrangement didn't make it past the first day. Puff pried open the lid on Cassie's gerbil cage and systematically devoured all seven rodents one by one, leaving only their heads, in a neat configuration under the living room couch. Discovering the slaughter with a corn broom, Edna frantically called Ma at work, crying out, "*H-h-h-heads! H-h-h-heads!*" when Ma came to the phone. Ma pressed for more detail but her friend carried on unintelligibly. Fearing the worst and knowing what mayhem her sons were capable of inflicting on the house, Ma shut down her register, hopped on her Schwinn and streaked homeward. She found Edna in a near catatonic state, pointing at the enchanted area under the couch. Ma bent down, exhaled droopily, swept the severed atrocities onto a piece of cardboard and flushed them down the toilet. She then held the fragile Edna until color returned to the woman's face, then drove her, in her own car, back to her house, where she helped her with her shoes, tucked her into bed at twelve-thirty in the afternoon and stroked her harp-string hair 'til she closed her eyes. By the time Ma hotfooted it back to Flynn's, the next shift was in and the baldheaded store manager was yapping on and on about how he docked her a day's pay and how she should let him know *right now* if she was serious about working there.

We asked Ma years later why she didn't just tell him to stick his lumpy-assed head in a diaper pail. She said she was tempted but what would it prove?

"It'd prove your were better than *that* spore," I said.

"I already knew that," she said, and adjusted her realistic-colored wig for a night out at Bingo.

Dee Dee led the way to Ma's room. I breathed in short little hiccups of air, trying to keep as much death out of my lungs as possible as we clopped down the corridors, passing the low-lit chambers of the doomed, the condemned, the gaunt. Their visitors looked up eagerly, as if they hoped one of us was a specialist from Austria with word of a cure.

Ma was happy to see us. She'd lost the ability to smile weeks ago, of course, but you could see it in her eyes.

8

A Turn for the Worse

When it comes to visiting someone in the hospital and providing them comfort and care, there is no one more useless than us. We just stand there, my gaping brother and me, ask two or three moronic questions and then look at Bob Eubanks on the TV. Even when the not-long-for-this-world patient directly *asks* us for something, we find a way to shit the bed.

"Can one of you get me a glass of water?" comes the feeble plea.

"Sure, Ma," one of us gets up from his chair. "Where is it?"

"In the bathroom."

"I don't see a cup."

"The cup is out here."

"Where?"

"Here. By my bed."

"Oh."

"I can't make the water come out."

"You have to push down on it."

"Nothing happens."

"Are you pushing the right knob?"

"Which one's the right knob?"

This basically goes on until the patient buzzes the nurse, falls asleep, or dies.

"You don't have to stay," said Dee Dee. "She's resting comfortably."

"No," I said, rubbing the fatigue from my eyes, "we'll hang a while longer."

"You really don't."

"Okay," and out we escaped like two cheats in a card game.

In the lobby sat Dally Schoerner, legs crossed, perusing one of those cross-the-street-to-avoid hospital magazines like *Disease Monthly* or *Living with Rickets*.

"Didn't expect you so soon," she said, lifting her theatrical eyes.

"Well, we did all we could."

She moved forward, real adult-like, resting her chin on her index finger like she was interviewing us for the laborer position, "How is she?"

"Oh, she loses something every day," I came up with. "How's Ca-Ca?"

"He's *resting comfortably*." She rolled her eyes as she reached for her coat. "They're gonna keep him overnight."

"They don't have a problem with that?"

"They have a problem with everything. You have to practically hypnotize the fucking hens. So where are we going?"

"We?" said Gully. "We are on our way to Braintree."

"Well now, how convenient is that? You can drop me at the Koala Inn."

The next thing I know I'm backing the van onto Tread Street, Dally's looking for a cigarette, and my brother's muttering something about hypnotism.

"Sorry," I said. "We don't smoke."

"I see," said Dally Schoerner. "So the yellow teeth and tuberculoid cough comes from watching too much TV?"

That was pretty much the remark that did it. Her superiority was coming through loud and clear. Up to that point, I'd been working up to asking her if she just wanted to bed down at our house. She could've had Ma's room, or even one of my sister's old ones—hell, she could have even bunked with us if she got lonely. But the lousy remark put an end to all that, and I couldn't wait to get to the Koala and be rid of her, which would have pleased my brother to no end. Night was falling as we crossed into Lower Mills. I snuck a glance at her in the mirror as she adjusted the straps on her boots. Her eyebrows were dark and exquisitely drawn, except that they weren't drawn at all, they just looked it. One of them was always slightly raised and its tail disappeared into her beret with a personality all its own. She knew I was watching too, you could tell. The way she gracefully moved her eyes and gazed out the window, like a trained actress, careful not to look into the camera. Phony as shit. I wished she'd never come back. I wished the streets weren't such a mess so we could be rid of her sooner.

"*Cops*," said my brother out of the side of his mouth.

"What?" I said, eyes darting like tree frogs.

"Cops!"

"Where?"

"On the street parallel. I saw the cruiser through the alley."

"Shit! Did they see us?"

"Christ, Johnny, they *musta*! We're the only ones *out* here!"

I've spent exactly two nights in jail, on separate occasions, and I wouldn't recommend it. Loud, too much light, slabs to sleep on, sarcastic judges in the morning—it's only fun the first time, and even *then*. But tonight, for some reason, is the *last* night I wanted to be jailed. This night cried out for someplace warm. Soft. Dimly lit. Don't ask why.

"Quick, pull down this street," said Gully, still doing ventriloquism.

"What's down here?" I obeyed.

"Just some place to duck for a minute if Toody and Muldoon start tailing."

We steadily toughed our way down the narrow strip, its snow-packed walls as claustrophobic as a bobsled run. I was doing okay, though, doing just fine. Turning again at the next street, a somewhat familiar locale, with white-covered wrought-iron fences, easy as you please, giving the wheel just enough play, trusting my touch on the brakes, quietly adding to my well-earned reputation as a skilled and daring master of motorized craft. And then we ran out of gas.

I knew it first, of course, because I felt the impotent emptiness in my right foot as the van slowed to a long, worrisome, red-lights-on-the-dashboard stop.

But I was determined to stay calm. Women liked men who stayed calm. I was calm.

"Don't fucking tell me," said my brother. "We're outta gas."

"Don't look at *me!*" I snapped. "You're the one who said we didn't have time to stop on the way to Gunther's party! You're the one who decided we should drive those two redheaded skanks to Leominster and you're the one who said, 'Fuck it, we can fill it tomorrow, it ain't gonna *snow!*'"

Otherwise, I was calm as a Christmas carol, and we all sat there in silence a minute or two, taking it all in.

"So," said Dally, "are we hoping to catch a stiff wind from the southeast or is one of us going to hike for gas?"

"Look, you phony, stuck-up, fake-accented—" started my brother, who turned to face Dally with that teeth-clenched Richard Widmark sneer of his and I interrupted before he got to the scene where he tries to strangle Sidney Poitier.

I said, "We gotta get out and push."

Being gentlemen and all, or hypnotized gentlemen at any rate, we let Dally steer while we pushed the van to a safe spot and called each other names. We pushed it backwards, both of us remembering this one bank of sludge around the last corner that did not contain a buried car. Right in it went, but the way it went in suggested that it would not be coming out, gas or no, without two or three good-sized boards and about a ton of sand. We climbed back in to regroup.

It was surprising how cold the van had become in just a few minutes. Clouds of breath mushroomed in the air and froze on the windows, sealing us off completely from the outside world. "We should probably move closer together, like maybe on the couch," I said, remembering this story Granddad once told over Sunday dinner, the one where he's in the navy, stationed in New Brunswick, Maine and he and his buddies are heading back to the base after a night on the town, in the middle of a raging blizzard. They've missed the only bus so they're on foot, and even though they're laughing and joking and having a heckuva drunken time, it's becoming more and more obvious they'll freeze to death if they don't find shelter. They find it in a junkyard, in an old DeSoto with no seats. All six of them pile in and huddle together, their ringleader, a big Georgian named Tex, convincing them that their combined body heat will keep them alive. And Tex was right.

Dally was taken by the story, you could tell. It was further pointed out, though, that the amount of body fat that hung from a Gullivan's frame wouldn't insulate a canary.

"This is how I see it," said my brother. "One of us could try to find gas while the other two stay here and freeze to death. Or we could figure that there's no gas to be found because nothing's been open for days and we all stay here and freeze to death together. Or we all get out and see if we can make it back to the house before rigor mortis sets in."

It was dark when we set out, two idiots in white smocks and Keds and a dark-haired girl in black. A streetlight flickered overhead and wind blew eerily in and out of the columns at the entrance of Loneberry Elementary, my alma mater. Dally stopped. "This is where it happened, isn't it? Right here on this spot. The murder of the football star." She pulled her collar tight to her throat, and seemed to imagine every aspect of the desperate scene.

The night Grady Gerfalts got stabbed was almost three years to the day Doody's father got shot. Doody had to go to Grady's wake too, which was way too wicked weird. All the kids who played Pop Warner football had to go—a show of oneness for a fallen comrade on the varsity. They went when Lummy Angelino broke his neck on a linebacker blitz and when Coach Clendennon had his cerebral hemorrhage in the shower. And they came and went together, wearing matching coats, and serious looks of concern.

"It was unreal," said Doody about the proceedings. "They cut his hair, for Chrissakes, shorter than the goddamn Smothers Brothers, and they polished his face like a wax peach."

We barely knew Grady Gerfalts ourselves. He was not someone who spoke to failed athletes like us. Our only connection, I suppose, was that it was he who hung Doody's long-lasting nickname on him, back in the fifth grade, when the then *Neil* Levine spectacularly crapped his white football pants whilst pushing the blocking sled across Hatch Field. Not since Babe Ruth has a nickname stuck so fast. He had no say in the matter. To friend and relation alike, he was, is, and shall ever be, Doody. Even the invitations to his wedding that never happened had the *Neil* in parentheses. Other than that, I can't think of another thing Grady Gerfalts ever said or did. Except score touchdowns.

Thing is, we didn't know Doody's father much better. He *did* own Saul's Drug—that we knew. He was a bit of a dick—that we knew too. "If you're gonna buy one of those, then *buy* one of those!" he'd bark as we drooled over the newly arrived comics. "If you ain't, then get the hell out!" Even if we reminded him that we were waiting for Doody, he'd give us the thumb. "Go wait on the curb. This ain't no public library and I sure as hell ain't one of them librarian broads."

We weren't allowed to go to his wake. Ma thought us too young to comprehend such things. She and Dad, who knew the guy even slighter than we, went in our place. Dad raved about the affair when they got home. "They call it Sit and Shiver," he explained. "They laugh and drink and make jokes about the dead guy and feed you like a horse. I feel like I've come from a Friars Roast!"

We ran into Doody the next day. He was pretty sad, you could tell, but it wasn't like he was crying or anything, or God forbid making us uncomfortable, so we sat with him on the stone wall and watched our feet as they bounced against the brick. After about three minutes of this eternity, Gully blurted, "So how did it happen?"

"According to Uncle Lou," he sighed, "two spooks walked in. One of them had a gun. That got the old man's attention like big-time. He says, 'If you're gonna shoot me with that gun, then *shoot* me with that gun! If you ain't, then get the hell out!'"

We could have dropped dead laughing right there, as you can well imagine, but we held back, steely-like, constricting every muscle in our body from the neck down. It was a good thing too, because Doody started crying a moment later, for real. And my brother and I cried with him, tears and sobs and everything, for a good twenty-five minutes. For *Saul Levine*. But we haven't since. I swear. Not once.

In later years, Doody seemed to find his father's unsolved murderers on every corner, especially the corners of Blue Hill Ave. and Columbia, where everyone was black and everyone was staring as our weather-bleached van and its kick-balls quintrophonic stereo blasted Richard Hell and the Voidoids out of its wide-open windows.

"Are you the dumb-assed niggers who put two slugs in my old man's chest?" Doody smiled at two guys on a stoop. "How 'bout you, fatboy?" he'd pretend to be friendly to the guy leaning against the fender of the Ford, "You the triggerman, or just the black-assed fuck who grabbed the vigg?" None of them were ever very friendly back, so we didn't feel so bad. Of course, truth be told, Doody didn't *exactly* get his hatred of blacks from his father being shot by one. Doody hated blacks because half the people in Morton hated blacks. Morton people said "nigger" as often as Morton dogs said "woof." I once sat in Spid's garage watching Dad's tailpipe get fixed and all I heard from under the truck was how the niggers were gonna take over this, the niggers were gonna take over that. "Let 'em in the schools, they take over everything," raved Spid, "Pretty soon you'll be living in Coontown." I was trying to think of one thing in town that would suffer by being taken over, and I asked Dad on the way home what living in Coontown would be like.

"I don't know," he said, "But I imagine you'll hear a lot of James Brown." But as we pulled into the driveway, he turned to me: "Don't pay any attention to Spid. Guys like Spid hear drums at night."

In our house, the only person who heard those drums was Granny, but that didn't stop her, in her pre-commode days, from yelling downstairs reminding Dad to play her number in the Nigger Pool. As for Spid, in the middle of his tirade, there was a honk out front and he had to climb out from under Dad's truck, swearing about his good-for-nothing sons who were at lunch. Spid went out to find a distraught black woman in a station wagon who had smoke coming out of the hood, and kids climbing out of the windows. He not only repaired the woman's hose but didn't charge her a dime, gave her directions, mentioned the weather, and patted one of her kids on the head. When he came back in and slid under Dad's truck, he said, "Niggers. Anything ya give 'em, they run it right to shit." There were lots of people in and around Boston who'd gladly sell rope to the lynch mob, but deciding which ones they were was tricky.

As for Doody, he'd pretty much calm down once we got through Roxbury, and, by the time we reached our destination—in this case, the Greyhound terminal on Stuart Street—he was back to his usual self. "Well, are we gonna rehearse or what?" he'd ask as we pulled up, and the event began.

The *event,* trotted out once every two or three months, had to do with the series of pay phones that ran the length of the terminal, broken up only by the newsstand, the soda fountain, and the ticket windows. When the New York bus came in—a vehicle sure to be loaded with weary, frenzied travelers—we sprang to action. I'd station myself at the first bank of phones. As the crowd made its way through, I'd carry on a loud, animated argument on the phone, laden with details, like: "You and your hideous curlers I gotta look at every morning it's no *wonder* I drink like a seal!" No sooner would the bewildered group advance past that unseemly scene when they'd be upon Doody at the second bank, engaged in the exact same conversation, word for spit-spewing word. By the time they reached the third, manned by Gully, most knew they'd been had.

Occasionally, this would end with a skirmish; more often with a uniformed banishment to the street, warned never to return. (Hence, the three-month hiatus.) Once, it ended in arrest for Disturbing the Peace. Doody, anyway—Gully and I got away. They shoved him in the wagon handcuffed to this large, muscular black guy, who had bloody marks on his face and was sobbing and carrying on about how was he gonna explain the whole crashing-into-the-building thing to his old lady and *goddamnshit* how was he gonna explain the blond wig and panties they were gonna find in the fucking car and *motherfuckin* how was he gonna explain to her how the fucking car ended up in Boston anyway? After a while, he composed himself and turned to Doody, "What you in for, man?"

"I had a very loud conversation about my abscessed hemorrhoids in a public pay phone," said Doody.

"Man, you in deeper shit than me."

They were put in adjacent cells. The guy offered Doody an oatmeal raisin cookie that his old lady brought in.

"Why? Don't they feed us in this fucking dump?"

"Not this time of night, man. You ain't gonna get nothin' in your belly now 'til after arraignment." Doody took the cookie. He agreed it was the best-tastin' motherfuckin' oatmeal cookie he'd ever had in his sweet-ass motherfuckin' mouth. "Old lady bakes all the goddamn time. All kindsa shit. You come over, man, you'll have cookies, brownies, and goddamn puddin' cake up your motherfuckin' ass."

"Be sure to leave me the address," quipped Doody, and he rolled up his coat and slept 'til morning. His mother bailed him out about nine.

"Nice chewin' with you last night, man," said the guy in the next cell. He stuck his hand through the bar to be shaken.

Doody turned and shook it, said, "Thanks for the righteous cookie, man," and went out to see his mother. It was the first person of African descent that Doody had touched.

"It felt weird," he said that night, as we hung van by Boston Common. "The skin, I mean. You know how you expect a snake to be slimy and then you touch it and it feels kinda good? It was something like that."

The whole thing was old hat to Gully and me. Dad sometimes let us tag along to watch him and Uncle Tut bowl in their Monday night candlepin league, whose members were overwhelmingly black. Guys bought us raspberry slushies and tossed us quarters for pinball. We shook lots of hands. Years later, in our short tenure at Frannie's Fine Foods, we learned, by Gully's count, sixteen handshakes. Old hat.

9

Love Is in the Air

"*A murder site is forever,*" said Dally Schoerner, as the three of us stood by the spot where Grady Gerfalts met his end. "The weeds may grow all around it, the snow may cover it, rain may wash away all the blood. It remains." But Dally wasn't the only one obsessing as we stood in the snow and stared at the steps of Ruslan D. Loneberry Elementary. I'd been obsessing about the place for years. After all, I went here, the only member of my family acquainted with its dank, asbestos-choked corridors. Everyone else, Gully included, went to St. Ukelele's with the nuns. The reason for this had something to do with Dad missing one of Dee Dee's payments. (It was later proven that the payment *had* been made, but in the back-and-forth between my parents and the archdiocese, I lost my spot and had to attend public.) I eventually *did* go to St. Uke's when I was older, but only for two marking periods; dealing with the Sisters of de Sade after years at Loneberry proved to be too much of a shock to my system, so I was returned. The *secular* son. Damaged from the first. The year I was away happened to be the year they killed Grady on these very same grounds, but I was too caught up in my own quibbles and quirks at the time to do much dwelling on the subject. I *did* play the scene in my head a couple thousand times, rest assured, imagining the helpless grid star falling to his knees, clutching his stomach as his two black assailants ran joyously into the night. "It must have been terrible," said Dally, and I shook my head in agreement, remembering Grady's blood on the hospital sheets. But the scenes running inside my head at the moment had more to do with the school itself, and what went on inside it. The hostile playground at recess where unsupervised pissheads punished the rest of us on a rotating basis for what their gin-drunken fathers did to them. I saw the half-dead coffee-drowned faculty, the blubbery principal Mr. Lucinda, the uniformly Irish lunch ladies, and, if I looked hard enough, I could almost see the straightaway stare of head janitor Eugene Bailes, taller than anyone else in the building, who hulked through the halls, broom slung on shoulder, barking things like: "Slow down, ya squealing hyenas—ya sound like a goddamn buncha *coons!*" (After the school was integrated several years later, his mutterings were reduced to slurs uttered in a decidedly lower voice out the side of his mouth.)

Lastly, I saw myself force-marched with my classmates to partake of the oral polio vaccine, which was said to be made of secretions from the testicles of monkeys, and came in teeny-weeny paper cups, a mouthful for each of us. Except for two kids: Amanda Blasingame, who got permission to do her swallowing at a private doctor's office on Furnace Brook Parkway; and Hednor Flack, the oldest boy in school by at least two years, who probably hadn't seen a physician since birth and had the sort of parents who hid from even the paperboy (which was me), simply refused to take the potion, saying, "Ain't no monkey gonna shoot no wad down *my* throat." Flack's mother, impossible to believe if you knew what she looked like, was supposed to be Principal Lucinda's sister, which helped to explain things. The rest of us in line all watched him as he walked away—pulling the collar of his dungaree jacket up around his sideburns—and saw nothing but polio, polio, polio.

"Shall we move on?" said Dally, whose idea it had been to stand here in front of the school obsessing in the first place.

"Don't let me hold you up," said Gully, who threw a snowball at the school as a parting shot. But turning headlong into the windchill with neither hat nor coat proved even worse than standing there. I started making a mental list of all the frostbitten body parts I would soon lose to amputation and had a vision of myself as a fingerless, toeless, earless curiosity whose picture would appear in the *Patriot Ledger* under the headline: LUCKY TO BE ALIVE, and who'd spend the remainder of his days licking envelopes for direct-mail advertising, nicknamed "Slurp" by his drooling, twitching, spasmodical colleagues.

But that's not the real reason I thought we should break into the school. The main reason, which I kept to myself, was because I needed to locate a toilet. (My digestive system, if I haven't mentioned it, governs my life. I ran away from home at age fifteen, again at sixteen, and once more at seventeen, with a mildewed old sleeping bag, a suitcase stuffed with Nabisco products, and attitude to beat the band. All three times I was forced to double-back to the house, holding my stomach, hobbling like a guy in a three-legged race. Not one to do his business just any old place, I passed up trees, abandoned shacks, hedges, bushes, two dry cleaners, and Spid's Sunoco, whose bubonic-caked restroom would take ten years off your life just by looking in the mirror. I made it back to the house in the nick of time, but, since technically I was still a runaway, had to sneak through the bulkhead and tiptoe to the tiny bathroom in the cellar. I sat down there in the dark, listening to my parents upstairs, thinking about home, and how comforting it was in times like these.)

• • •

"*I think we should* break into the school," I declared, the words hanging in the frigid air like underpants on a line. The idea was not met with resistance.

Surprisingly, my brother and I had never broken into a school. There was never much of a reason. We weren't thieves, really. The idea of loading up the van with electric typewriters and selling them to some fence in Revere never occurred to us, though it *had* been suggested by several of the lowlifes we knew. I recalled their advice, something about most school buildings being alarmed but not fully. You find a section that isn't, smash out a basement window with a chunk of concrete and you're in. We hiked around back by way of the road so as to minimize the amount of waist-high white stuff we'd have to bore through. A flickering EXIT sign beneath a weighted-down overhang stabbed a stream of red into the snow and we made our way to it.

The glass broke with a dull, muffled sound—not anything like what you'd expect. The high snow encased it like a room. No one heard it but us, guaranteed. Gully crawled in first. "Jesus, I think it's the home ec room," he said.

"Does it have a shithouse?" I asked, dying.

"I doubt it," he said, pulling open a fridge, "but it's got a shitload of chicken potpies."

"Don't get carried away, Chef Boyardee," said Dally, "your cops are gonna see that light a mile away."

Gully quickly shut the door but not before pulling three or four of the delicacies out. He began searching in the dark for a stove. I, on the other hand, was already out in the hallway, seeming to remember that the nearest boys' room was somewhere on this floor. The many EXIT lights lit my way as I ran, and I practically threw myself through the bathroom door, hit the light, and collapsed into the one stall. I recognized the graffiti at once, the many drawings of scrota, the phone numbers for blow jobs, the swastikas. Home.

Dally followed me in. "Lookit these urinals!" she said. "They go all the way to the floor! The only ones I've seen at Rutgers are those little fat things that come up to about here. Jesus, you could practically take a shower in these jewels. This is gonna be a cinch!" I had heard about the coed bathrooms they had at some of these colleges, but had never really thought about what that would entail, and what would happen if the only stall was taken. Dally didn't miss a beat.

I peeked through the crack in the door and saw her get into a catcher's squat with her back to the urinal. Her coat shielded everything, of course, but she seemed to pull something under and peel something back and—very tastefully, I thought—a single, driving, lengthy stream hit the porcelain behind her like a salvo of BB's. And all the while she's *talking*. "Y'know, I bet they've got phones in here. Lots of phones. I gotta try to find Ethel. I tried to call her brother in Brookline back at the hospital but got no answer. At the very least I gotta notify the police. Then I gotta find somebody to pick up Ca-Ca, not to mention the men in the little white coats for dear old Dad. I could be on the phone all night."

"When are you going back?"

"What? Back to my father's?"

"No. Back to school."

"Don't worry, dear, it's on my list. Hey, send a little toilet paper over here, won't you?"

"Toilet paper? For *peeing?*" (The minute I said it I felt like a dope; after all, I *did* have sisters.)

"Yeah, wise guy, for peeing. Hurry up."

"I'm having trouble."

"Just toss the whole roll over. I'll get it back."

"No," I said. "It's the kind that comes out one piece at a time."

"That crinkly little stuff that feels like math paper?"

"The same."

"Delightful. Okay, you'll have to make planes."

"Say it again?"

"Paper airplanes. Fold it up like a paper airplane and sail it over the top."

I did this. The first one hit the ceiling overhead and came right back and I ducked. The second attempt went over, straight down, and under the stall by my pulled-down pants. The third, I am told, soared across the room and into the barrel at the far end.

Others hit sinks. She mentioned she was almost dry anyway, when: "Bingo!" right into her fist it flew. Happily, she fixed her pants and stood up. "So, tell me the truth, Johnny, how long does your mother have?"

"A day or two, I guess. Maybe a week."

"Think of it. Soon, neither one of us will have parents."

I wanted to say something insightful, something about her father, maybe an anecdote from the old days, some tiny little memory about him that she could hold in her heart and clutch at anytime the hate got too big. Instead, a bowel movement the size of Kentucky rattled into the proceedings like a power chord by the Who.

"I think I'll wait outside," said Dally Schoerner.

We caught up to my brother, whose cooking could be smelled to the far reaches of the school. "You won't believe it," he said. "The audio-visual's right at the top of the next landing. Film canisters by the dozen. We're screening *Hombre* in fifteen minutes."

"We'll meet you up there. Dally's gotta find a phone."

"There's one in the nurse's office right above us. Works fine."

"You made a call?" I said.

"Yeah, called Worms, just to see what was going on."

"And?"

"Got the wife."

"What did she say?"

"She said: 'You fucking assholes have gotta stop calling here! Don't you shit-for-brains know this phone is *bugged?!*' Then she slammed it in my ear."

"So that's it?" I said.

"Well, I did call right back but all I get now is *busy,* so who the fuck knows. By the way, there's a shower in the janitors' room and it's hot as a bastard—I tested it."

Hot showers were essential to life as Gully. His hair needs to be washed every day, he'll have you believe, lest he be mistaken for a human clot of navel lint. He has rarely missed a day. When our plumbing went down years ago, he showered at Schoerner's. When our plumbing went down and the Schoerners were away, he withdrew from life, staying in bed until it was fixed.

The **windows** in the second-floor corridor upstairs reached to the ceiling. The moon spilled light on the courtyard outside, revealing the most awe-inspiring snowdrifts this side of the Arctic Ocean. Dally watched it with me for a minute, even put her hand on my shoulder, before disappearing into the nurse's room to make calls. She seemed to *squeeze* my shoulder too, I'm pretty certain. I wasn't sure how to read it; it could be as simple as: "Gosh, it's so nice to be here with my childhood chum looking out at the snow—I think I'll squeeze his shoulder." It could, on the other hand, mean: "I know fucking you would be like fucking a cousin but you look so handsome in the moonlight and the nurse's room also has beds." You just don't know.

The building was a din of hollow sounds—the submarine-like pinging of the many clocks, the constant hum of the Coke machine, the popping, tapping all-out war of the boiler-fired heating system— all of it alive as a midnight swamp. I wandered a little ways, down to the end of the hall, where the Main Office was and the main bulletin board and the main display cases. There appeared to be three or four replicas of the Declaration of Independence housed in one of them. It was hard to make out in the dark, but they were probably drawn by students—the kind who get A's. During my days at Ruslan D., a solid sixty-eight was about the top of my range. There was so much I didn't get; it was all so damn complicated. Wilmot Provisos, the Age of Phoenicians, math. It wasn't like I was rebellious or anything, more like stupid. The only thing I caught in any detail was Mr. Lucinda's morning announcements on the P.A., and that was only because he sounded like Johnny Most, nicotine-charred voice of the Boston Celtics. After that, I was lost for the day. Comprehension slipped slowly away like a darkening picture tube. Now, truth be told, I could follow the intricate Marvel Comics plots of Fantastic Four, and Reed Richards's perilous experiments with deoxyribonucleic acid, but start in with diagramming sentences and my arteries would harden. The problem is I didn't look stupid, or sound stupid, so my stupidity baffled them. There were numerous scheduled conferences with my parents. "I'm at my wit's end," Miss Buchanan might tell them, as I stared at some gum on the floor. "I *know* he's not stupid." *Lazy* was a word often used in my diagnoses and I wouldn't have disagreed. I slept a good ten hours at night, half the day in school and most of the afternoon when I got home. How they expected me to fit in all the homework was beyond me.

The marble-haired Miss Buchanan had been here, I'd guess, since the days when you could dip girls' pigtails in inkwells. In all that time she was never known to crack a smile. Her eyes twinkled a bit any time one of her fifth-grade dolts answered a question right and the corners of her creased mouth curved into this expression of forced cordiality in front of the parents on Open House. But the full-toothed wrinkle-stressed grin that lit up her face like the sun in the east—*that* happened only once, with *me*, the day she first laid eyes on the book report I'd turned in on *Captains Courageous,* the cover of which I'd illustrated handsomely, with crusty seamen of all rank and color peering suspiciously out at you from the main deck of their ship. The perspective was maybe a tad askew and misplaced shadows showed up just about anywhere—but the detail, from the stubble on a weather-beaten chin to the grain of the gunwales and planks, was rendered in breathtaking layers of realism, the same kind Ma used when she painted nativity scenes on our picture window at Christmas.

"Oh, John!" Miss Buchanan gasped. "This is simply . . . *wonderful!*" She flipped through the hand-lettered text inside, three pages' worth, every word and comma taken directly from the dust jacket. Then she turned to the back cover, where I'd drawn a panoramic masterpiece of the vessel cutting across an enormous setting sun, gorgeously shaded with almost every member of the forty-six-piece set of Benson's Colored Pencils I'd gotten from Aunt Fran in the mail. She practically hugged the report to her, her watery arms aquiver, her eyes welling up; and she called for Enid Rae Honigsblum, the smartest kid in school, to take over the class, while she paraded me to the office and proudly showed the flabbergasted Mr. Lucinda what I'd done. Then she took out a colored pencil of her own and put a big red A on the cover, the tail of which ran straight down through the captain's left ear, just like the title of a magazine would. Finally she unlocked the display case by the front entrance and hung the great work in there; curious personnel lining up to view it like it was the Star of India. Mrs. Dartfalling's kindergarten class from the basement floor even made a field trip out of it, bringing their snacks and everything.

It hung in there on Tuesday and Wednesday and Thursday and a good part of Friday, the day we discussed *Captains Courageous* in class. Miss Buchanan, delighted that she had awakened a love of literature in a theretofore listless bystander, naturally directed her questions to me. By the third one it became very apparent that the dust jacket had been the *only* part of the book I'd gotten to. Fifty years of washing blackboards and seventy-five years of curriculum-dictated life pulled down on Miss Buchanan's face like an overhead projection screen, and she opened her drawer, took out the key that I knew to be the one that fit the display case and stormed from the room, leaving no one in charge. When I got the report back five minutes later, the A had been violently crossed out and replaced with another (larger) letter, its imprint passing through all five pages. The wondrous expression she made when she first beheld it never crossed her face again—at least not in the presence of anyone *I* knew.

But I could still see that cover, even in the dark. And I could still feel the power it had—for a few days anyway—to raise Lazarus from the dead.

Dally snuck up from behind in her stocking feet and broke the trance by tickling me in the ribs. I would have described it as playful had she not given me a major myocardial infarction in the process. "Jesus!" I freaked. "Why don't you just grab me in the balls with a joy buzzer?"

"Don't get your hopes up, muscles."

"How'd you make out with your girlfriend?"

"Ethel? She showed up at her brother's all right, but they argued of course, and now she's Christ knows where."

"What about the fleabag?" I asked.

"Ca-Ca? Ha! I talked the brother into it. He's gonna check in on the little turd tomorrow."

"How'd you pull that one off?"

"I used the *vulnerable* voice. Another five minutes I'd have had him rotating my tires."

Without her boots and long black coat she looked a whole lot smaller and a bit less sophisticated. Almost like the Dally of old. It occurred to me, though, that I had carried on more of a conversation with Dally in the last couple hours than in the entirety of our childhood, which basically consisted of my brother or me serenading her with: *"Dally's got a mustache! Dally's got a mustache!"* followed by her chasing us down the street and pummeling us with her grandmother's green-and-pink umbrella. Now I just wanted to ask her out.

"So, feel like finding Gull and taking in a movie?" I suavely began.

"It's that Paul Newman thing, isn't it? The one where he plays the half-breed who has to protect this bunch of greenhorn clods from marauding Mexicans and he utters something like six lines in the whole fabulous production?"

"That sounds about right."

"Nah, I saw it once in the student union," she said. "I bailed when they had to change reels. I assume he gets killed in the end?"

"I believe he does."

"See? Now you went and spoiled it for me. Let's go for a walk."

"A walk?"

"Yes. I think it's time you took me for a fully narrated tour of your alma mater." And she curled her arm in mine, slung her coat and boots over her shoulder, and pointed us in a random direction.

To have the corridors to yourself, to roam them at will—something I only dreamed of when I went here. It took a Jewish holiday, as I recall, and a substitute teacher to give me my chance. The attendance list had to be delivered, in one piece, to the office. It was a task routinely done by Enid Rae Honigsblum, occasionally backed up by Stewart Krass—*trusted* pupils, the kind Miss Buchanan could depend on to not only complete the mission and come right back, but to even ask their beloved teacher after class if they'd missed anything in their absence. But today they were both home watching *Gumby* and Miss Buchanan was away at some conference in Lynn. Her substitute, Mr. Crimlisk, who was as thick as the turtles on the table, picked me. "Here," he said, "run this down to the office." There was no mistaking it, especially when he slid it right onto my desk. I took it in both my hands like a new pane of glass, looked right into Mr. Crimlisk's pickled eyes for reassurance and was gone.

I walked slow. Taking it all in. Some of the doors to some of the classrooms were open and some were closed. But everyone looked up as I passed—envious, you could tell. You couldn't *blame* them. There they were, all hunched together under fluorescent lights—learning, learning, learning. And here I was out in the hall. Not learning a thing. Who had the better life? You tell me.

Mr. Lucinda's bag-of-bones secretary, whose pinched, taut face was in the early stages of mummification, seemed to know me. "Why thank you, John. And how's your mom, and your sister Dee Dee, and your aunt Francine?" I think I remember seeing her at the house for one of Ma's Sodality meetings. I mumbled "Good" to all the questions.

I took the long way back. Climbed stairs I had never climbed and found myself on the third floor. The kids there looked up at me too as I passed, but only for a bored second. Being much older, they seemed not nearly as impressed with my night on the town, and looked quickly away. I reached the far stairwell by the legendary "third-floor shithouse" and started down. I heard the door creak open behind me. "Pssst!" came the whisper but I pretended not to hear it. "Psssst! Hey, paperboy!" it insisted, and I turned. It was Flack. Hednor Flack. Half in the shithouse and half out. Motioning me to come inside. He had the remains of a cigarette in his right hand. I had *heard* they smoked cigarettes in the third-floor shithouse but now I had hard proof. And Flack was inviting me in. Me. To the third-floor shithouse. To smoke cigarettes. And swear, I'm sure.

The floor was littered with butts as I entered the haze; there was an open window in the corner with at least a million more on the gravel roof outside it, some of them still burning. But only Flack was in here now. Flack and me. "Get over to the pisser and pretend like you're pissing," he said, and I did. I wasn't sure how this worked but I think I was running some kind of interference—he'd smoke and I'd pretend I was pissing. If some nosy teacher walked in, they'd clearly see that I was just pissing and they'd walk right out. Of course, they *would* see Flack smoking. I was trying to sort it out in my mind how my pissing was going to get Flack off the hook, when he came up behind me, right behind me, and breathed, "So, paperboy, what do they call you?" and all the blood went out of my legs. Suddenly my shirt was up and his penis thumped against the small of my back like the muzzle of a Colt 45. Just as suddenly the door flew open and Flack jumped to the other urinal and threw himself deep into it.

It was Mr. Lucinda. "What's going on here?" he barked, giving the place a good once-over.

"What does it look like?" spat an unfazed Flack.

"Mr. Gullivan—you have someplace to be?"

"Y-Yes," I said, and tucked in my shirt and fled. I was at the bottom of the first landing and a third of the way down the second flight before I even exhaled. Then I stopped. And glanced back up, my heart trying to punch its way out of my chest. No one had come out the door. I hid there a minute, in that place by the railing where I could see their feet if they came out, but nothing. Maybe I'd missed it. Maybe, in my panic, I'd missed Mr. Lucinda storming out of the shithouse yanking Flack by the ear. But *this* was the quickest way to the office—they would've had to come right past me. They were obviously still in there. I had a terrible thought. What if Flack had drawn a switchblade and killed Mr. Lucinda and was escaping through the open window and shinnying down the drainpipe? I slowly crept back up the stairs. One foot on a step, then two feet, then one foot, then two. At the fourth from the top I heard voices.

Sharp, echoed whispers, coming from inside. I couldn't make it out, but I knew who it was. It was Lucinda whispering to Flack whispering to Lucinda whispering to Flack. It was an argument. I thought I heard Lucinda say, "My *sister!*" three different times. Then I thought he said, "I can't protect you anymore! I *can't!*" Then I heard their feet sliding towards the door and I was down the stairs in two quick athletic leaps and sprinting back to Mr. Crimlisk like no one had run before.

10

The Trouble with Girls and Boys

My midnight tour of the school with Dally Schoerner approached the girls' locker room. The closest I had ever been to the girls' locker room was in the hallway outside its door. I often saw the girls go in and I often saw the girls come out, in a great hurried whiff of steam and cream-rinsed hair, and I would've given up Cheez-Its for a month for a glimpse inside. If it were anything like the *boys'* locker room, where the herd of us soaped up our balls under one gigantic pressurized shower head and came up with clever names for each other's penises like "Zorro" and "Manatee Head" and "Chewed-down number-2 Pencil," it would be something to behold.

"Silly," said Dally Schoerner. "The girls all have their own shower stalls, with little curtains and everything. See?"

She was right. There were about forty of them, all in neat little rows, all with curtains and benches and hooks for your clothes.

"Jeez, you get dressed in there too?"

"No, dear, we all just parade back and forth in the altogether and ask Sister Mary Alice Joseph if she's got any spare tampons."

I asked if she had ever longed to peek inside the boys' locker room back at St. Ukes's.

"Well, not to the extent that your depraved lascivious mind would allow, but I did run through once, on a bet. The idea was that I'd start at one end and Peggy Penn'd start at the other and we'd high-five in the middle as we passed. We collected fifteen dollars from the other girls and split it."

"Were all the boys in there?" I asked, my voice catching in my throat.

"Nah, they were all down playing bombardment. All, that is, but one."

"Who?"

"One Carl 'Worms' Faulkner. Came back because he was sick. How do I *know* he was sick? Because I saw his fat, white, bepimpled buttocks shuddering like dying cows as the rest of him heaved into the john. It was a sight I have never been able to shake. Years of therapy. If only the stall had had a door—was that too much to ask?"

Drops of water slapped loudly to the floor like random cracks of a whip. You could make out something—a cockroach, maybe a mouse—crawling out from behind a large receptacle of towels. Above it hung a corkboard full of rosters and hand-lettered notices for basketball practices, at least a week old. There was also an old news clipping of Aggie Ogden, Morton's most legendary female athlete, about to unload the javelin at the state meet. On the far wall a gigantic poster rippled from the blown heat radiating beneath it. The poster was of two muddied field hockey players in full pursuit of the ball. The two-inch block lettering said "COMMITMENT." One of the players, the blonde, could have easily passed for Wendy Pfisternak, a girl in my high school biology class, a girl who came this close to being *the first notch on my illustrious gun,* having smooth-talked my way into the backseat of her father's Ford Fairlane at eleven o'clock at night, in the parking lot behind the MDC rink, with the moon full, the breezes gentle, Cream on the tape deck, and the crickets chirping like mad. She was the first date I ever had who let me kiss her in places other than her lips and I was hell-bent on getting to as many of them as I could. Various parts of our clothing— a shirt here, a nylon there—were already dangling from rearview mirrors, strewn across headrests, and more were on the way. Virginity was in the balance and love was athump in the air. But for some reason—and for this I have no rational explanation—it suddenly reminded me of Peter Parker.

"Who's Peter Parker?" she asked, lifting my panting, oxygen-deprived face up to the moonlight to better appreciate my reply.

Incredulously, and in between gasping breaths, I explained that Peter Parker was the secret identity of the Amazing Spider-Man.

When not one spark of recognition appeared in her troubled eyes, I told her in one breath how Pete was your typical little bookworm-ish high school student who got accidentally bitten by a radioactive spider, acquiring that insect's proportionate strength and wall-crawling abilities—not to mention an uncanny sixth "spider sense" that went off like a three-alarm fire any time danger was near. He was only the greatest and most inspirational figure in the Marvel Comics Universe.

"Why does someone so great need a secret identity?" Wendy asked, removing my left hand from wherever it had been.

"Well, basically to protect his Aunt May, who he lives with. If everybody knew who he was, her safety would be greatly compromised and all manner of vile scum, from Kraven the Hunter to the Sinister Six, would kidnap her and hold her hostage and God knows what else."

"So why doesn't Peter arrange for Aunt May to be bitten by her *own* radioactive spider so she can protect *herself?*"

"At *her* age?" I cried. "Whattya, trying to *kill* her?"

Somehow I could sense a shifting of momentum. She began rehooking her bra in the back; the same bra that had taken me the entire first side of *Disraeli Gears* to disengage.

"This stupendous Spider-Man of yours—does he fly?"

"Don't be silly. Spiders don't fly. He did invent this super sticky webbing, though, that he squirts out of these devices on his wrists, enabling him to swing from building to building like Tarzan of the Apes." I moved in for a kiss.

"Doesn't his cape get in the way?"

"His cape? Are you kidding? Nobody in Marvel wears a cape. That's strictly DC all the way, man."

"You mean like in Washington?"

"No. DC Comics. You know, Batman, Superman, Robin the Boy Wonder in his little green pointy slippers? They wear enough capes to start a nunnery. Even Krypto the goddamn Superdog puts one on. And they've got no opinions about anything and nothing whatsoever to say."

"And your guys, of course, can talk your ear off." She seemed to be groping in the darkness for her blouse.

"You better believe it," I said, in an upright position. "Just consider the problems they face: Daredevil with his incurable blindness; Cyclops unable to remove his protective visor for even a second, for fear of annihilating all the other X-Men; Ben Grimm having to live his life trapped in the hideous features of The Thing! I mean, this is real-life stuff here. Of *course* they've got something to say!"

"And none of them wear capes."

"Right. Well, except maybe Thor; but he's a god, so that's another story entirely."

"He's God?"

"No," I said. "He's *a* god. The god of thunder, actually. Asgard is loaded with gods—Odin, Loki, Balder the Brave, the fair Sif—"

"So this is sort of a religion?"

I could tell this was not going in the ideal direction. I countered: "No, it's not a religion. It's just, well, the clothes all flung about reminded me of Pete . . . y'know, when he has to get undressed to, uh, fight . . . I mean, I dunno, I guess I'm just plain flat-out addicted, ma'am."

"Are there any inhabitants of this Marvel Universe that you're *not* addicted to?" she said, reaching for her shoes.

I had to think for a minute. "Well, I never cared a whole lot for Henry Pym," I said. "He invented some serum that turns him into Ant Man. For Chrissakes, aren't we puny *enough?* Why would anybody want to make himself smaller? And his *name!* Do you pronounce it 'Pim' or do you pronounce it 'Pime?' As far as I'm concerned anyone who walks around with an unpronounceable name should go to court and have it changed!"

"I see," said Wendy Pfisternak, who put on her sweater, lit a filter cigarette, and climbed back into the driver's seat.

On the way to my house she admitted that she read a lot of *Little Lotta* when she was a kid. And sometimes *Little Dot.* And occasionally *Casper.* She stifled a giggle as she thought of it, apparently revisiting a time of Barbie and Ken, thumb-sucking, and wearing pajamas with feet.

She dropped me at the foot of my street, by the wall. I didn't know there were people on the wall, otherwise I wouldn't have had her drop me there. There were people on the wall. "Pssst!" one of them said as I started up the hill. Out of the shadows came Doody, Floydie, Oatsy O'Carroll, and some other kid. They had beers.

"Where'd you guys get beer?" I said, borrowing a sip from Doody.

"From Oatsy's brother," said Doody. "Now tell me that wasn't Wendy Pfisternak."

I didn't deny it. It made them howl involuntarily. Wait til I get to the part about parking behind the MDC. Wait til I start singing the lyrics of "Strange Brew" while slowly pantomiming the unhooking of a bra.

"Holy shit!" they remarkably all said at the same time. "You made it with *Wendy Pfisternak?*"

"Well, not exactly," is what you are supposed to say at this juncture of the story. You've titillated them enough. You say, "Well, not exactly," and explain how it went wrong, how the cops or her grandmother showed up at the worst possible moment and you never saw two people get dressed so fast and how you had trouble zipping your fly because you got a boner like three feet long. They laugh, they drink, they belch, they give you a temporary nickname, and you get on with your life. Except I didn't say, "Not exactly." I didn't say anything. But you couldn't fool them. They saw it in my eyes.

"Look at his face!" cried Doody. "Look at his face!"

"You did it!" squealed Floydie. "You did it, didn't you, you son of a bitch?"

"Oh, he did it all right!" said Oatsy, and the other kid (Richie, I think) said, "He *definitely* fucking did it!"

And they all repeated, with *certainty* now: "*Holy shit! You made it with Wendy Pfisternak!*" And I didn't say "Not exactly." They laughed and laughed and screamed and screamed and belched me a new nickname and threw beer cans in the air. And I didn't have to walk up the hill because they carried me the whole way like Broadway Joe Namath.

I got a call a few weeks later. It was Wendy. Wanting to know if it was true that I told everybody in the zip code that I'd had sex with her in the backseat of a car.

"Well, not exactly," I murmured.

"And so it's simply a coincidence that a great number of my newfound suitors, who call at all hours of the day and night, mention your name?"

"Not exactly," I said, and started to explain.

She made me promise to recant my story to each and every one of the sex-crazed dirtbags I'd told it to. Then, in a much softer voice, she asked if one of the boys I'd talked to was Richie Calmetti, the basketball player.

"That's possible," I offered.

"Oh, John," she said sadly, before hanging up. "How could you?"

I pretty much did what I said I would do and met Doody and Floydie the next day. I told them about the *misunderstanding* and Doody said he never swallowed a word of my story anyway. Floydie said I wouldn't have known where to put it if I'd *had* the chance. Oatsy only came around once in a while—I'd run into him eventually. The problem was Richie Calmetti. I wasn't going to see Richie. Richie and his family moved somewhere west, taking tales about Wendy with him.

I saw no reason to bring up the story to Dally as we stood in the locker room staring at the poster of COMMITMENT.

The stairwell from the locker room down to the gym was darker than India ink. You could close your eyes and open them and it was exactly the same. I held onto the railing with both hands and Dally hung on to me—for *strength*. We talked each other through the inch-by-inch ordeal.

"Okay . . . I think we're on the landing . . ."

"Uh, yup, yup, we definitely are . . ."

"Careful . . ."

"Okay, now just follow the railing to the next flight of stairs . . ."

"Whattya *think* I'm doing?" I said.

"That's fine . . . I'm just making sure. Just keep hugging that rail."

"I *am* hugging the rail. You wanna come over here and see?"

"I *can't* see."

"Well, just take my word for it," I said. "I'm holding onto the fucking rail."

"Okay, I believe you—whoops—watch it—here're the stairs."

"I already knew that," I said.

"Okay, I'm just helping you—wait—here's another one—"

"Yeah, I know. They come in a series."

"Dear, you could cut yourself on that wit, it's so sharp."

Communication is vital in a crisis.

The door at the foot of the stairs led to the lobby, which led to the gym. I remembered the trophy case but had no recollection of ever looking into it.

"Come on," said Dally, "let's play some hoop." She'd found a ball in the corner and had already started in. There was just enough light from the EXIT signs to see the backboards; the rims and nets becoming slowly visible as the game developed.

She grabbed the early lead but I was coming on when, "Jesus," it occurred to me, "they're gonna hear all this dribbling and shit out on the street."

"You're right," she said, tossing the ball up into the bleachers, "I win."

She was always a pretty good athlete, and, even though we both knew I'd eventually win, it would have been a good fight. She did crew or something in college—old man Schoerner showed me a picture of her rowing one day while I was out front swearing at the lawn mower. *Good* athlete. But there was no doubt I would've beaten her if we'd finished the game. *No* doubt.

The subject of old man Schoerner came up as we lay atop a gigantic crash mat we found in the gymnastics room off to the side. We had not gone in there to *lie* upon the mat, we had gone to crash upon it—and we did, five or six times, swinging from the uneven parallel bars above it. "I could be good at this!" she remarked. "Watch!" And she went into this Cheetah the monkey routine with her feet on the bar, basically turned inside-out, pushed off with the boldness of a fifties-era hood ornament and landed with her butt on the mat. Then she raised her arms in triumph and played to the imagined crowd. The moon spilled in from the high corner window. The light fell on her cheekbones, her slightly raised eyebrow, her lips. The look on her face was exquisite.

Next to the uneven parallel bars was a toilet-sized receptacle full of ground-up white chalk. I dipped my fingers in as you might use holy water and considered making a sign of the cross. Instead, I put the chalk on Dally. A big stripe right down her arm. Showed up in the moonlight spectacularly. So she naturally reached over and put one on me. I reciprocated, she followed suit. Dribs and drabs. Funny stuff. Sexy, even. I then, without thinking, moved to her face and drew a mustache. The second I did it, I knew I'd done it. No! I wanted to scream, No! It has nothing to *do* with the mustache you had as a kid—I was just drawing a *MUSTACHE!* Not *YOUR* mustache! I mean, I know I put it *on* you and all, but it had nothing to do with *you!* I was just drawing a *mustache*! I knew she was gonna take it the wrong way.

Or maybe not. As calm and dignified as a nurse in the army, Dally methodically dipped both hands into the chalk. She started innocently, with glasses, drawing me a pair she called Poindexters, but quickly moved on to the moles. The first one she found on my left cheek and dabbed on the chalk good and thick. After that came the three on my chin, the two on my earlobe, the fourteen on my neck, all of it accompanied by that well-known musical number: "One dot, two dot, three dot, four dot . . ." She even threw up my shirt and made a dent in the dozens *there* before running out of paint. (I was relieved she didn't take things the wrong way.) The whole thing led to more chalk, then to tickling, which inevitably led to the collision of foreheads, and the both of us falling backwards to the mat, wailing to the ceiling in pain.

"Jesus, I miss my mother," said Dally, still rubbing her head. "I always miss my mother when I'm hurt. Don't you?"

"I'm not sure Ma'd do me any good in her present state," I said, checking my skull for blood.

"You know what I mean. 'There, there,' she'd coo in your ear, 'everything's all right.'"

"Let Mommy kiss it and make the boo-boo go away," I offered.

"Exactly. And she'd just hold you and rock you and hold you and rock you, trying to absorb your pain away, and it worked. It wasn't so much that she fixed you, it was that she cared so much, that somebody care *that* much that you were hurt. Was it all an act?"

"Excuse me?"

"Was it an act? Do they just do it because it's their job description, it's what's expected—the fathers take out the trash and the mothers pretend they give a shit?"

"I don't know," I said. "I never thought *my* mother was on the con."

"Well, your mother never ran off in the middle of the night with some leather-clad fuckstick on a Harley-Davidson. Tucks you into bed one minute and it's 'Born to Be Wild' the next. Grace Morgan Schoerner. Some mother."

I'd heard the Harley-Davidson story before. We all had. I remember old man Schoerner giving my parents the particulars one afternoon as he sat sadly on his steps, smoking the hell out of half a pack of cigarettes. I loved the part about the guy revving the bike's engine out front. How she ran down the back stairs with a suitcase, hopped on the back and they were gone. How her beautiful auburn hair whipped out behind her like a comet and she never looked back. My parents didn't know what to say. Dad sort of sympathetically tapped Schoerner's knee, and they left him there with his thoughts. Back in the kitchen, Dad had tons to say. "Good thing I was at work the other night. Me and Motorcycle Joe mighta met up."

"I doubt it," said Ma, putting the dishes away. "I *was* here. And I don't remember any motorcycles." It's possible Ma knew a little bit more about the situation than the rest of us, considering that she let Dally's mom sob on her shoulder right up til the day she took off. One of those serious sobs too, that gasping-for-air anguish that kids take on after they've caught a licking.

You could see that Dally knew a little bit about the situation too, because she stopped talking about her mother, put one hand behind her head and looked up at the elongated shadows on the ceiling. I leaned my chin on my elbow and watched her. Her eyes were sad and wet, but alive. Even with her big white mustache she was beautiful. Even with her old mustache she'd be beautiful. Then she looked at me. And saw the array of white-capped moles on my face and neck. And nearly threw up laughing for about five minutes. Once, when she had me down and was beating me with an umbrella and a falling crab apple hit me in the head, she laughed like this. It was good to laugh with her—she laughed from the stomach—and it was good to hold her, and to have her hands grapple me and poke me and pound on my chest and muss up my hair as she struggled for composure. I took advantage of the situation by going back to the well; I dipped my fingers into the chalk and drew breasts and nipples on Dally's shirt, directly over her real breasts and nipples. She laughed 'til she was weak. (You can't get moves like this in a book.) We were kissing in minutes, right after she blew her nose. Soft kissing, lips, then noses, then lips. Giving, wanting, her breath in yours, her lashes on your cheek. This was not the random Quaalude skank giving head on the black vinyl couch. This was something else. This was *something*.

And then she shot up like an ironing board.

"*That son of a bitch! That's* why she left! She never ran away with some biker—she was *broken!* She was broken by *him!* Him and his exposed *penis!*"

"Uh, I hate to bring it up, but he only exposed himself to your girlfriend last night. Your mother's been gone for years." (The power I have over women—one kiss and they start thinking about pervs.)

"No," said Dally, "There was another time. Omigod, it completely didn't ring until just now! It was bridge night, Wednesday night, a regular date my mother kept with the women from work, but this was the first one she'd ever hosted. They were laughing and cackling about some idiot supervisor. I was in the kitchen doing the dishes from supper. The door to my parents' bedroom was open and the small lamp was on, but I couldn't see in. Connie Edelson could. In the middle of a bid she suddenly jumps out of her chair, cards flying, drinks spilling, gasps, 'Oh Jesus! Oh God!' and starts fluttering to the hallway for her coat. 'Connie! What's wrong?' The other ladies chase her, but she says, 'Oh Jesus! Just tell Gracie I had to go!' and out the door she bolts. My mother never leaves the table. She gives my father the queerest look as he comes casually out of the bedroom, his head buried in a book about Great Danes, his favorite coffee cup in one hand.

"Two nights later the doorbell rings and my father answers it and goes out on the steps with some man. They're whispering, but I can hear whole parts of the conversation when there aren't any cars going by. The man says, 'You make sure to *tell* your little friend, if it ever comes out to say hello *again,* I will cut it off at the fucking roots with hedge clippers. Are we perfectly clear?' He points at my father once more before getting in his car and speeding off.

"'Who was that?' I hear my mother ask.

"'Oh, just some landscaper giving me an estimate on some maples,' he says, and goes out to feed the dogs. That son of a *bitch!*"

She pulled her knees up tight to her chest. I did the same, in support.

"My house became a whisper house after that," said Dally. "My parents spoke to each other in *whispers*. They'd use their regular voices if I was around, of course, but it was never anything more than 'What are we having, Grace?' or: 'The septic's acting up, Howard.' Any *real* talking was done in whispers, sharp and wrenching, behind closed doors—in the bathroom, the bedroom, the carport. After dinner he'd read the paper and retreat to his workshop. She'd help me with homework sometimes but mostly did crossword puzzles with the TV on and went to bed right after me. And she never played cards again—either at our house or anyone else's. I saw her sinking day by day, quivering, tugging at her hair, crying. And then she's gone. And she doesn't take me with her. And she doesn't say goodbye. And she leaves me behind with Nature Boy."

"Did Nature Boy ever show his 'little friend' to *you?*" I asked, my *own* little friend in a state of confusion and shock.

"Never! He never did anything funny like that. Barely touched me. Hugged me when I went away to school and I remember him giving me this little shoulder rub before my senior prom. He was draping a shawl or something about my shoulders at the time because he was upset with the low-cut gown I was wearing. 'My goodness, Daliah,' he said, 'we have standing in the community. For God's sake, I'm a *doctor.*'" She threw out both hands for emphasis. "Did he send me to boarding school because he couldn't take care of me or because he didn't want me to see his *behavior?*"

"I thought it was because of the note I sent over on the pulley," I said.

Dally pulled closer to me then. I put an arm around her shoulders and gave her rein. She pulled my free hand into her lap and clasped her hands around it. "All these years," she said, "all these years. Is she alive? Does she live three states away or is she right down the street? Would she even *remember* me? Do I care?"

"Are you gonna search for her like they do in novels?"

"I don't know. Maybe. I sure would like to talk to her."

"I'll help you," I said. "I have a van."

"And a brother," she smiled, and began kissing me on the neck, slowly, pretty much mole to mole.

"If you start singing, 'One dot, two dot,'" I breathed into her ear, "I'll be *joining* my brother."

"How 'bout if I hum it," she suggested, and did.

It became a movie then, a great movie, at times Rodgers and Hammerstein, at others the married paratrooper and widowed nurse stationed in Rome in 1944—forbidden, but irresistible. At any rate, it wasn't me. It wasn't me making love to this beautiful naked black-haired girl in a long, evocative, uncut scene. It couldn't be. I was not capable of it. This slow, assured, unselfish intimacy. I was simply not capable of having the kind of sex I was having. "Oh, Johnny," she cried out at one point, "Ohhh, *Johnny.*"

And I've already told you way more than you need to know.

11

School Crossing

Gully's janitor-room shower, a full-force onslaught so hot and luxuriant the memory of it shall, "warm my soul on the bleakest and rawest of days," was finally over. He had taken pains to secure a towel, a fuzzy green-and-white one he'd pulled out of the dryer in home ec. He then calmly got dressed, drank the better part of a quart of milk, grabbed a flashlight off the head janitor's desk, and entered the dark and disturbing muteness of the hallway. He had eaten four chicken potpies, screened parts of seven movies, slept for who-knows-how-long and was eager to find his companions. Up creaking and unfamiliar stairs he climbed, higher and higher, his flashlight showing the winding way—spidery shadows creeping into his uneasiness. He climbed to the third floor, to the landing by the third-floor shithouse, then into the corridor with all the science rooms and their science fiction test tubes and taxidermied mammals. Then he shone his light into some lecture hall with mineral charts on the walls and a skeleton seemed to spring right out at him, like skeletons do, and his heart screamed five years off his life. Soon he was back in the hallway, walking faster, yelling: *"Johnny! Dally! John!"*

I, meanwhile, was naked. One is never more naked, I observed, than when one is naked in a place where one shouldn't be naked. Such as, in the middle of the gymnasium where phys ed director Mr. Strimpel once put you and your sweating, farting classmates through burpies. Did I say *naked?* Naked is a bunch of geezers taking a sitz at the L Street bathhouse. *I* was nude. I was reminded of this fact when I woke up and found myself sprawled across a foam-filled crash mat, looking up at the taut apparatus of gymnastics. Dally was nearby, sound asleep, equally naked—but at least she had the sense to throw a coat over herself while I shivered with a smock from Frannie's Fine Foods as a pillow. But never had I awoken so pleasantly from dreams, though they were haunted, as is often the case, by demons, dragons, and Meredith the embalmed girl.

The sky was lighter, light enough to see Dally's face, and I wanted just to lie there and watch the lilt of her eyebrows for hours on end. But I couldn't. Because I had to piss. In a desperate way. One of those heavy, sloshing, if-you-don't-drain-this-vein-in-the-next-twenty-seconds-you'll-end-up-with-cirrhosis-of-the-bladder ideas. So I went walking. Naked, nude, and pink as a baby opossum. With socks.

The door up to the girls' locker room, the same door we'd come through earlier, was locked. So was the one next to it, the one that led to the boys' locker. So were the two bathrooms in the lobby itself. Now, truth be told, it wouldn't have killed me to crack open one of the exit doors and simply whizz into the frigid air, but a Gullivan demands more from life. A Gullivan, at the very least, expects to pee into a nice clean urinal in a cozy well-heated bathroom. Especially a *naked* Gullivan, who's already freezing his regions off. I walked back through the gym, checked on Dally, but she was still sawing serious

logs. It must be noted here that this provided me one more opportunity to don clothing, before heading out through the side door and
prowling down the stairs. I, however, declined the opportunity's
offer, and continued on my bare-ass way.

Instead of trying to find the boys' room I'd used earlier, I decided
to use the *girls'* room by the cafeteria. I mean, what the hell? I can do
anything I want. Who's gonna report me? The absence of urinals
was hard getting used to but a bowl is a bowl. "So now I've done
that," I congratulated myself, and felt free to not only shake the old
otter as I resumed my stroll down the corridor but even twirled it for
a while, helicopter-like, ready to grind up anybody who stood in my
way. Miss Buchanan's assignment: "What Does Freedom Mean to
Me?" came to mind, and I wished I could have another crack at it. Of
course, the sensation of things swinging freely as you walked was not
entirely new; my brother and I had given up wearing underwear
some time ago, when Ma laid down the law and refused to wash anything not found in the hamper. It was liberating. Things hung in
your pants like six-guns. Shoving your hands in your pockets took
on a whole new meaning—if you weren't grabbing something with
your left hand, you were scratching something with your right.
Those corduroy Levi's with the real thin, flimsy pockets? Ideal.
Everything was easier. Bodily functions? Bing-bing-bang. Freedom
was the word and the word was freedom.

But that was nothing. Swaggering ballickeys through the dimly-
lit corridors of Ruslan D. Loneberry at five o'clock in the morning
was the Emancipation Proclamation. The thing hung out like an
anaconda and I swung it with the nonchalance of Will Rogers's
lasso. Then I casually stretched a little bit, yawned, scratched myself
like a caged ape and decided it would be a good time to make my
way to the janitors' room and sample its much ballyhooed shower
facilities. I imagined Miss Buchanan suddenly appearing in my path
as I nudely sauntered across the cafeteria.

"Mr. Gullivan, I assume you have a hall pass?" she might say.

"Gee," I'd say, "I think I mighta left it in my pants. Will *this* do?"

(As for "What Does Freedom Mean to Me?" I remember what I wrote then: "We will never have real freedom until everyone is free; black, brown, yellow or red." As I got off the school bus that morning I saw Mr. Lucinda out front running the flag up the pole. Next to him was Eugene Bailes, head janitor, jabbing pieces of litter off the lawn with a long pointed stick. "Wait til we bring in the junglebunnies," he raved. "*Then* you'll see. This lawn'll look like a goddamn earthquake hit it.")

The janitor's shower was amazing. Torrents of scalding water bludgeoned you like a Gatling gun. Out loud you moaned, sighed, said: "Ohhhhh my Gawwwwd in fucking heavennnnnnnn . . ." The setup was unusual too; just a drain in the cement floor surrounded by a door and partitions that began two feet off the ground, taken right out of one of the lavs. Mounted on the wall, about eye-high, was a soap dispenser—the soap coming out red and syrupy and smelling like a million bucks. The shower was far enough in the back of the room, behind the lockers, to assure that nothing of importance got wet, but I had to turn on the light to find my way to it. The room was packed to the gills with toilet paper, case after case of E-Z-PLY 282, stacked to the very ceiling. Brooms of varying caliber and big, heavy-duty dustpans hung from nails. A large wheeled barrel stood dead center, loaded with trash. Sticking out of the barrel were two long fluorescent light tubes, gray and obviously dead, but still capable, I knew, of detonation. I knew because of the brief stint Gully and I did last summer as provisional city workers, assigned to clean out the attic of Roush Library. A job, that if done the way they wanted, would take about year. Hundreds of old beaten books and stuff, piles and piles of uselessness, under a half-inch of dust. They gave us these little paper masks to ward off black lung and they gave us this big receptacle to dump stuff into. We were then expected to lug the receptacle down three flights, hoist it up to the mouth of the Dumpster, dump it, then drag it back up for more. We made one of these trips. Then we climbed back to the attic, opened a window grand and wide, and sat out on the ledge for a good portion of the morning and breathed air. Jobs without much supervision are pretty good jobs, if you ask me. We knew we'd have to fill the barrel again, just to keep certain bosses off our backs, but neither of us saw much need to rush. Then I leaned my head way out and saw that the Dumpster we were slaving to get to was actually directly below, lined up almost perfectly with our window. "Whattya think?" I said.

"I don't have to think," said Gully, and dragged the barrel to the sill. Some of the trash never reached the Dumpster and blew across the lawn onto Tread Street, but the heavy stuff—old books, shelves, and cartons—hit the target like the bombs over Dresden. I found the fluorescent tubes in a side room, old grimy things about eight feet long, covered with decades of dust. Holding onto the window frame with my left hand, I leaned way out, took aim, and hurled one like a spear. It hit the lip of the Dumpster and exploded—a lovely explosion, sort of a muffled *pop,* the glass and filament flying. "Our morning, perhaps my life, just got a whole lot better," grinned Gully, who took the next toss. But he shot it right *in* the Dumpster, where it did nothing but sit there like a dud torpedo on the ocean's floor. We had to throw a book down on top of it to make it explode, and from then on, aimed only for the *side* of the Dumpster, where the Fourth of July resided. We developed a rating system based on intensity of pop and flash and I led 15–9 when we ran out of stock. "Jeez," I remember reasoning, "If old shit relics like these can kick ass like that, imagine what new ones could do." We snuck down to the second floor, found two cases of F96 Cool White Rapid Start in a closet and were halfway through the first one when somebody in charge of us drove up.

"Cause and effect," said a weary Ma, when learning of the partic-

dismissal. "Cause and effect. Often applied to babies ...ng their strained prunes to the floor just to see what will hap-pen. *Babies.*"

I thought of Ma now as I languished in the janitor's shower. The life she had. Losing Dad, her health, her hair. Retaining us. Having to send her two youngest daughters to live with ancient Aunt Fran because she couldn't take care of them. I thought of the people she comforted—Grace Schoerner, who cried on her shoulder for months, Edna LeRoi, who she hired to clean the house because her cancer-ridden husband left her penniless. What did anyone ever do for her? Not a whole lot. Now she lies in some hard cold hospital bed all by herself and just dies. And then I started crying. Uncontrollably. It just came over me. I wasn't sure if I was crying for her disappointing life or her agonizing death or for my soon-to-be motherless self, but I was carrying on like a baby, I can tell you that. Of course, you can get away with it when you're in a shower with the force of this one. Tears, snot, blood-rimmed eyes—washed away in almost *sacramental* fashion. Let it go. Cry, sob, moan, wail in anguish. This shower is Niagara Falls harnessed. Drowns everything right out.

"THAT YOU IN THERE, GENE?"

I hit my head on the soap dispenser and nearly gave birth. The voice was familiar. *Eerily* familiar. So was the stabbing chest pain it caused.

"GENE! I SAID IZZAT YOU?"

"Yeah," I managed. But I knew that voice. I just couldn't put my finger on it. And Gene. Who's Gene? Unless he means . . . of course! Eugene Bailes, the head janitor, racist as an Imperial Wizard.

"ARE YOU SURE IT'S YOU, GENE, BECAUSE IT DON'T SOUND LIKE YOU!"

That's when I knew exactly who it was. I said, "Whattya dumber than a goddamn COON? Of *COURSE* it's me!"

"WOWEE!" said Ward Belvoir, Dad's former helper. "THIS AIN'T LIKE YOU TO COME IN SO EARLY! SHIT, I THOUGHT *I* WAS EARLY! *YOU* THE EARLY BIRD WHAT GETS THE WORM TODAY, GENE!"

"Yeah, well I'm sick and tired of lyin' in bed every day like some melon-eatin' spearchucker. Now go get some *work* done!"

(I remember when Ward got the job with the schools. His mother was so proud. She credited Dad with the whole thing and dropped by out of the blue to tell Ma that. "Your Jim was a great man," she said, and Ma took the compliment to her heart as if it were a fallen serviceman's flag.)

But now *I* had Ward Belvoir to deal with, and he was two feet away.

"AREN'T WE GONNA HAVE DONUTS FIRST? WE ALWAYS HAVE DONUTS FIRST! DON'T TELL ME WE'RE NOT HAVING DONUTS!"

"Now where the hell are we gonna get donuts with everything closed? From the jigs on Blue Hill Ave?" I was fast running out of racial slurs.

"HELL, GENE, THERE'S ABOUT SIX DOZEN OF THEM WHITE POWDERED JOBBIES IN THE KITCHEN PANTRY. AND I KNOW I SAVED SOME OF THEM CRULLERS FROM LAST WEEK IN THE HOME-EC FREEZER!"

"Well get on the *stick* then, before they decide to open the damn school and let the JUNGLEBUNNIES back in!"

"I'LL GET 'EM!" said Ward, and rushed out the door. I shut off the water and frantically searched for a towel, wishing like hell I had thought of it before I got in the shower. The best I could do was somebody's wool coat hanging from a hook and my own socks. I dried off quickly and crept to the door. I stuck out my neck and peered down the hallway. A light came from a room, its door held open by a block. I heard rummaging. I threw on the coat and tiptoed

osite direction. The sound of the crashing tray behind me

hairs on my neck aflame and when I heard Ward scream,

WHAT THE FUCK! WHAT THE FUCK! WHAT THE FUCK!" I ran like hell. Took a hard right at the end of the corridor and another one further down. I heard Ward yelling, "GENE! GENE! THERE'S A NAKED GUY RUNNIN' AWAY WITH EDDIE'S COAT! GENE! WHAT THE FUCK! GENE! GENE?! WHAT DO I DO *NOW?!* HELP! HELP! *POLICE!*" I couldn't tell if he was chasing me, I was running so fast, my exposed privates flopping up and down like a Punch and Judy puppet show. I knew at the very least, if he *wasn't* chasing me, he'd be drawing conclusions fairly soon and be making calls to 911. I circled back to the cafeteria, practically killing myself leaping over the tables and chairs.

"Johnny!" cried Gully, meanwhile, *"Dally!"* each cry seeming more and more urgent as my brother roved from floor to floor. In the gymnasium he trained his flashlight on a figure by the bleachers, her bare legs and feet visible beneath a long dark coat. "Dally?"

"Yes. Now cease with the light unless you're here to read me my rights."

"Where's Johnny?"

"Haven't the slightest, dear. I got up to pee and he was gone."

"You slept here? In the gym?"

"Not out here, pops. In there, where the mats and stuff are. Very comfortable bedding, actually."

"So you and John *shared* this feathery love nest?" he asked, his flashlight sizing up the situation tidily.

"Surmise what you will," she said, locating her jeans in a pile that also contained my shirt, my pants, and a white smock stained in poultry blood.

"Shall I also surmise that you and my brother had, dare I say, *relations?*"

"Why don't you compile a list of all your questions and submit them in writing? In the meantime, would you mind getting out of my bedroom so I can get dressed?"

"Just my luck," muttered Gully as his light bounced from the ropes to the rings to the pommel horse, "My brother has the Last Tango in Paris while I'm having my blood frozen by skeletons."

"Come again?" said Dally, pulling on a sock.

"Skeletons. I had a run-in with one upstairs."

"A skeleton? What do you mean, a skeleton?"

"It was on a hook, okay, and it came out of nowhere, and I shit my pants."

Dally laughed. "You were frightened by a skeleton on a hook?"

"That's right. And, gosh, Dally, if only you'd been there to save me; if only you'd been there to pull me out of harm's way."

And then I and my naked (except for a black-and-red plaid jacket) butt appeared on the scene, yelling a warning about Ward Belvoir.

"Ward Belvoir," said my brother. "Now how do I know that name?"

"He used to work for Dad," I said, climbing into my pants. "Now he works here. And he's here right now. And he knows *we're* here. Which means that we are getting the fuck *out* of here like pronto!"

"The Ward Belvoir that used to say hum job? The Ward Belvoir who's retarded as a ring-tailed baboon?"

"The very one. Now hand me my shoes."

"Are you kidding? Ward Belvoir? This could be more fun than Paragon Park!"

"Get control of yourself," I said, discarding my newfound coat, still wet from the shower, and replacing it with my smock, nearly dry from its swim through the snow. "He is on the phone to the cops right now. We are going right out those lobby doors and getting as far away from this fucking dump as possible!"

"He's right," Dally agreed, pulling on a boot. "If they catch us all in here, they're gonna charge you with a lot more than ditching Monsignors."

"Relax," said Gully. "You two are under too much stress. I mean, a domestic partnership and all can't be easy in this day and age." He poked his head into the darkness of the cafeteria and inched his way out. We heard voices. And one of them was Ward's, going: "I SAW HIM GO RIGHT DOWN HERE, OFFICER, BY THE CAF!" Back up the stairs we ran, planning strategy as we went.

"We're fucked, we're fucked, we're *fucked*!" I said.

"No! We're going up this way, then across and back down!"

"I fail to see how that gets us unfucked!"

"All we gotta do is stay ahead of them. They probably don't believe Ward anyway—they'll give up in twenty minutes' time. I know this place inside and out. Just cool down and follow me."

I could have mounted a pretty strong argument, being that I actually *attended* the school, but Dally and I were a little vulnerable with the "romance" thing. We had no choice but to follow. We held hands, though, like adventurers running from dinosaurs. "Feel free to reach for *my* hand too, Dally," Gully dryly said, "Y'know, if'n you should get a'scared or somethin'."

"Yeah, sure, Gully," said Dally, "Let me know if you run across any more skeletons."

I was puzzled. "You saw a skeleton?"

"Your brother has skeletons on the brain," said Dally.

"Where?" I asked, as we slammed through swinging doors.

"Up there," he pointed to the ceiling, "Up in the science department. Freaked me outa my skin."

"What'd you think?" I laughed, "That it was alive?"

"Go ahead, wiseass, try it some time. Be in a dark hallway all by yourself, already *in* an advanced state of willies, and come face-to-face with a skeleton. You will scream like Tuesday Weld."

"What'd you do then?" asked Dally, "Jump out the window?"

"I considered it. But then I go up to the thing, y'know, and I go, 'Hey, bonesy, how they hangin'? Nice handshake you got there, cornfed—yer hip bone connected to yer thighbone? Yer thighbone connected to your ballsack?' And then I take him off his little hook, right, except I *drop* the fucking thing, he crashes to the floor, okay, and I've got bones from one end of the room to the other."

"You wrecked the skeleton?"

"I destroyed the skeleton."

"And you just left him there?" said Dally, "You didn't even try to put him together?"

"Lady, I ain't no miracle worker. There were bones I'd never heard of. I hung the skull back on its hook with a couple of femurs and a hand and a foot, and called it even."

Then Dally yelled "*Stop!*" and when we did, she shushed us and had us listen. There was a stairwell about fifty feet behind us and the cops were coming up it, taking two at a time. "They can hear our shoes!" whispered Dally, "They know where we are!"

"They're hearing *your* shoes," I said, pointing at Dally's boots. My brother and I wore sneakers, with the tread worn down to the very sock. They made about as much noise as Mingo's moccasins. Dally held onto me while she tried to slide off a boot, but the cops were on the landing, time was running out, we had to start *booking*. Even with boots on Dally could keep up with us, and Gully and I could run. She was enjoying it too, you could tell. There's something about being chased by cops, I can't describe it, but it's about as edgy as things can get. If they catch you, which is always possible, you are in for some bodily harm. The kind I dread most is when they grab you by the hair on your neck and make you swear to stuff. And some of the things they chase you for, like tipping over trash barrels, you wouldn't think they'd bother. But they do. Serious stuff, though—you can't predict how they'll react. It occurred to me, as I was fleeing with my gang through the school, that breaking into buildings at night was probably serious stuff. They could very well shoot us. Back down the stairs we flew, risking life and limb as we leaped.

At the foot of the stairs, Gully's flashlight caught something. A big metal door marked BOILER. He slowly turned the knob and led us in. Old grated steps wound their way to the cement floor and the air was thick as we searched out hiding places. All, that is, except Gully, who was hynotized by the place. He wandered about, his neck tilted back as if he were gazing at skyscrapers. Unimaginable treasures spoke out to him. The boilers, bigger than overturned buses, roaring like hell itself. Dancing flames reflecting on opposite walls. Dials, plates, chains, valves yammering like the lab of Doctor Doom. *Pipes.* Pipes connected to pipes. Pipes that went up and up and up. The operation held Gully in its sway. Things mechanical always did, especially enormous things with loud and spewing means of combustion. But the state he was in now I'd seen only once: when he was five and looked up and saw a blimp in the sky, flying much lower than usual. Insisting to his dying day that the pilot waved at him, Gully followed the slow-moving craft. Never took his eyes off it, in fact, as it led him through the backyard, under the fence, around Schoerner's kennels, out through the thicket, into the dirt alley behind Malstreum's, to Hempstead Street and places he had never been. Someone thought they saw a little boy crossing the tracks by Elligot woods.

The search party was organized in minutes, due largely to Ma's decree that: *"Everybody get out on the street! My Gully is missing!"* Every mother in the neighborhood joined in. (The fathers were all at work.) All the kids went too, and most of the dogs, none of them ever happier in their lives.

"Where was he last seen?" asked Grace Schoerner.

"What was he wearing?" asked someone else.

"Weren't you *watching* him?!" asked Eleanor Peeve.

All the questions were fielded by Rita Davis from Sodality, who held Ma's arm and took it upon herself to act as spokesperson and group leader. "Never mind who was watching who! Just keep your mind on your work. He's got blue sneakers, a red sweater and he's FIVE!"

Ma was basically a wreck. Every emotion possible crossed her face. "H-He was there one minute, playing with his GI Joe on the steps, and then he was gone!" The buzz from the crowd didn't relax her much, all the talk about bears being sighted and coyotes and snakes and wild dogs and red-tailed hawks and recently released mental patients and wolverines.

"Shut up with the theories!" yelled Rita. "And keep looking for clues! Can't you see we've got a distraught mother here?" The woods were up ahead.

The only man in the posse was Edgar Barntoy, who worked nights as a projectionist in the Combat Zone. He said, "Hey, looky here! Ain't that a little kid's footprint?" Everyone gathered round and agreed that it was. "I think it leads this way!" said Edgar, and we all followed.

"Isn't *he* the helpful one," Rita stage-whispered to Ma. "The *concerned* neighbor. Just wants to *help*."

"What are you trying to say, Rita?" asked Eleanor Peeve, half out of breath from the quick pace of the search party.

"I'm not saying anything. I just wonder about a guy home all the time in the middle of the day, is all."

"Rita, the man works nights," said Barb Weiderman.

"Yeah, and what does he do? Gets right down in the gutter showing that filth and smut. Night after night. I don't think any man who's seen *Nymphs of Berlin* two hundred times needs to be anywhere near a child of mine!"

"Rita Davis, that's an awful thing to say!" said Barb. "You don't know anything about Mr. Barntoy!"

"Well I know *perv* when I see it. Look at the look on his face. Look at the way he's motioning for everybody to follow. *Sooo* helpful. A real scoutmaster. The son of a bitch's gonna lead us right to the bod . . . I mean . . . *say,* what's going on up there?" Ma, who never smoked, grabbed the one right out of Rita's hand and took a long, hard drag.

They found Gully sitting on a log crying his eyes out. "I was watching the *blimp,*" he sobbed, as Ma swept him up in her arms. "And then I tripped on a rock and looked around and I didn't know *where I was!*" People clapped and started home. A lot of the kids were disappointed the excursion was over. I know *I* was.

"Why hello Edgar," said Rita Davis to Edgar Barntoy. "I hope we can count on a couple of your famous peach pies for next week's church social."

Dee Dee and I tried to make our brother laugh as Ma carried him home but we couldn't even get him to look at us. His eyes were fixed skyward, searching in vain for his blimp.

And his eyes were in their element in the boiler room; his ears atwitter, his mouth agape. He found that by tugging on certain chains overhead he could open valves and close them again, greatly affecting the arrows on the dials. "I have found my life's work," he said, as steam whistled over his head. "I must take a civil service exam at the next earliest time."

"What you need to do in the next earliest *second* is find a hiding place!" I yelled from behind a wheelbarrel, "The cops are gonna be here any minute!"

Ignoring me, he climbed metal steps to a platform, hoping it'd allow him a peek *inside* one of the boilers. Instead, something else came into view. An answer to all prayers. A means to get to Braintree. Gully's flashlight followed the chain-made tracks and snowy-edged puddles to the ramp at the far end of the noise-filled room, and the bolted bulkhead door above it. He then turned off the light, bolted down the stairs and said, "Everybody *out*! We got ourselves a *tractor*! *Look*!" Dally and I met him by the tractor and looked at it.

"I'm looking at a tractor," I said.

"Does it come with chickens and cows?" said Dally.

Gully stared at us in disbelief. "The fucking thing comes with a plow, okay? It has chains, seats, windshield, the whole works, and a ramp to drive it out! It has a fucking *plow*, for Chrissakes!"

"So you are suggesting," I said, "that we *steal* this tractor, which does what—nine miles an hour, while all the cops in the world are after us?"

"Unless you have a better suggestion, John-John, then that's what I'm suggesting. Now let's fan out and find the all-important *keys* to the fucking thing."

While Dally and Gully tore the room apart searching, I decided that one of us should climb back up the steps to stand watch, and I nominated me. I opened the door a crack and peered down the corridor. I saw the flashlights drawing closer, heard the shouts, *might* have heard: "THERE THEY ARE!" as the door closed behind me.

"Here they come, boys and girls!" I said, and leaped down the steps. "We gotta get outta here *now*!"

Out meant the ramp and we bounded up it together. As soon as the deadbolts were released top and bottom, the wind did the rest, one side of the thin metal door threatening to break out of its hinges as it violently flapped against the snowy brick outside. Gully grabbed something in one hand as we stormed back into the chill. I didn't know what it was until we were halfway round the block.

"You think of everything, dontcha?" I said, the cold air piercing my lungs as I ran.

"Thinking's too much work," panted my brother, as the gasoline inside the bright red can sloshed up and down with the same volatile uncertainty as our future.

12

Fists

Dad, in his younger, rawer, emaciated days, was a prizefighter. He boxed in the Golden Gloves as a featherweight, or so he told us, and often pulled out an old, brownish picture of himself: gloves up, in a menacing stare. It looked absolutely nothing like him. Could have been any malnourished Depression-era teenager with hair parted right down the middle of his skull. The mean expression didn't fit either; our dad was not mean. A cauldron of stress—yes. A seething, frustrated, lightning rod of exasperation—definitely. But mean? Even in his worst moments—trying to beat the panel truck to death with a tire iron while screaming every off-color word in existence in all conceivable combinations—he never really looked mean. His expression was more of a "Why are you *doing* this to me, God? What have I *done* to you to deserve this hell on earth?" We never, for one second, thought him capable of hurting a fellow human being. He never laid a hand on us in anger, never took any of us over his knee, never clipped our ears or slapped our sassy-assed faces. All that was taken care of by Ma, whom we feared like the Banshee of Cork. Dad, we feared not at all. As a result, we never swallowed his wild tales of knocking out Billy "Flophouse" Flavin in the fourth round in

Holyoke or his ten-round TKO of Mad Dog Mickey Sinise in Providence, Rhode Island. Rolled our eyes is what we did, and chortled into our cream chicken on toast.

Two incidents changed everything; I was present at both. The first occurred on the job. Four-thirty in the morning. Unloading the *Herald* truck, a nasty spring chill in the air, drizzle continuing to fall. The linebacker-sized guy who drove the *Herald* truck, Lou, was usually pleasant enough, if a little gruff. "How are you ugly pain in the asses doin' this morning?" he might ask, as he threw open his overhead door and laid out the heavy bundles on the runner for Dad, Ward, Gully, and me to lug inside.

On this day, though, he said nothing but "*goddamit!*" as he tore through his truck. The bundles were not brought to the lip of the truck as usual; they were hurled there as if he were building a dike with sandbags. A couple of them fell right off to the rain-soaked street below.

"Slow it down, Lou," said Dad. But Lou just muttered something beginning with an F and kept the onslaught coming. One of them hit me in the shoulder as I was trying to lift another one and almost knocked me down.

"Lou, I said slow it down!" Dad repeated.

But Lou just got redder and the Sunday *Herald*s kept rolling at us like boulders down a cliff. One of them flew right off the truck and hit Ward in the chest and sent him flying backwards to the curb.

"*Hey!*" yelled Ward. "WATCH WHAT THE HELL YER DOING!"

Lou came right to the truck's edge and said, "AW SHUDDUP, YA FUCKING GOOD-FOR-NOTHING 'TARD!"

Dad then climbed right up into the truck and, without warning, socked Lou square in the jaw. All the way back to the front of the truck he fell, back in the shadows where you couldn't see him. The guys and I exchanged fearful glances as Dad stood there, breathing heavy, both fists still clenched. Lou got up and moved forward, towering over Dad like Frankenstein. I thought about going inside to fetch our one weapon, the cracked Louisville Slugger under Dad's desk, when Lou put his arm on Dad's shoulder and said, "Jimmy, I'm sorry. I'm having a tough go-round right now with the wife. I didn't mean to take it out on you guys, honest I didn't. And the *kid*, Jim, the goddamn mouth on him—and all she does is *defend* him, can you believe that? Aw, why am I telling you, Jimmy, you got kids, you know how it is." Dad glanced my way and gave me a little wink. Then Lou came over to the edge, squatted down and apologized to *us*. "Here," he said, reaching into his wallet, "git yerselves some donuts when the old man takes you out." All the rest of the bundles he eased into our waiting arms like porcelain statuettes.

The second incident came at Dad's wake. Ambling into Lamb & O'Brien Funeral Home to pay his respects was Red Rand, the town drunk, maybe the *state* drunk, who was said to have been a contender for the welterweight crown, and had the cauliflower ears and misplaced nose to prove it. A lot of Dad's friends were acquainted with Red and he acknowledged each by going into a boxing stance, a gesture they more than happily returned. He did it with some of the older boys too, like Prick LaPinza, who looked mean enough at the moment to actually start *throwing* punches, and he did it with me and Gully when he got to the reception line, playfully jabbing us in the belly. He didn't do it with the girls, though, just gently tapped each one on the arm, but when he got to Ma, he seemed to undergo a chemical change. Taking her hands in his and fighting back tears, he looked deep into her eyes and whispered, in sort of a priestly way, "Oh, Betty, he was a fine fella. A man among men, he was. How many times he saw to it I got a hot meal in my stomach I can't count. Always made sure I had a place to sleep. He was awful good t'me, Betty, awful good. And the way he went—just *terrible*. Not a fit demise for a dog. Oh, he was a beautiful fella, dear; heaven's got herself another saint." Then he went over to Dad's closed casket. Red knelt, made a sign of the cross, and bowed his head real low. He got up, gave the box one last look, appeared to move away. But then he stopped, went into a crouch and began jabbing the air with his left fist. "Jimbo, you crafty sonuvabitch! I remember the night ya took out Flavin. Oh it was a work of art, it was. Bing! with the left. Bing, bing, bing, one round, two rounds, alla time with the left, then *bingo!* ya nails the son of a bitch right on the kisser and ol' Flophouse ain't seen that right comin' yet! The look on his face when they gets him to his feet—HAW! HAW! HAW!" Two well-dressed young guys from the funeral home, who knew a disturbance when they saw one, came calmly to the rescue and, real friendly-like, escorted old Red to the street, a gesture he didn't altogether appreciate. "I knew yer old man," he said to one of the guys on the way out. "*He* was a cocksucker too."

When my brother and I were growing up, Dad thought it extremely important that *we* learn to fight. The sessions, of which there were many, took place in the living room. Our sister Dee Dee, who was not invited to learn this manliest of arts, reclined on the sofa the whole time with her hands behind her head, taking it all in. Gully and I shared the one pair of boxing gloves, these heavy, oversized sacks of sweat that were always drenched inside and smelled like the chicken the dog dragged out of the neighbor's garbage. "There," said Dad, on his knees, "just hold the left out in front like this and deflect the blows, see? That's it. See how easy it is? Ha, ha, ha. *That's* it." It *was* pretty easy— you just held up your big fat mitt and he'd hit it. Of course, if he really *wanted* to hit you, he could do it without trying. A little "bing" with his open palm on the side of your head, then maybe a "bing-bing" on your cheekbone and a "bing-bing-bing-bing" on your temple, both cheeks and your chin. "Come on," he'd say, between the pepperings, "see if you can hit *me.*" You'd swing wildly for his enjoying-this-way-too-much face, he'd block it with his left and "bingity-bing-bing-bongity bong" you with his right until you had a full-blown nervous break-down, tore off the gloves and went screaming from the room. "Aw, c'mon," he'd holler after you, "I was just playing! Okay Gully, it's your turn—lace 'em up!"

My brother and I entered adolescence with several disadvan-tages, not knowing how to fight first among them. We also had fists the size of parakeet heads, rib cages that showed through our shirts and attitudes way too big to defend. When called upon to fight, which was often, we flailed, hands and feet flying, trying to hit some-thing, preferably something below the belt or maybe an Adam's apple, making weird and scary noises the whole time. Sometimes it actually worked. "You're crazy!" said Wallace "Bookworm" DeSault, suddenly quitting our epic battle behind St. Uke's. "And what's with the fucking screaming? For Chrissakes, my *eardrums* are shattered!" When facing somebody tough, somebody who *had* a good right cross, we either stayed there and died or fled, often the latter, in big leaping strides, through alley, glen, and glade. Our mouths, which had gotten us into the scrapes to begin with, would continue to flap, hurling back taunts and insults at our much slower pursuers.

"Suspended for fighting," I told Ma, who wondered what I was doing home from school at eleven o'clock in the morning. She gasped when she saw the blood on my swollen mouth and the dis-coloration around both eyes—no doubt sparing me my second beat-ing of the day—and she hurried me to the medicine cabinet for repairs.

Suspended for fighting. It had a ring. Not simply *suspended,* which could be for any number of inane infractions from skipping algebra to drawing nude cartoons of the principal and his staff on random blackboards. *Suspended . . . for FIGHTING!* It made you sound like something. Like a real badass dude from way back. *Suspended for fighting.* Forget that the closest you *came* to fighting was telling Lenny Schrade to "Watch it, fucknuts," as he bumped into you in lunch line. Forget the forty or so unanswered blows he then proceeded to rain on your head until a coalition of teachers, janitors, and lunchroom personnel pulled him off. Makes no difference. Lenny Schrade–Johnny Gullivan. *Suspended for fighting.*

But, as far as anyone knows, there has been only one Gullivan *arrested for fighting.* That would be Dee Dee. She achieved this distinction by nailing Aggie Ogden, Morton's own, right on the jaw after the living legend made a pass at our sister at a fund-raiser for the police department, of which Aggie was a cadet in training. I drove Ma to the station to bail Dee Dee out. She was still rubbing her right hand when they let us in. I got to pick her brain while Ma negotiated with the fuzz, who weren't too happy that one of their own had wound up flat on her back, dazedly looking up at the overhead fans at the K of C hall.

"I don't care if she's Sergeant Preston of the Yukon," said Dee Dee. "Nobody grabs my ass without permission."

"But Aggie *Ogden?*" I said. "That Amazon'd clean *my* clock."

"No doubt."

"How'd you learn to fight like that?"

"From Dad."

"From *Dad?*"

"Correct. All those nightly sessions in the living room where he'd pepper you and Gully with the lefts and rights until you ran screaming in terror?"

"Uh, yeah," I remembered, absentmindedly touching my chin, cheekbone, belly, and hair.

"Well, *I* paid attention," she said, going into a stance. "I saw how he did it. Nothing to it, really. You fake 'em down there, jab 'em up here and deliver the sermon, baby. Deliver the sermon and turn out the lights."

• • •

The sun was coming up as Dally, Gully, and I made it stealthily back to the van, which was parked in snow about a block from the school. I instantly regretted not removing the Red Cross insignia from the doors before abandoning the vehicle because there they were, for all to see, sparkling like beacons. Probably no one had noticed it yet, though, and I peeled them both off and tossed them inside while Gully emptied the contents of the gas can into the bone-dry tank.

"You might want to pop the hood and drop a little into the carburetor," suggested Dally. "I saw somebody do it once; started right up like a bomb."

"I'll save a couple drops," said Gully, rolling his eyes. "And, gosh, let us not forget to check our tire pressure before we leave."

Leaving, I knew, would not be possible, gas or no, until we found some sand or something to provide traction for the van's wheels, seeing as how they were pretty well set in the snow we'd pushed the van into. The car parked behind the van was buried under the snow, as were all the cars on the street, but as I brushed off the window for a laugh, I found the driver's door unlocked. "Dally," I said, "help me get the floor mats outa here and we'll put 'em under the van's wheels." (*I* had seen *that* done.) There was also a half bag of French fries on the console, frozen solid, but looking as seductive as a roast beef dinner at Durgin's. (Unlike my brother, Dally and I had not had so much as a crumb since entering Loneberry. Growling? My belly was ready to devour its surrounding organs.)

"If you let it sorta swish around in your mouth for a while like a lozenge," I said, passing a fry to Dally, "it becomes almost chewable."

"Mmmm," said Dally, reaching for another one, "you are truly my provider."

"*Cops!*" yelled my brother, ducking down behind the van. "Up there by the school!" Dally and I hopped in the strange car and got down real low. A white cloud of exhaust engulfed the cruiser as it hung the right and rolled slowly our way. They must have been the cops who'd been chasing us through the school.

"What's happening?" Dally wondered, as we sucked fries in our self-imposed igloo, the only visibility coming from the swipe I'd first taken at the driver's window.

"I can't tell, but I think they're inspecting the van; I can hear their engine right outside." I rolled down the window a crack. I could hear the back-and-forth crackle on their radio. "Shit! Why are they so interested in the van? Goddamit, I *took* the crosses off. There's nothing there that should've grabbed their attention."

"Silly, it's the only thing on the street not buried in snow. Their curiosity be *piqued.*"

"You're right of course. And Gully's gonna get pinched any minute now, if he don't freeze to death first." I casually rolled the window down another few inches and moved in slow motion for a closer peek. I could see the hood of the cruiser and the cop riding gun. I couldn't tell if the other officer was in or out. If he was out, he'd be stumbling onto Gully and his gas can in seconds. "I think we need to create a diversion," I said.

"A diversion?" said Dally. "You mean something compelling enough to take their attention off a suspicious vehicle that may have been involved in a break-in and also left Monsignor Burke at the altar? Look, sweetcakes, my clothes are on and they're staying on."

"No. We'll be like a married couple and we're like late for a court date or something and we blame each other for the car being buried."

"Oh, okay. Something like: You dumb shit! Ya hadda park the fucking thing right out front so's the plows can bury it! Sister's got a garage right down the street, but *nooo,* that's too far to *walk!* Right out front it's gotta go!"

I was impressed. "Coulda used you at the Greyhound," I said, needlessly making reference to an inside joke. "Okay, now let's slip out your door, crawl around the back and suddenly appear on the street, in full character." We gave each other the A-OK thumbs-up thing and confidently smiled. She still had a little chalk on her face, but it looked smeary and good. We both took fries for the road.

"Uggghhhh," Dally groaned. "It won't budge,"

"Whattya mean?"

"The door won't budge. It's all covered with snow."

"Lemme try," I said, flexing muscle. Exchanging places, I touched, nay, *groped* her in half-a-dozen familiar places before slamming my shoulder and all my strength into the door. "It won't budge."

"That's what I've been trying to tell you," said Dally.

I thought about rolling down the window and tunneling out, much like the attemped escape from old lady Walsh's, but I didn't think about it long. The gasping-for-air, going-down-for-the-third-time memory of it did little to inspire. "French fry?" I said, offering Dally another life-sustaining nugget.

"Shhhh!" she shushed. "Something's happening out there!" I heard yelling, dove across Dally's lap and rolled down the window the rest of the way.

"*Hey!*" bellowed the cop riding gun, half out of the car. "*Hey! Yeah, YOU!*" He was pointing far down the street, not at anyone in our party. "*Don't move a muscle, Puerto Rico, we're comin' TO ya! Hey! HEY! I said!*" The other cop jumped in and barked: "Unit seven in pursuit of suspect on foot!" as the cruiser sped away in a great whirring gale of smoke and kicked-up snow.

"Can we do the play anyway?" said Dally, as the cops disappeared round the corner.

"That was mighty close shaving," said Gully, as we all met in the open and exhaled. "Okay, let's see if this pig'll turn over and get the fuck outta here."

Surprisingly, it turned over on the third try, but none too convincingly, shimmying weakly with disease. I knew it'd have to warm up for a good twenty minutes before even trying to make it move. Then there was the problem with traction. We all got in and sat up front and took advantage of the faintly blowing heat. Dally was in the middle, concerned with something on the ceiling.

"Check out the hieroglyphics," she said, referring to Dad's notes all over the wall. "I never noticed it before. What does it mean?"

I pointed to the one over the door—*Kong 77g 67a15m W*—and translated: "It means the Congregational church gets seventy-seven *Globes,* sixty-seven *Sunday Advertisers* and fifteen *Christian Science Monitor*s. The *W* means it gets windy as a bastard—bring bricks."

She found one marked *Gun 18g15h.* Gully did the honors: "That's eighteen *Globe*s and fifteen *Herald*s for Gunther Malstreum. Who sucked. Called in half the time with asthma; Dad had to do the route himself."

"Your dad was probably the most overwrought, overworked person in greater Boston," Dally tsked. "You could see the hair he pulled out from the night before in his fists. He was always very nice to me, though."

"He was pretty nice to us too," I said. "It was inanimate objects who lived in fear."

"*And* penned-up dogs who barked all hours of the night," she said. "Y'know, I heard him that night. Woke me up raving out in the driveway. You know what I secretly wished? I was hoping he'd *kill* those goddamned dogs. I was rooting for him to hurdle the wall and stove in both their heads with a two-by-four. I hated those high-strung little shits as much as he did. They were Mrs. Livingston's dogs. Flisky and Flasky. They kenneled with us every time she sailed to Europe, which was only about eight times a year. Nipping, whining monsters. Yelped from the minute she left to the second she returned. She'd make a gigantic fuss every time: 'Ohhhhh, my *darlings,* look at your coats!

What have these heathens been feeding you?' I wouldn't have minded parting *her* hair with a board. And to think that these worthless slimes were responsible for your dad's death."

"Oh, there may have been another contributing factor or two," I said, glancing at my brother. Dad's death was caused by severe head trauma from hitting the wall, went the official report, but the doc in charge, with all of us present, told Ma that Dad's heart was so damaged, so weak, he couldn't fathom how he lived *this* long. All the things Dad was supposed to give up (cigarettes, coffee, his daily crucifixion at work) he did not. It is comforting to think of Dad's death as his own doing. But the look on his face when we wrecked his office that morning with Ward, I don't know. I just don't know.

Dally's eyes fell on a notation on the wheel well. "What's this one down here? *Lap?* And look—the thirty-four *Globe*s are crossed out, then the fifty-two, then the sixty-six, then the seventy-nine, all the way to a hundred and four."

"That, my dear," said Gully, "is the greatest paperboy in the history of the profession. The son our father wished he had." (I began to hum.) "A strapping, clean-cut young man who'd readily take on the routes of all the paper boys who quit, whose shoulders were broad enough to carry four full bags as he steamrolled through the streets, never tossing the paper in the hedges or rolling it up the lawn, but hand-delivering it to each and every one of the eagerly-tipping customers on his list. The Lap, my child, is for LaPinza. The natives have been known to call him Prick." Then he reached over and popped on the radio. *"Damn that teleVISION!"* insisted the singer of Talking Heads, and, partly to keep warm, partly to keep the dark vulture of insecurity at bay, the Red Cross Men of Knoll Road and Dally Schoerner of Rutgers started dancing, in close quarters, like those harboring demons. Soon, of course, we'd be hard at work—they, outside with the borrowed floor mats, pushing and shoving with all their might; I, in my usual spot in the cockpit, desperately trying to rock the van free—but for now, we were dancing. Dancing like the only thing that mattered was dancing. Dancing from deep in the soul, like Indians, our heavy breathing fogging the windows gray.

Then the passenger door flew open, light cut into the fog, and somebody, some hurried apparition of leather and intent blew right in, bounded across, landed hard in the driver's seat and turned the radio off. "Too good to be fucking true," he said, fumbling with every knob on the dash until he found *Defrost*. "Too good to be fucking *true!*"

"What the fuck is *this?*" yelled Gully, and the guy, who, it appeared, had not realized we were there, turned around fast. That's when we saw the white scarf.

"Pelo?" cried Dally. "You lousy son of a bitch!" And she went for him, but he pushed her back onto the couch. Gully and I charged him at the same time. Which is when he pulled the knife. Out of a *sheath*. The blade alone about six inches long. Guaranteed to make you behave.

"Well so, what have we here?" he grinned. "The two shitheads who lied to me earlier and the fucking bitch I'm gonna kill."

"Nobody's gonna kill nobody," said Gully. "And what's with this *familiar* shit? We ain't never seen your ugly ass in our lives."

"Uh, not entirely true," I intervened. "Mr. Pelo and I are somewhat acquainted, you see. You were still in the house with Monsignor last time our paths crossed. The other shithead was Doody, actually, an understandable mistake considering—"

"Shut the fuck up, dickface," spat Pelo, "less you want your *tongue* on the end of this blade. Now, I'm having a bit of trouble with the pigs right now, so let me tell you how it's gonna go. The first thing that's gonna happen here is the little bitch is gonna tell me where Ethel is. Then we're gonna drive to wherever that is, all of us together, one big happy family of joy."

"I don't know where Ethel is, you rotten fucking—"

"Yeah, and you don't know where the little dog is either, right? Fuckin' little shit just found his own way back to the cunt, right? Now let's move!"

"Uh, there may be one slight problem," I said. "The van is stuck."

"So we un-stick the bitch—let's *go!*" He started waving the knife. The blade curved at the tip; it would go in you like butter and take half of you with it on the way out. *Major* knife.

I had been at knifepoint once before. The day Timmy Mackey went planetary at Caddigan Park and got taken away in a straitjacket. "Someone's gonna get cut *bad!*" Timmy foamed at the mouth, knife glistening by my left ear. "Izzit *you*, Jonno? Whatta we think, asswipes, slice Jonno here like a fucking pear and leave the pieces in his old lady's *flower bed?* How 'bout we take a *vote?*"

The asswipes, which included Floydie, my brother, and Gunther Malstreum, seemed encased in ice, their mouths hung open, their breathing halted. They were to be of no help to me, I could see at once. I was about to be disemboweled before their very eyes and the horrible memory of it was already etched on their faces. Timmy's sixteen-year old forearm was choking my twelve-year old throat, close enough for me to bite it, and his knife was an inch from my eye. But I didn't bite him. I didn't do anything. I didn't cry, blubber, beg for my life, or struggle. What was I up to? I don't know, except that I hadn't been stabbed yet, I noticed, and Timmy was still threatening to hang my testicles on Major Caddigan's statue. Then two cops came onto the path and Timmy's sad-looking father was with them and you could tell he'd been recently widowed. I was resigning myself to the hostage phase of my captivity when Timmy threw his knife and started running, but the cops tackled him and dragged him to the wagon like a demented donkey and nobody ever saw him again.

"You have to treat the blade like a dangerous animal," I explained afterwards to my astonished peers. "Don't take your eyes off it, of course, but as long as you don't provoke it or startle it or basically

breathe in its presence, you stand a fair chance of living another day."
(Luckily, I was wearing my dark blue dungarees that day or somebody might've asked me about the large wet area that extended from
my crotch to about mid-thigh.)

The van moved. "For Chrissakes," groused Gully, "it *should* move,
with all *three* of us pushing on the bastard!" We thought about running, as if running were *possible* in this marshmallow world, but the
thought of the highly motivated Pelo running after us with a knife the
size of a bowling pin put us off that notion quick. Compliance would
do well for now.

Pelo was at the wheel (wouldn't be talked out of it) and the rest of
us were assigned to the bumper. The floor mats didn't work any mir-
acles. One of them got all mashed up deep under the tire and the
other one shot out behind the bumper in a blur of brown, never to be
seen again. Our idiot captor was rocking the van like I told him but
doing a miserable job with it. "Goddamit," I yelled, "you can't gun it
til you feel the momentum *this* way—you're going too early!"

I tried to reason with him at the outset, that I was the only one
capable of steering us out of this. *"Fuckin' MOVE!"* he insisted, and
out came the knife again. Dally also made a bid to be the driver, pri-
marily because that's where the heat was, but Pelo was pretty rough
with her too.

"So, Batman and Robin, what's the new plan?" she asked, as
crashing waves of slush slapped our bodies from the waist on down
as we heaved and hoed.

"I think we're fresh out," I said.

"Well, we better come up with something quick, especially when
he asks me again about Ethel."

"But you *don't* know where Ethel is," I said. Smoke came from
the whirring tires.

"Exactly. But he won't believe it. He thinks all women are no-good, lying, blue-balling tramps. I saw him shove hot pizza in the face of a chemistry prof who came to Ethel's aid and he kicked the hell out of three security guards getting away. Somebody's gonna get hurt here—I can promise you that. Somebody's gonna get cut!"

"Well, luckily, he can only stab one of us at a time," said Gully, spitting out a mouthful of snow. "The other two rush him and bring him down."

"You two against *him?*" laughed Dally. "*Ha!* Whattya gonna bleed all over him and hope he gets it in his eyes?"

Gully slipped and hit his chin on the bumper. "*Goddamit!* Okay, that's it! This fucking maniac can *have* the goddamn van! I'm done!" He started walking away.

"Are you kidding?" said Dally. "He'll chase you down like Genghis Khan!"

"Wait a minute," I said. "That's it! We *get* him to chase us!"

"Oh, good," said Dally. "I was wondering when inspiration would strike. When he stabs me, do you think you could tell him to aim for the throat so I'll die quickly?"

"No! You two walk off, making sure he can see you in the mirror. Meanwhile, I reach inside for the tire iron, he comes back here, I club him like a fucking seal!"

Gully stood before me. "You are going to hit him with a tire iron."

"Yes," I said.

"I see. Have you ever hit anyone with a tire iron? Anyone at all."

"Not really, but—"

"Because you're gonna hafta *brain* the cocksucker. You can't just *hit* him because that'll make him more pissed off than he already is *and he has something to STAB us with!* You gotta hit him as hard as you can, like you're felling a fucking tree! You gotta reach back with both hands and rain down on his skull like El Kabong!"

"Yeah, yeah," I said, "I get it already. I've hit guys before."

"No, guys have hit *you*. It ain't the same."

"I don't believe I'm listening to this," said Dally. "Okay, it's a plan. Your brother and I get out here and give him the finger, you slay the brute when he comes out, and we all live happily ever after. Let's do it. By the way, shall I do a dialect when I tell him to fuck off, you know, to give the role authenticity?"

"No," I said, "but you might employ sarcasm, as hard as that may be for you."

We all gave the van one more good push, then my coconspirators made themselves visible in the side-view mirror and set the bait. I heard Pelo ask what was going on; I heard my brother say, "Eat a bag of shit, numbnuts, you wanna move this pig you get back here and do it yerself!"

I threw open the back door and reached for the tire iron. The tire iron that was always tucked in the corner right next to the spare tire. *Always.* The tire iron that had no other purpose in life than to lie there next to the spare tire and wait for one of the other tires to blow. *No* other purpose. Except, I remembered, the other night, when the football we were playing with ended up under the van and we needed something to bat it out. The exact second that Pelo jumped out of the van and said, "Come the fuck *again?*" was when I realized where the tire iron was: on the lawn in front of Doody's house, under eight feet of snow.

In its place was a pail. The pail of golompkies given to us by the diabetic widow with the well-eared husband on Doberman Street. I grabbed for the handle. The sloshing weight took me by surprise. Much heavier than I remembered. Preserved-human-*head*-heavy. As I began to swing it, the voice of Jim McKay arrived in hushed accompaniment: "*. . . And with this attempt, his final attempt, Knudsen has his last chance for a silver medal in the hammer throw. . . . Look at the determination in his eyes . . . as he rears back . . . pivots like a screw . . . and uncorks a beauty into this warm Mexican night!*"

13

Red

Fact: the Stones go with everything. Even now, speeding through snowy streets on the way to Crawley Hospital with two bleeders in tow, the Stones demand attention. *"Dontcha know the crime wave's goin' up-up-up-up-UUUPP?!"* they wail through all five speakers, as the people behind me scream.

One of the people screaming was Gully who had ripped his smock into strips and was freaking out trying to tie a "goddamn tourniquet" on Dally. "I don't know how to tie the fucking thing! I got thrown out of Boy Scouts! I can't tie a fucking *shoe!*"

The other person screaming was Dally herself, who got cut pretty deep in the arm just before Pelo got hit with golompkies. "Calm the fuck *down*—I'm not *dying* here!" as the blood drenched through her shirt and pooled into each new strip Gully applied like a quick stroke of spray paint.

The body, or at least the *unconscious* body of Pelo was in the way back, one leg slumped across the spare. It was undetermined whether he was dead or alive. The pail of golompkies hit him in the side of the head with a sound as ungodly as a forty-pound pumpkin dropped from Ponky Bridge. He made a quizzical little "something's not right, here" expression before his arms and legs folded camp and the rest of him collapsed in a spectacular heap at our feet.

"Is he dead?" one of us said as he lay there in the snow.

"I dunno. Is he breathing?"

"Wouldn't your stomach move up and down if you were?"

"It would. Somebody check his pulse."

"Fuck this," said Gully. "Let's just give the fuckstick CPR and get it over with." He set his foot on Pelo's chest, pumped up and down a couple times and said, "There. We tried to revive him. Our conscience is clear. Now let's get the fuck outta here!" He picked up Pelo's knife and wiped the blood in the snow. "Uh—why do we suppose the blade has blood on it?"

"Shit!" said Dally, as a thin stream of red trickled out of the sleeve of her coat. "I *knew* he got me. Jesus, I think he got me *good*." She tore off the coat and revealed a gash on the fleshy side of her forearm about eight inches long. Then she felt woozy and my brother and I helped her into the van.

"Okay, let's go!" said Gully, slamming the side door.

"What about the fuckstick?" I said.

"The hell with him; the cops'll be back here any minute—they'll find his ugly ass."

"They're also gonna notice that the suspicious van they saw earlier is now gone. They *had* to've gotten the plate number when they were here. They'll be adding homicide to our ever-growing list."

"What if he's alive?"

"Then he tells them how we jumped him, bludgeoned him with baseball bats and left him for dead," I said. "All he hasta do is throw in all the racial slurs and they'll be chasing us with copters!"

"You're saying we should take him with us?"

"At least until we figure what to do with him. Get his head, I'll get his feet."

"His head has blood all over it."

"And his feet are covered with snow. Pick your poison."

"By the way," said Gully, as we emptied Pelo's carcass into the back of the van. "Do these scenarios just come to you or all they all out of *True Detective?*"

I got behind the wheel, kicked on the radio and rocked the van three good times, spinning slush, smoke, and rubber out into the street. I wasn't fooling around—not with cops all around, Dally losing blood and Gully freaking out. "*Ah bin SHATTERED!*" said the Stones as I rolled down the window, slapped the red cross back on the side and fishtailed back to the main road, "*Muh brain's bin SPLATTERED!*"

I glanced behind me and saw myself at nine or ten, in the same vehicle, with my brother and all my sisters, in the not-yet-light hours of the morning, coming back from the New York World's Fair. I saw Dad driving, punching in the lighter, unlit cigarette dangling from his lip. (As I recall, there was a newspaper strike; there almost *had* to be—how else could he have gotten away?) Ma, sound asleep, held Cassie in her lap as Maurice Chevalier crooned "Thank heaven . . . for leetle *garls*" on the radio—a safe song for our family as we traveled together in a perilous world, a safe song from a radio station that only played safe songs. Dad and I were the only ones awake as my family rolled through the predawn mist. The reason I was awake had to do with another song, *Ah Cain't Git No Satis-FACKshun,* which I heard for the first time that very afternoon on a transistor radio at a hot dog stand, its first five feverpitched notes attaching themselves to me like octopi. It remains my only memory of the New York World's Fair. Maurice Chevalier can croon all he wants, "Satisfaction" will lick at my brain forever. From the snugness of my sleeping bag I watched Dad, watched him flick ashes out the vent window and sip coffee with his other hand, whole seconds of time elapsing with nothing but a knee steering the truck. But never had I felt so safe. Behind the wheel he was John Wayne, tamer of a three-quarter-ton machine. It was where he belonged. I understood the power of it, identified with his mastery of it, picked up on its singular ebb and flow. In his gnarled and bitten hands I was safe.

And I had the gift, I could see that. I was to inherit the gene, Dad's gene, and I could feel my own hands on the wheel as he steered it, my own foot on the pedal, the truck's power surging right up my pant leg and on through the rest of me as the Rolling Stones bent into their guitars. It was my only passed-down gene. I got a little of Ma's artistic talent, I guess, but to develop *that* would take years of practice and classes and stuff. The driving just came to me. Bring it on—I can *always* operate a vehicle. Taking hard lefts, impossible U-turns, the louder the speakers the better. *"Go 'head . . . bite the bii-iiiiiiiiiiiiiiiiig APPLE!"* I was *born* to drive.

The Crawley Hospital once again came into view. Now back to earth, I remembered that we still had Pelo in the back. We decided to dump him out on a corner. If they found him, and he was still alive, the hospital was a mile up the street—they could probably save him. It was a humanitarian act and we were unanimously proud of it. Gully and I made the drop, sort of dumped him in a hard pile of plowed snow by a flashing yellow light. We had just swerved back into the street when the cops pulled up. "What's goin' on, boys?" asked the driver, who got out of the car while the other guy called in our plates. We already had committed enough acts to land us in jail, and now we had a body behind us in the snow with a caved-in head. I did not hesitate, though, in playing the trump card.

"We're on an emergency," I said, tapping the red cross on the side of my door. "The young lady has been wounded." The cop, a Boston cop, whom I did not recognize, poked his head in the window and saw Dally and all her blood lying on her back on the couch.

"Holy shit! What happened to her?"

"We're not sure. She came running out of nowhere flagging us down. It appears she's been stabbed."

"Jesus! Quick, follow us to Crawley! We'll give you an escort!"

But then the other guy, his hand still on the microphone, stepped out yelling something about our van being the one that ditched the priest.

"Of course we ditched the priest!" I said. "We got a lady losing *blood*!"

The escort was beautiful. Lights as blue as flame, not chasing us, but *leading* us for the love of God, the driver nearly as reckless in the snow as me. The gurney was awaiting us as both vehicles skidded into the drive-up to Emergency. The cops got out and passed Dally into the arms of the nurses themselves. "Wait here," one of the cops pointed at me. "We'll be right back."

"Good-bye, Red Cross men!" Dally called weakly after us. "My firstborn shall bear both your names!"

My brother and I just sat in the van for a few minutes looking out at the street. The radio was on low and stayed there. A delivery truck was spotted in the distance, suggesting the ban on driving was easing up. The wail of a siren was heard a couple miles away, but getting closer.

"So, where does this put us?" said Gully, examining the bloody tatters of his ruined smock.

"I'm not sure," I said. "Did that cop just tell us to wait here?"

"Uh, he said *something*, but I didn't catch it."

"Yeah," I said, dropping the van into *Drive.* "It's like he's got rocks in his mouth—you can't understand half the shit he mumbles." The siren was about three blocks away.

"Well, if it was important, I'm sure he'll catch up to us."

"Why, of course he will." I decided to bring the van around the side of the building and go out the back way. More cops sped by the front entrance and screeched to a halt farther down.

"I think they found numbnuts," I said, as other crime-solving units converged on the scene.

"Numb *Who?*" mocked my brother, cranking the radio. "Why, whatever do you mean?"

The back way was blocked off; a mountain of snow stood before us, left there temporarily by the two plow trucks that were trying to clear off the employee parking lot.

"I guess we're going this way after all," I said, backing up. As we came around, however, we saw the *other* cops, the ones who'd escorted us here and seemed to have a long list of unanswered questions. I pulled the van in under a great evergreen to wait the whole thing out. I knew how cops worked, though. By the time they roped off the crime scene down the street, got Pelo out of the snow and into Emergency, sniffed around for any witnesses, explained the situation to each succeeding cop who pulled up and thoroughly compared notes, we'd *all* be eligible for pensions.

"We have an issue," I said, "with gas."

"Agreed," said my brother, glancing at the needle pinging on E. "The two gallons I threw in ain't gonna last long sitting here."

I turned off the motor. "We now have an issue with frostbite."

"Not to mention lack of tunes." Floydie had rigged it so the stereo'd kill the battery if you used it with the motor off. All we could do was sit there and freeze.

The second part of Granddad's story about the huddling sailors in the DeSoto came to mind, the part told only to Gully, Dad, and me, away from the womenfolk, over Cokes at Brigham's: The sailors, one by one, begin drifting off to sleep. Until Dommy from Pittsburgh unconsciously lays an unforgettable fart, and Granddad and the others wake up in a panic.

"*Oh my God! It's mustard gas!*"

"*I can't breathe!*"

"*We gotta get outta here!*"

"*No!*" says Tex, the leader. "Only one of us is leavin'!" And he kicks open the door, grabs Dommy with both hands and throws him out in the snow, where he was still pretty much in a coma. Everybody laughs like hell, each intending to pull old Dom back in a couple minutes but they all transition into a snoring stupor as the laughter dies out. They don't remember he's out there until morning when one of them goes outside for a piss. They flag down a passing truck, rush Dommy to the base infirmary, where he loses three toes on one foot and two fingers on each hand. He has no hard feelings, though, and back home to his life in Pittsburgh he goes.

"It's funny," Granddad said. "It don't sound like much—a lousy three toes and a coupla fingers. What's the big deal, right? Until you look at some guy *missing* three toes and a coupla fingers. It looks like something half-human, half-crustacean. Someone who ain't never gonna set foot in public again." This was about as deep as Granddad was ever gonna get but we enjoyed the moment. We also never quite shook the image of no-hard-feelings Dommy and his fresh set of claws. More than once I had nightmares of the butchered sailor, scorned by his family, coming back to exact bloody revenge on his shipmates and their offspring. Frostbite, we learned young, was a thing to be avoided.

The ambulance on the other side of our tree started up and took off. We watched it speed down the ramp, lights flashing. We heard it slow down about where you'd expect and we saw it come roaring right back in a second and a half. You still couldn't tell if Pelo was dead or alive as they dragged him out on a stretcher, but then his arm, which had been dangling down dead, suddenly moved, coming to rest on his chest.

"Refresh my memory," said my brother. "Is his being alive a good thing for us or a bad thing?"

"Short term, good. Long term, we need to book passage to Guam."

Our cops went over and talked to some other cops who just pulled up. Once they started laughing and lighting cigarettes I knew it was gonna be awhile. The cold, meanwhile, was searing.

"Numbness in the toes—first stage to frostbite?" asked my brother, stomping the floorboards.

"It's the first step to acceptance," I was pretty sure.

"Okay, let's go see Ma."

"You wanna see Ma."

"No, I wanna see Worms Faulkner, but my brother plots against me at each and every turn."

"What time is it?"

"I dunno. It's gotta be at least seven."

"They won't let us in."

"Who won't let us in? Our mother is upstairs dying."

"They won't let us in—visiting hours aren't 'til eight."

"What time is it now?"

"We already had this conversation."

"Put the radio on AM. They give you the time til you're sick of fucking hearing it."

But the radio was on FM when I turned the key, and 'BCN was in the middle of a set that included Johnny "Guitar" Watson, Bowie, and Robin Lane and the Chartbusters. The time would have to wait.

The windshield was getting all fogged up again as we sort of bopped up and down to keep warm, hollering and stuff, but I thought I saw something. "Look!" I started to say, "Is that—?" But it all happened so fast, like a blur, and by the time I wiped the window with my sleeve of my smock, it was over.

"Is that what?" said my brother, his teeth chattering.

"Nothing," I said. But I could have sworn I saw Pelo, white scarf and all, blasting out the door they'd just carried him into, clearing all four steps without touching a one and disappearing into the deep snow at the corner of the building across. Maybe I didn't see anything, maybe it was the cold invading my brain, but the possibility that I *had* seen Pelo, hurtling through deep snow like a wolf after a hare, was not a comforting thought. And neither was freezing to death. I thought about Dally, right upstairs, and I thought about Ma too, two floors above Dally, her life soon to end. And I thought about the possibility of Gully and I dying first, right down here in the rusty old van Dad used to drive. And I started to chuckle to myself, never realizing how funny irony could be. They'd have to keep Ma alive long enough to attend our funeral. And then I just laughed out loud.

"What's so funny?" Gully shivered.

"Nothing," I continued to laugh, "Absolutely nothing."

The van, the panel truck, or the lousy good-for-nothing-goddam-shitfucking-hunk-of-tin, as Dad called it, was once brand spanking, right-off-the-lot new, part of a small business loan Granddad secured while Dad was in the service. Much like a farmer's new tractor, it was supposed be a symbol of prosperity, enabling Dad to pursue the American dream with a powerful, battle-tested machine. It came up a little short. The cancerous junk was generally more trouble than it was worth—and besides, the chicken feed Dad brought home set against the long dog hours he worked made the vehicle a symbol of all the injustice in the world. Ma had to work part-time at Flynn's and other cut-rate retailers just to pay for the truck's constant repairs.

The thing that was going to break the chains of poverty for my family was Ma's book, a book for children she wrote and drew herself. Everybody raved about Ma's talent for painting and she was recruited for just about everything. She was famous throughout the parish for her nativity scenes and anybody who thought up an idea for the St. Euclid's Christmas bazaar would expect Ma to put it into action:

"Betty? Patsy has a great idea for this beanbag game where you have to toss the beanbag through this hole, you see, but the hole is really a mouth, y'know, like a lion's mouth or a hippo's! (Louisa suggested we make it the Monsignor's mouth—oh, she's a stitch, that one.) Anyway, we were hoping you'd paint the faces. We're gonna need about twenty of them, we figure, and we should be able to sell them for twelve, maybe fifteen bucks a pop. Patsy's husband is sawing the pieces out of a big sheet of plywood and he could get them over to you by suppertime. Do ya think you could get 'em done by Wednesday? Also, could you man the booth for a few hours on Saturday? You're a big help, dear, no, a *huge* help. Also, are you going to design the banners again this year? Yeah, I wish we kept the ones from last year too, but you know how it is, out with the old, in with the new."

People basically swooned over Ma's artwork and happily forked over good money to obtain it. She was once hired by old lady DeLisle to paint goldfish on the walls of her dining room and got sixty-five bucks for it. Ma never had an art lesson in her life, either; it just came naturally. The mailman commented on her freshly finished picture window one year, saying, "Jee-zez, Mrs. G, if I had your talent I'd be living on Easy Street"—the implication being that he, with his superior smarts and drive to succeed would be able to do what she couldn't.

That got Ma to thinking: "I bet if I put my mind to it, I could make up a story for a children's book, draw all the pictures and sell it to Little Small-Fry Books for a pretty penny!"

Easy Street. The place we all wanted to dwell. "Will we have a color TV? A swimming pool? Our own bomb shelter? Collies?"

"Maybe," said Ma, but mostly she was doing it for Dad. She saw it as a way to get Dad out of the business she knew would kill him, with its all-hours-of-the-night-in-all-kinds-of-weather relentlessness. She was on the phone talking to Aunt Fran while treating my fresh Puff wounds with iodine—that's how I know. I might have been screaming too loud to catch every word (Puff's talons slashed right through my Little League pants) but I did hear Ma say: "I gotta get Jim out of the papers; this is the only way I know how. Yes, I'm sure it *helps* to have connections, Fran, but I'm just as good as the ones who draw those pictures, if not better. Some of them aren't any good at all—they're gonna say no to *me?* Yes, I know art supplies cost money but I've been saving for a rainy day, Fran, and as far as I'm concerned the rain's about to fall." Ma finished with me and shooed me away, but I didn't go far, no farther than the other side of the kitchen door, where I could hear the rest of her chat with my aunt. I heard her say in hushed tones, how she found Dad sitting in the truck in the dark yelling at himself and how he wouldn't come in and wouldn't talk to her and stayed out there all night. "He's at the end of his rope, Franny, I've got to do something." I always suspected that Dad's hatred of his occupation was extreme but it never occurred to me that he might be at the end of any rope. She was drawing to save his sanity. Maybe his life.

The book was to be called *Red,* and she worked at it while everyone else was in bed. I used any excuse to get up and peek over her shoulder, even the problem-with-my-penis excuse. (This was nothing particularly new; because Dad went to bed so early, Ma fielded *all* the penis-related questions.)

"Ma, my pecker hurts."

"Where does it hurt?"

"Right here, see? Feels like it's on fire."

"Don't worry. It's just a growing thing—it'll go away in a little while. Now go back to bed."

"But it's *burning,* Ma!"

"Go into the bathroom and put a wet facecloth on it."

"Can I watch TV while I'm doing it?"

"If you must, but only for fifteen minutes."

Ten minutes of *The Name of the Game* would usually cure the condition and if I kept quiet while Ma worked in the other room I could invariably hang in til the closing credits unless my brother came out to spoil things: "Ma, my pecker hurts too!"

"*Go back to bed, both of you!*"

But Ma's book fascinated us, Dee Dee included, and we came up with more and more reasons to traipse out to the sewing room and take a look. The ironing board was her easel and most of her art materials were ours—all those drawing tablets we got for Christmas, the watercolor sets we all had but hardly used. The only stuff she bought were brushes and this expensive fountain pen for lettering; she could make her letters look just like typeface. Ma wasn't mad when we snuck down; in fact sometimes she'd have us model a pose. The story concerned this neighborhood where all the boys played football and baseball and wrestled and swam, but never let the girls play no matter how loud they begged. "Don't be silly," the boys would say. "The only things girls play with are dolls!" Then Red moves into town, wearing a Red Sox baseball cap, and proving to be better than the other boys at everything. He can play sports better, fly kites higher, climb trees faster, and is even good at stuff the others never dreamed of, like pole-vaulting and logrolling and riding horses bareback. The girls are delighted that someone's put the conceited boys in their place, but when they try to talk to Red, he gets very shy and runs away. Then, in the middle of a horizontal bar-like giant swing dismount from a low-hanging tree limb, Red's cap falls off and a big gorgeous red ponytail plumes out and Red is revealed to be a girl. The last page has Red, minus her hat, uncorking her fastball in a smiling, happy, coed game.

We loved the book. The only one I thought was better was *Horton Hatches the Egg*. All those other things where tugboats or rabbits set out to see the world but end up being satisfied with home-sweet-home? Crap! *Red* was stupendous. The scene where she shinnies up the flagpole to retrieve the little girl's baseball glove that had been tossed up there by the boys? Priceless!

Ma went to the library and got the address to Little Small-Fry Books. She then wrapped up her collection of illustrations and text in thick brown paper, tied it with shipping twine, slapped a label and about a year's worth of stamps on it, and hauled it down to the post office. You could see her wince as the clerk pounded it with HANDLE WITH CARE and FRAGILE and she looked on with uncertainty as he tossed it in a basket with other things wrapped brown.

"You sure it'll be okay?" she asked the clerk, but he just gave her the "Lady-we-ship-this-horseshit-alla-time" look, and threw another package right on top of it. So we all walked home, me pushing the baby carriage, passing all the triple-deckers and small worn-out houses, laundromats and barrooms we'd soon be bidding farewell to. We stopped at Brigham's and Ma got us all a cone. A minor extravagance for a family soon moving to Easy Street.

Weeks passed. Not a word from the publishers. "Don't worry," said Ma, "They've probably got dozens of submissions to go through. Maybe hundreds."

"Maybe you should call them," said Dad.

"Oh, only amateurs would do that," said Ma.

"Oh," said Dad.

Meanwhile, more lucrative assignments flooded in: Bob Hitchner of the Knights of Columbus came up with a brainstorm to paint all the fire hydrants red, white, and blue for the Fourth of July—and could Ma do it? The Knights would supply all the paint. Ma said sure. Me and Dee Dee helped her with a couple of them, including the one right in front of the K of C Hall, listening to the Knights sing drunken songs inside as we slapped on the second coat.

Months went by; still nothing. I was home sick with the flu when Ma made the call. "Gullivan," she whispered into the phone. Then she had to spell it. Twice. Finally, after hanging on hold for about twenty-five minutes, they came back to tell her that, yes, they received it, and, no, there's no record of what happened to it. They told her to call back in a couple of days; they might have more information for her. So she did, and had to spell her name all over again.

Finally a letter from New York came in the mail.

> Dear Miss (Mrs.) Sullivan:
>
> We appreciate your interest in Little Small-Fry Books but are unable to use your submission at this time. Due to the sheer volume of submissions, we are unable to return any work not accompanied by a self-addressed stamped envelope.
>
> Sincerely,
>
> H.P. (or, the usual clown who doesn't know his ass from his elbow)

"See?" said Aunt Fran. "I *told* you you can't do this sort of thing without knowing somebody high up. Look, the girl who does my hair has a son who has a friend who works for Captain Kangaroo. I'll call her if you want me to."

But Ma just smiled and looked out the window for a while. When she called the publisher trying to get her originals back, the same lady said she never heard of her or her book. (She hadn't thought of making copies.)

"Are you saying," asked Dad that night at dinner, "that they just took all your beautiful drawings and threw them away?"

"That seems to be the size of it," said Ma. For a minute, judging from the look on Dad's face, I thought we were all gonna pile in the truck and head for Manhattan to right this great wrong. But a moment later he was lighting a cigarette and watching Huntley and Brinkley on the Admiral. And that was the end of any talk of *Red,* or any project similar. Ma had little time to dwell on *the way the world worked,* though. Clearing the dishes from the table, she went to the sewing room to paint plaster of paris puppies for Ladies Sodality.

And suddenly, nothing felt safe. What if Dad reached the end of his rope the same time Ma reached hers? What if they died? Doody's father died. All my grandparents died, two of them not even waiting for me to be born. Dad could easily die and so could Ma. *Bang!* Some boozehound runs a red light—*bang*—no mother, no father, no nothing. What happens then? Can you actually *survive* without parents? Will your teeth simply rot in your head from lack of brushing? And who will get you up in the morning? Will you even *get* up? Will you sleep the entire day until Woody Woodpecker at four-thirty, throw down two bowls of Cap'n Crunch, and go back to bed? Will you die *yourself* in six months' time, drowned in filth and neglect?

I went to peek at Ma that night as she painted. Not so much to see what she was working on, just to look at her for a second. No "my pecker's on fire" excuses to watch TV—I just needed to look at her. Her blue eyes rose to meet mine. I wanted to say a lot more than just "G'night" but that's all I managed. Feebly.

"Good night," said Ma, and I went back to my room to count moles.

14

VOWS

It is possible, for the most part, to casually stroll into any given workplace and not cause too much of a stir. Case in point? Right now, my brother and I are in the kitchen of Crawley Hospital, just rambling right on through. Everyone sees us—the guy lugging the sack of sugar, the lady pulling out trays of Jell-O, but nobody questions us, because we are walking and talking, rubbing our hands to get warm, stomping our feet to get the snow off, slightly bored, as if we show up every day. If we had been running, or worse yet, attempting to slip through the busy kitchen undetected, they'd be squawking like barnyard fowl: "Excuse me, what's your business here? You can't come through here! Where's Charlie? Somebody find Charlie! Tell him we got trespassers here!" Yet, if you walk and talk your way through like you own the place, doubt is created; nobody wants to take a chance interfering with the guy who owns the place. Doody and I once got in almost two sets of tennis on the grass at Whiteside Country Club before two guys in blazers escorted us out.

Our current plan called for us to elude security and work our way up to Intensive Care to see Ma. We weren't overly confident about leaving the van where we left it—under a snow-covered fir tree down below—but if the cops *did* find it, at least they wouldn't find us inside it. We figured they wouldn't have it towed either since the tow trucks'd be pretty much up to their ears with all the stranded cars on 128. Another foolproof plan in the making. So well thought-out, it lent itself very smoothly to a sidebar. I wanted to find Dally.

"Dally?" said my brother in amazement. "Dally? Christ, why don't we make time to look in on that little shitbum dog too. I'm sure a visit by us would raise its spirits *all* to hell."

"Oh, come on—she's been stabbed for Chrissakes."

"And what're you gonna do? Kiss it and make it better?"

"I just want to see her. I *need* to see her."

"Oh, Jesus," my brother rolled his eyes. "He gets his dick wet on a mat stuffed with foam and it's *Love Is a Many Splendored Thing.*"

On the top of the next landing, tucked away in the shadows, hung a monstrously large oil portrait of some fat archbishop in blood-red sashes and capes. His many rings squeezed the blood out of his sausage-casing fingers and the little red skullcap on his massive, jowled head looked like a bottle cap ready to go. He was posed as though he were blessing all that quaked before him. But the longing in his face, the way the fingers on his bejeweled right hand curved inward—he was Irv, the dispatcher at Morton Cab, my former boss, looking to get his palm greased—"unless you don't *want* no decent fares yer whole damn shift." It took us a long time to move on, reduced as we were to runny-nosed, chest-heaving hysteria. The cold had affected our brains.

We opened the door and let ourselves into the corridor. It looked like a floor loaded with patients. The kind we were looking for. I saw a nurses' station in the distance. I gave a sidelong glance to each room we passed.

"Are you telling me," said Gully, "that we're just gonna poke our head in every room in this shithole til we find someone we recognize?"

"Don't worry," I said, "we'll ask the nurse up here if she knows where they brought Dally." But when I looked back Gully wasn't there. He was around the corner, his eyes fixed on the tile floor, watching the pad of a custodian's buffing machine go round and round and round and round.

"You 'bout ready?" I said.

"Be right with you," said my brother, as he finished watching the machine buff wax.

The nurse up ahead seemed to remember hearing about the young woman with the stabbed arm and had a rough idea what floor she'd be on. Halfway there, we were interrupted by a rent-a-cop with a walkie-talkie.

"What's your business here?" he said, holding up his fat, pink hand.

"We're here visiting," said Gully.

"Zat so?" said the guy. "So how is it you came through the kitchen?"

"We didn't," I said. "Why would we go through the kitchen to get to the east wing?"

He didn't seem to know that and walked away shaking his head, trying to contact colleagues on his radio. We found Dally's room round the next bend. She looked sound asleep, and peaceful. Someone had washed the chalk off her face. We hovered over her bed and whispered, so as not to disturb her.

"Y'know," whispered Gully, "I think I stayed in this room once. The time I threw rocks at the bees' nest."

"Actually, I think it was *my* room," I said. "But I can't remember if it was the spray-paint-in-my-eyes incident or the barfing-out-all-my-organs affair."

"You don't have to whisper," said Dally Schoerner. "I'm wide-awake. The eyes, on the other hand, are closed and shall remain so. What brings you by?"

"Well," I said, "I don't know . . . I just—"

"Dally, we need to talk," said Gully. "I gotta know where I stand." Dally laughed and felt for my hand.

"So how are you?" I said.

"Me? Never been better. I could almost sigh."

"Didya hafta get stitches?"

"Oh, yes. There were stitches. How many are on a baseball?"

"Did they give you anything?"

"Oh yeah. They *wanna* give me Percodan. I say, 'Look boys, I can't do Percodan. I've *done* Percodan. I like Percodan. They gave it to me a year ago after my car accident—my Lord and *master*, Percodan. Give me something else.' But the sawbone says, 'No, it'll be all right,' and keeps writing the scrip. I say, 'Fine, but you gotta be okay with me coming back to rob you next week 'cause by that time I'll be on *smack*!' So they give me something else, so they say, but it feels a helluva lot like Percodan."

"So you're feelin' fine?" I smiled.

"I'm in a good space," she agreed. "Cops are a pain in the ass, though."

"They talked to you?" said Gully. "The cops?"

"Right in the middle of my getting stitches, can you believe that? Like I could concentrate on their damn fool questions."

A nurse came in so nobody said a thing. The long silence got awkward. *Too* awkward. All her shuffling in the drawers and checking this, that, and the other thing got me thinking she was stalling, maybe a plant for the cops, trying to get something on us. I had no choice but to start kissing Dally; I had to make it look good. Dally thought so too, I think, because the kissing was very convincing, her hand on my cheek a nice touch. The nurse seemed not to notice and left.

"Give me a second while I vomit," said Gully. "Now, as I recall, we were discussing the cops."

"I gave 'em Pelo," said Dally. "They asked and I gave him. Stabbed me with a blade about that long."

"Didya give 'em *us?*" asked Gully, feeling for the very blade in his back pocket.

"Now what do you take me for? I told 'em just what *you* told 'em—I crawled out in the street and flagged you down. My Red Cross heroes."

"How did you account for the golompkies to his brain?" I asked.

"I think I had a limb falling from a tree—something like that. 'All I know is that *something* hit him, officers, and I got away from his murderous clutches.'"

"They buy it?"

"I think so. Some orderly told me they were reading him his rights in radiology."

"So that should take a lot of pressure off us, right?" said Gully.

"I'm not so sure about that," said Dally. "They had about a thousand questions about the two kooks in the van and repeated each one about sixty times."

"What kinda questions?"

"Look, let's just say they're having a hard time with the concept that you just happened along, and, if anybody asks me any more fucking questions I'm gonna request euthanasia. Now why don't you just get along with your mission and leave me in peace."

I started to ask her if she needed anything, but she just raised her hand and dismissed us both. "Let's go see Ma," I said, and Gully agreed.

"Kiss her on the forehead for me," said Dally, and I promised I would.

On the way we saw a death scene. Three fat women and a skinny man stood around the bed of an old, old lady whose skin looked like it was made entirely of fingernails. You could tell she was dead. The skinny guy was sniffling, one woman was dabbing her eyes with a Kleenex and the other two were bawling like the corpse was Jacqueline Kennedy. I wouldn't have cried. Kid stuff.

My family and I were experts at keeping it all in. We shouldered deaths, wakes, funeral Masses, and burials like soldiers guarding the queen. We mourned into our pillows alone (at least *I* did) but nobody lost it in public, nobody broke down, we were a model for grieving families everywhere. "Those plucky Gullivans," folks would whisper to each other. "Nothing gets to *them*."

Something *did* get to us the day of Granny's burial, now that I think of it, a little chink in the armor that came in the form of a simple loaf of bread—the bread me and Gully were sent to bring back. It had dawned on Ma that: "Omigod, people are going to want to come back to the house after the funeral! We'll have to feed them!" She began defrosting the turkey she'd been saving for Thanksgiving and sent us to Flynn's to buy a family-sized loaf of bread for the stuffing. As far as I can recall, this had never happened before. Dee Dee was the only one trusted to take money from Ma's purse and bring something back with it, but our sister, on this occasion, was shaving carrots and peeling potatoes, so the assignment fell on us. We were very businesslike on the way to Flynn's, and there *were* distractions, let me tell you. A bunch of kids were running towards the bridge because a river rat the size of an armadillo had been sighted under it, but we stayed the course. Got the bread Ma wanted, got the change, got a nice smile from Julie Flynn, a high school cheerleader who ran the register, and went home. Something about Julie's smile, though, and the way the oversized loaf felt in my hand, got me thinking about football, got me thinking I could maybe *play* football, despite my ferret-like appearance, and I dropped back to pass. Gully caught the loaf in his chest, right under the street sign for Knoll Road.

"Go long," he said, and I ran an out pattern by the mailbox and caught it with one hand.

We then discovered that if you held it by the tie at the top you could swing it two or three times and *really* launch it. It's too bad our house was so far away—we might have made it home before the wrapper split down the middle and the individual slices flew into the dug-up dirt in front of Jenkins Oil. We did our best to stuff everything back in, discarding the eight or nine pieces that were *exceptionally* dirty, and tried to hide the lopsided jumble in the bread box on top of the fridge. We were back in our room by the time Ma found it. All that was in her came out, as she screamed up the stairs:

"You hate me, is that it? You hate school, you hate church, you hate my mother, and you hate me! You must! Why else would you do these things? You hate me! You hate everything! Well the hell with you both! You hear me? Do you hate FOOD? Good! Because here's all the food you're getting for the rest of the week!"

We could hear the bread hit the stairs but dared not to peer out to the hallway until we were sure Ma was back in the kitchen. When we finally slithered out and saw the array, especially the endie that landed in the hamper at the top of the stairs, it was too much. We fled back to the room, put pillows over our heads and laughed sobbingly for what must have been hours. There is nothing about our behavior—before, during, or afterwards—that I understand.

We got off the elevator and turned the corridor toward Ma's room. Though the hallway was darker than the others you could see the wear in our sister Dee Dee's face as she rose from her chair. She approached us, clearly shaken, her arms outstretched. While we were running around naked in schools and braining people with golompkies, Dee Dee and Ma visited hell itself.

"Is she dead?" I said, pulling my sister close.

"No, John, she's not dead. I'm so glad you're both here." She seemed to actually mean it. She then pulled us over to sit on a bench outside Ma's room, where she held both our hands and breathed in deep air for several seconds before speaking.

A peaceful death, the kind where you die in your sleep, had been arranged for Ma, but it apparently hit a snag. A snag in the form of a clogged tube that was supposed to be pumping fluid out of Ma's lungs so she could go out in calm. *"Dee Dee!"* She shot up like a jack-in-the-box, clutching at her blackened throat. *"I can't breathe!"*

Dee, who'd been sleepily watching a replay of the Celts game, had a brief major coronary and then sprang into action, dashing down the hall for the nurse.

"I, uh, don't know what to do," frittered the poor young woman, as Ma's purple face gasped for air. "It's never *done* this before!"

"It's never clogged?" said an exasperated Dee Dee. *"Ever?"*

"Well, they're usually dead by . . . I mean . . . I don't know what to *do!*"

"Well then get somebody down here who *does!*" roared my sister. "I know my mother's gonna die, sweetheart, but, by God, it ain't gonna be by *drowning!*"

The nurse ran from the room and other personnel soon ran back in, with brand-new tubes, brand new machines, and a white-haired doctor with a stethoscope and a reassuring voice. Soon it was quiet, Ma was back to sleep, and Dee Dee hadn't taken her eyes off her 'til the moment we showed up. She said a priest was now on his way up to administer last rites.

"A priest?" I almost dropped my coffee. "Did you say a priest?"

"Yeah," said Dee Dee. "A priest. That's who they use these days for last rites, John. The interior decorators just weren't working out."

"Uh, would you have any idea which priest might be coming?" I asked.

"How the hell would I know? Probably Burke. He was in here earlier."

"Monsignor Burke was here?"

"Yeah, he was here. Hard to believe, isn't it? People dead and dying and a priest. What a strange world."

I looked at Gully and he looked at me. No words were needed.

"Look, Sis," said Gully, "John and I are going to set down a spell in that men's room over there. Do you think you could come by and let us know when the coast is clear?"

"When what coast is clear? What the hell are you talking about?"

"Look," I said, "it would not be in our interest to run into Monsignor Burke just now. So how about it?"

"What did you two shitheads do—knock over the collection box?"

I took a very deep breath and was about to tell her the whole damn story, moles and all, when Gully grabbed my arm and nodded toward a cop fast approaching from the far end of the corridor. We were in the shithouse in seconds, peering through the crack in the door. The cop was a female cop and walked right up to Dee Dee, touched her arm and gently asked how Ma was. "Nothing's changed," said Dee, and turned her head to glare right at us. We closed the door fully and made quickly for the stalls.

"I could be wrong," said Gully, settling into his temporary refuge on the other side of my wall, "but that looked a lot like Aggie Ogden out there in the cop suit. Tell me I'm wrong."

"No, I'm fairly certain that was indeed Miss Ogden."

"I see. And did it seem to you that Miss Ogden and our beloved sister Dee Dee were, shall we say, more than just friends?"

"I did get that impression," I agreed, dropping my drawers to the floor. "Say, you got any toilet paper over there?"

"Sure," he said, tossing it over. "You're taking a dump?"

"I'm in the right place, wouldn't you say?"

"Jesus, whattya do it at will?"

"Oh, me and the ol' digestive system have an understanding—I take it to nice places and it lets me live."

"So, not to change the subject," said Gully, "but wasn't the comely Miss Ogden the same officer who got her clock cleaned by Dee Dee a while back?"

"I think you've got the chronology right."

"And now they're Rock Hudson and Doris Day?"

"Courtship is a funny thing."

"Fuck you. You mean to tell me that you knew Dee Dee was into girls the whole time."

"Well, I knew she weren't interested in nobody male," I said.

"Goddam. Did Ma know?"

"Christ, Ma knew when you had a wet dream. I don't think this sorta thing'd get by her."

"Can you imagine Dad? He'd have electroshock therapy and run away to the circus."

We were still laughing when the door flew open. Somebody had come in to piss.

All I could see through the crack was the solid black oxfords. But as I strained my position, I saw the solid black pants above them, the solid black jacket on top of that, and I didn't even have to take my eyes any higher to know that it was the Monsignor. The blackness in my soul I could feel right through my skin. "Forgive me Father for I have sinned!" I wanted to cry out. (The door in front of me, the sin-absolving prelate on the other side of it—I was *in* the confessional.) "It's been a *lifetime* since my last confession, Father, forgive me, forgive me, *forgive* me!" Penance? What would my penance be? Incant the Act of Contrition 475 times while walking barefoot on hot coals? What could possibly eradicate my thoughts and deeds since my last confession some nine years ago? Oh, to go back to that simpler time, that innocent time, when Saturday afternoon at two was just another boring chore that had to get done, cleansing yourself of sin in order to be worthy enough to receive Communion on Sunday. Confession. As far as I was concerned I didn't sin nearly enough to warrant my going. What if I went a whole week without back-sassing my parents, taking the Lord's name in vain or hanging with Doody down on the wall when I was supposed to be mowing the lawn? Coming up with stuff to confess was getting hard. But it was Doody who wanted to take it to another level, not me. It was Doody, who'd never set foot in a Catholic church in his life, who first sowed the seeds of sacrilege.

"Lemme get this straight," he said on that fateful day, "You kneel down in this dark booth and tell your minister all the heinous crimes you committed all week, he gives you a little punishment in the form of a prayer or two, and you're good to go?"

"Yeah, basically," I said, "except he's a priest, not a minister."

"What's the diff?"

"Ministers have wives. Our guys are married to God."

"Right. And the poor guy's gotta sit there in the dark all afternoon listening to this kid-stuff drivel? How does he stay awake?"

"The adults go to confession too, Doody. I imagine their stuff is a helluva lot more interesting, like cheating on their wives and ripping off stuff from work."

"Jesus. If I hadda bring my confession to Rabbi Schiff, I'd shit to my shoes. And you say the priest can't tell who's doing the confessing?"

"How can he tell? He can't see you. You're in the dark, for Chrissakes, separated by a screen."

"You don't say," said Doody Levine, and stroked his chin diabolically. And when I walked into St. Ukelele's that Saturday, my Hebrew friend was with me, dipping his fingers into the holy water and making a sign of the cross just like me. Father Gillipede, our then very young priest right out of the seminary, had been doing the 2–5 shift now for months. His still-wet-behind-the-ears befuddlement suited what we had in mind exactly. We found an empty pew a few rows from the confessional and waited, mentally going over the identical performance we were about to give. But first Doody had to get the lay of the land.

"So where's this boy-wonder priest of yours already?"

"He's in there—right behind that door."

"How can you tell?"

"See the red light over the door? That means he's inside."

"Gotcha. And the green light over the curtain on the left?"

"That means somebody's in there baring his soul. The light's rigged up to the kneeling pad. When they get up, the light goes off, fair game for the next sinner in line."

"How come nobody's in the one on the right side?"

"Don't worry, one of these gloms'll make a move any second. See? There goes Floydie's old man. You're supposed to stay here and pray awhile til you're right with God."

"We don't have to take a number or anything?"

"Jeezis, Doody, cantcha can it? I'm nervous enough as it is."

Funny, *Doody's* religion didn't interest me at all. I had my hands full with this one—I wasn't about to add to my chores. I remember having to go to Doody's bar mitzvah, an unending marathon of worship and bad singing every bit as boring as ours. And they made you wear a beanie. I rank beanies right up there with johnnies, if you know what I mean. Beanies, johnnies, jammies—there are things you just don't wear.

We moved up to the front pew so we'd be in good position to move. Just as Floydie's father came out, Doody got ready to take his place, with the understanding that I'd get the next one. As he rose from kneeling, Doody whispered, "I hope Cardinal Cushing's got a commode in there, 'cause he's gonna shit." You'd think Doody'd be satisfied just to *be* in the confessional, to recite the lines I taught him, to confess a couple sins, receive his penance and get the hell out of there. But no, Doody wanted to confess something lurid, something shocking enough to make young Gillipede think he had some real sin on the other side of the screen, something to stop him in his tracks, make him question his faith. He'd rehearsed this whole bit about these fantasies he had about nuns, how he can't get them out of his head, how all day long he has these visions about nun after nun hiking up their habits, parading to-and-fro in fishnet stockings, swinging rosary beads, singing "Real Big Spender" as they plop themselves down in his lap. Then I was to confess something in a similar vein, and before Gillipede realized he'd been had, we'd be halfway to Caddigan Park. The light went off in the left confessional, some fat lady came out of it, and I took her place.

In darkness I knelt. My heart was pounding as I waited. What if Father Gillipede can tell right away it's a put-on and gets mad? The panel separating me from him was closed, of course, to prevent me from listening to Doody's confession—something I would have given anything to hear—but *bang*, just like that it flew open, and I was on. *"F-forgive-me-Father-for-I-have-sinned—it's-been-seven-days-since-my-last-confession"* I mechanically began, and then launched into my prearranged soliloquy. But here's what I didn't know: Floydie's father, before vacating his booth, had laid down a terrifying fart, one whose fumes were thick and gooey and strong enough to attack your nervous system. Doody came out gagging for his life. Never did he kneel. When I got to the part about Mother Superior, Sister Mary Josephine, and Agnes Munn the church organist, I was on my own.

Deathly silence. I don't know what I expected, come to think about it, but I knew silence wasn't it. *Bang* crashed my window, a *terrible* bang, and I knew when the door flew open and *blammed* shut, rattling the entire confessional, that it hadn't been Father Gillipede at all—and I felt Monsignor Burke's wrathful, icy grip on my arm, a split second before I saw his white, ignited face, and he yanked me right through the curtain. Doody was still there kneeling in the pew, his eyes wide and wet as I was led away—Sacco taking his last long look at Vanzetti. The blood in my arm was cut off like a tourniquet as I was whisked out the back door, across the courtyard and up the dark staircase to Monsignor's office in the rectory, where the Inquisition would soon begin.

• • •

And now it begins again. There's no escaping it. Twenty-three years old, cowering in a hospital toilet, my brother in the next stall over, while Pope Innocent IV sniffed outside our doors. Something about the shoes, though, as I peeked again through the crack. They seemed small, boxy and small, a good deal squatter than Monsignor's size sixteens. In fact, now that I looked again, the distance between the tail of his black coat and the cuffs of his black trousers was about a half mile shorter than what you'd expect from Monsignor. And then, as he washed his hands in the sink, he spoke: "So, how you fellas doin'?" It was Gillipede.

"Hi, Father," I stammered, reaching for my pants.

"'lo, Father," mumbled Gully.

"Your sister told me where I'd find you. Are you actually doing anything in there or has it simply become your temporary home?"

"Well, one of us is probably legit," said Gully, unlocking the door to his stall. I followed him out a few seconds later.

"Well," said Father Gillipede, drying his hands with a brown towel. "How long has it been?"

"A lotta years, I guess," one of us figured, glancing at our shoes, the urinals, the stalls, anything but him.

"Tell me," he said, looking at me, "Can you actually get a comb through that mop?"

"I gave up trying, Father," I said. "But I can get Ma's brushes to work on a good day."

"Look at this," he said, whipping a comb out of his back pocket and taking two quick swipes through his rapidly balding scalp. "I could comb my hair with a house key. Drives me crazy. My boss is old enough to be my grandfather and he's got a mane like a polar bear. I commit the sin of envy almost every day."

When my brother and I laughed, he knew he had us.

"So, I understand you had some recent dealings with the boss;

something to do with hanging him out to dry at the widow Walsh's house?"

We basically just nodded.

"I'm sure you've got a perfectly good explanation as to how things went wrong," said Father Gillipede, leaning against the sink.

"We were forced to improvise," said Gully. "It sorta got away from us."

"I know how that can happen," said Father, glancing at his watch. He then looked off into space for a while, apparently thinking that we'd be impelled to fill the void by blurting out the details of the whole sordid tale right down to Worms Faulkner's prize-winning ounce of cannabis. But all we did was look into the same blank fluorescent space, not uttering a solitary word.

"Fellas, I wonder if you could do something for me," said Father. "I've got a couple people to visit, including someone over in Roslindale, and my little Rambler ain't rolling so good in all this snow. How'd you feel about chauffeuring me there in that big heavy Econoline of yours?"

"Jeez, Father, we'd love to," I said, "but our mother is, well, she hasn't got very long and . . ."

"I know, son, you want to be with her when she goes. Don't worry, she's got more time than you think. We'll be back in a couple of hours."

"What about the van?" said my brother. "We're like public enemy number one."

"Pish-posh. Who do you think's gonna get in your way with *me* riding gun? I've got a direct line to God. Let's go."

We stuck our heads into Ma's room for a minute, nodded to Dee Dee, and were back outside in broad daylight revving up the old beast for another run at immortality. Father Gillipede said he'd be happy to pay for gas at Spid's and also to spring for hot dogs and onion rings at Simco's in Mattapan Square. And he was all for crank-ing the radio, asking us if we had any Springsteen on tape. He wore his black hat in an unfortunate way, like Michael in *The Godfather*, and it made him look far more middle-aged than he was. "I know," he said, "but I hate the peach fuzz underneath it even more."

Father Gillipede had a tough time when he first came to Saint Uke's, but won everyone over with his judicious use of the word *shit*. He was put in charge of the teenage boys, reffing basketball games and the like, and they pretty much walked all over him. He'd make announcements about where kids were supposed to meet for the paper drive and he'd have to shout above the din—nobody paid any attention to him. Until, pissed off that a couple of his charges had been seen urinating into the flower urns in front of the church, he bellowed in the gym: "I'm sick and tired of this *shit!*" and had a cap-tive audience for life. He never even got in trouble for it. No one told.

"So what about heaven?" asked Gully from the couch, as we pulled the van out from beneath the tree and rolled out to the street like we belonged there.

"What about it?" said Father Gillipede.

"Is it real? The pearly gates, the wings, the harps, the sandals?"

"I guess we'll all find out when we get there."

"C'mon, Father, this is your stock and trade—is there a heaven and hell, or not?"

"It all comes down to faith, doesn't it? The substance of things hoped for, the evidence of things not seen."

"Okay, Mr. Evasive, do *you* have faith?"

"On most days, Gully. On some days, it's stronger than you can imagine."

"So you believe that when you die, you'll go to heaven and hang out with the Twelve Apostles and see all your old friends?"

"Yes," said Father. "Something like that. Sure."

"Okay, now we're getting somewhere. Now say I got a wife,

right—beautiful, blond, pure as the driven snow. Except she get her-self killed by some drunk driver on some lonely road in the middle of nowhere and I'm depressed and forlorn for years."

"Pure as the driven snow—I would be too."

"Okay, except many years later I fall in love with a redhead and we live to be old and gray. Now we're in heaven. Who am I with for all eternity—the redhead or the blonde?"

"Well, the redhead's old and gray, right? I think I'd go with the blonde. I mean, pure as the driven snow?"

"Oh, for Chrissakes, Father, you know exactly what I mean! Ma's gonna be reunited with Dad, right? What if Dad had one of them mortal sins on his soul that he hid all those years and he's actually in hell? Who does Ma see about that? And are they gonna be old and wrinkly or will they be like newlyweds on a cake? And do you eat nothing but Lynwood Pizza or do they make you eat *heaven* food?"

"'These are they which come out of great tribulation, and have washed their robes and made them white in the blood of the Lamb. Therefore are they before the throne of God, and serve Him day and night in his temple—and He that sitteth on the throne shall dwell among them. They shall hunger no more, neither thirst any more; nei-ther shall the sun light on them, nor any heat. For the Lamb which is in the midst of the throne shall feed them, and shall lead them unto living fountains of waters—and God shall wipe away all tears from their eyes.'"

"Uh-huh," said my brother.

"'And I saw heaven opened, and behold a white horse—and he that sat upon him was called Faithful and True, and in righteousness he doth judge and make war. His eyes were as a flame of fire, and on his head were many crowns, and he had a name written that no man knew, but he himself. And he was clothed with a vesture dipped in blood—and his name is called The Word of God.'"

"Well I'm glad to see they've got drugs up there, Father," said Gully. "If there weren't any drugs, I'd be staying right the fuck here."

• • •

Climbing the hill up Legion Highway was about the most ridiculous mission we'd been on yet; it was easy to see why Father had no faith in his little sedan. I also was confused as to why he wanted to go to Rozzie in the first place. It couldn't be to see anyone from *our* parish.

"She's an old college chum of my mother's," he explained. "Shut-in. I promised Mom I'd look in on her."

Funny, I thought I remembered a sermon Father gave at Dad's funeral where he talked about the day his mother died and how she died peacefully, with a smile tracing her lips, because she knew she was on her way to meet Jesus. Maybe I had that wrong, maybe it was some other priest, but I could've sworn it was Gillipede. I remember his voice cracking when he got to the part about his mother being too sick to see him serve his first Mass, but how he *did* get to serve her Communion, right there in her hospital bed, and how it was one of the finest moments in his life and how any doubts he ever had about his own faith disappeared the moment she passed. I didn't know if the story was a crock or if the story he was shelling out now was a crock, but my own faith, which had been solid as Gibraltar moments before, was now being rocked to its very core. "Hang a right before the light," said Father Gillipede.

And I said, "Sure, Father, whatever you say."

It was an apartment building, four stories high with an outside stairwell. A cigar-smoking lady in a pickup truck was halfway through plowing out the parking lot; most of the tenants were sitting in their cars in the street waiting for her to finish. The ones that weren't would wake up to find their cars even more buried under snow than they already were. "Sit tight, fellas, I'll be back in ten," said Father Gillipede, who skipped and glided across the street like Gene Kelly, trotted round the back of the building and climbed three flights, which was pretty tough going since the steps hadn't been shoveled all that great.

"Christ," said Gully, "I haven't spent this much time with clergy since Catechism."

"Who made me? God made me. Where is God? God is Everywhere."

"Good. We'll probably be picking *his* ass up next."

I noticed that one of the people waiting for the plow jockey to finish, a black guy in a beat-up yellow Gremlin, was smoking, and it was obviously not nicotine.

"Pant, drool," said my brother.

"Wanna ask him if he can spare any?"

"Nah. Walking up to some strange car and rapping on the window—number one, the poor fuck'll probably shit; number two, it's too desperate a move, too junkie-need-a-fix-or-he-die-right-here-in-street-like."

There is nothing more impeccable than my brother's logic. Which is why, when he spotted the phone booth on the other side of the apartment house, between what appeared to be a liquor store and a boarded-up gas station, it all made perfect sense for one of us to crawl over the mountains of snow with fistfuls of change in his pocket and put in a call to Worms Faulkner to see if there was still any chance of scoring his mythical bag of grass. "I'll go," volunteered Gully, borrowing my non-bloodied smock to keep warm.

"White Punks on Dope" was pulsing out of the speakers as Gully scampered (yes, *scampered)* on all fours, across the ten-foot ridge of hardened snow that was still in the process of being created. He was nearly dislodged as the plow slammed hard into its side, Gully hanging on by his fingertips, right below the dwelling Father Gillipede was visiting. He continued on his way and jumped down, his destination no longer visible, hidden by the ever-increasing height of the plow queen's leavings.

One by one, the tenants jockeyed their cars back into the parking lot; a couple of them, including the dope-fiend in the Gremlin, emptied their ashtrays into the snow before heading back inside. I entertained thoughts of combing through the debris after they were out of sight, but that would have crossed the line into *extreme* desperation and, besides, Gully had my coat. I saw his hands first, then his head, as he climbed back onto the ridge, which was higher now than before and even more precarious. He did the Flying Wallenda routine as he made his way back, wingspanning his arms for balance, carefully choosing each step. Stopping to catch his breath, he gazed up to see Father Gillipede—now pretty much level to his own position—in the open doorway of a brown-haired woman's apartment, engaged in a sort of eyes-closed embrace, their foreheads joined in a how-can-anything-so-wrong-feel-so-right moment of intimacy.

"I know he saw me," said Gully, stomping the snow off his feet as he tried to slap himself warm on the couch, "I know right fucking well he saw me." He was just starting in on Worms Faulkner's phone-slamming bitch of a wife when Father Gillipede climbed back in the van.

He gave Gully a real good long look as we pulled away, and he looked at me for a while too. Father Gillipede tossed his hat up on the dash, ran his hand threw his tuft of hair, rolled his tongue around in his mouth, gnashed his teeth and nodded his head up and down in time with the music, which seemed eerily mute. Then he gently turned down the stereo and cleared his throat.

"I'm leaving the priesthood. There. I said it out loud. I thought you should know."

Neither one of us knew what to say, so one of us, I'm not sure who, asked, "You in love, Father?"

He nodded. "Mary. Her name's Mary. Mary O'Brien from Holyoke, Mass. Went by the name of Sister Johanna."

"She's a nun?" asked Gully.

"Regular riot, isn't it?" laughed Father into his coat, as he leaned back in the seat. "The homecoming king and queen."

"She leaving the nunhood?"

"Yeah, sure. Of course. I mean, she already has. Almost a year now."

"Monsignor know about all this?"

"Oh, God no. Nobody knows, really. Only a close friend from the seminary and my brother Tommy. I've written a letter to the bishop, put a stamp on it and everything, but I haven't quite worked up the garbanzos to put it in the mailbox. I guess I just did, didn't I—I mean, spilling it to you and all. I'll try to tell Monsignor tonight. I've been trying to catch him in one of his kind and mellow moments, but he only has about one of those a month and I think I missed the last one."

This was the absolute closest we'd ever been to running our own confessional booth. My brother *had* to ask the obvious: "Have you, y'know, had, shall we say, *relations* with this girl, Father?"

The priest laughed, "Mary? No. No. Ha-ha-ha! We're saving ourselves for matrimony. Ain't that a kick?"

"Have *you* ever done the ol' down 'n dirty? I mean, with *anyone*? You can tell us, Father. We're all friends here."

"Ha! No, 'fraid not, Gully. Sorry to disappoint you. I'm, as they say, chaste as a newborn babe. So is Mary."

"Are you *suuuure*, Father?" teased Gully.

He sat up straight and leaned into both of us. "Y'know, guys, I'll take an awful lot of shit from you—you know that. But that's the end of it right now, clear?"

"Sorry, Father," we both said, feeling about this small.

"She's just a great kid, that's all."

"But the priesthood, Father?" I said. "You can just give it up? Just like that?"

"No, it's killing me. But I can't serve God and remain celibate. Not anymore."

"How come they don't change the rules and let you guys marry?" said Gully. "These Vatican accords they have all the goddam time—this shit never comes up?"

"Of course it comes up. But celibacy is not some inconvenience that gets in the way every time you catch a whiff of perfume. Celibacy is the knowing sacrifice you make when you're called to serve God. I've got nothing against celibacy, and I'm not resigning the priesthood so I can '*get a little*.' I've given my life to God and I'll continue to glorify him by devoting my life to Mary."

"What'll you do for work?" I asked. "Arm wrestle sinners in the Eire Pub?"

"We're gonna join the Peace Corps for a couple of years and then maybe open a bookstore on the Cape. The more I talk to you guys, the more I hear myself say it, the more certain it becomes."

"You shoulda come to us earlier," I said. "You'd have eight kids by now."

There was a disturbance at the intersection up ahead. Cops and everything. A small car had somehow worked its way onto a ten-foot pile of snow, its back wheels still spinning. Evidence quickly showed that it had been forced up there by a city plow. You could see the gash the blade had taken out of its side, and the bewildered expression on the old plow guy's face, as he took off his hat, ran his hands through his gray hair and tried to explain to one of the cops how the hell the whole thing happened, how he had the thing in reverse and how this guy came outta nowhere and tried to swerve around him just as he shifted forward. The doors to an ambulance were wide open as they tried to pull the unfortunate driver out the other side of the car.

"I think I'd better get out," said Father Gillipede, donning his hat.

"Can you hold that thought for just a sec, Father?" I said, spotting Prick LaPinza on his way over to the van. "We got trouble."

"Well, well," smiled the officer with teeth you could smell. "This day is getting better by the motherfucking minute! Thrashing the piss outta you two cocksuckers is gonna be better than a three-day stint with a Mexican whore!" His massive right hand was on his nightstick as he ordered us to step down from the van and lie face-down in the fucking street.

Father Gillipede leaned over. "Sorry, Officer LaPinza, there must be some mistake. The lads are with me."

"Jesus, Father! Saints forgive me—I didn't see you there!"

"That's quite all right, Officer. Now, tell me, do you need me out there?"

"Uh, yeah, Father, y'might wanna take a look at this guy. He's in pretty bad shape."

"How'd it happen?" I asked, as Father got out.

"Well, near as we can figure," said Prick, talking to me like a regular person, "the idiot tried to go around the plow as Tony was blade-down into his push. Ol' Tony's all broken up about it. I don't think he can drive." As he walked back to the wreck, he must have realized what he'd just done, and turned back and glared with great and seething malice.

"Nice fella, that Prick," said my brother, reaching for the radio.

"Helluva guy," I said. "We should invite him over some night to watch sitcoms."

As Prick did his surliest best to redirect what little traffic there was on the street, a well-dressed blonde in a beige coat and fashionable boots came up to him and started what appeared to be an argument, in very hushed tones. Holding her hand was a little boy about eight or nine.

"Who's the dish?" said my brother.

"Her? That's his wife, numbnuts. That's Mrs. Prick."

"Prick LaPinza is married to *that?*" said Gully, climbing in the front seat to get a better look. "How is it *possible?*"

"You're telling me you don't remember Ellen? Ellen Pagano? They've been together since they were kids. She was the head cheerleader when he was playing ball. Ellen Pagano, for Chrissakes!"

"I was like twelve when Prick LaPinza played football. I wasn't exactly glued-in to his career."

Ellen turned finally and stormed away from her husband, the little kid struggling to keep up as she pounded through the slush to her car, which had a FAHNS REALTY sign on the door. The paramedics loaded the accident victim into the meat wagon; Father Gillipede had a quick word with Prick before coming back over and getting back in. "He alive?" said Gully, rolling back onto the couch.

"Yeah, but barely," said Father. "I started giving him the last rites, but this old guy, his father, I think, came running up and said, 'Get the hell outta here, ya goddamn vulture!' So I did."

Prick shot me another look as we drove away. "Take a good look at that face, Father," I said. "You give up being a priest, you ain't gonna be able to call off the dogs like you did today. He'll be kicking your civilian ass like he was ready to kick ours."

"I know," said Father Gillipede, placing his hat back on the dash. "Don't think I don't know. We'll probably have a lot of trouble with cops, Mary and I, seeing as how our lifestyle will mostly consist of tooling round town in our shitbox van, smoking hash, and raising hell."

I said "ouch."

"So, Father," said Gully, "as you look back on your life as a cleric, what was your finest moment?"

"That's easy, Gully," said Father. "On the day after I was ordained, I got to drive the Cardinal back to Boston. His driver was called away on a family emergency, as I recall, so straws were drawn and I got the job. Didn't say two words, the Cardinal. Just sat in the back of the Caddy and read papers. And then we got a flat. Out on some back road in the middle of nowhere. I'd never changed a tire in my life. I grew up in the north side of Philly—we didn't even *own* a car. The Cardinal stood out there in the cold and told me what to do, talked me through it, in a soft voice, how to loosen the lug nuts while the tire's still touching the ground, how to keep the nuts in the hubcap so you don't lose 'em. A guy in a pickup came by and offered to help, but the Cardinal said, 'Bless you, son, but we've got things under control,' and waved him off. He thought it was important that I learn this skill. Afterwards, he had me stop at this little sub shop for lunch. We ate in the car and yakked the rest of the way. I never had a better day."

"What about the worst moment?" ventured my brother, knowing instinctively how to kill a vibe.

"I guess that would have to be giving last rites to Grady Gerfalts," frowned Father Gillipede. "I knew the minute I saw him he wouldn't make it. Too much blood. And his poor mother, God rest her soul, clinging to my arm and wailing, *wailing*. I *knew* the kid too. Great kid. Saw him play football a dozen times. Tight end—must've caught ten passes a game. He was a teammate of your friend LaPinza back there. You know what got to me most? His hands. They were the tiniest hands I have ever seen. Like a child's hands. It nearly broke my heart to hold them, cold and lifeless, as I prayed over him. How he ever caught all those passes with those tiny little hands I'll never understand." Father looked at his own hands ruefully, as if somehow they'd failed him at a crucial time.

I wanted to say something sympathetic so I offered, "They never caught the bastards that did it, did they?"

The haunted priest looked at me as if he hadn't fully heard what I'd said, but then just shook his head and said, "No. No, John, they never did."

Then Gully chimed in with, "I heard they grilled every black kid from here to Grove Hall and came up with zilch."

"That's about right," said Father, "but I never thought much of the investigation. I always thought they went in the wrong direction."

"Whattya mean?" said Gully. "That the killers weren't black?"

"All I ever heard, in the papers, on the radio, in the street, was that Grady was killed by some rivals on another team, some bad blood that had spilled over from the field. But I was on the sidelines both times we played the black schools. I don't recall any bad blood. It always made me wonder. Still does."

The mere mention of a conspiracy theory of any kind had me

licking my lips, but something else was unfolding at the next corner. A little girl, not more than ten or eleven, was flagging us down, pointing to something in the snow.

"If it's last rites she wants," said Gully, "lemme take a crack at it, Father. Just gimme yer hat and coat—you can stay in here and keep warm."

Father didn't say anything, but gave my brother the same look he'd given both of us earlier. Even *I* gave him the look. The girl was in anguish as we pulled up.

"*My dog!*" she shrieked. "*My dog!*"—her hand gripping the handle of a red leash that led to *what?* A gigantic pile of *snow?* "H-he was just sitting there, taking a *pee!* And then the *thing* came and I said *stop! stop! stop!* but he didn't *hear* me and Toby got all covered *up!*"

The *thing*, a beeping, yellow front-loader, was already scooping up snow a block away as if it had a brain of its own, no conscience, and no oblivious city worker in its cab. Father got down on one knee and tried to quiet the girl: "There, there. Now, are you saying that your little doggie is under all that snow?"

"*Yes!*" Her nose touching his, her arms outstretched. "*Yes! Yes! YES!*"

"Okay, fellas," he turned. "We got work to do." But my brother and I were already on the job, scraping and boring like Rodents of the High Country. Somehow sensing that a shovel would prove pretty handy about now, Father Gillipede dashed into the nearby drugstore and borrowed one from the druggist, which led to the druggist himself throwing on a coat to see what all the commotion was, which led to two or three pedestrians and a couple motorists getting out to look, and, before we knew it, we had a good-sized crowd. Naturally, we literally threw ourselves into the work, immersing our bodies completely in the snow, shovel be damned. They cheered when Gully mentioned he felt a leg, and a few of them reached in and helped out when I mentioned I felt another one.

"Okay, on three!" directed Gully. "A one, a two, a *three!*" and out through the snowy birthing canal came Toby, frozen solid and apparently dead.

Everyone looked at the carcass (a basset hound I think) and everybody looked at the poor sobbing girl, who fell to her knees in despair. Father knelt down and began brushing the snow off the dog; me and Gully and some other guy joined in, rubbing the animal, hoping to revive it with the miracle of heat. Nothing. We all stood up, scratching our heads; some of the crowd began to disperse. Father put his arm around the girl and asked her where she lived. Gully nudged the dog with his foot—sort of what he did to Pelo earlier—and Toby came suddenly alive, springing up on all fours, shaking the snow off like crazy. You could see his partially frozen tail wag as the girl fell all over him and kissed his face, which wore a panting expression of: "Okay, that was fun, now where do I shit?" The remaining audience members applauded, giving Father Gillipede most of the credit, of course, but a couple did shake my hand and someone slapped Gully on the back, and the little girl and her dopey dog were heading home into the hazy afternoon sun, as we—we three brothers in Christ—sped through plowed streets, windows rolled down, waving at random citizenry like Lindbergh at Paris.

It's weird how you drive down familiar roads and recognize half the people, even though you haven't seen some of them in years. One of the people who waved back I recognized as Lumpy Ribek, an old classmate, whose picture I once drew for all to see with big lumps coming out of his head. (That ill-fated book-report cover that gained me all that notoriety in fifth grade, led to a lot of poster work in years to come—I was very popular during class elections—and that led to the plum assignment of caricaturing the members of the school's hockey team for the winter-spring yearbook. Being a junior high yearbook, it wasn't much—just a lot of Xeroxed pages held together with stapling pins—but it was the talk of the hallways, and most of the talk was about the hockey players, who were delighted with the project, taking turns peeking over my shoulder as I worked on the creations in the cafeteria during study hall. For a minute I felt like one of them, like a jock. Everyone loved the little details I threw in and the liberties I took—like rendering Iggy Preston toothless and giving Buddy Cortez cauliflower ears. But for the team's star, league-leading goal scorer Oatsy O'Carroll, I pulled it all out. Being in the middle of all the action and one who poo-poohed the idea of masks, Oatsy's face was often marked up by the sticks and pucks that routinely met it, so I drew it that way and then some, condensing an entire medical history into one cartoon, covering every inch of his face with stitches, bandages, scars, and axes to his skull. All agreed it was the masterpiece of the series and people began counting days to the yearbook's release.

Oatsy O'Carroll's mother was a guidance counselor in the school, which meant, like other staff members, that she got an advance copy of the yearbook. To say she was displeased doesn't come near it. It took the principal and three department heads to calm her down, and an unholy stink was raised. She made them substitute a photograph of her son, which held up the yearbook's release a whole week. It looked ridiculous. There were the other hockey players with the crazed bloodshot faces I'd given them and here was Oatsy, strikingly handsome, as if he were posing for a trophy. Oatsy felt bad about it, embarrassed about the way it set him apart from his teammates, and everyone else felt bad about it because the drawings looked really stupid now, and some people blamed me for the whole thing instead of Mrs. O, which made me feel worse than all of them, causing me to lose a great deal of interest in art. From then on, doodling in my notebook was all that occupied my time. I turned them down when they bothered me with requests. I wasn't about to end up like Ma. Hell with 'em.)

• • •

We dropped Father Gillipede at the corner by the rectory. As he stepped down into the snow, Gully wasted no time reclaiming his rightful seat up front and already had one foot on the dash. The soon-to-be ex-priest pushed the door closed, made sure it was tight, put his hand on Gully's arm and said, "Boys, I thank you, as does Mary, my love."

"So, Father," said Gully, "If I should suddenly take up an interest in reading in the next ten years, and I find myself down the Cape, and I decide to look you and the better half up—can I still call you Father?"

Gillipede laughed. "Do you remember that story from Luke, where the twelve-year old Jesus spends the day in the temple, fielding question after question from the doctors? I wish you two could've been there to ask some of those questions. That, I would've liked to have seen."

"We mighta stumped the little whippersnapper," said Gully.

He laughed again. "Anyway, my name is Larry. You can call me that. Just don't call me Centipede, which is what they called me in grade school."

I leaned across. "Your name is Larry?"

"Larry Gillipede?" grinned my brother.

"Yup. Larry P. Gillipede from Philadelphia, Pee-ay." He nodded, tipped his hat and pushed away from the van, looking for a second just as young as he did when he first walked into St.Uke's.

"Good luck, Father," we said simultaneously, and left him on the curb. Gully turned up the radio. It was *"God Save The Queen."* Gully cranked it.

I suddenly, as is often the case, needed a shithouse bad. No time to hunt for someplace comfy, either—the future was now.

"So go back to the rectory and pound on the door," Gully suggested.

"Oh, yeah," I groaned, "Forgive me, Father, but get outa the way."

So I pulled over near a dug-out fire hydrant and ducked into an alley. The alley had a lot of snow piled up at the entrance, but once you climbed over it and got in between the buildings, the snow was nary a dusting. In fact, at the spot where I ended up dropping my drawers, the ground was completely bare, as if you crossed a time zone and stepped into another clime. No wind or nothing. I love crapping in peace. And I love thinking while I'm crapping. I didn't get very far into thinking this time, though, because as I lifted my head and let my eyes run up the wall, I saw a body (if I'm lying I'm dying) hanging right above me from a pole. I almost swallowed my tongue. Then I saw that the body wasn't an actual body, but one hung in effigy, and that it was supposed to be Judge Garrity. I could tell because he wore glasses like Judge Garrity's and because the white paint on the front of his gray suit said: *Judg Garity*. I'd heard they hung Judge Garrity in effigy a lot but this was the first one I actually saw. His order to integrate the schools by busing did not go over well and he was blamed for all that followed, including the toothless, white drunks who tried to tip over buses with black kids inside. Since little of it affected cozy Morton, I never gave it much thought. But I remember Dad thinking about it, years ago, *before* Garrity got famous. I remember him raving all the time about the punks on Boston's school board who paid for their elections by keeping everything white. He knew all the loudmouthed Southie pols too. "If these bums could get away with it, they'd bring back the slaves," said a disgusted Dad one night at the TV "The damn courts'll have no choice." I looked at Dad for a minute. There was something going on with Dad that you just didn't see in anyone else, and I don't mean the times he went homicidal on the truck. We were working with him one night, a very hot night—it had hit 100 that day. Ward got heat-stroke chasing squirrels at the golf course so I had to take his place on Dad's runs and we had to take Gully too because we couldn't very well leave him alone at G & Son. Dad dictated as he drove and we counted out *Globe*s and *Herald*s between stops and readied bundles. But the side door was latched wide open and the cool, delicious air swept over our faces and Dad let us dangle our legs over the side, something Ma would never have to know about. The gray street passed below, fast and flickery, like the TV screen when 38 goes off the air. The rest of the town sweltered. You could practically hear them toss and turn as tiny circular fans whirred in every window. I sat facing the back, Gully the front, shock absorbers taking everything the road had to offer, world rushing by. The truck looked so alive from this vantage. No one else had a ride like the panel truck and no one else rode in it at three o'clock in the morning with windows and doors wide open. The truck panels looked white as bone, immortal, like it was running on its own, like it would run forever.

Then, in the shadows by a tree I saw a black man and woman struggling and I saw him throw her to the ground. "Didja see that?" I said to Gully, who hadn't. The truck then did a complete U-ey and Dad rolled up close to the guy. I had to strain to see anything now that the action was on the other side. The guy glared at Dad but said nothing. His shirttail was out and he was breathing heavy. The lady was just getting up and pretty mad. The guy glared at Dad again. "This ain't got nothing to do with you, man."

And Dad said, "Go home."

The lady had gotten to her feet and was looking for her pocketbook and was missing a shoe. The guy looked at Dad again. "You don't know what's going on here, Jimbo, it ain't none of your business."

Dad said, "Go home."

The guy started shaking his head and put his hands on his hips. "Jimbo, I'm telling you for the last time, stay out of it, it ain't got nothing to do with you."

"And I'm telling you to cool off and go home before the cops come." Dad held out his cigarettes, but the guy waved them off.

"Yeah, Jimbo? And what am I supposed to do with her? Yeah, I'm talking about *you*, you bitch!"

"I'll get her a ride," said Dad, "You just head thataway and keep walking." About two minutes later, he shrugged and did just that, disappearing round the corner by the light. Dad offered the lady a ride but she'd hear none of it and grabbed her shoes and took off into the park. I watched Dad as he held his half-empty coffee cup in his teeth and turned the truck around. This was his world, the streets at night, and I caught a glimpse of it. While the rest all slept and heard drums, he was out there, talking and smoking with those the rest only heard about. And we all just picked up where we left off, dictating and counting, the soothing breeze at our chests. Next to sleeping with Dally, it was my favorite night.

"What'd you fall asleep out there?" said Gully, when I finally came back to the van.

"No, I simply came across Judge Garrity hanging in effigy, that's all." And, with Melvin and the Bluenotes throbbing from the speakers front and back, I aimed my big, muscular machine for the open road and let it do the rest.

Two songs later, we were pulling up to the longest light in greater Boston, the four-way at the corner of Mallard and Tread. You could grow a beard. There wasn't anybody around except some guy in a delivery truck trying to back into an alley, and I thought about just punching the light, but rescuing dogs with Father had put me in a righteous and law-abiding mood, so I stayed put and waited. The delivery truck couldn't make it—too much snow piled up against the alley's walls. Disgusted, the driver got out, threw open the cargo doors like he wished they'd blow away and started angrily piling boxes onto a hand truck, knowing he was destined to have just as hard a time pulling the load over the curb behind him. This, we knew, could easily have been us, had certain fates conspired.

"Did you ever think what it woulda been like?" I asked Gully as we watched.

"What what woulda been like?"

"If Dad had lived long enough for us to take over. What do you think it'd be like?"

"You mean like if we ran the whole thing?"

"Yeah—Gullivan and Gullivan Distrib."

"Jesus." My brother ran his fingers through his hair. "Newspapers. Refresh my memory—they come out every day, right?"

"Right as rain. Seven days a week."

"And they come out really early, right, like three, four in the morning?"

"Pre-dawn, baby. And again in the afternoon."

"Waking up every day while the whole rest of the world's asleep?"

"Day in, day out."

"Well, Dad's still alive, right? In what would you call it—semire-tirement?"

"Well, he'd get us out of bed, if that's what you're driving at, but it'd be our gig."

"Uh-huh. And how long do you think it'd be before the schedule interfered with our life and we leave one afternoon with Ward Belvoir in charge? Or maybe drag Red Rand outa the cellar in a pinch? For Chrissakes, we'd run it to ruin in about a week."

"Yeah, but suppose we got handed it—dontcha think there's a chance we mighta got responsible? That we woulda been forced to step up after all?"

"Well, hypothetically—"

"And there's two of us," I continued. "Imagine if we kicked ass. If we got so ambitious that we branched out—into Boston proper, into Revere, the North Shore."

"You mean, like with guys under us? Like employees?"

"Employees? Managers, even."

"I love it! Hey you, yer fired! Hey you, leaning against the water-cooler with your head up your ass—yer fired! Clean out yer locker and screw!"

"In one door and out the fucking other."

"Know what I'd do?" said Gully, "I'd hire all black guys. Nobody else hires the sonuvabitches—I'd hire 'em all. My entire workforce—nothing but brothers."

"What about Doody? Certainly we'd have a position for him?"

"Depends on his references. Of course, we'd have to be assured he could coexist with all his darker-skinned colleagues."

The guy with the crates was just getting over the nutty he took after losing his load in the snow, and had just piled the last crate back on his hand truck when a door opened behind him and hit him in the head. The last and final straw. He was still kicking things and throwing things as the light finally changed. Dad's similar temper came to mind as we drove by, and dogs who barked all night.

"Y'know," I said, "we probably woulda been good at it."

"Probably."

"Imagine coming home with a big wad of cash and throwing it right on the table for Ma."

My brother let out a little laugh and took his foot off the dash. "You're talking a whole lot about fate here, my friend, a whole fucking boatload about fate." He reached for the volume knob and turned it up. The Ramones were doing "Rockaway Beach" but I wasn't really listening.

Because that's what bothers me most, I guess. Fate. I'm about fed up to here with fate.

Now needing a place to piss (my bladder runs neck and neck with my digestive system in terms of inconvenience) I pulled the van over and trudged behind Weaver's Cut Flowers at the foot of the bridge, commemorated always as the birthplace of Puff.

Commemorated also as the place of my first actual job, this after-school thing Dad arranged with Mr. Weaver to keep me out of trouble since I flunked out of sports. Gully joined me back there, writing *"Gina Loves Gully"* in the snow, for which he also provided narration. The shop was out of business now and the greenhouse was all boarded up. It seems funny, but there was a time when I thought the floral trade would be my life's path. I loved the fragrance of the place as I swept stems off the floor and I couldn't get enough of the greenhouse and its warmth. Olaf, the old guy who ran the greenhouse, I could have done without. The brown teeth, the spittle on his grizzled white face that held age and disappointment like cave moss, the way he barked out orders like the Captain in *The Katzenjammer Kids*: "Get der hoses und vater der goddamn begonias den pick oudt der pests from der geraniums!"

And picking out der pests was the part that could make you reconsider everything—the pests being slugs the size of prunes who clung to the walls of the clay pots like bloodsucking fiends from hell. You were supposed to pry them loose with your *fingers*, for God's sake, then destroy them by tossing them into a small pail of lime. Now, even if they didn't bite—and Olaf assured me they didn't—the very *look* of them filled you with dread. To attempt to *touch* their squishy, secreting, eelish-like hides was unthinkable. Holding a small spade at arm's length, I'd try to scrape-scrape-scrape the monster to the lip of the pot, then flip it onto the slate floor to stomp the Holy Christ out of it with the heel of my Hush Puppy boot. Sometimes I'd inadvertently flip a slug into another plant and have to start the whole unpleasant business all over again. On a good day, I could rid the premises of an easy six or seven, woeful enough to get demoted to the delivery truck, where I was put under the wing of this doofus named Dale, who was five years out of high school, wore one of those little-kid hats with the earflaps and scratched his head nonstop like he had the mange. Also his nose ran, his gums showed when he yelled things out the window to every female we passed, and he called *me* Slick. "Women," he was fond of saying, "Can't live with 'em, can't bury 'em in a shallow grave and expect to get away with it, right, Slick?"

And here I stood, all these years later, at the age of twenty-three, pissing behind the same greenhouse I used to piss behind every day when I was fourteen. I felt like I hadn't been anywhere at all, like I'd been stuck knee-deep in the snow here forever. The Ramones were still playing when I got back in the van. Joey's age when he founded the band? Twenty-three.

The doctors said Ma wouldn't last the night and a family vigil was maintained. Gully and I were supposed to be at the hospital around suppertime to take over for Madgie and Cassie but got there a hair late, finding it necessary to load up at Flynn's with supplies for the long haul: Fifteen comic books, a *Mad* magazine, *Boston Phoenix*, two sacks of Wise potato chips, three liters of Pepsi, one pink and one white Snowball, a chess-checkers-backgammon combo and two psychedelic-colored yoyos. Madgie jumped up when she saw us and hugged me for a very long time as a machine next to Ma's bed murmured.

"Oh Johnny, it's so awful," she wept. "It's just so *awful.*"

"I know," I whispered, gritting my teeth so hard to ward off any tears, they ached. I peeked at Gully, who was hugging Cass. *He* was gritting too, you could tell. It was like a private cry between brothers—almost *liberating,* if not for the pulled muscles. (Don't ask me where we get this stuff, unless it's from never having seen Dad, Granddad, Uncle Joe, Uncle Tim or Uncle Tut cry once, in all the years we knew them.) The girls reminded us Dee Dee would be back at midnight to relieve us, and left. My brother and I settled in.

The reason the quacks were so sure this would be the end for Ma was because they'd sealed the deal earlier with a morphine drip, a heart-wrenching procedure Dee had signed off on, and Ma had been in a coma all day. Her jaw was stuck half open and little whoops and yelps emitted from her mouth at the rate of five or six a minute. Her remarkable blue eyes, wide open and frozen still, seemed almost to be pleading—but not the way you think. More like *reasoning*. More like the time she was summoned to the rectory in her blue scarf and curlers to pick up her eldest son, who'd been detained there by Monsignor Burke for something he'd said in the confessional, something to do with his having erotic dreams about every nun in the parish. Ma sighed, leaned across the Monsignor's vast oaken desk and quietly implored, "He makes things up, he makes things up, God help me Father, he makes things up."

I sat down next to Ma's bed and touched her sad bald head. She'd been referring to herself lately as "Mr. Clean" and even acted out scenes from the commercials featuring the chrome-domed dynamo. Her energy level, up until her recent downslide, had been almost scary. She even got up and helped Gina Sookey with the laundry. I was right there eating Cocoa Puffs when she turned to Gina and whispered, "You be good to my son, Gina," and went back to bed, leaving Gina with the most surprised expression I'd ever seen. And Ma got downright wise with the doctor who called wondering why she missed one of her chemotherapy sessions: "I've decided to save it for something useful," she told him. "Like declogging the bathroom sink of hair. It is very good with hair."

I felt bad about the wig. It was not an attractive wig, completely not Ma's color, and somebody said it was previously owned. Her real hair, up until she got sick, wasn't much to look at either, though, sort of a tight little perm that stood still when she moved. But if I concentrate really hard I can remember the hair she wore when we were little, how long and flowing it was, long and brown and blond and flowing. And I see her behind the wheel of the panel truck, the wind just catching the blondish lock above her eyebrow. And it must be Shoe Day because the only time Ma drove the panel truck was on Shoe Day, the last weekend in August, hauling us to Maloof's to get shoes for school. And it was breezy, one of those breezy, willowy summer days that you hated to waste on something like Shoe Day. Our plan had been to sleep til three and were dismayed to be rousted at noon.

The guy who measured our feet was named Rudy, according to his name tag, and we had him hopping pretty good, ol' Rudy, bringing out box after box. He had black hair with a gallon of Wildroot in it and I stared at the mass of it as he tied yet another pair of clunky brown things on my feet. There were a couple guys at school who wore Dingo boots and I drooled at the Dingo boot display when we got there. But I knew I wasn't coming home with Dingo boots because Dingo boots made no sense. I was coming home with regular shoes. Brogans they were called. Ma made no distinction between old feet like Dad's and young, ready-to-rock feet like mine. Both would wear the same shoes—brown, tied, and sturdy. I asked Rudy if I could see something in a loafer, but Ma saw no sense in that either. "You'll have them one day, step in mud, and come home in socks. You'll get those."

Rudy started tying Dee Dee's new saddle shoes, but he was looking right up at Ma's blue eyes as he did. "Say, haven't I seen you at St. Euclid's?" he asked her.

"Probably," smiled Ma, who was trying to keep an eye on all of us.

"Yeah, you sit up front. I see you at Communion, we pass each other. I'm coming back, you're going up, ha, ha, ha, ha, ha."

"Well, I've probably got my head down," said Ma, being nice about not remembering him.

"Yeah, you sure do, but I don't," said Rudy, "I see you every week."

"Isn't that something," smiled Ma, who *knew* the guy was flirting. The only flirting I'd ever seen in real life was in Elvis movies, and *this* was flirting. I snuck a peek at Ma as I walked back and forth in my new clodhoppers. She looked almost pretty, like Eva Marie Saint, and you could tell she wouldn't let this guy lick her shoe, but she seemed to be getting a kick out of him just the same. He even made her giggle with a little crack about Monsignor. Ma—the object of *flirting?* I'd never imagined the like of it. But then, what about all the dates she had with Dad? He must have been flirting all over her. She probably flirted back. It was strange to think of it. She'd always been just Ma to me, and to Dad she was always just "Honey, I'm home." I never imagined Ma as anybody's girlfriend. Rudy put his hand on my shoulder and asked, "How they feel, champ? A little tight? Ahhh, they'll loosen up." Then he gave Ma a wink and hauled our many boxes to the register.

And look at her drive that truck on the way home. How small she looked in Dad's seat, way up high like that, trying to handle something so immense. But how confident she looked doing it, shoulders back, gripping the wheel with both hands, spinning it, spinning it— she could spin the wheel like the roulette guy at Casino Night, her blue eyes watching everything, clear and unafraid. And she honked the truck's horn if somebody dawdled at a green light—and the truck had a horn like the bark of a big dog, demanding that space be cleared. And when space did open, she took it, letting out the reins, allowing the van's big motor to gulp what was due it.

The clear blue eyes were all Ma had left now and they were as still as the rest of her as the hospital bed slowly claimed her. The little pips and yelps were still coming out of her, like they had been for hours, we'd been told, but it didn't take very long to get used to it, and hardly distracted us from our comic books at all. I almost died laughing at the Don Martin section in *Mad*. Gully broke into the Snowballs, devouring one in seconds, starting in on the other.

"Dontcha think you should pace yourself?" I said, "We could be here all night."

"You eat *your* Snowballs," he chewed, "I'll eat mine."

Suddenly, just as I reached for the chips, Ma's breathing seemed to change. The series of yelps became fainter . . . and fewer . . . and I started . . . counting . . . and . . . counting . . . and . . . counting. I looked at my brother and he looked at me and we both dropped our papers and went close to Ma's discolored cheeks. A barely audible breath. A moment later, another. Another moment. And nothing. Nothing. *Nothing*.

"What do you think?" said Gully.

"I think—*fuck!*" I said.

"I think one of us should go tell the nurse," said Gully.

"I'll go," I said, and I went and did it, real adult-like. Then I decided to call my sisters, who were all staying at the house. And I did that too. "She's gone," I steadily announced, as if I'd done everything possible to save her. My voice was deeper too; the situation seemed to call for it. But I still felt just like me. Is it possible that that's all maturity is? Speaking better? Is it possible that everybody in the world—the monsignor and president included—is just a dumb, stupid kid acting like a grown-up because they can sound like one and look like one? It almost seems easy.

The nurses were very quick and efficient, shutting down machines, yanking out this and that, arranging everything just so. Before they left, one of them gently touched two fingers to Ma's eyelids and closed them. Just like that. And we were alone. Standing over our mother, each of us holding a hand.

"Didja see that?" whispered Gully. "She just closed Ma's eyes with her fingers."

"Yeah," I said. "I always thought that was just something Doc Adams did on TV."

"If I'd known it was *that* easy," said my brother, "I woulda done it myself when we *got* here."

That, of course, triggered things. And then the Gullivan brothers, at their dear mother's deathbed, in the dim, whistling stillness of the IC unit of Crawley Memorial Hospital, started laughing. Softly at first, then harder, then ridiculous. One of *those* laughs. A long, loud, secreting laugh from long ago. A *Sunday* laugh. The kind we used to do in church.

There are those who say—and Father Gillipede is among them—that when a good person dies, the body's spirit hovers around awhile before heading off to the afterlife. *Believe* it. I could feel Ma's eyes on the nape of my neck as I stood there and lost it. I could practically hear her tsk-tsk: "Look at them two birds, true to themselves to the very end." She was fighting off a smile too. You couldn't fool *me*.

15

The Red Skull

Orphaned. I couldn't speak for Gully but I felt heavier. Waking up for the first time parentless would take some getting used to. My bones seemed pulled-down and dense, worn-out from lugging this old body around for as long as they have. I felt suddenly *experienced*, as though I had wisdom to pass down to the next generation.

Some of that generation, sisters Madgie and Cassie, I could hear in the kitchen rattling about. The conversations we had last night after Gully and I got back from the hospital were indescribable. There we were, the five surviving Gullivans, sitting around the kitchen *talking*, for God's sake, like adults at some adult gathering. I'd known these people all my life but didn't know the first thing about them, it became painfully clear. Dee Dee had somehow managed to graduate college, Cassie broke her arm in a field hockey game last fall, and Madgie had some guy in a parked car expose himself to her while she was walking home from school and then had to get out of bed to give a description to the cops who came to Aunt Fran's house that night. How did we miss this stuff? What, no one can pick up a phone?

But I'm telling you, it felt good to be with them, good to lean against the washing machine and recall old times, good to talk about Ma. They did comment about the condition of the house, and how they had to do a lot of cleaning and a lot of laundry, and "How often does this Gina character come over, anyway?" They had to go out and buy food for the fridge, which was bereft of everything but two frozen pizzas, a pack of baloney, and a half-drunk liter of Pepsi. They had to buy cat food. But they did very little in the way of condemning, I thought. Dee Dee even praised us for moving the rabbits to the cellar: "I'll admit, I was expecting to find them frozen solid under a tomb of snow, but, imagine that—you came through for them. You saved their little lives."

"Aw, shucks," said my brother, who could've been tempted to tell all about our heroic rescue of Toby the basset hound, but didn't. Instead we looked our sisters square in the eye like equals and reminisced far into the night. Using grown-up-type voices. And words we'd only seen in print. They all slept in their old rooms, which meant that I'd have to put on pants to pee.

I peeked out the window before turning in. A plow was going by, quickly and easily, putting the finishing touches on Mallard Ave. There'd be lots of half-wits with radials out on the road tomorrow, I knew for a fact. I tossed and turned for a while, finally fell asleep, and had a dream about Kevin White, the mayor of Boston. Yes, the usual spawns from hell chased me down alleys, and the face of the embalmed girl I saw at fourteen appeared like she always did—but never before had I dreamed of Kevin White. *My* mayor. So closely do you identify with Boston when you live in the bordering town that you think of *your* mayor as Kevin White. I was with him, as his driver, of course, and I was at his side as he traveled through the city solving problems the storm had caused. As *hail-a-fellow-well-met* as there was, shaking hands with everybody, slapping cops on the back, charisma oozing from every pore. If *I* slapped someone on the back they'd probably turn around and wonder why I was touching them. But Kevin White, he could make you run through brick walls. Remember when the Stones got arrested in Rhode Island and he single-handedly sprung 'em so they could play their gig at the Garden before the 15,000 fans there burned it down? Whose balls did he have to bust to pull *that* off? Our fair hamlet of Morton had selectmen, as I recall—three of them, I think—but I couldn't name one if you tortured me with fire ants.

"So, Johnny, my boy," Kevin White asked me in my dream, "How soon can you get us to Codman Square?"

And I said, "Faster than you can say Louise Day Hicks, your honor." And he laughed heartily as we sped away.

I woke up alone. Alone with Wild Bill Hickock and the rest of the silly cowboys shooting at each other on my wall. I had no idea what time it was but I heard a lot of activity downstairs and smelled some pretty good smells. I also heard one, maybe two voices I didn't recognize, and was trying to make them out when Gully came through the door.

"Okay, maybe you can explain it to me," he calmly began. "How is it that Worms Faulkner is married to that fucking bitch?"

"You got her again?" I said, reaching for my dungarees.

"I couldn't even get a *word* in. I clear my throat and she hangs up on me. We're gonna have to make a personal appearance."

"Sounds reasonable," I said. "Who's downstairs?"

"Uncle Tut just came over with a sponge cake and Aggie Ogden's making omelets."

"Yeah right," I said, "and Puff is playing with a little pink ball."

"I'm telling you. Aggie's wearing Ma's apron and she's making omelets. I just had one. Fucking delightful." He started counting tens and twenties on his dresser. "How much gas we got?"

"We're loaded," I said. "Father Gillipede filled it up, remember?"

"Sublime," said Gully. "By the way, I talked to Doody. He wants to go too."

"Sounds like our course is set," I said, pulling on a flannel shirt.

"Isn't it always?" said Gully, and I followed him downstairs. We were also going to the Crawley to see Dally, but I thought better about announcing it just yet.

Uncle Tut was holding court; Madgie and Cassie were getting quite the kick out of him as he demonstrated the little butt-wiggle Dad used to do before releasing a bowling ball. "Johnny me boy!" he cried when he saw me, giving me a big hug. "God, you don't put on an ounce, do you?" Aggie Ogden was cleaning up after breakfast and asked if she should put on another omelet.

"Sure," I said. "If it's not too much trouble." Dee Dee reached for the eggs, not troubled at all, it seemed, and cracked them for Aggie. Gully was back on the phone, whispering to Gina Sookey. Also in the house was Ellen (Pagano) LaPinza of Fahn's Realty, who was in the living room, on a stepladder, measuring the width of the drapes over the picture window. Her young son in boots was with her, scratching Puff's ears, unaware of the danger he was in.

Uncle Tut got up and motioned for me to join him out in the hall. "I heard what happened with Morton Cab," he said, in a low voice. "You're gonna need a job. Here." He slipped an address in my pocket with the name of a guy who ran this ball-bearing mill in Mattapan. "Good buddy of mine. Give you the shirt off his back. Get your arse down there by noon and the job'll be yours."

This was interesting. I hadn't seen Tut (who was not our real uncle, just an old bowling crony of Dad's) in what—five years? And he knows my entire employment history, right down to my last previous discharge? And he somehow *gives* a goddam? He was right, though, about my needing a job. I was down to about my last sawbuck. It was time.

"You got a jacket?" asked Uncle Tut, glancing down the hall toward the kitchen, some weird conspiratorial urgency in his voice.

"Excuse me?" I said.

"A jacket. A sport coat. Do you own a sport coat?"

"Uh, not that I'm aware of," I said, figuring that'd put an end to it.

"Jesus, Mary, and Joseph," sighed Tut, slapping himself in the forehead. "Come on, then—we'll trot upstairs and pick out one of your old man's!"

We've *had* jobs, my brother and me, plenty of them, but never anything with sick leave or Blue Cross/Blue Shield or three weeks' vacation after a year. For most jobs, we were hired out of sheer desperation: "When can you start?" they'd excitedly say, looking around for an apron or a smock or a pair of long rubber gloves.

"Uhh, tomorrow?" you might say.

"How 'bout today?" they'd insist, holding some stained garment up to your shoulders to see if it would fit. "Now go find Tommy in Waste."

But Tut's great lead would be the first job interview either one of us had ever been on that required you to show up in a jacket. The jacket we picked out, I must say, looked pretty snazzy. It was a dark blue corduroy number that I remembered Dad wearing at my confirmation. A little big in the shoulders but not grotesquely so. It would also solve the problem of what to wear at Ma's wake tomorrow night. Tut hugged everyone good-bye and left, his work here done. My two younger sisters left with him—something about meeting the guy at the funeral home to pick out Ma's casket. You could hear the traffic noise when they opened the door. Cars were out, all right. For God's sake, Uncle *Tut* was out.

Breakfast was amazing. Aggie's omelets were loaded with onions, peppers, and cheese, and there was this other delicacy filled with pineapples. Dee pitched in with homemade bread. It occurred to me that it may have been the first real breakfast I had eaten in this house.

Gully and I never got up in enough time to eat anything Ma had on the stove in her bacon, eggs, and oatmeal days, and we've been subsisting on Cap'n Crunch and strawberry-flavored Pop-Tarts ever since. I sipped my freshly brewed coffee, as Dee Dee, Aggie, and Ellen Pagano LaPinza buzzed around my head, standing on chairs, taking notes, measuring every inch of the place with a tape measure that shot rapidly back to your hand. Aggie operated it from her hip, like standard issue. Dee Dee waited until Gully was off the phone before getting down to the business end of the meal.

"How would you feel," Dee Dee began, "if Aggie and I moved in here?"

I tried not to gulp. "You mean move in, as in move in and live?" I said, seeking clarification.

"Yeah," said Dee, "And we'd bring in furniture from both Aggie's apartment and mine, and lay some new carpeting, maybe hang some pictures, fix the roof."

I looked at Aggie Ogden mostly, because I knew what Dee looked like, and then I looked at Dee. They were both smiling these little smiles. I could see, that with Ma gone, it was gonna be a lot easier to get kicked out of the house. The house we'd lived in all our lives and slept in fourteen hours a day. Dee Dee and Aggie, with Ellen LaPinza's help, had come up with this deal with the bank where they take over the mortgage payments and pick up where Ma left off. Seemed perfectly legal and cut and dry, I thought, as I glanced at the soon-to-be notarized document. Gully and I were wondering how all that financial stuff worked anyway, and, since we hadn't contributed dime one to the overall upkeep of the house to begin with, had no real desire to get involved now.

"And we want you both to know that you can stay here as long as you want," said Dee Dee, as she leaned forward reassuringly and touched us both on the arm, *"Years,* if it comes to that. This is your house and you'll always be welcome. Nothing's changed." I thought about that. It was tricky enough maintaining our lifestyle with Ma around, now she's back and there's two of her. And one of them's in law enforcement. No, everything is just like it was, all right.

"Which room would you sleep in?" I asked, *"Ma's?"* Just the idea of it, with saints and crucifixes looking down from all four walls, would shame anyone to repentance.

"We haven't really thought about it," said Dee, "We'll have to see where we are after the renovations." A major face-lift was in the offing, apparently, and our new landlords were anxious to get to it. Our bedroom held a prominent place on the list. Dee Dee asked if we could move our valuables and some nonessential furniture to the garage before we went out, so they could get in there and look around. Aggie pointed to some boxes we could use.

"I got a better idea," said Gully. "How 'bout me and John make our own arrangements and pick up the payments instead."

"Yeah," I said, "and you'd be welcome any time, Dee. You could even stay in your old room."

Our sister just smiled and nodded toward Ellen, who read aloud from a prospectus on the property, which made mention of various liens and judgments and Ma's payments being about ten months in arrears. I sort of remembered Ma on the phone with shysters in the last few months, and, though the tone *did* seem urgent at times, I never thought it was anything to get lathered about. The payments after refinancing, Ellen explained, would be set at $449.57 a month.

"I see," said Gully, who recently made a cool sixty bucks the week before last helping Floydie's father tear down some garage. I followed him upstairs.

Ellen Pagano LaPinza's son, who apparently followed Ellen everywhere she went, busied himself by going through some of the boxes of our prized belongings—mostly just stacks of Marvel comics and shoes and stuff—which had been set aside in the living room for further transport to the van; the garage being grossly unsuitable for such treasures. The kid, who we named Little Prick (without his knowledge, of course), seemed pretty *un*-Prick-like in his behavior. He was rugged enough and ruddy-faced, but very quiet and polite, and even asked an occasional question as we went by. "Wow!" he gasped, pointing to the dastardly villain on the cover of *Captain America*. "Who is *this* fiend?"

"That," I said, squatting down, "is none other than the Red Skull, the personification of Nazi evil, Satan in dark green."

"God," he said, "I've never seen anything like him. His eyes are like molten steel."

"He's scary all right," I said, taking the glossy gem from the kid's oddly undersized fingers to get a real nice look myself. Then I said something else, something completely unexpected: "How'd you like to keep this comic?"

"You mean it?" His eyes got wide.

"Yeah," I said, riding this new twinge of benevolence like a horse through a meadow. "You promise to take good care of it?"

"I'll treat it like a baby," he said, receiving it in his tiny doll-like hands and keeping it perfectly flat as he tucked it gently under his sweater.

My brother was not amused. "Am I hallucinating," he said, as we lugged a bookcase to the garage, "or did I not see you give one of our comic books to Little Prick?"

"Yes," I said weakly.

"And not just any comic book, mind you; not a random *Jughead* or, God forbid, a *Stumbo the Giant,* but a *Cap!* The Cap with the *Red Skull* on the cover. You went and gave Little Prick the *Captain America* with the Red Skull's sneering *face?*"

I nodded, beginning to realize the magnitude of my act.

"I thought I knew my brother," muttered Gully, as we jockeyed the bookcase into the corner by the old freezer, "but it turns out I have no brother at all." The rest of the comics went straight to the van and the mission was resumed.

• • •

We pulled up in front of Doody's a few minutes later, the picture-window color wheel in full flight. He had our long-lost tire iron in his fists. "Blind-assed plow jockey took out half the front lawn. Thing was sticking up in the air like an arrow."

"Now we are *fully* armed," said Gully, in his plotting-to-take-over-the-universe voice, twirling Pelo's knife as Doody threw himself onto the couch.

"Jesus, where did you get that thing?" said Doody. "Put it away, you crazy fuck, before we all end up with a glass eye."

"I'm a *baaaad* man!" said Gully, stabbing at the air.

"Yeah," said Doody, "all fruits and vegetables tremble at the mention of your name." And he made the sign of the Z, *swish-swish-swish,* which naturally lead to us lustily singing "*The Horseman Known as Zorro*" all the way to Crawley Hospital.

"Are we giving blood?" wondered Doody, as we pulled under the familiar facade.

"I'll be right out," I said, slamming the door behind me and bounding up the steps. I saw my reflection as I went in, the reflection that included the dark blue sport coat that used to be Dad's. No wonder all the gloms in the world wear these things, I said to myself, and strolled smoothly into the gift shop, where I saw my reflection again in the cooler where the cut flowers were kept.

"How much for one of these calla lilies?" I asked, reaching for my last ten.

"Eighty-nine cents," the old lady beamed, no doubt astonished that someone other than she knew what these things were called. "Shall I put in a sprig of baby's breath?"

"Please," I said, using another word that apparently came with the coat. The lady asked if I'd like to write something and I said sure and took down a little card, touched the pen to my lips for a second and then wrote: *I love the way you look in chalk, you raven-haired tomato.* The lady took it, put in its tiny envelope and stapled it to the rest of the wrap. I tucked it under my arm like Robert Mitchum and took the stairs two at a time.

Dally wasn't in her room. A nurse came in and told me that they had just taken her down for a bath. (Yes, I felt moles.) "How long will that take?" I asked.

"Oh, not more than half an hour," she said. "Can I find you a vase for the flowers?"

"Please," I said, my voice as deep as a city judge.

I was debating whether or not I should wait for her when I looked out the window and saw the van down below. I still had the Red Cross sign sticking to my door, plain as all day. "Shit!" I said, almost knocking down the nurse as she returned with the vase, and I ran all the way down.

"I can't believe I left this out here," I said, ripping off the cross and throwing it in the van as I jumped in.

"Jeez," said Gully. "Dontcha think it might come in handy?"

"Whatta we, gonna *call* attention to ourselves? Even the *Boston* cops are after us!"

"Christ, Johnny," said my brother, "two cruisers have gone by since we've been out here. They didn't seem interested at all."

"Yeah," Doody agreed. "Maybe your newest family member, the lady cop, took care of things. And, by the way, where's my other red cross?"

"It's back there somewhere," said Gully. "Maybe under the couch."

"Okay. And the armbands?"

"Jeez, Doody," said Gully, "whattya want—the *world?*"

The idea that Aggie *had* taken care of things was intriguing. To suddenly have connections at City Hall. The world at my feet. I tugged the lapels of my dark blue corduroy sport coat and aimed the van for the street. Right away, my brother was confused about the flight plan. "You're scaring me, John. This is not the way to Braintree, John. Talk to me, John."

"I have a stop to make in Mattapan," I said. "Uncle Tut set me up with a job."

"Now you're *really* scaring me."

Crossing the line into Boston was more punctuated than usual because of the difference in snow removal. Having deeper reserves of manpower and overtime pay, Morton's streets were pretty clear by this time, while Boston's looked like the only path had been made by motorists repeatedly driving over it. It was getting warmer, though, and things were starting to melt. Tut's ball-bearing mill was not far from the Neponset Bridge. I shook my head as we rolled up. Hopeless and bleak, it was one of those old, dark, dirty places you wouldn't ordinarily enter on a dare.

The employment office was on the second floor and I plodded my way up the grimy staircase, loudly questioning the need for a damn sport jacket. You had to talk to the lady through a hole in the glass, another development worth questioning. "Which position are you applying for?" she asked, as bored as an ungulate.

"Uh, I'm not sure," I said to the hole. "My uncle set it up."

"Who are you here to see?"

I took out the piece of paper. "Uh, I think it says Ed Steib."

She handed me a form. "Fill this out at the table and bring it back here."

Luckily, there were pencils at the table. There was also another guy, a salesman I think, all dressed up in a suit and tie, looking at a collection of newspaper ads on top of his briefcase. The monogram on his case said he worked for *Morton Sun,* which came out once a week and which I had never read. "Ahhh, these deadbeats'll never buy anything," he said, apparently to me. "I don't know why I bother coming here every week."

"Heh, heh," I said, and continued working on my application, which didn't take all that long, considering my checkered employment past. I brought the paper back to the lady behind the hole and went back to the table to await further instructions. There were other pieces of paper on the table, I noticed, so, not willing to let a perfectly good pencil go to waste, I began to draw. Naturally, penises came to mind, or breasts, but I controlled myself, what with the talkative guy in the suit right next to me, so I drew my character, this toothy, dumb-looking, bloodshot, bulbous-nosed, cross-eyed squirrel that I'd been drawing since I was about ten. I usually had him smoking a cigar or wielding a golf club or both, with a tail that looked like it had been through war.

"Man, that is some squirrel," said the briefcase guy, leaning over for a closer look.

"Heh, heh," I said, and gave the rodent sneakers, *Keds* actually, with about four inches of tread.

"Ha! Ha! Ha!" laughed the guy. "That is some funked-up fucking squirrel!"

Then the lady in the hole called me by my first name and told me to haul my application down the hall to the last door on the right. I left my squirrel on the table, cleared my throat, straightened my jacket, hiked up my pants and went in, noticing that the line on the form that asked: POSITION YOU ARE APPLYING FOR had been filled in: *Sweeper.* And the guy I was trying to dazzle with all my late father's finery hadn't a tooth in his head. Like *none.* I watched the lit cigarette protrude from his sock-puppet mouth, its long ash dangling like a charred Slinky, and as he chomped on it, it went up and down, up and down, from the top of his insipid face to the bottom, and he's asking *me* how I happened to get booted out of Morton Cab, and I'm explaining it to him, actually going into detail, trying to justify my words and actions to a guy who looks like a mammary gland.

"So, tell me why you want to work for us, Mr. uhhh, Gullivan," he said, with only one eye open because the other one was engulfed in a rising column of smoke—and I wanted to ask *him,* Like how do you lose *all* your teeth? I don't mean a couple incisors that *anyone* could lose by saying the wrong thing to some jiboney out in front of Pope's Pub—I mean every last *one* of them. Like somebody just reached in up to his elbow and hauled them all out in one motion like a spring-loaded bear trap. How is this *done?* And even though I could tell he was about to offer me this godforsaken position, I came right out with it. I actually *asked* him, and he snuffed what was left of his Lucky into his hubcap ashtray, flung my application onto this unhappy heap by the radiator, leaned back on the slats of his knotty pine swivel chair and proceeded to tell me about his *drinking* days, and the time he runs into this falling-down-drunk dentist in some hole-in-the-wall in Revere, and how they get to laughing, and how he happens to mention this toothache that he's had for like three years or something, and how the dentist's office is like a block and a half away, and how they laugh and laugh and take turns with the gas and get to be about as giddy as geese as each tooth is yanked out one by one by one like removing spent bullets from a machine-gunned man. He remembers coming to, in sticky puddles of his own gore, wishing he could shut his eyes and never wake up again—when he spots the ossified dentist at the foot of the chair and, enraged, begins beating the good doctor with his own tools. He managed to beat up a good part of the office too, before the cops came, and, though he did get a complete set of falsies out of the deal, when he wore them into work that first day back, somebody said he looked like Francis the Talking Mule and he never wore them again.

"So, like how do you chew your food?" I wondered.

"I manage," he said, and fired up another butt and looked at me through the haze for a long, uncomfortable minute until I got up and left.

"How'd it go?" asked Doody, as I climbed back in.

"Oh, they're gonna lemme know," I said.

"So, like, we could conceivably be on our way to Braintree now?" asked my brother.

"We very well could," I agreed.

"Praise the fucking Lord!" he exalted, and cranked some serious sound.

Some days you really feel like driving, if you know what I mean. This was one of those days. Even with the stereo full-blast, you could feel the slushy crunchiness underneath, the uncharted vastness of the lanes before you. Even with the Gang of Four jumping up and down through all five speakers, you could still hear Ma's voice telling you to wear your heavy coat, your green rubber boots, and be nice to people. The traffic was thin but more and more cars were venturing out, ridiculously high piles of snow still on their roofs. The drivers looked frightened, gloved hands gripping the steering wheels in strangulation. Not me. Index and middle finger, nothing more, nothing less. I had a good van under me, a good, old, been-through-it-all sonovabitch of a warhorse. I had trust.

Worms Faulkner lived in a pretty nice mustard-colored ranch house in the suburbs. It always struck me as a little out of place, what with all the neighbors cavorting about on their lawn tractors and their cranberry-hued golf pants. But Worms hired neighborhood lads to keep the hedges trimmed and the old guy across the street even waved at the endless procession of degenerates who darkened the Faulkners' door.

"Oh, Jesus," sighed Worms' wife when she saw it was us who rang the bell. "*Worms! WORMS! Ya got a coupla shitheads at the door, here—Take care of 'em!*"

"So you leave 'em right out on the steps? What the fuck is *wrong* with you?" You could see him coming down the aisle as we huddled on the porch. He was wearing shorts, as usual, his colossal tanning-booth belly protruding from his unbuttoned Hawaiian shirt, flip-flops on his hideous, toes-pointed-in-all-directions feet. "Christ Almighty, it's the Gullivan brothers and their rabbi Doody Levine! If I'da known you was coming, I woulda took a shit!"

"Hey, Wormo," I said, "what's happening?"

"What's *happening*? *Speed Racer*'s happening, my friends, followed by *Kimba the White fucking Lion!* Come in, come in, come in!" Shaking off the cold, we followed him downstairs to the TV, his pinch-faced wife glaring at us from the kitchen.

"So, to what do I owe this unexpected honor?" asked Worms Faulkner, falling fully onto the couch while the rest of us made do with the overturned crates and beach chairs that were scattered about the cellar.

"We were hoping you'd have some stuff?" said Gully.

"What—the Dominican? Fuck, that shit is long gone, my brothers. Weren't you supposed to be here day before yesterday?"

"We got sidetracked, Worms," I said. "So somebody else picked up the last ounce?"

"Somebody else? Hell, no—I smoked the fucking shit."

"You smoked it?" cried Doody. "All of it?"

"Every last crumb. We ain't fucking around here, boys. The Wormy One's gotta *maintain*." He got up to escort us out. "Look, I got some more shit coming in Wednesday. Gimme a ring."

When we got to the front door, Gully played the trump card: "Look, Worms, we're in a bad way here. Our mother just died."

Worms laughed out loud. Then he looked into Gully's eyes, then into mine, then back at Gully's. "Jesus! You ain't kidding! How the fuck did it happen—did she get hit by a plow?"

"No," I said. "She was sick, Wormo. Cancer."

"Cancer? That's some harsh shit, man. Had an uncle died of cancer. Sonuvabitch looked like a bag of fucking assholes when he died."

"So you can see how much we're hurting," my brother choked up. "Is there nothing you can do?"

Worms thought for a moment, running his hands through his long, stringy hair. "You wait here for a second." He went back downstairs.

His wife hollered down after him: *How long are these fucking jerks gonna be in my house, Worms?*

"Gimme a goddam break, Jeanette—their old lady just croaked! Cantcha show some respect for the fucking dead?"

Jeanette poked her head around the corner, saw us, muttered, "Sorry for your loss," and ducked back in the kitchen. Worms reappeared in the hall. He had a tiny white film canister in his hand.

"Okay, it ain't much," he said, pressing it into Gully's hand, "but it might getcha through the night." Gully reached for his wallet but Worms wouldn't hear of it. "Now get the fuck outta here before I start fucking bawling."

The old guy across the street was sanding his walk and stopped to wave at us as we climbed back in the van. "What'd we get?" I asked, turning the key.

"Looks like enough for a coupla bones," said my brother. "Now all we gotta do is stop somewhere for rolling papers."

Gully talked a little bit about Gina on the way back into town. She was into a lot of things, he said, things like religion and philosophy and reincarnation.

"You mean that shit where you don't die and go to heaven," Doody said. "You just come back as something else?"

"Yeah," said Gully. "Gina's convinced she's coming back as a bird."

"A bird would be nice," I said. "Flying all over the frigging place, swooping down to spear some food, eating it in the tree of your choice. Of course, with my luck, I'll come back as Phil the fucking canary and wind up in a cage with a mirror and half a foot of shit."

"What if you came back as a worm?" said Doody.

"No," said my brother. "What if you came back as a worm and you *knew* it?"

"You knew you were a worm?" I said.

"Yes."

"Jesus, you'd be *begging* the bird to eat you."

"You'd *dance* for the fucking thing."

And to think that we hadn't even broken into the stuff we got from Worms yet.

Just outside of town, Doody suggested we pull over at that 7-Eleven just before the rotary to buy the papers. "And I know for a fact they got Table Talk pies," he said. "*Cherry.*" I jammed on the directional and slid in in front of a fire hydrant. Gully stayed with the van while Doody and I went inside. Doody knew exactly where the pies were and grabbed two for each of us while I searched out some Pepsi. There were only a couple people in front of us in line and I could swear that the girl at the register—a toothsome, freckled redhead with a *Veronica* nameplate—was giving me the eye while she rang up somebody's Slim Jims. You could hear the manager's voice, coming from somewhere under the counter, giving her a hard time:

"Goddamit, Veronica, I've told you a thousand times about your personal stuff down here." A hairbrush appeared on the counter, then deodorant, then a mashed-up pack of Winstons, then Visine. The phone down the end of the counter rang; the manager got to his feet, scolding the girl to keep her stuff in a box out back where it belonged, and went to answer it.

"Jesus, Veronica," said Doody, who always struck up conversations with clerks, "you work for a real douchebag."

"Tell me about it," said Veronica, handing Doody his change but looking directly at me.

"Why don't you quit?" Doody continued. "Why don't you just shut down your register and tell him to stick his *ass* in a box out back?"

She leaned over to whisper, but it was *me* she was whispering at: "This is my last night, you wanna know the truth, only he don't know it. You see that ramp over there? I'm gonna be at the bottom of that ramp tomorrow morning at eleven o'clock, hitchiking my way to Cali*FUCKING*fornia. You guys wanna tag along, that's where I'll be."

"Damn, sugar," laughed Doody. "That's too early for me."

"Ain't that a shame," she lamented, batting her blue-tinged lashes practically in my face. "Ain't that a goddam shame."

This new phenomenon of women throwing themselves at me like I was Roger Moore was starting to make me wonder.

Meanwhile, Gully was up to his ass in cop. A real belligerent one, who tapped the van's bumper with his nightstick and gave Gully the signal to move on. Gully pointed at us inside the store. But the cop wasn't interested in anybody in the store—he was interested in Gully getting the van the fuck outta there right now. Gully rolled down the window to try to explain that the person who drives the van would be back in a matter of seconds, but not a syllable reached his lips.

"*Are you fucking DEAF?*" wondered the cop. "*Get this ugly-ass piece of shit OFF MY STREET!*" the last three words accentuated by his stick against Gully's door. Gully adjusted the rearview mirror and saw the terror of machinery in his own face. He then grabbed the wheel, gunned the motor, and, without even looking, screeched rubber and snow out to the center of the street.

I heard the first car hit and saw the second. The van went up on two tires and gracefully swayed there for an hour-like second, before crashing glassily to its side and skidding into the rotary like a refrigerator down a slope. Everyone ran to the wreck, some hollering encouraging things like: "*He's gotta be dead!*" or "*He DESERVES to be dead—didja SEE the crazy fuck?*"

The cop, a guy from one of the cars involved, and Doody and I started climbing up the van's axle, just in time to see the passenger-side window begin to unroll. Gully's dopey bloody face and shoulders emerged from it like the victorious commander of an armored tank division. He looked at the very nice crowd that had gathered, then drunkenly zeroed in on the cop that started it all, and said, "Well, how'd I do, fuckface? Everything off your street now nice and tidy?" And then he collapsed back down the hole.

Spid's wrecker arrived the same time as the ambulance. I jumped back there with Gully and watched them strap him in. He was out of it but breathing. One of the EMT guys told me that breathing was a good sign. (Imagine sharing something that technical with a civilian.) They wouldn't let Doody ride in the ambulance, so he figured he'd just mooch a ride from Spid. I looked through the back window as we pulled away, sirens blaring, and took one last gander at the Gullivan & Son panel truck, lying on its side, mortally wounded. It got smaller and smaller until it was just a toy, one of those little Tonka toys you always see over other kid's houses, just little crummy toys, lying there on the rug with the puzzle pieces and the army guys, wheels up in the air. I closed my eyes, just to get inside it one more time, and all I could hear was Ma's voice, telling me to get up because she needed to lie down and could I ride up front with Dad?

"Sure," I said, and even held open my sleeping bag for her to crawl into, then accidentally stepped on Madgie's head on my way to the front. She cried, but only for a minute, and I was riding with Dad.

"Well if it isn't John Cardinal O'Gullivan himself," said Dad. "Sleep well?"

"Not too," I said. "Got a song in my head that won't go away."

"That can happen," said Dad, snuffing out his cigarette. "Happened to me once. 'The Cauldron on the Moor.' Saw a witch do it in this Halloween play in the fourth grade at St. Catherine's. Scariest thing I ever saw or heard. Had that damn thing in my head for twenty-five years."

Dad pulled into some flea-bitten truckstop with gigantic neon signs. "Need anything?" he asked before climbing out, and I shook my head *no*. I glanced back to see my family, snoring away with their usual fits and starts, so tired from our long day at the World's Fair.

Ray Charles was singing "Georgia" on the faintly playing radio. Dad came back in and handed me a honey dip and a Styrofoam cup of coffee. "Four sugars, right?" he grinned, and I said thanks, unaware, til that very moment, that he knew I drank the stuff. We swung back onto the road.

"Pssst," whispered Dad, "watch this." He purposely turned off the headlights. We entered utter and total darkness. The temperature seemed to drop. No streetlights lit this forsaken stretch of highway, no neon signs, not another soul to be found. The only sense that you were moving at all came from the pavement rushing beneath. My heart pounded as I put down my coffee, my bulging eyes adjusting slowly to the blackness, making out tree lines as the road sucked us into its gaping maw.

"Whattya think?" asked Dad.

"It's exciting, but *scary*," I said. "Aren't you afraid you'll hit something?"

"Yeah, but if you really concentrate, you can see, *see?* You can't see very good, I'll give you that, but *look,* there's a fence . . . and here's a big tree . . . and I think that might be a stop sign coming up . . . yep . . . I think that might be a—"

"*Jim!*" cried Ma. "This is doing absolutely *nothing* for my peace of mind!"

"Whoops, sorry," said Dad, who quickly switched the lights back on, illuminating the entire landscape—and I hadn't realized til that exact minute that I'd been holding my breath the whole time.

Dad and I exchanged glances and chortled a little, sipping coffee in silence as the panel truck, sturdy and workmanlike when it wanted to be, transported us home.

The irony of it all, is that after Dad died and the van was ours, it ran like a dream. It was like a horse, I guess. You had to love it to make it run.

• • •

The blood that Gully had all over his body came from two little cuts on his head, it turned out, and he put up with the stitches and all the fuss about glass in his hair, and the splint they had to put on his two broken fingers and the wrap they wound round and round his damaged ribs. "I never knew you could turn a vehicle over and live to tell the tale," he hoarsely said, as they helped him into his bed. "I'll be damned if I know what I was afraid of all those years—driving is *tit*."

"Dee Dee says she'll swing by and get you in in time for the wake," I said. "That is, if they say you can go."

"They *got* no say," he said. "Van pretty much done for?"

"Dunner than shit," I said. "Looks like they're gonna total it."

"Damn. What about the shit inside? Have they issued a summons yet?"

"Doody took care of it. Spid let him go through it before he hauled it to the yard. Found your knife too, which he promptly tossed in the Neponset River."

"Tell him I'll fucking sue," said Gully. "What about the comics?"

I shook my head sadly. My brother then said nothing for a very long time, winding and unwinding part of the sheet round his thumb and forefinger. As I got up to find a bathroom, he quietly uttered, "I could be getting married."

"Married?" I said. "Married as in married with a wife?"

"Forget it. I don't wanna talk about it." He tried to roll over.

"You mean Gina? Gina Sookey?"

"No, ragnuts, I'm gonna marry Doody."

"Wow," I said. "And this is gonna happen soon?"

"I don't know," he shrugged. "I just thought it up tonight."

"So Gina has no idea?" I grinned.

"I wouldn't say *that*, exactly."

"Jesus," I said, "I didn't know you were so close. I thought she was just someone you humped in the van."

He rolled his eyes. "The van my ass. She has an apartment, John. She has two cats named Cobalt and Claudine and a mother named Antoinette. There's a shitload you don't know."

"I can see that. But Gina Sookey? This is the girl you wanna spend eternity with?"

"I don't know about no eternity," he said, "but she treats me good, Johnny—is that okay with you? You, of *all* the moony-eyed shitheads in the world?" He then grimaced in pain as he turned to the window and frowned.

"Somehow," I sensed, "you don't look ready to break out in song."

"Well, it's *sad,* for Chrissakes. Love, I mean. It's sadder than anything in the world, when you think of it. You let somebody into your life, whom you will eventually lose. Another cruel joke to savor. Why do we do it? Why do we let it in?"

"It comes with the species," I started to say, but Gina appeared in the doorway then, tears running down her face, crying, "Oh my *god!* You're all right! Oh, baby, they told me what happened—I thought you'd been *killed!*" She ran to him sobbing and held him tight, his taped-up fingers caressing her back, his face buried deep in her long auburn hair.

After several minutes of invisibility, I just said, "Seeya, kids," and went upstairs to find Dally. The nurse said they released her. There was someone else in her room.

So I took the elevator to the street, stepped outside, pulled up the collar of my sport coat and hailed a cab that was parked at the corner. I had never hailed a cab before. I had been the *hailee,* dozens of times, but never the hailer. It felt good back there, roomy and warm, and it made me feel older. Mature. Like you *should* feel if you were old enough not to have parents. I gave the driver all the bills in my wallet and had him drop me a block from the house, so I could get a little air before turning in. Also so I could stand outside Schoerner's for a few minutes hoping to detect some signs of life in the darkened windows. Nothing. My house was pretty dark and silent too. I crept through the back door, bent down and scratched Puff's ears for a few minutes, then gave her some milk. There was a note on the kitchen table in Dee Dee's handwriting. It said for me to call some guy named Higgins at the *Morton Sun*. I brushed my teeth in the upstairs bathroom and fell asleep hard, nightmares haunting every breath.

16

Squirrel

Poor Ma. Not poor *dead* Ma, because Ma was good and ready for death, she'd been dying so long. Poor Ma right now, stuck here at this wake. I tried not to look at her as I fulfilled my duty with my siblings in the receiving line. I couldn't look at her. There are three distinct images of Ma that find space in my head. The faintest is the young mother with the fleeting blond hair who helped me with homework and made blueberry pies. Then there's the dead mother with the skin-bald head and heavenly, mesmerizing eyes. And this Ma, the one in the casket, the one least like Ma than the rest. Sadly, it is the image of this Ma I will take to my grave. What did they do to her? What did they do to her face? They had her skin powdered up to the color of a clay pot and the corners of her mouth were drawn up in this macabre semblance of a smile. Do they learn this in embalming school? Do they need for us to think of the dead as being happy? Does that help us to get through it, knowing that our loved one is simply delighted to be in that box, tickled pink to be lying there in front of all the world's gawkers, her mouth twisted into a disturbing smirk? Why couldn't we just kiss Ma on her cold, blue forehead like we did in the hospital and bury her that night? Why must we put her through this?

"Mark my words," whispered my brother to the rest of us from his chair. "If any of you allow *me* to end up in that state, I shall come back and haunt you the rest of your days."

And that causes me to look at Ma again, and there it is, I have to start all over again. I have to strain myself now, as the picture of Ma steering the panel truck with the wind in her hair becomes weaker and fainter and less specific. The third Ma is winning out.

My brother did well in the chair. Because of his cracked ribs, he couldn't stand by the casket with his siblings—he got to sit. And everybody who showed up, I mean everybody, had heard about his terrible accident and wanted to know all about his brush with death. "You mean to say that the van was on its *side*? How ever did you make it out *alive*?" People promised to pray for him, I swear to God. With my sisters and me it was just: "Sorry, so sorry, so very sorry" right down the line. But Gully offered something they could touch; someone who had looked death right in the eye and was here to testify. It was as if the wake was for *him*. Even old man Schoerner had soothing words to impart to my brother. He didn't know anything about Dally, though. I asked him. He just shook his head and looked away.

Ward Belvoir showed up with his mother, who had to be ninety. They were both crying, and my sisters, especially Madgie, greeted them with heartfelt compassion, as if the Belvoirs themselves were there to be comforted. I was amazed how Madgie did it, how mature she looked when she took Ward's hand. Ward, for some reason, stopped crying when he got to me. He stood there snuffling for a few seconds, seeing something, he didn't know what, and some weird memory seemed to be formulating in his head: a naked guy, I'm sure, running away with Eddie's coat. Then Gully broke in with: "Ward, old buddy, howaya?" and I was saved.

People seemed to be having a good time; Uncle Tut was over in the corner demonstrating bowling strides to Gina Sookey, who must have turned and rolled her eyes at Gully fifteen times. Ma's old Sodality chums were cackling about the nativity scene Ma painted for the church one year with the two goats who looked just like Monsignor Burke. And then I spotted Doody at the door. He came in like Rodney Dangerfield. I could just make out what he muttered to the two old morose guys on the couch: "Jeez, fellas, who died?" Floydie was with him, wearing a plaid sport coat. Judging from the expressions on their faces, they had not waited to sample the wares in Worms Faulkner's film canister. The girls, who always liked Doody, were very happy to see him. He gave Madgie and Cassie big hugs, then went into a boxing stance before giving Dee Dee one too. Gully and I got the two-handed handshake bit and Floydie followed him right down the line with sorry-sorry-sorry-sorry. The clock on the wall said eight-fifteen. Forty-five minutes to go.

To relieve the boredom of shaking hands with all these strangers and near-strangers I looked at the flowers. There were tons of them, big showy arrangements, colors bursting. I have a kinship with flowers, I admit it, an *irrational* kinship, especially with funeral flowers. They way the glads and ferns swoon up to make this fiery backdrop for the roses, the orchids, the mums, who hold the epitome of sadness and sex in their slightly open lips as they slowly climax and die. But so hard did I lose myself in these particular flowers that another funeral home appeared to me, the *basement* of another funeral home to be specific, one I crept into when I was fourteen. And I saw myself being taken there, in Mr. Weaver's flower truck, riding up front with Doofus Dale, a full load of flowers behind us, whose ribbons said *Niece* or *Daughter* or *Merry* in gold script, a detail I paid little attention to at the time. I *do* remember trying to block out Dale's commentary about the women we'd see on the street or the ones in cars we'd regard from our high perch in the truck. "Jesus, lookit the pie tins on that one! Mama-lama, tittie and tape, I could rock her cradle right to the frigging *grave!*"

The previous day's *Herald* was on the floor of the truck and I snatched it up and tried to bury myself in the batting averages of the Red Sox but Dale called my attention to a story on the front page: TEEN TRAGEDY, which featured a photo of a mangled car, a bunch of tsk-tsking cops and three smiling yearbook pictures, one on top of another, a girl and two boys, all blond, all beaming with life, all cheapened—as only the Herald could do. The girl's name was Meredith Grimes. She was pretty and everything but you might not have noticed it if she hadn't been dead. Dead, she was unforgettably beautiful. A smile unlike any other, shrouded in mystery and sadness and fate.

"Quite the dish, ain't she, Slick?" said Dale.

"She's pretty all right," I said, not able to take my eyes off her.

"Pretty? What kinda word is that? That, my friend, is the finest piece of dead young fur you're ever gonna get near in your lifetime."

"Yeah, Doofus," I muttered, "you *wish* you could get near her."

But then his attention was turned to some hitchiking girls and he whinnied "man o man o man!" and pulled over to pick them up, saying, "Get in the back, Slick, and learn from the master." Except that one of the girls was actually a guy, and the one that wasn't sat up front, and they had a German shepherd too, and it jumped in the back and sniffed at my crotch, and Dale put the moves on the girl, dripping innuendo, and everyone else in the truck chortled, and by the time we dropped them off in front of Ashmont, the dog had lifted his leg and urinated in every single arrangement.

It was then I caught the name on one of the bouquets. In the flowing gold script that only Mr. Weaver could do, it said: *Merry*. And so did the one next to it. And I knew at once who Merry was and what had happened to her and where we were going. I moved back up front and studied her picture, my eyes returning again and again to the photo of the wreck, imagining her perfect hair and teeth in the middle of it. Her mother was quoted in the story. Her daughter had a smile that'd light up a room, she said, and that God must have had a reason to take her so soon.

And then we were there, pulling into the circular driveway of Roger P. Hempstreet & Sons. A series of little, solemnly-lettered signs directed us to the door around back marked *Floral Deliveries.* (Which, Dale let me in on, was always open.) We parked behind the hearses, grabbed two arrangements each, plunging our thumbs into the cold synthetic slush that prolonged the flowers' lives, and headed down the stairs. A plain white room off to the side was where you stuck them; we threw them in with the others and went to get more. But Dale, at the foot of the stairs, said, "You mind getting the rest, Slick? I gotta go find the undertaker guy and get a signature." He yanked a wrinkled piece of yellow paper out of his pocket to show me, then turned down the dark hallway and in through the swinging doors. Jesus, I said to myself, there's about twenty of them. But actually there were only ten—and a couple of them weren't even that big—and papier-mâché doesn't weigh much anyway. I was done in no time. I checked out some of the displays and compared them to ours. There was one in the corner that took Mr. Weaver to school. A large portrait of Virgin Mary, eyes heavenward, completely surrounded by orchids, like about eighty of them, each living in its own little tube of water. Had to cost an arm and a leg. The trouble with orchids, of course, is that they don't stay fresh very long. These were already turning brown underneath and would have to be touched up with spray paint to have any chance of making it to a second night. Only those of us in the trade pick up on such details.

I could only entertain myself for so long looking at flowers back *then* and I started to get a little antsy about the Doofus and where the hell he was. I poked my head around the corner and peered into the shadows. Then I stepped into the hallway. Then I looked at the swinging doors and wondered if I could see anything through the porthole-type windows. I couldn't. I pushed the door open a crack, and eased myself into the darkness, the door rolling off my fingers and back into place with nary a stir. My every step was slow, deliberate, moccasin-like silent. I could hear my heart. Light was spilling from a room across. I inched closer. There was a figure at the far end of it, hunched over a table. His back was to me, but I made out the bluish folds in his smock, the silver shine in his hair. The undertaker? Embalming somebody? But then he turned abruptly to something at his right and screamed, *"What the hell do you think you're doing? Who are you? What right do you have to be in here?"* And he charged from the table and out the side door.

I saw it all at once, the whole of life in a second of time. Her pastel skin, her tiny blue-gray breasts, her hair, her hair, her *hair*, and Dale's wild-eyed jackassed face flailing in my direction like a man on fire. I stepped aside, undetected, as the undertaker yelled after him, and I took one last look at Meredith Grimes, quietly, calmly, all by myself. And I felt neither shame nor arousal. Nor did I feel fourteen. I felt almost elderly. Like I was looking down from high up and miles away. For it wasn't a naked girl I was looking at, nor a dead girl, nor a famous dead girl whose picture was in the paper. It was like a Renaissance painting of a naked dead girl, more unreal than real, more immortal than alive. A naked dead girl who never decomposes, whose beauty never wanes. And though I was with her for only a moment, it was like I was meant to be there, which, I'm sure, makes no sense whatsoever. But I have never felt closer to any person since, alive or dead.

Then my sister Dee Dee nudged me and I realized that old Edgar Barntoy, the Combat Zone projectionist who lived down the street, was shaking my hand and offering condolences and going on and on about Ma, and I remembered where the hell I was.

But something was happening. Aunt Fran dashed in from the other room, shushing everyone up with: "The *Monsignor's* here! He just pulled *up!* He's here right *now!*"

Uncle Tut, who seemed to have knowledge of these things, came over to Ma's casket where me and my siblings were and moved us aside, as Monsignor Burke bounded in, his head down, escorted by no less than five Knights of Columbus, with swords and plumage and high black boots. The last one in was Father Gillipede, who held the Great Book open as Monsignor loudly read from it. Then he led us all in familiar prayers and implored the Lord our God to take this wonderful, brave, nurturing woman to His bosom. His oration voice was as barbed-wire horrific as ever, but he said some pretty nice things about Ma. He called her artistic talent a gift from God and said she never stopped giving it back. When he was finished, Tut gently pushed us back into place and the priests came down the line. Gully was first to receive them and I was second.

"Very sorry," said Monsignor, taking Gully's hand. "Peace be with you." He then did the exact same thing to me. That was it. We got more out of Floydie. Of course, when he got to Dee Dee, it was Paul's Letter to the Corinthians. He was delighted to see her, taking hold of both her arms. He congratulated her on college, thought it was wonderful she was keeping the house in the family, wanted to be sure she was in touch with her spirituality? Dee turned to me and shrugged, as he chatted amiably with the girls.

"Peace be with you," said Father Gillipede to both of us; then he winked and whispered, "I *told* him."

"What'd he *say?*" My mouth dropped open.

But Father just shook his head and winked again. Before he moved on to Dee Dee, he drew close to my ear and said, "He wants to see you outside."

I got a drink of water and went out through the side door. It had started to snow again, but it was a warm snow, falling wispily from the dark sky, settling on my corduroy forearms like feathers. I figured Gillipede had it wrong until a small black Buick by the mailbox flashed its headlights. I stuffed my hands in my pockets and walked over. He wants to talk to me? Fine, we'll talk. A fat guy with red hair got out of the driver's seat and went around to open the back door. Monsignor was sitting there like Al Capone and motioned me in. "Jeesh," I said to the fat guy, "you fellas ain't thinking of taking me for a *ride*, are ya?"

"Come in and sit down, John," said Monsignor, and I did, the guy closing the door behind me.

Monsignor rubbed his chin for a minute, quietly observing some of the mourners passing by, then said, "I understand that you and your old white truck have parted company?"

"The van? Yeah, Father, I guess you can say the van is no more."

"Pity. So many, many years it rolled. Fate is a curious thing, don't you find?"

"Heh, heh," I managed to say. I guess he was trying to imply that we defied fate by biffing His Holiness in the first place, thereby bringing the destruction of the van on ourselves.

"Y'know," I said, "my brother and I are really sorry for what happened at the Walsh lady's house. It wasn't supposed to go exactly that way."

"What was your *A* plan?" wondered Monsignor. "Having *me* crawl through the snow instead?"

"Well, no, but—"

"Never mind, John. What's done is done. I got another ride about ten minutes later and Audrey sliced me another piece of pie while I waited."

"Well, okay, but we're still really sorry and—"

"Tell me John," Monsignor stopped me with his hand, "do you *believe* in fate?"

"Me?" I squirmed. "Jeez, I dunno. I never really thought about it."

"Well, think about it. Do you believe things happen for a reason or do you think it's all just a series of random occurrences?"

"God, Father," I said. "I don't know what I believe. Maybe I don't believe in anything."

"What about God? Do you believe in God, John?"

"You mean the God who dragged my mother through hell for two and a half years before finally letting her die? Oh, yeah, Father, let me get down on my knees and exalt Him as we throw the dirt on her tomorrow." (This wasn't entirely factual; Ma wasn't exactly getting buried tomorrow—they were gonna store her body somewhere until spring thaw—but I was on a roll.)

The Monsignor laughed out loud. "My God, John Gullivan, you sound just like your father."

"Dad?" I said. "Whattya talking about? He never missed a Mass, or a confession or anything else."

"Going through the motions, lad, just going through the motions. Your father had no more faith in God than that mailbox out there."

I tried to recall some incident from my childhood to support this assertion, but, other than his habit of taking the Lord's name in vain two hundred times a day, came up with zilch. "He told *you* all this, Father? Like, he admitted it?"

"Oh, yes," smiled Monsignor. "Many, many times. I can't tell you how much I looked forward to his visits."

"But why would he go to such lengths to pretend? He manned the collection basket, for God's sake! He knew the Gospels like the back of his hand."

"All of it done for you, lad. You and your siblings. It was frightening to him that his lack of faith would be passed down to you. He knew that his way, going through life with no faith at all, was a terrible way to live. So he played a little make-believe, if you will, in the hope that his progeny would believe for real."

"Great. And I suppose my mother was a heathen too."

"Your mother?" Monsignor chuckled. "Son, your mother had more faith in her little finger than the three shepherd girls of Fatima."

"And this gets her what, exactly? A hideous death? Lemme get this straight: Ma believes with all her heart, Dad fakes it, both die like dogs. Gosh, Father, which path should I take?"

Monsignor chuckled again. "My God, you even have his voice. I could swear dear old Jimbo was sitting here right now."

"Don't worry, Father," I said, "he ain't here. That's the other thing too. He ain't up there either, is he? Ma thinks she's going up to have corned beef and cabbage with him tonight and he ain't gonna be there, is he?"

"I'll tell you, John," said Monsignor, touching my knee. "When I get up there in a couple of years and find out that Jim Gullivan's not amongst the angels, I'm going to have some strong words to say to somebody, I'll tell you that right now." I saw the fat guy toss his cigarette and look at his watch. Monsignor took my hand. "Pray with me now, won't you John?"

"Uh, okay," I mumbled. He must have sensed that I only knew about three prayers by heart, because he picked one, the Our Father, and he squeezed my hand tighter and tighter as we repeated our little duet three times through. Then he signaled to his driver to get back in and I reached for the handle. "One thing's for certain," I said, climbing out. "There ain't no way *I'm* gonna see no gates of heaven."

"Don't be so sure," said Monsignor. "The God I know has no intention of casting you into the fire. Not for anything you've done up to this point." He nodded to the fat guy and his small black car sped away.

In its place, standing in the middle of the street with a suitcase in each hand, was Dally Schoerner. She said, "Hey."

"Hey," I said back, and she dropped the bags and came to me, holding me warm and intimate as she buried her nose in my neck.

"Are you taking a trip?" I finally asked.

She nodded. "I'm going back to school tomorrow. Taking the Greyhound."

"Do you want to go inside and see Ma?" I asked, seeing that the funeral home was pretty much emptying out.

"Is it an open casket?"

"It is."

"Then I think I'll pass," she said. "I don't much care for the wax museum thing, you know? I'll pay my respects at the funeral tomorrow."

My sisters came down the steps then and Madgie and Cassie practically shrieked when they saw Dally. They were hugging and kissing her before they even got to her, so excited they were. She tickled them just like the old days and they all danced up and down in almost biblical jubilation. Dee Dee suggested we pick up a couple pizzas at Lynwood and all go back to the house. Doody said he'd grab some beers and volunteered Floydie's car for the run.

It was a nice night. Everybody present had at least one good story to tell, several I had never heard before. When it was over, Floydie and Doody went home, the girls went to bed, Gully picked up the phone and stretched the cord all the way to the pantry so he could have privacy cooing to Gina, and Dally and I were left to ourselves in the kitchen, with logistical problems to solve.

Dally couldn't go home, that was out of the question, but she couldn't exactly sleep with me up in my bedroom either, not with my brother snoring five feet away. Even if Gully agreed to sleep on the couch, I was pretty sure I didn't want Dally to see our room with its socks and squalor anyway. *She,* of course, could sleep on the couch, but that would leave me pining up in my bedroom like a caged caribou. Getting a room was suggested, but that would involve transportation, of which there was a decided shortage at the moment. So we grabbed heavy coats, boots, and a few odds and ends and set out walking. Singing and walking. Singing and walking all the way to Ruslan D. Loneberry Elementary, where we ended up climbing through the selfsame window as before.

"Are you sure we should be doing this?" said a suddenly nervous Dally, as I kicked in the thin piece of plywood that had been temporarily nailed there to plug up our original hole.

"Hell," I said, "it's not like we're gonna steal anything. Besides, we're taxpayers, aren't we?" This last comment seemed to quiet all fears, even though I hadn't consciously paid a tax in my life.

An hour or so later, sent on a mission to find tea, I ended up in the principal's office, which, like just about every door in the place, was unlocked. Naturally, I put my feet up on the desk. The nameplate that got kicked to the floor in the process said MR. STEVENS. (I don't know what ever happened to Mr. Lucinda. Croaked, most likely.) To my great delight, I found that by flipping a couple of switches on Mr. Stevens' console and fiddling a little with dials, you could make 'BCN come in over the P.A. system. I kept it on low, which is generally against my religion, but I didn't want to attract the attention of anyone out on the street as I loped down darkened corridors, miming the stormy chord progression to "Seasons of Wither," my imaginary Fender slunk low to the ground.

I found the tea in a cabinet in the faculty lounge. *Lipton.* Earl Douche or whatever it was I was sent for was preferred, but they didn't have any. Then I *made* the tea, strange as that sounds, standing over the stove in the dark pouring hot water, still moving to Aerosmith as I plop-plopped the tea bags in. (Tasting this stuff—that would be another first.) I put both cups on a brown lunchroom tray with a jar of sugar, a little bowl of cream, and spoons. I thought it best at this point to shut off the stereo, but hummed something wicked as I walked, keeping myself company on the long hike back, the linoleum feeling invigorating on my socked feet. EXIT signs lit the way.

"How was the shower?" I asked, setting the tray on the nurse's desk.

"Marvelous!" said Dally, drying her hair with a green plushy towel. "Just like you described it. Say! Take a peek in the bedroom and see what I found!"

I could see the TV's blue glow from right where I stood. "Where'd you find it?"

"I wheeled it in from one of the classrooms down the hall. We only get one channel, though. It's the late, late show."

"What's playing?" I asked.

"Hombre," she said. "I believe he gets killed in the end."

I pushed a small table into the room and put the tea on it. We had a very nice bed. We'd taken two of those leather benches the nurse lets you crap out on when you're nauseous, stuck them together in one room, harvested the pillows from all three rooms and threw two old sleeping bags from home on top. There'd been some planning on this caper, boy; Dally almost died when I came up with the condom, helping me put it on and everything. Afterwards, we glided out to the corridor, in bathrobes I also brought from home, and looked at the moonlit snow in the courtyard. I wanted to tell her I loved her, like they do in stories, but I was afraid she'd just smile back. Then I'd be a fool for life. Later, when we were watching TV in bed, I almost said it again. Luckily, Paul Newman was on the screen for inspiration. Paul Newman doesn't say much. Never do you see what makes him tick. He just looks away. Checks his weapons. Grunts. You can't *pry* it out of him. Paul Newman is the way to go.

"I can't believe you have to go back to *schoool,*" I pouted, in the dinkiest voice that ever came out of a mouth. Paul Newman gave me a disdainful glance and looked away.

Dally smiled. "They're giving me ultimatums, Johnny. I gotta go back." She took a swig of tea. "And *I* can't believe we're burying your mother tomorrow."

I must have been making the saddest face imaginable, because she said, "Awww, honey," and snuggled up real close, put her head right on my chest. She *had* to feel my pain. Losing my mother and my girlfriend in one fell swoop. Could I survive it? Then she said it: "You will of course, come to visit me."

"Of course," I muttered, minimally. "How does that work?"

"Well, sleeping with me at my place would be out," she thought. "I have roommate issues. We'd have to improvise."

"That could be interesting," I said.

"I mean, nothing *this* lavish," she said, with a sweep of her hand.

"That goes without saying," I said. What I wanted to say was: *I love you, I love you, I LOVE you! I don't want you to go! I want to kiss you and kiss you and kiss you, and caress your feet at night! I want to wake up every morning smelling your hair!* But how could I say such things? Ask her to give up her life's goals and stay here in Morton with me? What the hell did I have to offer? What did I have to make her even *think* of giving up everything's she's worked for since St. Ukelele's?

"I got a job," I said.

She lifted her head. "Really?"

"Yeah. Some editor guy down at the paper wants to print this squirrel I drew. Right on the front page."

"Make me understand," said Dally, excited but confused.

"They're gonna have the squirrel holding up a sign that says: TWENTY-FIVE WEEKS TO TRICENTENNIAL BASH; then next week the sign'll say TWENTY-FOUR WEEKS and so on, right down to the big bash itself. Did you know Morton was three hundred years old? I sure as hell didn't."

"They're gonna pay you for this?"

"Damn straight. They're gonna give me ten bucks a week for as long as it runs."

"Wow, Johnny, them tens is gonna add up quick!"

"Tell me about it. And I don't have to lift a finger the whole time."

She laughed from the belly, nearly falling off the bed. This is when I loved her the most, I think, when she laughed from the belly. No one laughed like Dally—not Doody, not Gully, not Ward Belvoir. She got such joy out of it, and the joy entered *my* bloodstream; and to think that I was the one who provided it. When she finally composed herself, she said, "I want you to send me a copy every week. I'm going to cut out every one of your squirrels and tape them on my wall."

"That's a lot of squirrels," I said.

"I like squirrels," she said, and began kissing me in that way of hers, that Dally way, tantalizingly slow and tempting. I reached on the floor and fumbled all around for my other condom (I'd planned for *this* eventuality too), but by the time I returned, she was already exhibiting the early stages of slumber, those adorable little jerks and tremors she does that make you fall in love all over. I kissed her on the forehead, got up and turned off the TV, then walked down the corridor to pee. On the way back, I stopped again to look at the snow. It was still coming down, but lightly, nothing to get excited about. I reached way down with both hands and forced the ancient, rattling window upwards. Down on one knee, I stuck out my head and took the courtyard air far into my lungs. If I was the praying type I could see myself praying right now. But who was I kidding? This thing with Dally wasn't going anywhere. I might be good for a laugh or two but no girl like Dally was going to frame any five-year plan around me. Back at school she probably has one of me a week. Then I closed the window, felt my way through the nurse's room and climbed back into bed. A thin stream of streetlight angled down through the blinds, across the tiled floor, out to the corridor.

I had one hand behind my head as I gazed at the ceiling, the other hand on Dally's bum. But things weren't so bad. Tomorrow morning I will sit in church with my brother and my sisters and a lot of other people who seem to love me, and I will say good-bye to Ma. Then I will hopefully borrow Dee Dee's car, or perhaps we'll just take the subway, and I will walk Dally to the bus station, and I will kiss her on the steps, holding up the other passengers, who won't be the least bit mad because they'll know true love when they see it. Maybe I'll mouth the words *I love you,* as the bus pulls away, and quite possibly she will mouth them back, and I will be certain, absolutely certain, of sleeping with her again. I gave her bum one last, good night squeeze, and closed my eyes. And then something, I wasn't sure what, began eating at me.

"*Holy shit!*" I shot right up in bed. "*Holy fucking shit!*"

"Whatizzit?!" cried Dally, jumping up in absolute terror, struggling desperately to discern where she was.

"Ward Belvoir!" I freaked. "Ward *Belvoir*! We can't just fall asleep and expect to get up in time to be outta here before he comes in!"

"Oh, Jesus," sighed Dally, letting her whole body plop back down on the bed. "Go over and look in my blue suitcase. There's an alarm clock in it."

I did this. Rummaged through the whole thing. Emptied everything out. Nothing.

"It's not in here," I said.

"What?" came the disembodied voice on the bed.

"The alarm clock. It's not here!"

"Jeeshush Chrisht," she slurred. "Are you in the blue suitcase?"

"Yes!" I snapped. "It ain't fucking here!"

"Try the brown one."

I did. Found it in three seconds. It was a *National Velvet* alarm clock. On its broad face was a handsome picture of the legendary horse with the young Elizabeth Taylor stroking its forelock. Liz's hair was as black as a Monsignor's shoe. I had never once heard

Dally go on about horses, or even mention motion pictures about horses, so I figured that whoever bought the clock for Dally must have done so because of her striking resemblance to Liz. I turned the clock around, reached over and found a Bic in my pocket to light the scene, and studied the intricate mechanisms.

"I think I'll set if for five-thirty," I said.

"What?" Dally moaned.

"Five-thirty. I think I'll set the alarm for five-thirty."

"Make it five." She rolled over. "Your friend Ward . . . *Yawn* . . . is a bit unpredictable . . . *snort* . . . as I recall."

"Five it is," I agreed, and jumped back into bed.

My hand was back on her bum, her arm was draped across my chest, one of my feet was touching one of hers, and the returns were in and I was elected president. Soon I was sleeping, soundly sleeping, I kid you not, my lungs sloughing away like underwater apparatus. *Fully* asleep. *Me.* Johnny Gullivan. With a woman at my side who looked like Elizabeth Taylor. Who was willing to sleep with me again.

In my dreams, people I knew came in and out but not one jackbooted regiment chased me, no precancerous moles danced round my head like moths, no ravenous house cats latched onto my barelegged thigh and tore sinew from bone. Instead, I dreamed of Ward Belvoir, and the day he met with Mr. Lucinda about the janitor job. Except that it wasn't Dad who drove Ward to the interview. It wasn't Dad who did all the talking as Ward squirmed in his chair and scratched under his arms. It was me. It was my hand Mr. Lucinda shook, it was me Ward's mother hugged.

Little Prick was in my dream too. I saw him lying in bed, rereading his *Captain America* for the dozenth time, trying to make sense of the Red Skull's unfathomable hate. Then I saw that the boy had something else in his lap, a much larger book, one that he'd found in the attic. It was a Morton High yearbook, class of '69, and something in its pages stared back at him, something that spoke to him and him alone, something that scared him even more than the Skull.

Lastly, I dreamed of Gully. I saw him in a garden of white flowers, framed by a trellis of gardenias, down on one knee. He was in the midst of proposing, it looked like, in a very grand and dapperly way.

"Let me think about that," winked Gina Sookey, who was already wearing a wedding gown, a smile wide as springtime showing through the veil. "Let me think long and hard about that." In the meantime, they danced, cheekbone to cheek, heart to breast, as Maurice Chevalier sang about them and children laughed. Round and round they spun, until they were dancing above the garden, above the clouds, Gina's dress swirling in the rarefied air.

The alarm blasted off at five, as arranged, gripping my body in piranha-like seizures, as you might expect. But they only lasted a second or two. Not much more than that.

17

And Leave the Driving to Us

Dee Dee's car, this little gray thing, Japanese-made I think, had the shifter on the floor, which might make you mistake it for a standard, which would have made it a lot more interesting to drive. To make the stupid thing work, you had to compress this little button on top of the shaft, a procedure my sister took great pains to explain, along with about a million other things that I may be unfamiliar with, including some rule about feeding it unleaded gas, whatever that was. You could see her displeasure in letting me borrow the little pisspot too, but it was for a good cause, giving Dally Schoerner a lift into town. Take Dally out of this equation and I may as well have been asking for kidneys.

"How do people drive these things?" I said, all bunched up in the driver's seat with my knees practically in my face.

"Silly," said Dally, "There's a lever underneath that lets you slide the seat back. See? Ba-boom."

"Oh," I said, and Mickey-Moused the seat back two or three knotches, acquainting my lungs with oxygen once again. It felt weird driving roads in something so small and vulnerable, like the whole world could shit right on your head if it cared to. But you could really feel the road underneath—it was right there. The snow and slush seemed to splash up against your legs and I winced every time we scraped bottom. I never paid attention to these dinky little windup toys when I was high up in the van, but now I realized how many of them there were out here—little people in little cars, with little or no control, and horns that sounded like ma-ma dolls. Catastrophe waiting to happen. But in *my* hands? Be serious. Child's play.

I still had on the tie I'd worn to Ma's Mass that morning, but I'd had enough of it by this time and pulled it off over my head. But when I tried to stuff it in the pocket of the corduroy sport coat I was also still wearing, I found something else in the pocket, a Red Cross armband.

"Shit," I said, "I was supposed to give this back to Doody but I forgot."

Dally took it out of my hand and put it on her wrist like a bracelet.

"It looks good on you," I said.

"It does, doesn't it?" said Dally, who admired it from every angle as if it was a bauble I'd gotten her at Maloof's. "I think I should keep it."

"Pardon me?" I said.

"I should keep it. I should wear it. Every time I look down at my wrist, I'll see you. It will be a constant reminder of our love."

You heard it. I didn't just make it up. She used the love word. Our situation, whatever it was, or whatever it might turn into, was definitely *ours* now, not just mine. Hearing it said out loud sent blood to a whole lot of places in my body and made each mole pulse in turn. "Keep it," I said.

And Dally said, "I will," and dropped Doody's armband into her bag.

Dally had held hands with me in church earlier, a sign in itself that we were more than just the sex thing. In fact, at one point during Father Gillipede's sermon, as he was talking about some sweet little thing Ma once did, Dally touched her lips to my cheek, ever slightly, just for a second, and I knew something even then.

The most challenging thing about all this dead and dying business, though, is the great amount of church involved. No sooner do you make it through the wake with all its handshaking, stiff-upper-lipping and bowing before clergy than you're right back at it the next morning, sitting in a pew in the front of the church, the pre-tied knot in your necktie and your two-sizes too small white shirt strangling what little life you still have right out of you.

"Why do we have to go to church?" I remember asking Ma one Sunday morning when I was still too young to have a say.

"Because that's what God wants," she said, smearing a quick-hardening agent all over my cowlick.

"God cares if we go to church?"

"Oh, yes. God cares very much that we go to church."

"But everyone's so bored and sleepy when they go there. Can't God see this? What good does it do God to look down and see that?"

"What God sees is his people doing the right thing," said Ma, who had an answer for everything. "Sometimes you do something because you should, and that can be far more rewarding than avoiding things that bore you. You'll understand it when you get older."

But the older I got the less I understood anything. And I spent about as much time in church as a mackerel spends on shore. It's possible that the last time I set foot in St. Uke's was at *Dad's* funeral. Everything looked pretty much the same, and smelled the same too, a danky combination of smoke, perfume, and intestinal gas.

And there was Jesus where he always was—high above the taber-nacle, nails in his hands and feet, head hung limp and stringy. God, I felt sorry for him up on that cross. I did when I was ten and I do now. The way he had to die, all naked and slow, calling mournfully out for his father. How he could've stopped the whole thing early on but let the scumbags kill him anyway, making the mother of all sacrifices on our behalf. And we somehow are worth it? The whole of us—nothing more than scheming apes with addresses—are worth saving? And all this talk about a Second Coming—doesn't he know how that'll go too? He'll get everybody all worked up all over again and somebody—Nazis, the Klan or Christians Against Christ—will stick him back up on that cross, and we'll all cut and run like a billion scared rabbits the instant the first nail meets hammer. What the hell does Jesus see in us?

Luckily Dally was stroking my hand through the whole Mass, making me think quieting thoughts. Our entire seating arrangement was innovative, now that I think of it. Gully sat on the other side of me and Gina Sookey was stroking *his* hand. Dee sat in the row in front of us with Aggie Ogden at *her* side. It was unclear whether or not *they* were stroking each other's hands, but I bet all the teary-eyed mourners behind us were craning their necks to find out. I had to hand it to Aggie and Dee. It was pretty ballsy of them to appear publicly this way, considering that the only person in the whole building who might have approved of their flowering romance was inside the casket dead. I can hear Ma now if Dee had come to her: "You're in for a lifetime of heartache, honey, but don't let them get to you. Don't let 'em tear you down." She most likely would've tsked a little too, just to make her editorial opinion clear, but Ma was never in the business of judging. She must have tsk-tsked me three thousand times, but hardly ever wagged her finger.

And what did I get from this, what life lessons have I learned from Ma? You tell me. Gully and me—we judged *everybody*. I was doing it right now, right here in church, looking around at all these sniffling frauds and knowing exactly what they were whispering about the way Ma dressed and the shitbox that sat in our driveway and the questionable offspring she raised. Only a few of her close friends showed up; the rest of them were either dead in their own right or gone away, like Grace Schoerner.

But, you know, it did feel rewarding to be in church this morning. It felt good to stand up for Ma. I *was* a good son. *We* were good sons. And believe me, there was a moment when it could have gotten away from us, the moment when Aunt Fran, sitting between Madgie and Cassie, had a pippy little sneezing attack that differed only slightly from the opening cackling notes of "Wipe Out" by the Surfaris. I know for a fact if The Lady With The Mole had been sighted among the grieving gloms assembled, there would have been hell to pay.

Father Gillipede, in one of his last acts as priest, gave a real nice talk, in a real convincing voice, even mentioning how upstanding Ma's kids were, particularly singling out Madgie, who'd served as family spokesman with a maturity that belied her years. It was she who'd decided that me and Gully should be pallbearers and I took my place directly opposite Uncle Tut, who winked at me Irishly as we carried Ma to the hearse. You're telling me she wouldn't have been proud?

"Boy," said Dally, as we passed the buried fountains and ice-encrusted walkways of Boston Common on our way to the Greyhound, "You Gullivans are so damned stoic. The only one crying was your old aunt. Did you all take something?"

"We grieve in our own way," I said, thinking back to my all-out weeping-willow release-valve breakdown in the janitor's shower the other night, "We all said good-bye, I'm sure."

"I know I did," said Dally. "I was glad to be given the opportunity."

I knew what she meant. She never gets to say good-bye to anybody. I asked her about trying to find her mother.

"I don't know," she sighed, slipping some lever down below that made her seat tilt back like a lounge chair, "I don't know if it's in me. It's not like I didn't have mothering."

I'm wasn't sure what she meant by that. She didn't get much of anything from old man Schoerner.

"Johnny, do you remember when you could see my facial hair, you know, right here above my lip?"

I shrugged like I didn't know what she was talking about, as my brain filled up with solid images of Charlie Chaplin, Groucho Marx, and Guy Williams as Zorro.

"It was your mother who helped me bleach it out. I asked her about it one day in the backyard and she came over that night with a bottle while my father was at Rotary. In five minutes it was over. I looked in the mirror and cried. My hair looked like everyone else's hair, a little line of invisible fuzz. It was like meeting myself for the first time. Even my name sounded good when I said it. I wasn't Dally anymore. I was *Dally*. Yeah, I said good-bye to your mother."

Duke and the Drivers were on the radio as we rolled down Tremont Street. They were singing about the hole in your love bucket and how you go about fixing it. It was pretty good preaching, if you ask me, and a good tune to hold hands with as the snow crunched beneath us.

The Greyhound terminal. While Dally was over buying her ticket for the noon bus, I cased the joint. I was very familiar with the terminal and its layout, having done my share of mayhem there with Doody and my brother. I could tell which people were waiting for a bus, which ones were waiting for someone to get off a bus, and which ones were just there to sleep. The same clinically depressed old guy in the newsstand sat where he always sat, his wrinkled little head framed by the latest red-fleshed issues of *Skank* and *Meat* and *Hot Dripping Lesbos*. All his newspapers had front-page pictures of people digging out from the storm. I leaned my elbow on one of those trash cans with the swinging, scum-sticky doors. Not far away was a fat, frantic, middle-aged couple engaged in a very trying conversation on one of the pay phones. They were a typical couple you'd run into just about anywhere, especially the guy, who was packed into a trussed-up suede number with belts, buckles, and a fake fur collar. His hat was one of those little porkpie things, checkered, and it sort of teetered on his boar-sized head like a saucer, ready to slide right off as he yelled into the phone, all pink-faced and exasperated, trying to reason with (who I gathered) was the churlish son or daughter on the other end of the line. I don't remember what the lady was wearing, but I do remember her face, and the rings of dyed hair around it. And I remember how sad she looked as the conversation unfolded, cupping her ear close to the receiver, biting her lower lip with worry and regret. For a second it moved me. When Dally came back I asked if she wanted to play a game before her bus was ready.

"What game would that be?" She pretended to be interested, checking her reflection in the facade of the pinball machine.

"Okay—this is how it works. See that bus that just pulled in? I go over to one of them telephones, see, and I make like I'm having this really loud obnoxious conversation, jumping up and down, the whole nine yards, while you go to a phone further down and start doing the exact same thing, word for word."

"I see. And this does what for me?"

"That's immaterial," I said, "It's what you're doing to them."

"Who's them?"

"The people passing by. If you do it right, you seriously fuck with their heads."

"So this is an activity you've engaged in before?"

"Well, once or twice," I admitted.

"And it works every time?"

"Yeah. Pretty much. Of course, it helps to have three of you. Then you can *really* fuck with their heads."

"And that's the whole bit? You're not leaving anything out?"

"No, that's it," I said, "The key is in getting the words exact."

"I get that. So what you're telling me is that these poor, road-weary, saddled-sored wretches climb down off the bus, get their already frazzled heads seriously fucked with and then are turned loose in a strange city to be driven around by strange cabdrivers who may or may not speak the same language?"

"Well, when you put it like that—"

"Gosh and golly, John, you'd better get to a patent office as fast as you can with that idea, before some sharp-eyed entrepreneur beats you to it." She then went over to buy cigarettes, her stride there as sarcastic as the rest of her. She had spoken about smoking cigarettes a couple times since I'd been with her, but I'd never seen her actually smoke one. Just having them was the thing, I remember her saying, just having them for that dark and loneliest moment, when you'd claw through carpeting to get a drag. I watched as she paid the guy, tucked the cigs in her pocketbook, and asked for directions to the lady's room. Then I watched the fat guy on the phone clutch at his chest, watched the phone drop out of his hand swinging from its cord and saw him go down hard, collapsing to the butt-littered floor like a sandbag in rehearsal for a hanging.

"*Herb!*" screamed the lady, flying on top of him, her tiny hands trying to pry him over. "*Help us! For Chrissakes, somebody help us!*" A couple of sleepy people looked over and a guy looked up from his paper, but the only one in the vicinity, it appeared, was me, and it was clear she wanted *me* to do something. As hysterical as she was, she implored me quietly with her eyes, looking right into them. She wasn't *asking* me to do something, she *expected* me to do something. She saw something in me that made her *think* I could do something. One thing I did know was death, and the thing that bothered me most about death was sadness, and I didn't want this poor fat lady to have to go through it. I dropped down, yanked Herb's large carcass over and started slapping his face. Short taps at first, like a doc on a newborn's butt, but they got more meaningful as it went, and forceful, until they were open-palmed slaps across the face like Patton with the GI, sending Herb's hat flying. I felt on my fingers the bilious ickiness that oozed from his gaping mouth, but on I pressed, as passersby stared in wonderment, slapping his face harder and harder, spanking his fleshy cheeks with a left and a right, slapping, slapping, slapping, trying to beat the life back into his cod-colored complexion: *Live, damn you, live, live, LIVE!*

"Get out of the way!" cried Dally, who moved in close to the deceased, knelt by his mouth, listened. Then she ripped open his collar, felt for something on his neck and made her diagnosis. "Get on the phone and call 911!" she barked to some gawking traveler, "Tell them we got a guy in cardiac arrest—no pulse, no nothing!" The gawker understood his assignment and dashed to complete it, not about to miss too much of *this* spectacle.

Dally quickly found a spot on dead Herb's chest and, with fingers entwined, began pumping on it, methodically, sharply counting the reps. At fifteen she moved over to his run-over-by-a-truck face, tilted back his head and dove in, putting her lips fully over his, forcing two quick breaths into his lungs. (Going out on a limb here, this could be the single most revolting act I have ever witnessed, neck and neck with the communion rail tongues.) Pulling free of his mouth, Dally climbed back on his chest with a sense of purpose I'd never seen on anyone and repeated the whole disturbing thing. God, the look in her face. And the look on the lady's face as she watched, her nose just inches from Dally's, trusting her with all her heart and tears. I desperately wanted to jump in and help.

"Should I pull off his shoes?" I asked, as Dally disappeared into the guy's massiveness and came back up, nearly out of breath as she attacked his chest. Hadn't I seen that somewhere—pulling off the victim's shoes? Cowboy movies maybe. I wanted to be helpful, I really did. There was something about the guy, something about his gently sobbing wife. I didn't know these blobs from Major Mudd, but the way she looked down at him, the way she cried over his bulged-out jiggling face, even *I* didn't want him to die. I asked again about the shoes.

"No," Dally panted, "But you can do this part." She took both my hands, turned them over and showed me how to find the guy's sternum. "Now thread your fingers like this and put the heels of your hands right about here and start pushing down, one, two, three, that's it, all the way to fifteen." And away I went. I couldn't believe how easy it was, no harder than dribbling a basketball.

"Where'd you learn all this?" I said, pumping away.

"*Count!*" she commanded, and I did. Was I doing it right? I think so, or at least Dally made no effort to correct me, but the guy's color was as scary as the churning sea and hope did not present itself on his face. Not a glimmer of hope did I see. Neither did the lady, I don't think, as she sorrowfully repeated his name. Behind her I saw the phone, dangling from its cord like the still-smoking weapon that did the deed. I couldn't tell if there was still a voice coming out of it, what with all the commotion, but I hoped they were still there. I hoped whoever it was was still listening, hearing the anguish his/her actions unleashed. I hoped they'd feel guilty the rest of their lives. The lady took her husband's hand and said good-bye, you could really hear it. So heartfelt it was as she whispered in his ear that she loved him. All hope was lost, yes, but if he was still alive by some invisible thread, maybe he could hear her say it this one time, maybe he could feel her last kiss on his meaty hand. Death would separate them forever, but love, even dumpy, middle-aged love like theirs, is for eternity.

But that was the lady. Dally was another story. Dally was not giv-ing up. She kept putting air in him and blowing up his lungs and I held up my end over here. Her determination was like that of a medic's in some old war movie. *They're not dead til I say so! Keep 'em alive, no matter the mortars exploding around us.* And I was right there with her, believing with all my heart, believing in *her.* I kept pumping on his chest and she kept blowing in air and I kept on believing. I wasn't gonna let her down. I was through with letting down. I let Ma down, I let Dad down big-time, I let Miss Buchanan down and Wendy Pfisternak and various priests and nuns and just about everybody else. I let down my little sisters, who only lived with Aunt Fran because I was too much of a dickhead to take care of them, and I let myself down. I wasn't letting Dally Schoerner down. Not today. If she was going all night I was going all night. I refused to look at the guy's face, though, because its very deadness made my arms feel weak and inadequate. I just concentrated on my count of fifteen.

"Has anyone called an ambulance?" yelled someone with a suitcase from the ever-growing peanut gallery.

"Has anyone called for help?" yelled some horse-faced guy with a duffel.

"Has anyone told you you're uglier than a rain-soaked turd?" I muttered out the side of my mouth.

But Dally ignored it all. She had the focus of an athlete, like that photo her father showed me of her in the crew boat, rowing with all her might. *In sixth place at the turn? No problem—we win it at the wire.* She directed me with hand signals, counting the pumps along with me, making me hold up while she checked for respiration, then locking onto the guy's fleshy lips, their eyes both wide open as she blew, then signaling me again for another round. I had my weight into it now, boy, practically doing front supports on the guy's chest. It was a little like plunging the toilet; sooner or later you feel something give. But nothing was giving here. And the wife was hanging on, breathless, and I knew that as soon as Dally threw in the towel, the lady'd collapse in unforgettable grief, sobbing and sobbing and sobbing. But Dally wasn't throwing in any towel and neither was I. As long as she was ready to blow more air into this poor bastard's useless lungs, I was there with the muscle, ready to deliver another payload from the bellows. She stopped the rhythm only once, pushing her soaking wet hair off her glistening face, then reached for a very deep breath and gave the guy two more shots. But you could see she was weakening, becoming light-headed, dizzy. Another couple rounds was all she had left. Get the bugle ready for taps. I thought about offering to trade roles for awhile, letting me do the mouth-to-mouth, but the moment passed; one taste of the slobbering stiff's saliva in my mouth and I'd be sure to vomit all over him *and* his wife, and *then* where would we be? I started coaching Dally instead, egging her on like two iron-pumping buddies in a gym: "Come on girl! You can do it, baby! Just two more, sugar! Give it what you got, baby, give it what you got!"

And then, wait a minute—did I just see, did I just, did I just see his stomach heave? *Something* moved, and I wasn't the only one who saw it. Everyone got very still. We all stared at him, Dally, the wife, me, the bystanders, afraid to blink, afraid to breathe. Is it like this when you strike oil? Something, then nothing but you know it's something, then something else, a quiver, perhaps a tremor—and then Herb's lips moved, his eyes stretched wider than possible and his body came forth with a cough of cinematic proportions, as if a dozen strangling devils were expunged at once into the Greyhound air—horns, tails, and all. "*Oh, Herb!*" cried his wife, almost afraid to touch him. He then wheezed for another breath, fear in his eyes as he stared up at his wife, staring at her as if she was on the other side of some invisible barrier, like she was on top of the layer of ice he was under and he knew he couldn't get there. "*Oh, Herb!*" His wife broke down, and she kissed him on his eyebrows and on his ears and on his balding head, as he wheezed for more air and coughed out more death. "Oh, Herbie, don't ever leave me, don't ever leave me again."

Dally, still kneeling across from me, her chest moving up and down, couldn't believe it. "It worked," she slowly grinned, "It really worked. Johnny, we did it! We actually *did* it!" She stood up and leaped over, reaching to hug me like battery-mates after a no-hitter. And she held me like you're lucky to be held if you live to be ninety. I didn't let her down, she was telling me, I was bound to her.

Over Dally's shoulder I saw legitimate rescue personnel with stretchers and everything come bounding through the big glass door in front; cavalry arriving long after the fort is captured. I was all set to give them the whole rundown so they'd know how to treat the guy from here, and I looked around to see if any reporters had tailed them, clearing my throat to give them quotes and quips. But the EMT's voices were loud and Marine-like bossy, clearing all civilians, including us, far away from the perimeter. I was all set to protest this ignorant shabbiness, when two distinct sounds were heard. The first was Dally's bus being announced over the public address and the second was the guy on the floor dying all over again. In mid-gasp, he seized up like capital punishment, dug the heels of his Florsheims hard into the linoleum and was stricken as dead as a head-on collision with God. It was as if an arsenal of warheads and pitchforks had come up through the floorboards and pierced all his organs at once. The professionals pounced all over him, of course, hooking him up to every piece of hardware they'd hauled in, slapping a mask on his drooling face, yelling out: "*We're losing him!*"

The lady didn't cry, either. She saw him die good and dead this time. Cattle prods, voltage or enough TNT to blow the Bridge on the River Kwai wasn't going to bring him back. They called Dally's bus a second time.

"Come with me to the little girl's room," she said, fumbling in her pocketbook, "I've an overwhelming need to brush my teeth."

Boy did she brush, and I didn't blame her, lathering toothpaste from her chin to her eye sockets. She spit with such force I was afraid she'd hit her head on the sink. And, I don't know how to explain it, but I'd never felt so intimate to anyone the second before she washed it off, throwing herself in the water like a desert-parched cowpoke at a horse trough.

"By the way," she said, reaching for paper towels, "You were wonderful out there."

"No, you were *unbelievable*," I said, "Where *did* you learn all that?"

"Oh, some camp my father sent me to. Years ago. Never thought I'd actually use it—none of us did. We routinely referred to the practice dummy as 'the Doomed.' But it worked! Can you believe that? It worked! We saved somebody! We pumped life back into the lifeless!"

"That may be true," I said, "but all we gave the poor fuck was twenty-six seconds. It ain't like he stood up, quit smoking, went on an asparagus diet and finally read *War and Peace*. He lived for a crummy twenty-six seconds."

"It doesn't matter, Johnny, don't you see? For a minute he breathed. For twenty-six seconds he got to look into his wife's eyes one more time. We gave him that. He got to say good-bye."

Funny, if you asked me, I thought he was saying something else as his eyelids blinked bewilderingly, something like: "*Why are you assholes doing this to me?*" But I was willing to give Dally the benefit of the doubt.

The ambulance had backed right up to the door by this time and they were wheeling Herb to it, his wife running alongside in her heels, he still dead as a desk on the stretcher. I ran Dally to her bus, threw her suitcases into the baggage bin underneath and kissed her good-bye. It was a nice long deep kiss too, surprisingly, mindful as I was about the essence of corpse on her lips.

On the steps of the bus, she turned to me. "There's something

I've been meaning to ask you for some time now," she said, "The tomato in 'raven-haired'—what does it mean?"

"I'm not sure," I said, "but I think I'd know it if I saw it."

"And you see it in me?"

"Oh, baby, I see it all over you."

She smiled, and reached in her pocketbook for the red armband. "Here," she said, "Give this back to Doody. I've got more than enough to remember you by."

She waved from her window as the bus pulled away, and blew me a little kiss, too, her mouth making the sexiest **O** I have ever seen. I returned the wave but it had some thought behind it. It wasn't one of those flappy little, bye-bye-bye productions you see all the time. I barely pulled my hand out of my pocket, in fact, and let it hang there by my belt. Just a single move, up and down, thumb still in my pants. Cool? There is *nothing* this cool. And this is the picture she will take back to school.